A BLACKBIRD IN DARKNESS

A BLACKBIRD IN DARKNESS is the stunning new novel by the already celebrated author of A BLACKBIRD IN SILVER, and although this serves as a sequel to the previous book, it can also be read on its own, for it is a fascinating fantasy story in its own right.

Three intrepid warriors search for the mighty Serpent, determined to kill it. Their task is weighed with worldly problems, for if they fail, the Serpent will destroy their lands forever.

From the Blue Plane to the Black Plane via the harsh Tundra wastes they encounter a host of diverse and mysterious figures like The Lady of H'tebhmella, a tall beautiful ethereal creature surrounded by a blue light, and Arlenmia, a statuesque figure with piercing luminous turquoise eyes. Not to mention a Silver Staff, a mystical city and a magical ship. Ashurek, Estarinel and Medrian knew that whatever they encountered, they could never relinquish hope, until their mission was finally completed.

About the Author

Freda Warrington was born in Leicester in
1956 and studied graphic design at
Loughborough College of Art and Design. She
has worked as an in-house designer for a local
building company in Hitchin. She is now a
freelance designer and lives in Leicester. Her
first book, A BLACKBIRD IN SILVER, was
published to triumphant acclaim, and is a
prequel to this fascinating story. A
BLACKBIRD IN AMBER is the recently
published sequel.

'Enjoyable readable fantasy . . . many cuts
above the average'

Anne McCaffrey

A Blackbird in Darkness

FREDA WARRINGTON

NEW ENGLISH LIBRARY
Hodder and Stoughton

First published in Great Britain
in 1986 by New English Library
Paperbacks as an original
publication

Reissued 1988
Third impression 1988

British Library C.I.P.

Warrington, Freda
  A blackbird in darkness.
  I. Title
  823'.914[F]   PR6073.A7/

  ISBN 0-450-40161-8

Printed and bound in Great Britain
for Hodder and Stoughton
Paperbacks, a division of Hodder
and Stoughton Ltd., Mill Road,
Dunton Green, Sevenoaks, Kent
TN13 2YA (Editional Office: 47
Bedford Square, London WC1B
3DP) by Richard Clay Ltd.,
Bungay, Suffolk.

For Hazel, Colin and Hannah Rose,
John Richard Parker and Carolyn Caughey,
with love and thanks

Contents

1 The Quest of the Serpent   11
2 Medrian of Alaak   34
3 Forluin   56
4 The Shana's Lie   80
5 'I was alive here'   114
6 The Domain of the Silver Staff   144
7 The Past and the Future   168
8 Children of the Worm   195
9 'At the Staff's Mercy'   213
10 Across the River   237
11 The Mathematician   266
12 Hrunnesh   294
13 The Last Witness of the Serpent   326
14 The Arctic   352
15 'They must open their eyes'   379
16 Night Falls   406
17 The Far Side of the Blue Plane   445

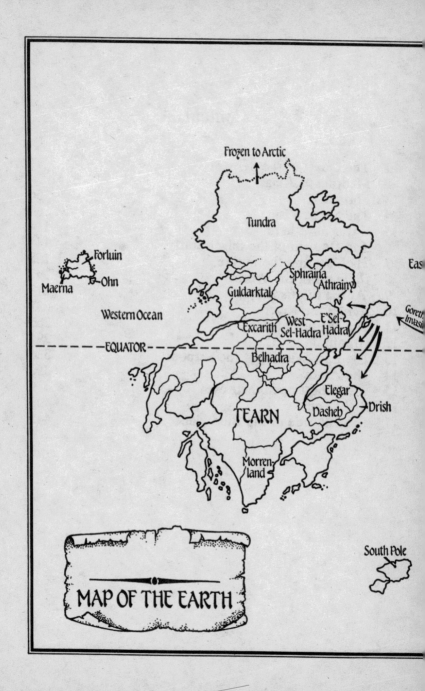

Frozen to Arctic

Tundra

Forluin
Ohn
Maerna

Western Ocean

Sphraina
Athrainy

Guldarktal

East

E'Sel
Hadra

Goreth
invasi

Excarith

West
Sel-Hadra

EQUATOR

Belhadra

Elegar

TEARN

Dasheb

Drish

Morren-
land

South Pole

MAP OF THE EARTH

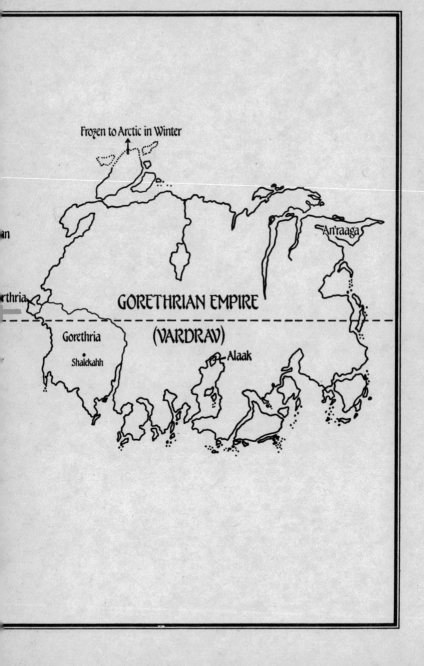

Frozen to Arctic in Winter

An'raaga

GORETHRIAN EMPIRE

(VARDRAV)

Gorethria

Shalekahh

Alaak

...an

...rthria

1

The Quest of the Serpent

As FAR as the eye could see, the Blue Plane H'tebhmella stretched in all directions. It was quite flat, but shimmered with a myriad aquatic blues, like a facet of an infinite sapphire. Islands and spires of crystal rose everywhere out of the shining water, some clad in iridescent vegetation and some displaying the simple beauty of unadorned rock. Above stretched a clear, pale sky. It was always cloudless, for it was not a true sky as such, but at times its gentle amethyst light would deepen to a rich blue twilight, responding to the mystical rhythms of the Plane's existence.

The Blue Plane was the only place that offered refuge from the Serpent-dominated world. Because it existed in a separate dimension from Earth the terrible Serpent M'gulfn could not touch it, and here the three travellers who had set out upon a Quest to destroy M'gulfn were resting and waiting.

The three seemed unlikely companions. Estarinel was a gentle young man from the once-peaceful island of Forluin, Medrian, a small, white-faced Alaakian woman who persistently maintained a shell of grim secrecy about herself, and Ashurek was the tall, dark-skinned Prince of Gorethria whose evil deeds – though long renounced – had made him a dreaded figure throughout the world. They had first met at the dwelling of the sage Eldor, the House of Rede, which lay on the dull, rocky continent at the South Pole. From there, they had boarded a ship, which should have sped them straight to the Blue Plane, but the Serpent, understandably, had no wish that the mission against it should succeed. The journey to H'tebhmella proved arduous and complex, several

11

times thwarted by agents of the Worm who sought to destroy them or bend them to its will. Only at the last moment, when death seemed inevitable, had they escaped to the Blue Plane. Now, even as they recovered amidst the healing beauty of H'tebhmella, there was no avoiding the knowledge that this peace could not last, and they would soon have to return to Earth and continue the Quest.

Perhaps not for a few days, though, and Estarinel, not having seen Forluin for a year and knowing that he was unlikely to survive the Quest, craved one last glimpse of his country.

'I told you that Arlenmia could not have made the Serpent attack Forluin a second time,' Medrian said. 'Can't you believe me?'

'Yes, I believe you,' Estarinel answered. 'It's not that. It's – a feeling. I must see Forluin as it really is: not the lying, distorted visions that Arlenmia showed me, but the reality.' He and Medrian were walking together along the shore of a shimmering lake. Great horses, blue-green like sea-washed boulders, swam languidly in the water. Just inland stood a line of graceful trees with trunks of indigo glass and leaves like flakes of lapis lazuli and onyx. Shy, unearthly animals raised their delicate heads to watch the two humans pass by.

'Well, as the Lady of H'tebhmella has permitted it, I suppose it is all right,' Medrian said quietly.

'And you will still come with me?' She looked round at him and the pain and longing in her eyes, as always, made him long to wrap his arms round her and kiss her misery away. But if he so much as took her hand, she would draw away from him as if his concern only made the pain worse.

She did so now, saying shortly, 'Yes, I want to. But don't press me, or I may change my mind.' And she turned her back on him and walked away between the trees.

Estarinel watched her go, feeling troubled. All through the first stage of their journey she had been withdrawn, cold and enigmatic, her behaviour at times contradictory and inexplicable. His own reason for wanting to slay the Serpent

M'gulfn was clear enough: it had attacked and devasted his beloved country. And Ashurek's reasons, although more complex, were also known: he had come to understand, through his love for the sorceress, Silvren, that the Worm was the root of the monstrous cycle of events in which he had been ensnared. Only by killing M'gulfn could the evil be ended, and also it was his only chance of freeing Silvren from her imprisonment in the Dark Regions.

But from the beginning, Medrian had refused to tell Estarinel and Ashurek anything about herself. The most they knew was that she was from Alaak, a small island belonging to the Gorethrian Empire. The Alaakians loathed their Gorethrian oppressors, so Ashurek had never trusted her. Shared misadventures had bonded the three together and Ashurek's hostility towards her had dispersed, but still her motivation remained a mystery, and his suspicion of her was only submerged, never lost.

Perhaps Estarinel, by contrast, was too trusting. Medrian had at times actually warned him not to rely on her or confide in her, lest she betray him in some way. But behind her emotionless, even callous exterior, he knew that she was undergoing some internal torment for which she could find neither relief nor comfort. And his concern for her had gradually become love; love that he could not show, because she would only recoil from him, beseeching him not to question her, not to show her affection.

Here on H'tebhmella, where they said it was impossible to be unhappy, she was still as cold, as locked away from him in her misery. Yet she was also subtly different: the sinister, dark quality she possessed had faded into a spiritual abstraction, which seemed a contradictory mixture of hopelessness and unconquerable determination.

Estarinel, Medrian and Ashurek had been on the Blue Plane for three days. Without their timely rescue from the dreadful Castle of Gastada, they would certainly have died, but already the healing aura of H'tebhmella had restored them to health, cleansing illness and closing wounds as if their unspeakable ordeal had never happened. The memories remained, but it all seemed far in the past, incapable of touching them in this distant domain of blue crystal.

On the day they had arrived, the Lady of the Blue Plane had spoken to them at length about the existence of the Earth and Planes, and how the Serpent had come into being. She had told them that although the creature was virtually invincible, if it did not die, disaster awaited the Earth and universe. The Guardians, neutral beings who tried to balance the energies of the cosmos, were preparing a weapon known as the Silver Staff to be wielded against M'gulfn, but even so, the Serpent would only be vulnerable as long as it did not regain its third eye, the Egg-Stone that Ashurek had found and lost.

Certainly there was no chance of the Egg-Stone being recovered, for it had fallen deep into the laval mass of a volcano. But there were other unanswered questions: Miril, the strange bird-like creature from whom Ashurek had stolen the Egg-Stone, had warned that unless he found her again, the world was doomed. And it was also said that the Serpent possessed a host, an unknown human into whom its spirit could flee if its body was attacked. That, above all, made it indestructible. Yet even the Lady herself seemed to have no answer to these mysteries.

And even if we find the Silver Staff, and Miril and the rest don't matter, we are still fallible humans, Estarinel thought grimly. How can we hope to face the Arctic weather, let alone the Serpent's cunning and power?

He found that as his body returned to health, his mind was becoming increasingly restless. He was more apprehensive now than he had been at any other stage of the Quest; it had been easier to bear all this dreadful knowledge when he was ill and in despair. Now it seemed that however much he twisted thoughts and possibilities in his head, it only made their situation seem worse and worse.

Ashurek had said he felt that they were not acting of their own volition at all, but being manipulated by invisible powers of the universe. The more he considered it, the more Estarinel could believe it. It filled him with a frustration that was

14

too turned in upon itself to become anger, although he could feel the truth of it in everything. Eldor had withheld knowledge from them. He thought the Lady had not said as much as she could, and even Ashurek might be keeping certain things hidden. As for Medrian – he shook his head. In his darker moments, he felt something was indeed manipulating the Quest, thrusting three humans into an impossible situation with the minimum of help or advice, as if they were puppets, and Ashurek and Medrian were reluctantly in league with the heartless puppeteer.

I only came to help my own people, to try to save Forluin from being destroyed, he thought. How did it all become so complicated? When he thought of the beautiful island he had left behind, the gentle and loving people who had been undeservedly ravaged by the grey Worm, his confusion and unhappiness twisted ever more tightly within him. It was hard to grasp just how savage and uncaring the world outside Forluin was, and he wondered if he could withstand this awful realisation for long enough to continue the Quest.

'Estarinel!' The sudden call made him start and look round. Approaching him along the shore was a tall woman with shining chestnut hair and humorous eyes. She carried herself proudly and her face was bright with cheerful courage. Lost in thought as he was, for a moment he could not think who she was. Then he remembered.

'Hello, Calorn,' he greeted her, forcing a smile. She was the warrior whom the H'tebhmellians had assigned to help in the next stage of the Quest.

'I thought that as we will be travelling together soon, it would be as well if we got to know each other,' she explained with a friendly grin. 'But you seem troubled. If you'd rather not talk now . . .'

'No, it's all right. I would be glad of your company.'

'Good. Let us find somewhere to sit.' They walked along the shore until it curved round and rose into a knoll of crystal-blue rock. Estarinel looked around for Medrian, but she was out of sight; he did not notice Calorn's eyes on him as they seated themselves on the knoll.

She was wondering if he had changed much since starting the Quest; she imagined that he must have been less thin, perhaps younger-looking, and without the haunted darkness in his eyes. He still had the clear, beautiful features of a Forluinishman, but there were certain ineradicable lines and scars on his face now, and his black, slightly curly hair had grown very long, giving him an almost wild appearance. It was a look both of determination and despair.

'Estarinel, you seem so downhearted. Hasn't H'tebhmella brought you healing? Aren't you happy here?'

'Too happy,' he sighed. 'Perhaps that's the problem. From the time the Serpent attacked my land and all through our journey, I've never really had time to think. Now I can't stop thinking . . .'

'Would it help to tell me?' Calorn asked. He hesitated, but then he saw the friendliness in her clear amber eyes and he knew he could trust her.

'I don't know, Calorn. It's the beauty of this place, and knowing what is happening to Earth and what we have to face when we set off again. And I've made a decision to visit Forluin before we go, and I don't know if it's right. Then this waiting for news of the Silver Staff is terrible, and there's so much we don't know . . .' He was silent for a moment, staring across the lake at a crag of aquamarine-hued rock. 'But what troubles me most of all is Medrian.'

'Why? She seems so self-possessed.'

'She seems it . . . but there is something wrong with her, something terribly wrong, and she can't or won't tell us what it is.' He shook his head and smiled half-heartedly. 'I'm sorry, Calorn, I shouldn't burden you with this. There's nothing anyone can do.'

'H'tebhmella could bring you peace of mind, if you'd let it,' Calorn suggested gently.

'I daren't,' he replied. 'I'd just lose all heart to carry on, if I let myself forget.' Just then he saw a small boat drifting across the lake. In it were Medrian and the Lady of H'tebhmella. He watched the vessel until it was lost to sight, wondering where they were going and what Medrian was

16

telling the Lady that she could not tell him. 'Well, and what of you, Calorn?' he said, trying to sound cheerful. 'You heard all about us when we arrived here, but I still don't know anything about you.'

She pulled a face. 'There's nothing to know, really. I'm just a warrior who's been assigned to help you in the Quest.'

'Don't tell me you're going to be even more secretive than Medrian,' he persisted, and the genuine interest in his gentle eyes got the better of her.

'Well, if you insist . . . I come from a world that some call Ikonus, a lovely green world,' she began. 'I was always restless for travel and knowledge, even as a child; the feeling drove me to the greatest place of learning in the world, the School of Sorcery. I didn't study sorcery itself – it was too esoteric for me! – but the more basic arts, soldiery and the Ways between worlds. But a disaster befell Ikonus—'

She faltered and Estarinel said, 'If it's painful, don't—'

'No, it's all right. I was just thinking, it is a long story and strangely interconnected with events in your world; I hadn't realised it until now. You see, Silvren and Arlenmia were at the School of Sorcery at the same time as me.'

'Silvren and Arlenmia?' Estarinel echoed incredulously.

Calorn paused, then said, 'I'll tell you about it later, because I think Ashurek would also be interested. For now, I'll just say that it was Arlenmia who brought ruin to my world.'

Estarinel stared at her, stunned. 'I can believe it,' he muttered. 'Go on.'

'Well, Ikonus was dying, or at least very sick – but when I offered my services to the Sorcerer, to help heal the damage, I was told there was nothing I could do. In one way I was angry; in another, oddly relieved. I used the knowledge I did have to leave Ikonus and explore other worlds. I've never been back.

'I made a decision that even if I couldn't help my own world, at least I could try to help others against people like Arlenmia.' She smiled. 'Ironic, isn't it? After years of travelling and fighting, I eventually arrived on H'tebhmella,

17

and gave my service to them. I suppose I am a mercenary of sorts,' she said thoughtfully. 'My reward is being able to believe that I'm fighting for the right side. I know how important your Quest is. I believe the Lady told you that my job – because of my knowledge of the Ways between worlds – is to guide you to the path into the domain of the Silver Staff. It's vital that I don't fail you.'

Estarinel looked at Calorn for several moments before replying. He suddenly saw her in a new light: a woman who had turned her back on her own ruined world without bitterness, and gone forth with cheerful courage to fight other people's battles. Would I be capable of the same thing in her place? he thought. If Forluin is doomed, can I leave her behind and forget?

He knew the answer was no.

He had already proved it, in deciding to go back there before finishing the Quest, and although he felt his decision was wrong in every way, he could not resist his compulsion to return.

'Do you really feel so responsible for us?' he said eventually. 'This isn't your world, and you hardly know us. It can't really matter to you if you fail.'

'I have not undertaken this mission lightly!' she responded heatedly. 'I made a vow, to myself and to the Lady, to serve the H'tebhmellians. I would not have taken this task upon myself if I did not mean to devote myself utterly to fulfilling it! Believe me, it will matter to everyone if I fail. Estarinel,' her tone became softer but no less firm, 'you must trust me.'

It will matter to everyone if I fail, his thoughts echoed.

'I do trust you,' he told her. 'Forgive me, Ashurek's cynicism is catching. Can you tell me anything about the Silver Staff and the journey to fetch it?'

'Certainly. I'll tell you all I know,' she said, smiling as he responded with an ironic grin.

'Thank goodness. I was expecting another cryptic, "That knowledge can wait." '

'What I know may not be that helpful to you, but I'll do my best,' Calorn laughed, pushing her chestnut hair off her face. 'I don't know the origin of the Silver Staff, how it came into being or why. I hardly know what it is, except that it is a weapon of vast power. Over the millennia thousands have quested after it and only a few have been found worthy to use it. The conditions for its use are that the Quester is clear of purpose, and facing a vast enough evil to absorb all the Staff's power. If it were used against a lesser evil, or used wrongly, it could destroy a whole earth.

'The Guardians have always kept watch over it, but the Staff itself chooses who may use it. It chooses by – well, by setting tests for the questers. Those who fail are generally driven mad.' The words seemed to scrape through her throat as if she was reluctant to speak of what she had learned. 'But this time, things are different. The Guardians are using the Staff to capture the lost, positive energy of Earth, which can destroy the Serpent. The Lady told you of the great energy that split into two parts, the negative forming itself into the Serpent, and the positive spinning out into an ever-expanding ring. The Guardians' theory is that the ring must reach a nadir of its power, and pass into another dimension, or disperse altogether.'

Estarinel said thoughtfully, 'So they're trying to take advantage of a crisis. We have to destroy the Serpent now, or never.'

'Yes . . . I suppose you are right. It's their only chance to capture the power and bring it back to Earth. If they fail – the positive power will be lost and the negative will be supreme.'

'But why do they need us, three mere humans, to collect the Silver Staff and slay M'gulfn? Surely they're more suited than us . . .'

'Who knows?' Calorn joked darkly. 'Perhaps they are not clear of purpose. Will you let me go on?'

'Sorry . . . it's just that the thought of these Guardians . . . never mind.' He could not bring himself to express the coldness he felt at the idea of the Guardians, who manipulated people and things with such impassive callousness. Sometimes, in flashes of foresight, he thought he had seen them: blank-eyed, grey figures seen through red glass. They terrified him. At least he could hate the Serpent, but they made him too afraid even to hate them. As Calorn continued, speaking of them and the Staff, he felt pierced by a white and silver needle of ice, and he did not know if the pain was fear or prescience.

'Their belief is that when the power passes into another dimension, it will be on a different scale so that it will emerge as a small sphere. They hope to use the Silver Staff to locate and absorb the power. You see, the Staff is the only object that can act as a vessel for that energy, in order to physically bring it back to Earth and attack the Serpent with it. But even the Guardians can't be certain that the Staff will accede itself to their service, or that their theory will prove correct. So, we wait for news.'

'I hope it won't be long,' Estarinel murmured. 'If I understand you rightly, the Silver Staff is being prepared for our use – but only if we prove ourselves worthy of wielding it?'

'Yes, apparently.' Calorn cleared her throat and went on almost uncomfortably. 'The Guardians told the Lady that the Staff will still have to test you, there's nothing they can do to prevent it. And the tests will be arduous and dreadful, even unfair. The only help I can give is to show you the way from Earth into the Staff's domain; once you are within it, the Staff will have control. It is a sensitive entity. I've really no idea what will happen.'

Estarinel took a deep breath, as if the air of the Blue Plane could instil him with courage.

'Well, it seems that no help is freely given; it must always be fought for. I didn't expect anything different. At least there are three of us to face its tests, and perhaps persuade it—'

As he spoke, Calorn's gaze flinched from his face, as if she was loath to tell him the worst news yet.

'Oh, Estarinel – no, oh dear, I'm sorry,' she floundered. 'I hoped you wouldn't ask, so the Lady would have to tell you instead. Only one of you can go – the Staff will only permit one. The Lady has chosen you.'

'Has she?' he almost gasped. 'Just me, on my own? It's not that I'm afraid – I am, but that wouldn't stop me – only surely Ashurek is far more fitted to the task than me. He's used to fighting, and supernatural beings – it's been his way of life.'

'Ah, but is he clear of purpose?' Calorn asked cryptically.

'Yes – far more so than me!'

'I doubt it. The Lady is wise. Remember, his main desire is to free Silvren. Do you think he really cares about anything else? And he bore the Egg-Stone for a while, which may have done more damage than we know.'

'What about Medrian? Her purpose is clear, quite untainted – I can see that in her eyes, in everything she does.' He lowered his head. 'Not that I could bear to see her set off on her own . . .'

'There must be other reasons why she is unsuited. Don't look at me like that – I know nothing about her.'

'I just . . . don't want to fail. If we fail at the very end, if the Serpent wins, all right. What else could we expect? But if I deny us all even a weapon to attack it with . . . deny Forluin a future . . .' he trailed off. Calorn looked at him, suddenly made inarticulate by the extreme sympathy she felt for him. She still felt cool and detached about her mission; it was her ability to work with such objective dedication that made her so valuable to the H'tebhmellians. But she was still affected when she saw how deeply involved others were.

'I'm sure the Lady has made the wisest choice,' was the best she could manage.

'It's all right, I'll go,' he murmured. 'I'm glad you told me; I'll have time to prepare myself. But I just don't know if I have a purpose at all now. When it first happened – when I left Forluin – I felt numb. I couldn't take in what had happened or imagine what I was setting out to face. I still can't – do you understand? I can't take in what happened! I saw that dreadful creature and I think it will kill me if I see it again. I really can't conceive of attacking it. I must've been mad to even think we could try . . . and now, when I don't feel numb, I feel grief and confusion. Do you call that clear purpose?'

He saw that Calorn was distressed by his outburst, but he still had to try to make her understand how he felt, if only to help himself. He could not tell Medrian and Ashurek. It was not that they did not care; on the contrary, they understood how he felt so well and with such grim sympathy that no words could make it any clearer.

'So how can I fool the Silver Staff?' he continued. 'I want the Serpent dead. Its venom is destroying my country . . . I still mean to kill it. But it's not that easy. I can't be objective about this Quest any more . . . or about Medrian and Ashurek. It was easier when they were strangers, but now they're friends—' the words sounded like sand in his throat. 'More than friends . . .'

'Estarinel, are you asking me for an answer to how you feel?' she asked softly.

'Yes – yes, I suppose I am. Well – do you have one?'

'I've only found one for myself. I can cope because I've never felt any ties, not to my parents or world, or to any other person or place or thing. It's not that I don't love, but I can let go.'

He nodded thoughtfully, then sighed.

'I'm frightened, Calorn. I don't mind admitting it. I'd be a fool if I wasn't . . . and I'm pretending I need an answer to give me strength to finish the Quest. Well, the truth is . . . I'm just trying to find a way to stop myself suffering, to bear the knowledge of what happened to Forluin.' He paused, staring out across the Blue Plane, then continued, 'But why should there be an answer? Nothing can help me accept what happened – it is impossible to bear. I can't keep on assuming that for some reason the Forluinish have a creation-given exemption from misery.'

'There's another way to cope,' Calorn said hesitantly, 'which is to stop thinking and act instead.'

'I know. I've thought about that too, and I can't do it. The Silver Staff – it's just a dream, we can't assume that anything, anywhere can offer us real help. The only way for me is the hardest, to see the pain through without trying to find ways to lessen it.'

Calorn put her hand on his shoulder, trying to reassure him and show that she understood, but for the first time she felt her own optimism dulled by dread. And she thought, yes, that is the only way, and it will destroy him.

Ashurek was walking along the edge of the lake, his head bowed in thought. When he glanced up and saw Calorn and Estarinel seated on the knoll ahead of him, he hesitated; he had no desire for company, and purposed to avoid them. But they had already seen him, and when Calorn waved and called out a greeting, he changed his mind. Perhaps it would be better to find some diversion from his haunting thoughts of Silvren; after all, brooding could not help her.

Throughout most of the Quest, he had managed to suppress his grief at her loss. He had once been a prisoner in the Dark Regions himself, and knew intimately the fear, torment and wretchedness that Silvren was undergoing. The Dark Regions were the hellish domain of the Shana, who served M'gulfn; until now he had accepted that he stood no chance of rescuing her until the Serpent was dead. However, the Lady of H'tebhmella's appalling disclosure had changed that. She had told them that the Regions did not exist in some vague, distant limbo, but were actually cleaved to the far side of the Blue Plane. Each Plane, being flat, was two-sided, and the Lady had hinted that H'tebhmella's other side had once been even lovelier than this. But by some ghastly, supernatural trick the demons had contrived to place their own evil kingdom there.

On Hrannekh Ol, they had gone from one side to the other through a tunnel in the Plane's fabric. And although Ashurek knew that H'tebhmella was sealed against the Shana's power, that no such tunnels could exist here, still he could not rid his mind of the obsessive knowledge that Silvren was there, imprisoned and in agony, just out of his reach . . .

He climbed up the knoll and seated himself by Estarinel and Calorn, greeting them with the merest sombre nod. His tall, lean frame was no less imposing for being clad in H'tebhmellian clothes of deep blue.

'I'm glad of a chance to speak to you,' Calorn said cheerfully. 'Estarinel and I were just talking about the Silver Staff.' Ashurek appeared quite uninterested in this; if anything, his baleful eyes became more introspective. She persisted brightly, 'And I was telling him about my being at the School of Sorcery at the same time as Silvren and Arlenmia.'

The change in Ashurek's expression as she spoke was startling; his green eyes met hers, brilliant against the dark, brown-purple sheen of the skin. His face, with its high cheekbones, straight nose and grimly set mouth, became so menacing that she began to feel distinctly uncomfortable.

'Everywhere it seems I meet people who know more of Silvren than do I,' he said in a low voice.

'But surely you knew—' Calorn floundered, unnerved by his intense, inescapable glare.

'I know that Silvren travelled to another world to learn how to use her sorcerous powers. But of her time there she told me nothing. She never cared to speak of her past, so I did not insist. However, I would like to learn more of the experiences that made her so reticent. How well did you know her?'

'Hardly at all—' Ashurek's expression became more dangerous at this. Calorn refused to let herself be intimated by anyone and made a determined effort to recover her composure. 'I should explain that the School had a hierarchical structure. The Sorcery students were the School's élite, so those of us who studied lesser subjects knew all of them by name, although they might not know us. I would recognise Silvren anywhere, but I exchanged only a few words with her in ten years there, and I doubt that she would remember me. She was quite small – a little taller than Medrian, I think – and her hair and skin were deep gold in colour. Her eyes, too.'

Ashurek nodded. 'And Arlenmia?'

'She was tall, extremely beautiful in a strange way; her

24

skin was like marble – almost as if she was a perfect statue brought to life. She had extraordinary hair, all shades of sea-green and azure, and large eyes the same colour. And such a graceful way of moving that no one could help noticing her.'

'I think you know that Arlenmia is a fanatical and dangerous woman,' Ashurek said. 'Only recently did I learn that it was she who sent the demon Diheg-El after Silvren. As you know, that demon eventually caught up with Silvren and she is now its prisoner. Yet I have also heard that she and Arlenmia were once friends; naturally, I find it somewhat hard to believe.'

'Well, it's true. They used to go everywhere together, like lovers. Most of the Sorcery students were natives of my world, but Silvren and Arlenmia were the only ones from their respective worlds. Arlenmia had been there for a year before Silvren arrived, and had made no friends at all. And Silvren was very young – fifteen or sixteen, perhaps – and rather shy. I think they were both lonely. They became close friends and remained so for ten years – although some said they had frequent arguments.'

'What about?' The fierceness had left Ashurek's eyes, and both he and Estarinel were listening to Calorn with rapt interest.

'Metaphysical things. The nature of good and evil,' Calorn replied with a dismissive shrug. 'Arlenmia had some strange ideas. I know that she was different from the other Sorcerers. Each of them had been born with the ability to draw sorcerous power from the Earth through themselves, and they were at the School to learn how to use their magic properly; that is, with restraint, and only for good. I heard that Silvren was the only one ever born on her own Earth with these powers.'

'Yes, that is so,' Ashurek said. 'She always said that she had been born out of her time, because by rights her power should not exist until the Serpent is dead.'

'Well, apparently Arlenmia had no such intrinsic power. Instead she had this strange ability to draw power through mirrors, and she had been given special dispensation to study

25

at the School. But some of the tutors disliked or distrusted her, and because of that they made her feel that she was different, inferior, not a true Sorceress.'

I am no sorceress, I can only work through an unbroken mirror . . . The words echoed in Estarinel's mind.

'Because of that, I believe Arlenmia grew to despise the tutors,' Calorn went on. 'Silvren abided by everything they said, and Arlenmia did not, and so they disagreed. But their affection for each other was genuine; Silvren was the only one that Arlenmia trusted and confided in, and everyone said that although Silvren was well aware of Arlenmia's faults, she was so sweet-natured and loyal that she found it easy to overlook them.'

'Oh, that is Silvren,' groaned Ashurek to himself.

'I don't know whether Arlenmia planned what happened . . . or whether it was done on the spur of the moment, in anger. The School of Sorcery had a kind of icon of power, a silvery sphere that hovered perpetually in the sky above it. It was called the Ikonus – which is why my world is sometimes called Ikonus – and it was revered as – how did we say it? – "a symbol of the perfection of pure, uncorrupted Sorcery exercised in the service of Good". Every student had to take an oath upon it that the arts they learned – even the arts of war – would only be used in the service of goodness.

'But Arlenmia believed that the Ikonus was more than a symbol. She became convinced that it contained vast power, and secrets which the tutors were selfishly guarding for their own use. She thought the power should be released, so that all could benefit by it. It's not hard to surmise that if she ever thought of attempting such a thing, Silvren must have dissuaded her, perhaps many times.

'Each year, the sorcery students who had successfully completed their ten years of study participated in a ceremony at which they received the white robes of fully fledged Sorcerers. (I finished my own training in soldiery and Way-finding in the same year as Silvren.) Arlenmia had stayed at the School an extra year to wait for her friend, but just before the ceremony, the High Master informed her that as she could only draw her power through mirrors, not through herself, she was not a true Sorceress and therefore could not don the white robe.

'We heard later how upset Arlenmia was by this: distraught, humiliated and outraged. Understandably, I suppose. Even Silvren could not console her. The ceremony went ahead as planned and I remember vividly that Silvren received her white mantle without a trace of joy, because Arlenmia was not there. If only someone had thought to find out where she was!

'The ceremony took place outside, and the sun was shining on the School so that it glittered like a palace of diamonds. No one foresaw what was about to happen. The first we knew that anything was wrong was when the sphere Ikonus began to rock drunkenly in the sky. Then a white light poured from it, more dazzling than the sun. I was half-blinded, and all around me people were screaming. When the light faded, the sphere had gone. But from where it had been, a rumbling darkness was surging across the sky, like a thundercloud, until it was dark as night . . .' Calorn broke off, swallowing hard.

'And this was Arlenmia's doing? What had she done?' Ashurek prompted.

'We found out afterwards. While everyone was busy with the ceremony, she had gone to her room and worked through her mirrors to release the "secrets" of the Ikonus. Some said she never meant any actual harm, only to steal the power and flee . . . If that's what she intended, she'd made a terrible mistake. The Ikonus was no mere symbol, but neither did it contain the marvellous secrets she desired. The High Master described it as the work of centuries, "a sphere that captured and contained all the dark, negative forces which otherwise would have tainted our sorcery, a filter through which only good energies could pass". That was why we revered it. But within it was only blackness, and that blackness spread around my world like a blanket. It became perpetually cold and dark, and the plants, animals, everything began to die . . .'

'And what happened to your world?' Estarinel asked gently. 'Were they able to save it?'

Calorn took a deep breath and steadied her voice. 'The Sorcerers believed they would be able to heal it eventually. But it would be a long, hard task, one in which only a few possessed the sorcerous skill to help. By now much of the damage will have been healed . . . I hope.'

'What became of Silvren and Arlenmia?' Ashurek enquired with a touch of impatience.

'As soon as the High Master realised what had happened, he and the tutors rushed to detain Arlenmia, but she had already vanished. When she saw the havoc she'd wreaked, she must have used her skills to flee the world. No one knew where she had gone. But a few weeks later Silvren, who had been distraught, vanished as suddenly. A couple of the tutors said good riddance, she had been as foolish as Arlenmia, but most were distressed, because they had wanted her to stay at the School and become a tutor herself. I don't think even the High Master understood why she had followed Arlenmia. And I have only realised it myself since I met you, Ashurek.'

Estarinel looked round at the Gorethrian and said, 'When Silvren spoke to me in the Glass City, she said, "Arlenmia brought another world to ruin before this, and it is my fault she came here." '

'Yes, I remember,' said Ashurek heavily. 'I understand well enough, Calorn. In all innocence, she must have told Arlenmia about this Earth and the Serpent. In her desire for power or knowledge, no doubt Arlenmia did not believe that the Serpent was evil; or at least, she probably decided to come and see for herself. And as soon as Silvren realised where she'd gone, she followed her to find out what she was doing.' Ashurek pondered this for a minute or so. 'She must have found Arlenmia and confronted her. When she discovered that Arlenmia planned to serve and worship the Serpent, Silvren would have been horrified. She must have tried with all her strength to make Arlenmia see that she was wrong, and when she failed, I expect she warned Arlenmia that she would use her sorcery against her. Therefore Arlen-

28

mia sent the demon after Silvren, to prevent her from sabotaging her plans for the Worm's supremacy.'

'Poor Silvren,' Estarinel exclaimed, 'to be so cruelly betrayed by someone she thought her friend for so long.'

'Aye,' Ashurek agreed, gazing moodily downwards. 'And to feel it was her fault that M'gulfn had gained an ally of such power. Often it seems that the harder someone fights the Serpent, the more they do to aid it.'

'I'm sorry this was such a revelation to you,' Calorn put in. 'I had thought you would've known most of it already.'

'Don't apologise. I'm grateful to you for telling me. It puts much in perspective.'

'I know it must be terrible for you, to know that the Dark Regions are on the other side of the Blue Plane, so near, and yet so impossible even to consider rescuing Silvren,' Calorn said, and immediately wished she had not spoken. The hellish light returned to Ashurek's eyes; he glared at her for a moment, then stood up abruptly and strode away. Calorn stared after him, feeling a sudden conflict of duties and emotions.

'I always seem to say the wrong thing to him,' she murmured.

'Don't take it to heart,' said Estarinel. 'It's hard to say the right thing.'

'I only wish . . .' she said thoughtfully, 'I wish there was something I could do to help him.'

Estarinel replied, 'The only thing that will help any of us is for the Quest of the Serpent to be completed, and you are helping in that, Calorn.'

The small boat carrying Medrian and the Lady of H'tebhmella drifted gently through water that was as clear as liquid glass. The vessel was made of a pale, smooth wood and pulled by a water-dwelling horse with arched neck and delicately tapering head. They sailed a long way before mooring and stepping onto an island of sapphire and indigo crystal. As Medrian and the Lady crested a rise in the shore, they saw a long vista of weird and beautiful formations, like joyously leaping water frozen in its carefree dance. There were arches and knolls and spires of shining rock, shimmering in every shade of blue and violet. Mist that was like sparkling heliotrope light drifted between them, but the drifting seemed somehow meaningful.

Medrian had to swallow a tightness in her throat as she saw the landscape. She could not say why she felt moved, except that the mist seemed sentient, moving among the rocks as if greeting old friends with infinite tenderness. The formations themselves seemed to return the greeting, bowing imperceptibly with love and gentleness in every line of their forms. At the same time, the strange, still dance of light and stone was so unearthly, so far above and beyond her that she knew she could never touch or share in their communion.

All that love, she thought, and I am condemned to feel cold for ever.

As if reading her thoughts, the Lady placed a comforting hand on Medrian's arm and led her down the slope into the strange landscape. There was a light in her grey eyes, like the sun shining through spring rain, as she said, 'Everything, even rock, has a spirit. In places the soul of H'tebhmella shows itself in more than external beauty. Don't be – envious. No human can hope to feel such pure and unhuman emotion.'

Medrian dropped her eyes, shivering.

'I am not envious,' she said. 'I have had enough pure and unhuman emotion to kill me – the Serpent's hate.'

The Lady's hand fell from Medrian's arm as if even she had no reply to this, no answer for her pain. She was silent for a long moment. Then she said, 'Medrian, forgive me.'

'My Lady, I should not have—' Medrian broke off, biting her lip. 'You asked me to talk with you, but I don't know whether I can. I'm so unused to being able to speak freely. It's difficult.'

'Then there's no need, if you don't wish it,' the Lady responded gently. 'Let us just walk for a while.'

They went on in silence. The soft blue mist swirled around them, attaching itself to them in motes of azure incandescence. Their hair – the Lady's silken brown, Medrian's black – floated in the charged air, full of blue sparks. The Lady had faith that Medrian would, eventually, find words to express the misery that had been locked within her for so long, and so find release for it. *This time on H'tebhmella is the only happiness she will ever know,* the Lady thought sorrowfully, *but while she is here no consolation, no joy will be denied her.*

Medrian, however, had no expectation that confiding in the Lady would help her. Kind and wise as the H'tebhmellian woman was, she was not mortal. She glided through the weird landscape at Medrian's side, tall, beautiful, crystalline – and so distant. There was a gulf of sapphire between them, no human warmth. *I cannot bear this alien beauty,* Medrian thought, *it can't be real . . .*

Without knowing it, she had discovered H'tebhmella's paradox. The Blue Plane was viewed as a kind of paradise, enigmatic and unattainable. Some strove for years to find an Entrance Point to it, and the few who succeeded found it all they had dreamed of, and much more. Yet no one ever stayed there for more than a few months. The H'tebhmellians had never forbidden anyone from living out their lives there, but perhaps the Blue Plane was too perfect, its unearthly beauty too alien. Sooner or later each person would feel a restless need to return to a more normal, spherical world. For that reason H'tebhmella remained, in actuality, unattainable, and so its legendary enigma was perpetuated.

Since the initial relief of arriving here had faded, Medrian had been assailed by self-doubt and indecision. They were enemies she had never had to fight before and she was afraid, because to lose the battle would destroy her. She ached to ask the Lady a question, but she could not seem to frame it.

'Won't you tell me what's in your heart?' the Lady murmured, sensing her struggle.

'I don't know. I would, but—' With sudden, heartfelt bitterness the confession burst from her, 'Oh, I wish I had never come here.'

31

The Lady turned to her, a look of enquiry on her clear, compassionate face. 'Medrian, why?'

'All my life I have dreamt of being free of the Serpent,' she said, her voice icy and flat as if she was fighting to retain her composure, 'I know it's said that M'gulfn cannot touch the Blue Plane in any form, but I still could hardly believe it when I came through the Entrance Point – and I was free. I still can't believe it – it feels so—' She shuddered with remembered dread and revulsion. 'It's heaven to me. And I can't stand it.'

The Lady's rain-grey eyes were full of sorrow as Medrian went on, her voice hoarse with loss, 'It's heaven I can never have. I can't afford to let it touch me, any more than I can afford to let the Serpent touch me. I have to harden myself to it, so that I can bear to go back into the world and finish the Quest. If I accepted freedom, I would be finished—'

'Medrian, you must not doubt your strength,' the Lady said gently. 'If you accept the small amount of comfort we can give you here, I believe it will increase your strength, not undermine it.'

'When there's no hope, how can there be any comfort?' she exclaimed savagely. 'I'm sorry, my Lady. It's selfish to think only of my own hope – I forsook that many years ago. I have received healing here, and without H'tebhmella the world would have no hope at all. But no one can help me. Not even – not even you. I've accepted it.'

The Lady felt inwardly stilled, almost stunned, as though the very fabric of the Blue Plane had shifted beneath her feet. What a fool I have been, she reflected, I thought I knew everything. Now, the revelation. Medrian is unhappy on H'tebhmella; even we, here, cannot really touch or ease her misery. Have I deluded her, as well as myself? Must the Serpent triumph?

Now the Lady of H'tebhmella knew; there was nothing left with which she could reassure or even console Medrian. She could not even tell her not to be discouraged, because she already was; despair was all that kept her going.

The Lady could look into human souls as into crystal, and

she shared deeply in their suffering and devoted all her strength to alleviating it. Yet it had always seemed to her that people had an insubstantial quality that she could not quite touch, any more than a rock can grasp the sea that washes against it. She knew she could never cross that essential barrier, for she was H'tebhmellian, immortal. And now, faced with this Alaakian woman, whose soul was as intangible as a shadow, the Lady felt the void more acutely than ever. All her compassion, strength and wisdom had failed her; she felt wordless, powerless. Diminished. I cannot heal her. M'gulfn had won.

When the Lady spoke at last, there was a quality of inner exhaustion in her voice that Medrian had never heard before. 'I accept that you feel like this, but I wish you would tell me your story, so that I can understand more clearly what has brought you to this depth of hopelessness.'

Medrian hesitated, and the Lady felt sure that she would refuse. But at last she said, 'Very well. I will tell you, because you are the only one to whom I'll ever be able to speak freely. Not that relating it can change anything, but it might restore my strength of purpose.'

Emotionlessly, the words falling from her lips like cold, white pebbles, Medrian began to describe her life, a nightmare such as even the Lady could not have envisaged.

2

Medrian of Alaak

MEDRIAN DREAMED.

She dreamed that she was lying in snow under a black dome of night, and the light of stars was burning around her – stars that quivered with mocking pain, like the fragments of a shattered crystal.

She dreamed that her body was long and loathsome, a thick grey cord of knotted muscles covered in a colourless, flaky membrane like the discarded skin of a snake. She felt so, so heavy, as heavy as pitchblende, and at her sides leathery wings twitched feebly, impotent of flight. Yet within the core of her body a latent energy vibrated, radiating along every muscle rope, as slumbrous and fierce and deadly as the power at the earth's heart.

The snow felt lukewarm and ice crystals grated against her skin membrane; the feeling was both irritating and deeply familiar. She rocked the weighty body from side to side, groaning faintly as she failed to lift her lead-heavy head. Unfamiliar, nightmarish sounds rent her lobeless ears; someone was singing, though she had never heard a voice before, or any sound except the fall of snow and the creaking of ice, and the moaning of the wind in the stars.

Medrian dreamed she was the Serpent.

Or rather, it dreamed and she was forced to share it, seeing through its eyes and experiencing its feelings and thoughts. Its thoughts were wordless images, vivid and explicit and nightmarish, redolent of age-old, unforgotten terror. For the Serpent suffered its recurring phantasm of aeons ago, when it had been the only living being on Earth, and the Guardians had come to rend it of its power. And Medrian was entrapped in the nightmare, no longer knowing that she existed as herself. She was the Serpent, and to her the dream was real.

She lay upon the roof of the world, safe and inviolable in her domain of sighing, snow-filled gales. Of her origins she remembered nothing; she had always been there, past and future were just a grey tunnel of eternity. She – the Serpent M'gulfn – was in perpetual symbiosis with the Earth, her Kingdom and home.

Until this moment.

Grey figures stood before her, their shapes both vague and chillingly real through her three Serpent's eyes. They stood upright; they each had a torso and a head and four limbs but each was shrouded in an ashen robe. She had never seen – never seen anything but snow. One of them was singing. She had never heard—

The song seemed to pinion her long Worm-body to the ground as if each word was a lead arrow. All the appalling power of the Serpent was rendered impotent by the song – she could not fly – could not even raise her head – could do nothing but groan.

She saw them flinch back at the terrible sound of M'gulfn's voice, but the song grew stronger and she weaker. They advanced upon her. The words of the song made no sense, for she had never heard words before, but still they purged her every sinew of its strength. Now a throbbing, sick sensation filled her dim consciousness, terrifying in its very unfamiliarity.

For the first time, the Serpent felt fear.

To the Serpent, fear was not a word; it was a feeling. An image of bones crushed to dust, skin flayed from nerveless muscles. Medrian thrashed in the prison of her dream – rocked her Serpent body and groaned as the figures glided closer, filling her trinary vision.

Her three eyes twitched and rolled in their sockets, muscles spasmed as if trying to draw the orbs back into the dark recesses of her skull, there to hold them safe. The effort

35

speared her optic nerves with pain, but her eyes remained vulnerable—

Pain!

M'gulfn-Medrian saw the flash of metal before it cut under her centre eye, continued to see it even as the eye was dragged from its socket. And when the nerves and muscles were severed, the flash continued as a scream of white fire shafting through her head. Through that blazing agony, her two remaining eyes saw the figure step back, clutching the small blue orb as if it was a deadly creature that would inflict a fatal bite if he did not hold it firm. No flesh-fibres hung from it. It did not bleed.

My eye!

The white sword of pain rent her skull with impossible pressure. Her struggles were useless. A long, long age passed before she knew that the hurt was not caused by metal struck through her head, but by nothingness. The socket was empty, there was no knife. No eye.

Now there was no dread song to pinion her against the snow; the Serpent's vast energy was returning. Soon pain was forgotten, fear a blurred, hollow memory. And Medrian-M'gulfn felt rage. With a roar, she lifted the thick body into the sky on trembling, primeval wings. But beneath her, the only witness to her ponderous, dreadful circling was the wind sighing across the ice-plains like the weeping of the world.

The figures had gone. And with them, her precious eye.

The Serpent screamed its torture, its frustration and rage; screamed until even the wind dared not challenge its voice. Images exploded across its primitive mind.

They have taken my eye, the thought-pictures said.

Men will come to the Earth. The world will teem with their small, frail bodies that are made in the image of the Guardians – head and limbs and torso. I have always known that men will come, I have always waited for their coming and I can still wait – what is a million years to me but the drifting down of a single snowflake? They have taken the eye with which I could have looked into the hearts and minds of men, bent their petty wills to mine and made them see that I am supreme on Earth; I am the Earth.

They have tried to take my power. The next time they come, they will try to slay me.

They shall not slay me, not *me*!

Emotion tore apart the Serpent's mind then, sparked and ran like fire along every sinew of its body, like tinder that had been poised, dry and flammable, for the ignition of insult and pain. Its body thrashed, scored and engulfed by the flames of emotion.

The emotion was hate.

Hate. Medrian writhed in the dream, the cosmic intensity of the Serpent's malice filling her lungs with burning pain.

The Guardians, I hate. Men, in their image, I loathe also. When they come into existence, I shall despise them doubly.

The image of hatred was more terrible than that of fear. It was blood and rage and violence, and worse; it was grief and despair and desolation; and overlaying all, the grey of escapeless eternity.

Men will come to the Earth and because the Guardians have taken my eye I cannot see into their hearts and they will not worship me. But I have other powers. With my two remaining eyes I shall keep watch over the hideously dry, warm lands where they will live. I can hold sway over the elements.

I have boundless power. I can make for myself helpers who will instil chaos into their existence. And – grim triumph shook the Worm's body like an earthquake as the idea came to it.

I can take for myself a human in which to hide my mind, so that I can move unseen among men, learning their words and ways and weaknesses. In the second body I can hide when they try to slay me. And then I can still – even without my eye – see into their hearts!

My enmity is as boundless as my power.

Men will evolve upon the Earth – my Earth, the invaders! – seeking life and joy and hope. I will give them confusion and pain and death.

And at the end of all, desolation.

In the whirling vertigo of its thought-images, the Worm did not notice, or took for an ache in its empty eye-socket, a small subconscious stone of doubt. If it had looked, it would have seen a chilling vista of eternity: the Earth, stripped of all life and beauty, and itself, lying alone and motiveless upon the dead husk for ever. But it did not look. It had already found too much diabolic joy to care.

Desolation.

'It wasn't the first time I had the nightmare,' Medrian told the Lady. 'Nor the last. But I remember that time because it was the turning point. I struggled awake, trying to scream. My lungs were burning with the stench of smoke, and my side was knotted with cramp; I couldn't think where I was, what had happened. But then the dream faded and I remembered . . . I was sitting in the bottom of a rank, weed-choked ditch, concealed by black trees. There was smoke drifting through the branches, and I could still hear the occasional faint shout in the distance. There was a man lying with his head on my lap, my Commanding Officer . . . and he was near death.

'Alaak had lived under Gorethria's rule for centuries, but never accepted it. The rebellion was inevitable, well-planned we thought. The army was drilled in secret for years. I was seventeen and had already been a soldier since fourteen. We could not have trained harder, been more devoted . . . and yet, in one fell afternoon, it was over. Gorethria crushed us, just one division, led by Ashurek. Half the population dead, the rest waiting for the Gorethrian army to sweep across them – and me, a survivor crouched in a ditch, wishing I had died with the others.

'By rights, I should have done. I had taken a deep sword thrust in my side, yet it had not killed me. There was no blood. And my Officer, even as he lay dying beside me, could not forget how he had always disliked and distrusted me.'

Even now, eight or more years later, the memory was still unpleasant. 'Why did it have to be you with me at my death? Why you, Medrian?' the Officer had gasped. 'Like a bloody basilisk, you are, always have been. I don't think you've ever given a damn about Alaak, or anything else. You fight like an automaton. You take a death blow and do not die. Are you human?' he demanded fiercely. 'You must be as sick with hatred as Meshurek and Ashurek and the rest.'

Hate! Images of desolation reeled across her vision. She longed to cry out, no! I don't hate. All this has happened because something . . . something loathes us all – the Serpent M'gulfn. But the words turned to clogging dust in her throat. In bitter silence, she gave him water and tried to make him comfortable.

'Forgive me,' he whispered at length, his breath failing. 'It is not you I hate; it is Gorethria. Damn them to hell! Do we not even deserve to live? I am not afraid to die – I'm proud to die in Alaak's defence. I have done my utmost, it is my only fit end. But you, soldier – I feel sorry for you. You are going to escape, and live. Have you done your utmost?'

'It wasn't long before he died,' Medrian said. 'Then I had no more reason to stay in the ditch . . . but no real reason to leave either.'

She had remained with his body for a long time, staring through the spiky black branches of the trees at the white sky as if seeing a reflection of her own blank detachment.

She waited, hoping to die.

She felt numb, as if what had just happened to Alaak meant nothing to her. Her throat ached with numbness. She ached for oblivion.

'Have you done your utmost?' The words echoed at her like an accusation. If he was me, Medrian thought, he would go down and seek out stray Gorethrian soldiers and kill and kill until at last they slew him. Then he would have done his utmost. But I cannot. I don't have enough hate.

She shivered and pulled the black jerkin back on. She stood up, her legs nearly buckling with their cramped weakness; the

39

sword-wound in her side pained her, but it was rapidly healing. There was little honour she could do her dead Officer, except to compose his body and cover him with fallen leaves. Then she scrambled up the side of the ditch and emerged on top, a dirty, battle-weary figure.

She stood up boldly, as if hoping a nearby Gorethrian would see her and fell her. But all was deserted. The acres of shimmering grass that swept across to the feet of stone hills were blasted by fire and battle. There were bodies everywhere, tragic scars on Alaak's stark beauty.

Medrian moved among the bodies like an expressionless puppet, seeing person after person that she knew. Why me, she thought, why did I survive? Did I not do my utmost?

Then she found her horse.

It was a crow-black, sinister beast that had seemed to choose her as its rider, and though she had felt repelled by it, she had been unable to drive it away. Now it lay dead, a great splash of blood congealing on its side. She had been riding it when she was struck, she did not remember it being injured. Its wound was in exactly the same place as her own.

Oh, ye gods.

It died in my place.

Bastard! She screamed inside her head. She fell to her knees, pounding uselessly at the horse's body as if she could make it suffer for depriving her of death. But it just stared back with a glazed, cornflower-blue eye.

She recoiled, agony bursting across her chest. Her stomach knotted, her limbs felt like fast-flowing, dark flood water. The wound in her side opened in a flower of pain. The iron self-control she had willed herself to all her life broke; her numbness burst into thrashing life and all the ice of her soul was crushed, melted and borne away by the flood of her grief.

Oh, my family, she thought. My mother and father and brother, down there in the village with the Gorethrians marching upon them. I can do nothing to save them. I will never know if they live or die. If only I could have loved them, and they me.

40

Oh, Alaak! Oh, Gorethria! Why couldn't you just leave us alone? Was it too much, that even one small crumb of meat should fall from your mouth?

You have done this, you mocking, hating Worm. She raged in fury and grief until her throat was a raw, bloody cavern and her guts were curdled with pain. She struck the ground until her nails were ripped and her hands bleeding, but all the time she was inflicting physical pain upon herself to deaden that dreadful agony in her head that always came when she dared to feel emotion.

All gone, gone; my family and home and land before you gave me the chance to love them. And now I will never have that chance, never. Great, racking sobs ravaged her body, shook her as if they would break her apart. She clawed at the ground and then rolled over, wrapping her arms around her head.

Never, never. All gone.

When she struggled to her knees again, she was screaming. As the nightmare sensation in her head grew worse, her cries weakened to throat-tearing rasps of air. She was scratching at her head as if to pull her brain from it.

The grief and the hideous agony became intermingled, one soul-destroying entity. Long years ago she had steeled herself to an emotionless, ice-cold existence, for if she felt or showed one flicker of emotion it opened her mind to the ghastly presence of the Serpent. It would come crawling through the steel wall into her brain, tormenting her, mocking her, letting her feel the eternal grey horror of its being.

Medrian was the Serpent's human host.

That an immortal being so complete in power and so alien should place its mind to exist alongside that of a frail human was unthinkable. It could have only one result: torment and madness and eventual destruction for that unfortunate human. So had all its previous hosts ended, though the Worm had kept their physical husks alive into old age. But Medrian had in childhood found a way to resist it. She had cut her mind off from it. She had concealed all her thoughts in ice, frozen all her feelings so that eventually the Worm could not

41

touch her. But if ever her coldness warmed for an instant, it would lash back at her with threefold fury.

Its evil, grey mockery flooded her now, like thick-flowing acid she was helpless to wash from her body. It clung like spiders' webs round her face, in her head – a suffocating nightmare of madness.

No! This is what I have always fought against!

No, Medrian, said the Worm, *you have let me in and you are going to be sorry you kept me out. I loathe you as much as you loathe me*.

No! I will feel my grief – let me feel my grief, I've never been allowed to feel anything till now – I won't be denied—

I will not be denied either, my Medrian, said the Worm.

She writhed in her struggle against it, squirming in the blood of dead warriors as she fought to release her misery without suffering the Serpent's torment. She failed. M'gulfn was laughing at her pain. Even as she poured out her despair it seemed to ring with hollow mirth, as if death itself were dancing with skeletal glee at its own existence.

When her mother had hugged her as a child she had had to hold herself stiff and cold and unresponsive, lest the Serpent throw her down in a fit of agony. Eventually her mother had ceased hugging her.

She gulped down air into her lungs and held it there. She took her arms from her head and stretched them out as if they were stiff with tetany. She held her head up and looked across the pale battleground and thought of coldness. Frozen steel and white ice came to encapsulate her mind until it was a polar wilderness.

It took a long time. The Worm was reluctant to release its hold; it retreated with agonising slowness, clutching at her brain with desperate tentacles. It was whispering, *you can't do this to me, I must see your thoughts and make you suffer, suffer . . .*

But at last it was over. Her violent emotions were under control and M'gulfn felt no worse than a reptile coiled in her brain, pressing persistently against the wall she had brought between its mind and her own.

She relaxed her spasmed muscles, falling forward like a rag doll. Her first long breath emerged like a groan of absolute despair.

She pressed the heels of her hands against the earth, enduring the grit in her raw wounds like a penance. Never, she told herself with determined finality. Never again.

She rose and looked about, as if making sure no one had seen her frantic struggles on the ground. The long plain of grass was still deserted. A warm wind from the Empire blew ash before it, lamenting towards the distant villages whence the Gorethrians had marched.

She could not bury the dead. She would not follow the Gorethrians and ambush them one by one till they killed all the old and young in retribution. She would not try to find her family.

She must leave Alaak behind.

She must stop the hatred in another way.

Wearily, she began to trudge the leagues to the shore, there to find a boat and sail the straits to the Empire.

I will not rest, she told herself, until I have done my utmost.

Even if she had known it would be eight years before the Quest of the Serpent was even begun, she still would not have turned aside in despair. She was in despair, but she froze herself against all such feelings and went steadfastly on. She did not care if it took a lifetime to fulfil her goal. Her one aim was to stop M'gulfn's evil and bring an end to her own misery.

Her eight years in the Empire were weary and soul-eroding. It was a vast continent and she had many countries to cross on her way to Gorethria. She trudged through jungles and tropical forests teeming with strange creatures, waded dangerous rivers; she crossed volcanic mountain ranges and arid plains of sand. She met electric storms, burning winds and floods; she fought strange creatures and was once captured by dark warriors of the Empire. Her only companion through these dangers was another crow-black horse which had forced its sinister faithfulness upon her. She knew it was a creature of M'gulfn, which it was using both to protect her and intimidate her. But she tolerated the beast, and a dark love-hate relationship developed between them.

The horse died when, in one of her darkest moments, suicide seemed the only escape from the savage, blue-skinned tribe who had imprisoned her. When she tried to kill herself, it died in her stead. Crying in terror that she was a supernatural being, a demon, one of the Shana, the tribe drove her away and she ran into the hills, laughing with hollow irony at her plight.

A few days later a third raven-black horse came to her. Grinning like a fiend driven mad by its own evil, Medrian mounted it eagerly and drove it at an exhausting gallop towards the heart of Gorethria.

Each adventure only seemed to shape her for the worse, and she felt she had aged twenty years in those eight. The Serpent never ceased to fight her, creeping at her in nightmares, whispering to her through the wall, its mutterings like shouts in the silence of her mind. Only in great danger or physical pain did it withdraw – whether it was enjoying the spectacle of her external suffering, or whether it was actually afraid to share her pain, she did not know. Each battle left her more despairing, but also stronger, colder, and more determined.

The most difficult task of all was moving unseen through Gorethria itself. At first she travelled only at night, but when she neared the cities she found herself clothes such as a slave would wear, and became adept at skimming through the streets as if on a vital errand for her non-existent master. The horse was no problem, for slaves were allowed to ride; a mounted, well-dressed slave was a sign of a wealthy master. And they were allowed in public buildings, even libraries.

Medrian came at last to the first goal of her journey: the glittering capital city, Shalekahh, and the vast library annexed to the palace. Here she hoped to find knowledge, and perhaps an answer to her own need.

The sight of the palace, with its porcelain-white painted

walls, chilled her. If it was possible to feel colder than she already did, that edifice sealed her icy destiny. It stank of demons. The thought of Meshurek, hunched on his throne in the grip of the Worm-serving Shana, nauseated her. She did not at that time know Meshurek's tragic story, but the demon-presence around the palace was tangible to her senses. It underlined what she knew, that the Serpent was behind this savagery and misery.

She entered the echoing, vaulted halls of the library like a thief, but went unchallenged past the tall, ornately dressed librarians. She moved along shelf after shelf of books, searching for any information she could find about the Worm. But either scholars had been afraid to write about it, or the works were not taken seriously enough to be kept under the history or science sections.

She went deeper into the library, ignored by the dark-skinned Gorethrian men and women studying there. At last she found a small, dim side-room with a sign over the doorway that read, Astrology, Religion and Superstition. The shelves were crammed with manuscripts and books, many in rough unmarked covers as if they had only been bound, years ago, when they arrived at the library. Volumes were stacked on the floor as well, but the dust that plumed up from every book she touched showed how little the section was used.

She soon found out why. Many of the books were rubbish, mere myth and speculation. Others, more sinisterly, were in Gorethrian so ancient that only scholars could have deciphered it, but all the same, they had an aura that terrified her. As her eyes glanced over the alien text, the odd word that she understood would scream out at her, filling her with the dread of finding a meaning behind an incomprehensible nightmare. Laboriously she worked her way through the books, fighting a panic sensation that she would never escape from the room.

In the writings of ages past, [she read in a great calf-skin volume] we find mention of a mythical creature called the Serpent or Worm M'gulfn. The origins of the belief in this creature are obscure. It is possible that such a being did once live, and certain people saw it and told others; in the retelling, such stories inevitably attributed the being with ever more awesome supernatural qualities. So myths are born. Even in the author's lifetime there came a tale from the far North of the Empire, that a great grey monster had flown down from the Arctic and devoured many of them and laid waste their land. It can only be assumed that they were using symbolism as the best way to describe a devastating storm—

Medrian slammed the book shut in disgust. The pompous rationality of the author contrasted sickeningly with the hideous reality that she knew. The words seemed like the laughing of a ghoul. Abhorred, she dropped the volume. Her heart sank as she began to realise that none of the authors had the knowledge she needed – what the Serpent was, and if it could be killed. They did not even understand that the need existed.

The light was failing when she at last found a book she could understand. It explained, straightforwardly, the creation of the Earth and Planes, and how the Serpent itself had come into being – just as, years later, the Lady of H'tebhmella was to explain it. Medrian read it avidly, and she knew, from the faint reactions of M'gulfn suppressed deep within her, that it was true.

Men, animals and plants have evolved upon the Earth [the book said]. Their existence owes nothing to the Serpent. So where do the Shana, whom men call 'demons', fit into the plan of things? Undoubtedly they are not natural beings and they live in a separate Region that is not of the Earth or Planes. We conclude that the Serpent made them itself. It has abundant energy; it has every reason to resent man's presence on Earth; and so it has created beings of its own to torment and eventually master the human race which it hates.

Now this to me offers conclusive proof that the Grey

Ones, or Guardians, do exist and have intervened on Earth at times. The Shana have great power and are loathsomely evil. There is no reason why they should not have run riot upon the Earth and destroyed everything millennia ago (then, of course, they would have risen up against the Serpent and it, in turn, would have destroyed them); except that the Grey Ones, for the Earth's sake, have placed what restraints they can against them. The Shana's Region has been moved from under the Earth to outside it, and they can only come when men call. The summoning is arduous, and but few have the knowledge of it; and the Shana now have to offer something more than torment to the summoner or they would never be called at all. But they are still dangerous, and the Grey Ones' intervention has only made them, and the Serpent, more vengeful in the long run . . .

This was all new to Medrian; she read to the end of the small book feeling that she had at least learnt the external truth, even if she never discovered the internal.

The next book slid into her hand as if it had been waiting for her. It was a volume of only about twenty thick handwritten sheets carefully bound in dark leather. There were three or four different handwritings, all very old but more or less legible. Even in the fading light she could read the words easily, as if they were glowing with their own ghostly light, and they conveyed to Medrian the feeling of a distant, haunting dream whose subject had been forgotten, but whose terror and mystery still called to her across an abyss of years. The book was called *The First Witness of the Serpent*.

I walked with Eldor across the snow, [the first writer said]. I don't know where I was. We could have been in the Arctic, or anywhere. The snow was flat and the night sky like crystal. I felt that the Earth was very young, though I know this cannot have been, so perhaps the whole thing was a dream. But at least in the dream Eldor attempted to make rational the rest of my life, which has been a phantasm of terror, and for that I bless him. I asked him why the Worm has made my life a nightmare.

Medrian read the words with a thrill of dread, suddenly knowing that they had been written by a previous host of the Serpent; it was as though she had written them herself, so intimately she knew the pain behind them. At the same time she felt M'gulfn stirring within her; its emotions revolted her, but this one was new. She cautiously lifted the mental screen between them, so that she could glimpse its thoughts. Grimly, she read on.

'Understand,' Eldor said to me, gently as to a child, 'the Serpent is not just a living creature. It is a solid manifestation of unearthly power. When the Earth itself was curdled from the vast cosmic forces of the universe, the energy produced by that creation struggled to separate itself into two parts. In that dreadful conflict the Planes were struck into existence; and when they at last diverged, the negative part of the energy spun in upon itself, until it birthed itself into a creature of cosmic powers – the Serpent. And the positive energy whirled outwards into an infinite ring that long ago passed beyond helping us . . .'

Within Medrian, M'gulfn's strange emotion became stronger. She could not yet identify it, but gasped at its intensity; it was like – like a frantic possessive jealousy, yet there was more to it than that.

Even the Guardians [the writer continued], have been unable to destroy or even restrain it. Eldor told me, 'They tore an eye of power from its head, but that has only filled it with rage and malice, made it aware that it has enemies and so more dangerous. So do not torture yourself with thoughts of destroying it; such a thing is impossible, and it would only revenge itself on you for thinking of its death.'

I despaired when Eldor said this, thinking there was no hope. I could only hope for death, though with the knowledge that the Worm would then seek a new host for itself, make another's life agony, and another's, and on and on. But Eldor did give me hope – only a small thought, intangible, but it has kept me sane enough to write these words, if ever they may be of use to another.

He told me of the bird Miril. 'She is a tiny fraction of that lost positive power,' Eldor said. 'The Guardians captured the dot of energy to guard the stolen Eye, but they did not create Miril from it; she created herself. She is beautiful, and sad, for she knows she cannot keep the Eye safe for ever. One day the Serpent will find a way to unleash it upon the world, and at last regain it, and dominate the Earth with its grey horror. But she is still the World's Hope. The sun does not shine brighter than her outstretched wings, and the crystal rocks of the Earth are her tears . . .' so said Eldor.

Sweet Miril, Hope of the World, I keep you in my thoughts; you alone the Serpent cannot dominate, you are our only symbol of love and freedom until the end of time.

Medrian dropped the book into her lap with a stifled cry, then sat white-faced and swaying like one who is very ill, or drugged. Another emotion flared from M'gulfn's mind into her own like a gout of flame: loathing of Miril. It was more than loathing – the repulsion of complete opposites, tainted with hate and even fear. M'gulfn despised Miril, would tear her from the sky and devour her if ever it could. Medrian cringed, trembling, under the force of that hate, feeling she was being devoured herself.

She reopened the book and read on. The next hand was spiky, wild and demented in form. But she recognised in acute detail the fractured images of his suffering.

'This black snake comes to me, it came out of my child-hood, hiding in the corners of my room and in my head, I see the Worm-form of it, the grinning Snake that bites my head with razor-teeth . . .' As she forced herself, shuddering, to read to the end, she seemed to be drifting down a long twilit tunnel of horrified revelation – and at the end M'gulfn was waiting, waiting for her to see the truth and surrender in her despair.

The next writer seemed to have written her account in secret and in a great hurry, having no time for detailed explanations or anything but objectivity.

I am a woman of Morrenland. I am in prison. No one will believe my experience, but as it is true I must write it. I was in the army that went North, at the King's command, to destroy the Serpent. The King thought it a heroic exploit to add to his glory. How little he knew of the truth. Still, I had no power to tell him.

We sailed to the Arctic and marched across the snow. The others went proudly, joking and laughing bravely at the cold and at the spectres the Serpent sent to haunt our path. But it was tormenting me, and I could not speak aloud to warn them all and turn back the insane mission.

In due course we found the Serpent. It was smaller than we had thought, grotesque, lying in the snow as if it could not move. The others grew arrogant, thinking they could overpower it.

But at our first attack, the Serpent rose up on wings and circled us, spitting down acid. Several died in that first attack. All the time it was raging its furious glee in my head. I could stand no more. I prayed to be killed quickly.

At its second attack, it snatched the rest of the soldiers in its jaws in several swoops, chewed them and dropped their broken bodies in the snow. I did not escape, but alas, I did not die. When I came to myself, lying in the bloody snow, all my comrades were dead and the Serpent was staring at me like an impassive gargoyle amid their crushed bodies. I was in terrible physical agony. My arm and leg were broken, my head cracked, and my body rent from throat to abdomen by its stinking teeth. My skin burned with its venom. Then I understood that I should be dead, but the Worm was keeping me alive.

50

I cannot bear to describe what it said to me as I stood there, how it laughed at my misery and pain. I don't know why I didn't go mad, but that would have been too easy an escape. It berated me, then it forced me to walk – with my leg broken and my skin in shreds – all the weary miles through the bitter Arctic, across the Tundra and down through Tearn to Morrenland. I felt every detail of the pain. I was a walking corpse, animated by the Serpent.

I came to Morrenland and went before the King. The Serpent forced me to report the failure of the mission, with all its derision in my voice. Their fear of me was obvious; I must have looked and behaved like a Serpent-possessed ghoul. The only thing they could do with me was imprison me, and impose the death sentence for desertion.

Now I await the hanging. I hope the Serpent will let me die, although if I do – sorrow for the hangman! I feel composed now, the Serpent is distant. Strange that I am so calm and rational, as if my very lucidity is a manifestation of madness. I am only sorry that I will die having learnt nothing, except that fighting the Serpent is foolishness. I have never suffered fools.

The woman finished her account with a bold underline. Below, in a black, erratic scrawl, were the words,

Sorrow for the hangman indeed! Sorrow, sorrow, sorrow!

And that was all. But Medrian knew that if the host was killed, the Serpent would enter the body of the killer; to her, the spidery writing was a perfect graph of his torment.

She stared at the blank end-paper of the book as if willing words to appear on it. She felt bloodless, raw, her lungs full of grit. There must be more, she thought. Is this all there is? I haven't found everything out yet. What about the thousands of other hosts there have been?

Then she realised.

The truth was inside her, waiting to be explored. All the

51

knowledge and memories were in M'gulfn's mind, if she only had the courage to look at its thoughts. She had already felt some of the memories, in that strange emotion like jealousy. The Serpent, although it had treated all its hosts with despicable cruelty, apparently also felt an attachment for them, a sick, possessive love. She recoiled inwardly as she recognised that. Distorted by evil as it was, it was not a parody of affection. It was real.

Closing her eyes and leaning back against the shelf of books, she let herself drift down the Serpent's corridor of memories. She saw every detail, though clouded by its consciousness, of its long solitary existence in the Arctic snow, the stealing of its eye by the Guardians, all its many hosts, the few hopeless missions to destroy it, the giddying flights across the world that left it torpid and exhausted . . .

She reeled away from its mind, fighting to re-establish her own identity. She had learnt . . . she had learnt more than she had ever desired to know. She had felt blood in her mouth . . .

She staggered to her feet, wavering like a dying tree in a cold wind. I've learned the truth, what have I lost? I never had any hope anyway, never any hope, she kept telling herself. She tucked the book, *The First Witness of the Serpent*, under her jacket and smuggled it from the library with the ease of an adept thief. The librarians were just locking the doors. Outside, all was darkness.

Medrian wandered from Shalekahh and eventually left Gorethria's borders, not knowing or caring where she was going. She wandered as if blind, numb to almost everything outside or inside herself.

She was so stricken by the truth she had discovered at last that she ceased to function. The Serpent could not be suffered to live. Yet it was, she now knew, indestructible. Even she could not endure such a depth of despair within herself, and so instead she stopped feeling and thinking.

She let the horse carry her where it would, staring ahead as it plodded on. If anyone spoke to her, they were ignored, and sometimes she sat and stared at the unmarked last page of the book for hours, as if searching for some unforeseen revelation there.

But a nightmare came and shook her out of her stupor. A confusion of impressions, something that the Serpent was experiencing physically, flickering back through its mind to hers. It was preparing to fly, to attack, although it had not moved for centuries.

No!

Like the painful first cry of a baby, her awareness, her thoughts and feelings and nerves, screamed back into life. Don't attack – not Forluin – not anywhere—

But the Serpent did not listen to Medrian. It flew and ravaged a peaceful island, while she endured the nightmare of vague impressions – blood, and death, and vertigo – until at last it returned to the Arctic and lay in torpor, brooding sickly on its victory.

And Medrian lay awake on the hard ground, wide-eyed and shuddering throughout a long night, while the horse grazed impassively close by. It is not just my suffering – it is everyone's; and the hosts – there were thousands before me and there will be thousands after me, and I can do nothing—

When morning came, Medrian had made her decision. She filled in the last page of the book, turning increasingly grey as she wrote as if she was engraving her own future into the most appalling story of horror ever written. When she had finished she tucked the book beneath her jacket and secured it there with a belt. Then she mounted her horse and rode to the nearest port. I have been a fool, she thought. I have learned the truth, and lost even the hope of hope, but what does that matter? It doesn't matter at all, it means nothing. But Alaak's suffering – Forluin's – mine – I can only try – I said I would not rest until I had done my utmost. It's all I can do, there's nothing else left.

She found a small ship to take her to Eldor, because she did not know where else on Earth she could go. The sage, at least, might know something that could help her, if only in the small way that he had helped that previous host by telling him of Miril. Later, she was surprised to find that

Eldor seemed to have been expecting her, that a Quest was to take place and in due course Estarinel and Ashurek arrived to go with her. It was as if pre-ordained. She had not expected such concrete help, in spite of what she had written in the book; and although her struggle against M'gulfn had hardly begun, let alone ended, she found a kind of peace in knowing that she faced a final journey.

But when she first arrived and met the grey-haired sage, she could not speak. The Serpent would not allow her to explain what she was. But Eldor, as soon as he saw the small dark-haired woman, whose face was as white and cold as quartz, needed no explanation. He recognised the shadows in her eyes and he recognised the thin book she was clasping in her hands. When he reached out and took it she seemed to uncurl herself grimly from the volume, like a witch who had learnt terrible spells therein.

He turned its few pages and found a new hand on the end-paper, compressed and erratic as if the writer was struggling against a persuasive power to express herself. He read,

The Serpent has nightmares.

I have lived alone with it in the quiet void. I have heard its thoughts, seen its snowy home through its own eyes, dreamed its dreams. I have seen desolation. It makes me afraid.

It possesses me, though I struggle to defy it. But escapeless bleak eternity cannot be denied for ever. Once I spoke to it, offering my surrender to its will if only it would stay in its cold domain and not fly South to feast upon innocent flesh . . . *No*, it said to me, *your long silence has caused me pain. Now the bargain does not suffice.*

Never again will I offer it surrender. Though the denial has been colder than the frozen wastes of space, it is ice that can never be thawed again. When the grey desolation of the Serpent overwhelms me at last, as I know it must, my coldness will burn it. The Serpent should not have made me more desperate than itself. It has lost me for all time.

All say the Serpent must win. I have perceived this through the inescapable nightmare of my life. But the Serpent, too, has nightmares. It must have cause; and if not, it will be given cause before I die.

I am Medrian of Alaak.
I am the Last Witness of the Serpent.

3

Forluin

MEDRIAN WAS leaning against a spindle of blue rock as she finished speaking, tracing the facets and angles of its glittering surface with her fingers. She murmured, 'It is so easy to dream of staying here for ever . . . and so treacherous. For I know that I must leave here and resume the Quest, and when I do . . .' she turned round in the mist, a slow, graceful movement like the strange calm of madness. 'It will be waiting for me. Waiting for me.'

'I had thought your deliverance from M'gulfn whilst on the Blue Plane to be a welcome respite,' the Lady admitted sadly. 'Now I see that it may only serve to make things harder for you in the end.' Medrian nodded, her eyes dark with suppressed dread. 'Estarinel and Ashurek do not know who you are yet, do they?'

'No, of course not,' Medrian replied with a self-mocking smile. 'The Serpent would not permit me to tell them. How can the host protect it, unless she is silent and anonymous? At the House of Rede, I thought Ashurek would kill me when I refused to say anything, but even if I had been able to speak, I still would not have done so. Because they must not know until the very end.'

'Yes, you are absolutely right in that.'

'In a way, I'm surprised they haven't guessed. The times M'gulfn fought me, and I almost betrayed the Quest . . . but they still don't know. Perhaps it's because they suspected Arlenmia. And Ashurek believes I came upon the Quest in despair, after Alaak, which is partly true. I don't know what Estarinel thinks about me. Strange, I never cared what

56

anyone thought of me – until Estarinel . . .' Again the question leapt into her throat, but she could not force the words out.

'Medrian, there is something you need to know, is there not? Don't be afraid to ask me,' the Lady encouraged her gently.

Medrian spoke swiftly, before doubt stopped her. 'Well – I am free, for the first time in my life. But the Blue Plane is not Earth – it's so beautiful it's painful to me. I just wondered – what it would be like to be free of the Serpent on Earth, just for a little while. So I could know what it's like to be – normal.' She uttered a dry laugh. 'It's something you said – that the Serpent had "overlooked" Forluin. If I went with Estarinel – is it possible that M'gulfn could not touch me there?'

Oh, Medrian, the Lady thought. This little I can do for you.

'What I said was true. The Serpent attacked Forluin physically, because it cannot exercise power of mind over the island. You can go there in freedom.'

'Thank you, my Lady,' Medrian murmured.

'As to whether your visit is right or wrong,' the Lady added, her eyes shimmering with tears, 'that you must decide for yourself.'

Ashurek and Calorn stood together on a promontory of rock that rose only a bare few inches above the glassy surface of the water. Several yards before them, on the very end of the promontory, three H'tebhmellian women – including Filitha and the Lady – circled a cloud of sparkling blue light, coaxing it into a cohesive sphere with strange, metallic instruments. With them stood Medrian and Estarinel, both wearing H'tebhmellian clothing of pale blue silken material, Estarinel breeches and a loose shirt, Medrian a long dress gathered at the waist and sleeves. They were waiting anxiously for the Exit Point to be completed.

Due to a peculiarity in the complex orbit of H'tebhmella's

Entrance Points, they passed across Forluin more frequently than anywhere else on Earth. A rare conjunction would allow Estarinel and Medrian to return to the Blue Plane in a few hours' time.

'Estarinel doesn't look at all happy at the prospect of visiting Forluin,' Calorn observed.

'What have any of us to be happy about?' Ashurek said gruffly.

'Being in H'tebhmella?' Calorn suggested.

'This can last only a few days more. The idea of attacking the Serpent makes me far from unhappy, but there is still Silvren . . .' he stared down at the soft blue-green moss beneath his feet. Calorn could sense how powerless and restless for action he felt. She was eager for activity herself, and longed to find some way to help him regain Silvren. There was nothing more dear to her soul than a dangerous mission with a satisfying outcome, like a successful rescue.

Ashurek's green eyes were bright with danger against his fine-boned, dark purple-brown face as he glanced up at the H'tebhmellians again. Calorn's thoughts dwelt for a moment on his evil and bloody past, then dismissed it. I know the man, not his reputation, she thought. The H'tebhmellians have spoken no ill of him.

She opened her mouth to speak, but at that instant Filitha called out that the Point was ready. Ashurek and Calorn went forward to watch their two companions leave.

'In eighteen hours' time, an Entrance Point will pass the place where you emerge. Be ready – you must not miss it!' the Lady was saying. She kissed them both on the forehead. 'Now go, with my blessing.'

Estarinel and Medrian stepped into the cloud of blue light and disappeared.

'I don't know that his decision to visit Forluin was wise,' Ashurek muttered. 'Still, as long as they don't lose their courage to continue . . .' He turned and strode swiftly along the finger of rock back to the shore without waiting for any of the others, obviously eager to be alone.

Calorn watched him for a moment; then she made a decision, and started after him.

Estarinel and Medrian emerged from the Exit Point onto the soft floor of a wood. The change in their environment, in the very touch of the air, was so great that both stood still for several moments, stunned. The atmosphere had lost its crystal clarity, but taken on a warmer feel, pleasant and earthy. Late sunlight filtered down through the trees, outlining each leaf with silver and flooding the space between the trunks with a bronze haze.

'It's summer, just as if I'd never left,' said Estarinel. 'How strange to think a year has gone by. The voyage from Forluin to the House of Rede took several months; I never really thought of the seasons changing here, while we were out on the sea.'

'Do you know where we are?' Medrian asked.

'Yes. Trevilith Woods. My home's about an hour's walk, that's all. I spent so much of my childhood in here—' a rush of memories silenced him.

'Come on, then,' Medrian said, but Estarinel stood still, as if rooted to the spot.

'I don't know,' he said emptily. 'I don't think this was a good idea – to go back in the middle of the Quest. I feel I've gone in a large circle and been nowhere. It's wrong. I don't want to see anyone – what can I tell them? I've nearly been killed several times and achieved nothing? Yes, I'm back but the Quest still hasn't begun, I have to go away again. Oh, they'll understand if I explain . . . and then they'll feel fear for me, and reliance on me, as if *I* could save them – all of them – just me. It was the easiest thing in the world to set out on this Quest – now it's become the most difficult to carry on. It's not fair on them to have to rely on me. I don't want to remind them, when perhaps they're starting to forget. I shouldn't have come back.'

Medrian looked at him for several seconds. She felt very strange, as if she was floating. The Lady had spoken truth;

M'gulfn had no power over Forluin, and for the first time she was free of it on Earth. But she still dared not relax, allow herself to feel anything or behave any differently. She could not let herself show sympathy for Estarinel.

'It's too late,' she replied quietly. 'You've made your decision. Come, we can't stay here for eighteen hours.'

He stared into her dark eyes, wondering why he was able to hold her gaze when before it had filled him with coldness. She had always, in her own reserved way, supported him through the worst moments of the Quest; now she was in his land, and must be able to trust him as he trusted her.

He sighed and tried to smile.

'You're right, as usual. This way.' As they began to trudge through the wooded glade, he added, 'I'm glad you came with me.'

She did not reply. She walked in silence beside him, the hem of her H'tebhmellian dress brushing the earth. She felt almost dreamlike, but she had never had a dream like this before; it was at the same time heartrendingly real, making the rest of her life seem a bizarre nightmare. She could appreciate the feel of the leaf-mould beneath her feet and the touch of breeze on her face, the silver-bronze sunlight and the rough, rich texture of tree-bark without suffering the Worm's mocking punishment for daring to love something. For the very first time, she experienced normality, and it was everything she had hoped for.

They came from the ragged edge of the wood onto a broad meadow of grass and bracken whose green fronds filled the air with a fresh aroma. Estarinel increased his pace and they ploughed through the knee-high growth, through a small copse and out onto a green hillside. A patchwork of fields and trees stretched before them, coloured green and amber and honey-gold in the late sun. Nearby a couple of sheep grazed, and a single bird called forlornly from the sky.

Forluin, Medrian saw, was beautiful.

But to their left, the sunset was a splash of garish carmine, like a wound in the clouds. And she could not fail to recognise the greyish haze drifting along the horizon.

She felt Estarinel shudder at her side. For a few minutes he could not speak, so sweet, familiar and homely was this view to him. How often he had ridden and walked and run over this beloved landscape, that was only less dear to him than his family. But he also recognised the Worm's grey haze, polluting the sky and distorting the colour of the sunset. The curse had not left them.

'This area – my home – was just South of the worst of the attack,' he began to explain, the words like grit in his mouth. 'The neighbouring farm was crushed – ours just escaped.'

'I remember, you told me,' Medrian said hurriedly, trying to spare him the pain of talking.

'You can't quite see the farm from here,' he went on, 'but it's only a couple of miles more.'

He led her down the hillside and along a path overhung by great golden beeches.

Eventually Medrian said, 'Forluin is beautiful – the loveliest place I've ever seen. Even now.'

'Normally . . . before,' he answered with hollow sadness, 'the meadows and copses would be teeming with life. Birds singing, deer among the trees. There were sheep and horses everywhere . . .' he shook his head, unable to continue.

They skirted another clump of trees and followed a well-worn bridle path along a hedgerow. At last they came out onto a broad, undulating meadow and Estarinel almost broke into a run.

Fixed in his mind was the image of the bowl-shaped valley when he had last seen it: still green, the old stone farmhouse sitting contentedly on the valley floor amid vegetable gardens and meadows as if nothing had happened. And beyond, at the open end of the valley, had been blasted trees and the ruins of his friend Falin's farm. His family's escape had been that narrow.

Suddenly, the prospect of seeing his beloved parents and sisters again swept all doubts from his mind. They were, at the last, all that was truly important.

'Come on!' he called to Medrian. 'Here's the rim of the valley.' He ran ahead of her and at last gained the green lip

61

of the Bowl Valley from which he could see every detail of his parents' farm.

Medrian, trying to keep up with him, saw him stop. She saw the sudden rigid disbelief shake his body; she gasped with the effort to make herself catch up, see what he had seen.

The valley was grey, a bowl of blasted ash. Trees lay in grotesque ruin, like scorched bones scattered across ground that seemed to be rotting in acid. The ruin wreaked by the Serpent's grey poison extended up the sides of the valley to within a few yards of where they were standing; what remained of grass and hedges was slicked with glutinous grey venom. A stench of desolation, tangible to the skin and eyes, came up from it. It carried the Worm's hate; an undeniable destiny where sickness and misery became the same thing. And in the centre were the crumbled remains of Estarinel's home.

The ruins looked so still and sad, like a small animal that had died of fear.

At first Estarinel was so devastated, so stricken by bitter incredulity, that he could not move. He felt paralysed, numb; a steel wire was tightening around his throat, causing blood to burst blackly across his vision. His head swam with confusion.

'How—' a whisper rasped from his throat. Then a tide of anger, of horror and grief flooded him like a scream of ultimate denial. No! No! The word became his being, animated him like a crazed puppet into a stumbling run down the valley. The soul-shattering shock of grief thrashed through his limbs as if it could only find release down in the Worm-ruined house.

Medrian was after him in an instant; she threw herself sideways at him to knock him off course, then seized his arms and tried to pull him to a halt. He struggled with her, his eyes wild; he did not seem even to recognise her.

'Stop!' she cried.

'Let me go,' he whispered hoarsely. He tried to break free of her, but she hung grimly on to him.

'No!' she shouted frantically. 'If you step in that stuff, it'll kill you. Don't you understand? It's acid – poison!'

He stared at her, shaking convulsively, but he was seeing Sinmiel, Falin's sister, dying in a pool of venom. Dying, because she had not watched where she was walking and had stumbled into the Serpent's flesh-eroding effluent.

With a hoarse cry, he broke away from Medrian and ran raggedly up to the top of the valley, then started round the rim towards a small, undamaged, stone cottage.

She raced after him; the Serpent's smell had caught in her throat and she was coughing, gasping for breath. She could not match his hell-driven pace. She saw him enter the cottage, then dash out again a brief moment later. She cut across towards him, but he still outran her, tearing across the meadow and down a path between dark trees which looked like skeletons, rigid with dread.

At last she lost sight of him. She ran to a gasping, sobbing halt, half-doubled-up with pain in her ribs. She fell to her knees as she tried to recover her breath; and now she was weeping, tearing at her long hair with white hands.

For the first time, her grief found release without the mocking interference of M'gulfn, but she was hardly aware of that. Estarinel . . . her thoughts twisted in an incoherent mass of grief. Oh, by the gods, what can I do . . .

When she at last began to recover, she pulled herself upright and sat back on her heels, looking at the twilight descending over Forluin. She was trembling, her breath escaping in rough sobs.

'And did I not have another reason for coming here?' she said to herself. 'It wasn't just to be free of the Serpent. I needed to torture myself with guilt . . . to see the agony M'gulfn had caused so I could truly understand what it has done. What *I* have done, because I was so unable to dissuade it from doing this. Unable . . . oh, Estarinel, I should have tried harder. I didn't know . . .'

She dragged herself to her feet, dusted off the pale blue dress and brushed back her hair with her shaking hands. Then she strode on down the path Estarinel had taken.

It wound through fields whose Northern edges were scorched with ash. When the vista was clear of trees, she could see the dim greyness of the distance, and knew that the Worm had done its work thoroughly there. Whole tracts of Forluin had been laid waste; and its venom had the ability to spread, insinuating itself through the ground to continue the destruction long after the Serpent had returned to its Arctic home.

Cold and desolate, she found herself on the fringes of a small village. Six or seven stone cottages clustered around a green with a well in its centre. Lights danced in some of the windows as twilight fell, but outside it was quite deserted. She felt sure Estarinel had been heading for this village, and would reappear if she waited for him. Meanwhile she had no intention of knocking on a stranger's door, so she wandered across the grass and stood by the well, looking about her.

The love and care with which the cottages had been built was obvious, as was the careful tending of the green and the paths that wound around it. Flowers and shrubs had been encouraged to grow everywhere. There was an atmosphere of warmth and gentleness about the village that she had never sensed anywhere before, least of all in Alaak.

She hugged herself against the chill in the air. Strange – she rarely felt cold, at least not physically.

This is just the sort of place, she thought, that the Serpent would most despise and wish to destroy. Not the place, but the people and the feeling. I wonder why it waited so long?

She shivered. She could make no sense of the turmoil within herself. Free of the Serpent, the ice she had held against it in her mind had automatically melted. The comparative warmth made her feel she was burning inside, and each flame was a different emotion. Most consisted of a mixture of grief and anger – grief for Alaak's fate, her family, for Forluin and Estarinel; anger at M'gulfn, Arlenmia, Gastada – the causes seemed endless. There was fear, too, dread so chronic that it paralysed her if she let her mind dwell on it. And somewhere there was love and concern for another human being. That feeling was so alien to her that she hardly realised what it was; the gentle strength of it hurt her more than the burning of the other emotions.

She had never been foolish enough to imagine that in subduing her feelings for many years, she had destroyed them, but neither had she expected them to return with such force. Since her outburst near the farm, after Estarinel had run from her, she had been stunned by that internal violence.

Now she stood motionless by the well, thankful to have at least a few minutes to order her thoughts and re-establish her self-control.

How strong am I? she asked herself. It would seem not at all, without the Serpent to make my strength essential. Freedom! What made me think I was free for these few hours? I must steel myself against my own feelings, just as I have to against M'gulfn, before I betray myself . . .

Estarinel must not suspect I am any different. That would only make the rest of the Quest impossible. I have to be cold, as always.

She knew it would be difficult to show no sympathy and concern over the fate of Estarinel's family. Her indifference could only make it even harder for him to bear. He had never believed that she was really as icily callous inside as she appeared to be externally, but perhaps he would believe it now; perhaps he would begin to hate her. She swallowed against the knives in her throat. It would be better so. Then the Quest could be completed.

Falin, for no particular reason, got up and looked out of the window of his cottage. In the middle of the green, by the well, he saw what he at first took to be not a human, but a statue. Surprised and puzzled, he stared at the figure in the twilight until he realised it was in fact a small and slender woman, standing very still and with an air of total self-containment. That alone told him she was not Forluinish, even before he noted her face and colouring.

He opened the door and went out to her. She looked up as he approached, but otherwise did not move. Her delicate-featured face was white, contrasting sharply with her large dark eyes and black hair; she looked familiar but he could not think how he knew her.

'My name is Falin,' he began hesitantly. 'Do you need any help at all?'

'I'm looking for Estarinel,' she said simply.

Falin felt as though the earth had tipped under his feet; his head swam with shock and confusion. What did she mean, who was she?

'Estarinel—' he said, his mouth dry. 'He's not here. He went away months ago.'

'You don't recognise me, do you?' the woman said.

'I'm not sure . . .' He was beginning to remember her, but that brought more incomprehension and growing fear.

'We met at the House of Rede,' she said. 'You were one of his four companions.'

'And you must be Medrian. I'm sorry – you look different. But what are you doing here? I thought—'

'It took us longer than we expected to reach the Blue Plane. When we got there Estarinel wanted to come back to Forluin for a brief visit, before continuing the Quest. The Lady gave permission, and for me to come too.'

'Oh, ye gods,' said Falin, pulling his fingers through his long brown hair. He was very pale, Medrian noticed, with the tense, strained look of someone who could not sleep. 'And did he take you straight to his farm?'

'Yes,' she answered flatly, 'and the farm was not there. He ran down this way, and I lost sight of him.'

'Oh,' Falin sighed in distress. 'His family were all killed. Why didn't he come to me? I know where he will have gone – we'd better go up and find him.'

Medrian said nothing as she followed him between the cottages and along a path winding up a grassy slope.

Falin was trembling as he walked, shattered by the arrival of Medrian and the news that Estarinel was here. It was only a few days since the farm had collapsed, undermined by the Serpent's poison, killing Estarinel's family – including his own beloved Arlena. Since then he had barely slept – dreaded

66

the moment when Estarinel would return and he would have to tell his friend the awful news. He dreaded facing his dearest friend's grief – he knew he would be unable to bear it, after everything else.

Even more he had feared that Estarinel would never return at all. Thoughts raced through his mind – he had never, ever expected him to come back so suddenly, and if he understood Medrian correctly, they would be going away again, a second parting in so much more pain and despair than the first.

His thoughts then moved to Medrian, and he glanced sideways at her. He suddenly realised just how cold she seemed, how icy and emotionless, as if nothing had happened, and she did not care if it had.

Just who was she? Had he really entrusted his friend to this person who seemed as uncaring and treacherous as ice?

These thoughts were becoming unbearable, so he broke the silence.

'There's a long barn – it was the wheelwright's but he gave it over after the Serpent came, for use as a – well, a place of rest. We have laid all the dead there. I'm sure E'rinel will have gone up to see if his family—' he fought the tightness in his throat.

'And are they there?' Medrian asked in the same matter-of-fact, chilly voice.

'Yes.'

They reached the low stone barn and entered. Each side of the long building was lined with low wooden pallets where many of those slain by the Serpent had been laid. All were covered in cloths of pale green and had leaves and yellow flowers twined in their hair. There was nothing grim about the barn; the atmosphere was like the clear twilight of a spring evening, cool and quite peaceful.

At the far end Estarinel was kneeling by a pallet, grasping his mother's hand. His face was far whiter than any of the corpses' and he looked too numb with shock to be able to weep. Very slowly, Falin approached him, Medrian a little way behind.

'E'rinel,' Falin said softly. He flinched as his friend looked up, the terrible grief in his eyes just as Falin had imagined it would be, time after time. He went up beside him and Estarinel stood up, and the two embraced each other without speaking.

Medrian looked at the bodies of Estarinel's family. She recognised Arlena, Estarinel's sister, a tall silver-fair girl who had also been at the House of Rede. Their mother was similar, though fair in a warmer, more golden way. Next to her lay a man who was obviously Estarinel's father, he was so like his son and did not look much older. The younger sister, Lothwyn, also resembled her brother in her darker colouring. Her face was gentle and sweet.

Strange how suddenly and infinitely more real Estarinel seemed to her amid his family, as if before he had been no more than a spectre whose path had happened to cross hers. How different her perception was without M'gulfn – it was both painful and wondrous to realise that people mattered to each other, existed and suffered in a vital way that she had not understood before. It was as though she had known abstractly – but only now did she feel the truth of it. She no longer felt detached.

I must stay detached! she thought, turning her back on Estarinel and Falin so that they could not see her face.

She recalled how his family must have died, crushed by the collapsing farmhouse. The others there had, presumably, died in the Serpent's jaws, or been consumed by its venom, or died of illness caused by the ash it had left. Yet there seemed not to be a mark on any of them, nor any sign of decay even in the bodies that had been there the longest.

A terrible feeling swept through her, a terrible vision hung crucified across her brain; figures in a grey landscape, frozen under topaz glass in eternal, agonised worship of the Serpent—

She then found out just how hard it was to hide her feelings without the Serpent's dreadful presence to make it essential. She had to struggle not to run or cry out, clenching herself until at last her horror subsided and her face was expressionless again.

It's only a feeling, only a feeling, she told herself. There must be another reason why the bodies were perfect. Don't think of it. They are dead – even the Serpent could not—

'E'rinel,' Falin was saying, 'come back to the cottage. We can talk there. You'll feel better after a drink.'

'Tell me how it happened,' Estarinel said hoarsely.

'Yes – when we get back. Come on.'

Darkness was falling as the three left the barn and gently closed the wooden double doors behind them. Falin supported Estarinel as they went, for he was too faint with shock to walk properly. But Medrian walked ahead of them as if they did not exist, cold as alabaster.

Falin found himself disliking her, though it was a most un-Forluinish reaction to dislike someone on sight. Still, nothing had been the same since the Serpent's attack. It was also un-Forluinish to feel fear and misery, to know hunger and illness – to find that even the love he shared with his many friends in the village was edged with the pain and dread of losing them also.

But at least that most Forluinish of traits, the love and concern they felt for each other, had not been diminished by the Worm. In that respect it had not conquered them and never would, even if they all died eventually. So he could not understand this strange woman, who had come with Estarinel yet had not spoken a word to him, who kept her back turned to him, and whose face clearly showed – he thought – that she felt nothing, absolutely nothing at all.

Perhaps Falin's feelings towards her were also tinged by jealousy of a sort. She had been Estarinel's companion for several months, while Falin and his other loved ones had been separated from him, not knowing how he fared or whether he was alive or dead. And he had an idea that whatever they had been through together, they were not going to tell him. He felt somehow excluded by their relationship, and angered to think that Estarinel might have come to feel love and friendship for her while she was apparently quite indifferent to him.

69

He must try not to pre-judge her, though that was difficult when Estarinel's life was at stake.

In a few minutes they were inside Falin's cottage. He moved around the room lighting up lamps, then stoking a dying fire until a warm light flooded away the darkness. The floor was covered with rugs of russet, gold and green, and the creamy walls bore several small tapestries. On either side of the stone fireplace dark wood doors led off to other rooms.

Estarinel sat in a chair by the fire and gratefully drank the wine that Falin offered. Medrian sat opposite. He looked at her once, but she was not looking at him, just staring into the fire.

Gradually the wine steadied him; his muscles unclenched and he felt the colour returning to his face. He felt almost unnaturally calm as he said, 'This is your aunt Thalien's cottage, isn't it?'

'Yes,' said Falin, sitting down on the floor near him. 'Edrien and Luatha were staying here too, but they wanted to go back to the coast. Thalien went with them because she wasn't feeling well, and thought the sea air might help. So I'm here alone now.' He was fighting the constriction of tears in his throat as he spoke. For the first time Estarinel noticed how pale and strained he looked. After losing his own family in the Serpent's first attack, he had virtually been 'adopted' by Estarinel's. And of course there was Arlena – he should have realised that Falin had as much cause to be in despair as he had.

'Falin, I'm sorry. We shouldn't have appeared out of nowhere like this. I was just thinking of myself . . .'

'I dreaded having to tell you,' said Falin. 'I don't know what made me think you'd come to me before you even went to see your own family, especially as you wouldn't have known where I was living. It only happened a few days ago; I've just been too confused to think straight.'

'Tell me what happened,' Estarinel said gently.

'Well, your father,' Falin swallowed hard, 'he died not long after you left. They told us when we arrived back from

70

our voyage. It was the fever that the Serpent brought, it's nearly always fatal.

'But there was no warning of what was going to happen to the farm. It was as though the Serpent's poison had seeped through the ground and dissolved the mortar; it must have fallen so suddenly that there was no way your mother and sisters could escape. Lilithea woke in the morning and it had happened. She rushed to the village to tell us. We were able to get down into the valley and bring their bodies back here, but soon afterwards the Serpent's venom flooded in and covered everything. We can't get rid of it. It kills. Oh, if only I'd been with them they might not have died!'

'Falin, it's all right,' Estarinel said, grasping his friend's hand. 'More likely you'd have died too. Where is Lilithea? Her cottage was empty.'

'She's all right. She went South, to stay with her parents.'

At this, Estarinel visibly sagged with relief. At least she and Falin had been spared so far.

'On the voyage back from the House of Rede,' Falin went on, 'Arlena and I were together most of the time. We decided that the Serpent mustn't win, and the best way to defeat it was to go on living and making the very best of life. We were going to marry in a couple of weeks' time . . . that creature won't rest until we are all dead, will it?'

Medrian stood up suddenly, as though a hot ember had leapt out of the fire and burned her. She paused, then said quietly, 'Do you have somewhere I can rest?'

'Yes – yes, of course,' said Falin, getting hurriedly to his feet and opening one of the doors. He showed her along a short corridor to a room with rugs strewn on the floor and a patchwork blanket across a low bed. Again he wondered what she and Estarinel had been through since he had stood among the cold mountains of the Southern Continent watching the two of them, with Eldor and Ashurek, dwindle to nothing in the Antarctic half-light. He lit a lamp for her.

'There's water in there, if you want to wash,' he said, indicating a side-room. 'Would you like something to eat? Sorry, I should have asked before . . .'

'No,' she said, staring at him with those heartless eyes. She seemed about to say something to him, but just added, 'Thank you.'

Falin rejoined Estarinel and sat in the opposite chair with a sigh. Perhaps Medrian was just being tactful; he certainly felt more at ease now she was gone.

As if reading his thoughts, Estarinel said, 'Don't think ill of her. She's very unhappy.'

Falin nodded, thinking that he really had no right to form any opinion of her.

'How long can you stay?' he asked.

'Just tonight. We have to return to H'tebhmella in the morning. Did Medrian tell you?'

'She told me a little, not much. I realise the Quest is not over.'

'No, it isn't. Falin, I should not have come back; I realise it was wrong of me. It will only raise new fears and perhaps false hopes, for you at least, even if no one else knows I've been here. I just had to know how things were . . .'

Falin looked at him, noticing that his friend looked older, world-weary and haunted. There were scars on his face; what battles had he been through?

'Then you'd better know everything. That venom that the Serpent left is like a living substance, it spreads through and over the ground, killing everything it touches.

'I think we'll have to evacuate the village soon. It spreads in sudden rushes, without warning. So many animals killed, farmlands ruined . . . Eventually it will cover the whole of Forluin. We're doing our best with what's left, but it's only a matter of time. That's how things are, my friend.'

Estarinel felt hollow with misery, as though there was no ground beneath his feet and never would be again. But for Falin's sake . . .

'There *is* hope,' he said, trying to sound convinced. 'The H'tebhmellians are helping us . . . forgive me, I don't feel I can speak of it, or all the things we've been through so far. But there is hope.'

Falin tried to smile.

'It's all right. I don't want to know yet. I'd rather wait until the Quest is over and then you can spend hours by the fire, or out on the meadows, telling us everything that happened,' he said with forced bravery.

'I will come back,' Estarinel said.

'Yes. You must.' And they looked at each other, sharing memories of their childhood and families, all the friends and animals and places that had made their lives in Forluin so happy and beautiful, until the Worm came.

They sat by the fire for another hour or so, but there was not much else they felt they could say to each other. At last Estarinel stood up and wished Falin good night, saying he would look in on Medrian before retiring, to see that she was all right.

Falin settled the fire and put a guard over it, then doused all the lamps except one, which he took into his room. Once in bed, he extinguished that as well and lay for a long time, staring into the darkness.

He was desperately worried about Estarinel. He was exhausted and possibly disheartened by the first stage of the Quest and on top of that had had the terrible shock of his family's deaths. Yet Falin noticed how unnaturally calm he had seemed since arriving back at the cottage. Something within him was suppressing the grief, allowing it no expression in tears or anger. If he continued to contain his misery, Falin thought, it would eventually destroy him. He would be unable to continue the Quest on which Forluin's future depended . . .

Falin came to a decision then. He had the same grief to contend with, but he had had longer to come to terms with it. He finally believed the nightmare was real, and he had not suffered Estarinel's mental and physical anguish on the first part of the Quest. He knew that the Serpent's death was not a matter of revenge, but of Forluin's survival, and he would do anything to spare his dearest friend left alive from further suffering.

They should have sent me in the first place, he thought. My family was already dead, I had nothing to lose – except Arlena. I am ready to go in his place.

With the decision came release from the terrible anxiety that had gripped him for days, and he closed his eyes and slept soundly.

Estarinel knocked softly on the door of Medrian's room, then hesitated, realising the calmness, which had descended upon him apparently from nowhere, had come from inside himself, solely to protect Falin from the even greater distress his grief would have caused. Out of Falin's company he no longer felt calm, was starting to tremble. He hoped Medrian would be asleep, so that he could sit with her for a few minutes and then leave.

But she was sitting on the floor, hugging her knees to her chest and gazing at the softly glowing lamp.

'Medrian,' he said quietly. 'I should have waited for you by the farm – you could have got lost. I wasn't thinking . . .'

She did not look at him, just stared at the lamp as though he was not there. He realised it was pointless to apologise, that she must understand well enough the distress that had caused him to run blindly to the village without her; for all her coldness, she was not insensitive.

He felt dizzy, suddenly affected by the way she looked so self-contained and utterly alone. It was as though there were swathes of darkness around her, like the wastes of space, and anyone who ventured into that darkness would die of cold before they ever found Medrian at the centre.

He did not know why she needed to hold herself so apart from everything, protecting herself in layers of callousness. She had often shocked him, even terrified him, as though behind her coldness she was the Serpent itself, and he had never been able to hold the terrible darkness of her eyes. But in spite of that, she had always fascinated him – he had never felt repulsed even by her worst hostility. At the heart of her iciness he sensed a misery so great that it had become her whole being, and he had longed to draw that out of her, replace it with love and hope.

But she had steadfastly refused all his attempts to comfort

74

her, as though she found any kind of comfort deeply painful. But perhaps he had not tried hard enough; perhaps he had been afraid to discover that he was wrong and that she really was formed of solid ice, with only petrified evil at the core.

This thought grew in strength. She was proving it herself, for she had shut herself away from him more completely than ever, at a time when even a word to show that she understood his loss would have helped. He was falling; Falin could not catch him, for he was falling too. But Medrian could have done, because in spite of what she appeared to be or what she actually was, he loved her.

They had faced death and danger together, many miles from his beloved family and home. And now his family were gone; only Medrian was still there.

His head was spinning; he stumbled to the bed and sat down on the patchwork cover before he fell. Something was constricting his chest, he could hardly breathe. He put his head in his hands, looked down at the floor – and there saw a rug that his sister Lothwyn had woven. It was a simple thing, one of her first attempts at weaving when she had been a child. He had forgotten that she had given it to Falin's aunt, Thalien, who had been especially fond of her. And here it still lay, in pride of place by the bed, loved and cherished because Lothwyn had made it.

Oh, Lothwyn, my little sister, he cried inwardly – and in a moment of pain so intense it seemed to be a dazzling light, he came to understand, as Falin had done, that the nightmare was real. Inescapable. To be lived through to the end – never to be woken from.

Medrian saw the rigour of his body and the distraught lines of his face. He looked like a man who was being buffeted from every side by cold winds and could find no refuge anywhere. And I am one of those winds, she thought. She hugged herself tighter, reminding herself of her decision. She could not afford to weaken. Let him think she didn't care; it was better in the long run.

She thought he was going to weep, but he did not; he

began to talk, as if beyond caring if she replied or even listened.

'I was glad, in a way, to show Forluin to someone who'd never been here before,' he began, his voice flat but tinged with bitterness. 'Even as she is now – you saw that part of her is still beautiful. You mustn't think we were unaware of her beauty and took our good fortune for granted. We gave thanks all the time – in every aspect of our lives. We cared for the land and all the plants and animals, and especially for each other. We gave Forluin all the love and respect we were capable of. She bestowed on us everything we needed to be happy, so we thanked her by being happy. Life was that simple.

'But we must have gone wrong somewhere. We were unaware of the possibility that it could all be taken from us. We were complacent. We never thought—' he hardly raised his voice, yet it rang with anguish, 'we never thought that our happiness and good fortune were due but to the grace of the Serpent in refraining from attacking us for so long!'

I must be cold, cold – he must not suspect I am different, Medrian told herself frantically. She could see how more and more desperately he needed some kind of comfort from her. She felt sick with horror at her own cruelty. But she could not pretend, could not offer a few trite phrases of consolation while remaining cold within. She knew if she said one word she would be lost. Loathing herself, she willed her mouth to silence and her eyes to lose focus.

'My little sister, Lothwyn, wove this rug,' he went on. 'When all this first happened, it seemed like a dream. Surely no one could have a nightmare this bad and not wake up. But when I saw the rug just now, I realised – Lothwyn and the others have made me realise – it's real. When I saw the Worm lying on Falin's house – when it stared at me and I saw that it had blue eyes – that was real. How can we hope to defeat something that has so much hate?' He was shuddering with revulsion at the memory of the Serpent. How well Medrian knew that revulsion, and how familiar she was with the Serpent's hate; she had known them, day in and day out, through long years of misery. Oh, he needs my help – I must not . . .

Estarinel saw her face grow even colder and, in his misery, felt stirrings of anger.

'Where does the Serpent get its hate from, Medrian?' he almost shouted. He saw her flinch as though he had accused her of some terrible crime and regretted his words immediately.

'Tell me,' he said quietly, 'the only thing that will stop the Worm's venom from destroying all of Forluin is if we kill it, isn't it? M'gulfn's will gives the poison its power.'

She nodded, her eyes glittering like jet.

'Then – could it be that the Worm has taken revenge on me? If I hadn't set out on the Quest, my family would have been spared?'

But Medrian did not answer. Her face became whiter; she could have been carved from snow for all she seemed to care.

He dropped his head onto his arms, pain and sorrow overcoming him. This was the worst time he had ever known, the coldest and most desolate knowledge he had yet had to face. It seemed only Medrian in all the world had the power to rescue him from despair, and she was using that power to torment him over the brink of darkness. The only way he could save himself would be to turn his love to hate – was that what she was trying to do? – but he knew that would never, never happen. All that was left was to surrender himself to the abyss.

But Medrian was shaking as though a polar wind was blowing on her. I've made my decision, she kept telling herself. I knew it wouldn't be easy. Oh, but this hard! How can I watch his pain, and do nothing? Have I grown as cruel as M'gulfn? I cannot, cannot sit and watch him be totally destroyed by sorrow – no more—

'No,' she said, and he started and looked up at her. 'The Worm is not that clever, it won't have specifically attacked your family. There's nothing you could have done.'

And just as she had known it would, her resolve collapsed utterly as she spoke. She began to sob, tears of sorrow, for

Estarinel and for Forluin, running down her cheeks. Like a crippled woman she uncurled herself and crawled across Lothwyn's rug to him, pulling herself up off the floor and into his arms.

She hid her face against his neck and whispered, 'Oh, I'm so sorry – sorry – sorry—' over and over again, as though the attack on Forluin had been entirely her fault. Estarinel rocked her, stroking her head, his own tears falling into her hair as he embraced her. He did not stop to wonder why she had changed so suddenly and completely; it did not matter. He was happy to accept her comfort with unquestioning relief and love as she drew him back from the void into light and warmth.

Medrian was thinking, this is mad, coming to Forluin was mad, I must have known what would happen. What a fool to think I was strong enough! She wept as if she would never stop, flooded by sorrow not only for Estarinel but now for her own lightless existence, made terrible by the Serpent. And by fear and dread at the thought of completing the path upon which she had set herself. I would never have coveted these few hours of freedom, she told herself severely, if I had known they would only mean surrender to terror and self-pity, all the weaknesses that jeopardise the Quest . . .

But it was too late. Estarinel needed her, she could not have done otherwise. And now she was discovering something she had never been able to feel before, the exquisiteness of being held in someone's arms, something beyond mere comfort. The need to release her misery was submerged by a stronger need that felt like starvation: the craving to love and be loved. Oh, ye gods, I am human – even I – even after all that's happened to me. To waste these few hours would be insane – they are all I'll ever have. I may never defeat the Serpent now, but if I have just one moment of love and joy to remember, it can never defeat me either . . .

Estarinel kissed her, made joyful by her sudden warmth in the midst of his grief. Whatever had made him love her, the elusive self she had kept sealed beneath Arctic ice, was real; all the love she had been denied from giving or receiving, all her life, was flooding her now like a storm. Again he did not ask why; he ventured into the darkness and at the centre, at last, he found Medrian.

4

The Shana's Lie

CALORN FOLLOWED Ashurek, at a distance, for a long way. He went along a mossy shore that was only a few inches above the blue water that lapped it, half concealed by strange jade- and aquamarine-carved trees. The moss glittered with water within the imprints of his feet.

She was fairly sure he knew she was following him. He left the shore and crossed a breathtakingly high, delicate bridge that arched across the water to join an island of faceted cerulean rock. When he reached the far side he turned and waited for her, staring at her grimly.

'You've been trailing me like a hound. What do you want?' he demanded, but Calorn faced him unrepentantly.

'I want to know where you're going,' she replied.

'Oh? I wasn't aware that I was answerable to you in any way,' said Ashurek.

'But while we are here, we are answerable to the Lady, and I think she'd be none too pleased if she knew what you are planning,' Calorn said pleasantly.

'Don't anger me, Calorn. You're not indispensable to the Quest.' He turned away from her but she caught him up, ignoring the dangerous intensity of his face.

'Maybe not, but you won't find the Silver Staff without my help, and nor will you find what you're looking for now.' Ashurek stopped and turned to stare at her again.

'You'd better explain yourself, and quickly. I've no time for conversation.'

'It's obvious enough to me, ever since the Lady told us the Dark Regions are on the other side of the Blue Plane, that you've thought of nothing except going through and rescuing Silvren. Well, is that what you intend?'

'What of it? It's true the Lady wouldn't approve. She would most likely expel me from H'tebhmella. But unless someone tells her, she won't know,' said Ashurek. 'I suggest you go back the way you came, and remain silent.'

'Ashurek, I was not going to tell her. On the contrary, I want to come with you.'

'You—'

'Yes. How do you plan to find a Way through to the Dark Regions? Sometimes mere determination isn't enough. All my training has been to find Ways from world to world, plane to plane.'

'Nevertheless, I can find the Way unaided. Calorn, you are wasting time—'

'Can you find it? I know where it is already. And you are going the wrong way.'

Ashurek looked at her bright eyes and unclouded face, and began to realise it would be easier not to argue with her.

'You'd better show me. But I cannot let you come through with me. It is a more terrible place than you can imagine.'

'So what?' Calorn grinned. 'I never was very imaginative. I am coming with you, every step of the way, for I know you will need all the help I can give.'

'By the Serpent,' said Ashurek, 'you are as insane as I. Come on then, let's waste no more time; we must be back before Estarinel and Medrian return, and we are missed.'

Calorn led him off to the right, over another bridge and down a long, precarious causeway of rock. Horses swam past them on either side, and he wondered, briefly, if the animals had the ability to tell the women of H'tebhmella where he and Calorn were going. More likely the whole Plane was sentient, and in truth no one could go anywhere upon it without the Lady knowing. They climbed around the base of a great mushroom of rock, and came at last to a strange landscape of gnarled, indigo stone.

The sweet calm of H'tebhmella was still tangible here, but the shining blue water that covered most of the Plane was not visible unless they climbed up on the rocks. That was unusual, for the vast lake could normally be seen from anywhere on the Plane. More strangely, Ashurek could sense an introversion about the rocks, as if they were leaning in towards each other to conceal a secret about which they felt faintly sad and ashamed.

Calorn was looking about, moving from rock to rock and touching each one in passing as if it could show her what she was searching for.

'It's here,' she mumbled as she passed him. And although Ashurek could feel and sense that she was right – that there was a concealed Way to the far side of the Plane very near – he knew that without her it would have taken him days to locate it, days he did not have.

Now Calorn was circling a single stalk of rock, probing it with her fingers. With an expression of deep concentration on her face she located a thin rim of stone concealing a shallow depression that apparently led nowhere.

'Here – come on, quickly,' she said.

Ashurek pressed himself into the depression and found that, behind the overlapping rim, there was a black gap just wide enough to squeeze through sideways. Calorn was close beside him as he pulled himself through into a small, dark cavern.

As their eyes adjusted they found that all was not pitch dark. A soft, twilight-blue illuminated the little cave, though whether it was light filtering from outside, or the rock itself that glowed, they could not tell. A thin passage led steeply down in front of them. The cavern had a still, neutral air about it. It seemed fully aware of the secret it held, the fistula running through to the Dark Regions, but as well as the sad shame it felt, there was a pride that it was protecting H'tebhmella, preventing the Shana from ever coming through to this side. The balance between these two feelings was a stoical neutrality that would not allow itself to express either joy or pain.

Ashurek shut his mind to the feeling that by entering the cavern he was somehow betraying H'tebhmella. He set off swiftly down the narrow tunnel with Calorn following. And so, unarmed, they made their way down to the Dark Regions.

The tunnel hardly seemed to be intended for use by humans. Just as on the White Plane, when the Questers had crossed from one side to the other, the shaft turned vertically down and there was a sickening shift of gravity beneath their feet.

But unlike the White Plane, the shaft was not a round, wide tunnel. In places they had to crawl, in others it was barely a few inches wide and they had to squeeze through in danger of getting stuck fast. Ashurek was made anxious not by fear of the narrowness of the tunnel, but by frustration at the difficulty of moving at any speed towards his destination. He had no idea of how long the shaft was, but now they were on their way, he had no intention of turning back, however far it was.

But it seemed H'tebhmella was not as thick as the White Plane. In less than two hours they felt the nearness of the Dark Regions. The shaft was made entirely of the fabric of the Blue Plane, and where it opened upon the foreign matter of the Dark Regions it cried silently in protest, like a slender throat screaming its revulsion at the unutterably, incomprehensibly vile. Ashurek had to fight to stop himself pressing his hands over his ears, as if that could keep the terrible scream out. Looking round, he saw that Calorn was struggling too, her face tense. He hoped her courage would hold.

Now the dim blue light that had lit their way had blackness seeping into it, and the way grew even narrower and more difficult. It seemed to Ashurek that the tunnel really was a throat, swallowing and constricting itself against the entry of that blackness.

He turned to Calorn and said, 'Prepare yourself. We're there.' But at their next step, their hope of entering the Dark Regions slowly and cautiously was torn away. Gravity spun beneath them, drew them into a vortex: they were falling with sickening speed through darkness. They could have been anywhere, transported to another universe, spinning through space.

Calorn had automatically relaxed her body in preparation for the impact when they hurtled into a black swamp. A shudder of pain jarred through her as she landed. But there was also a sensation of bouncing, as if the surface was slightly elastic and had absorbed the worst of the impact. She stretched out her hands and touched the black substance to find it had the exact texture and resilience of flesh.

Gagging with revulsion, she snatched her hands away, but it was not the touch of the surface that revolted her. She could sense a terrible evil lying underneath, permeating the whole of the swamp as water fills a sponge. An almost inaudible gibbering filled her ears, as if a million imps lurked below the surface, a sick swarm that could extinguish the brightest hope with their mindless cruelty. And she could feel herself sinking down towards them as if into a viscous ink. The ground was sodden with evil; she had not known such depravity could exist, such soul-consuming emptiness. But among the supernatural malice of the black imps hid human weaknesses that also led to evil: guilt, jealousy, irresponsibility. And the swamp was sucking her down, like an amoeba, to join the infinite horrors within it.

. Calorn was brave when faced with something she could fight. Now she was paralysed, but still her instinctive self-control prevented her from voicing her terror. As levelly as she could, she called, 'Ashurek.' She trembled as the sound of her voice reverberated horribly, as if some venomous monster had spoken the word within her own skull.

At first there was no reply. Her whole body was stiff with revulsion and denial as she felt the swamp drawing her further into itself. No, she screamed to herself, the Quest, the Silver Staff, Silvren – my life can't just end, meaninglessly, now—

Then, out of the darkness somewhere above her, she heard the Gorethrian's voice. 'Calorn?' The tone was normal, lacking the terrible echo. 'I can't see you.'

84

'Ashurek,' she gasped, unable to still the shuddering of relief in her voice. 'In the swamp – I can't move.'

In seconds he had located her, had grasped her arms and was hauling her to her feet. He was astonished at the reluctance with which the swamp gave her up. It clung to her like latex, finally relinquishing her with a dreadful sucking shriek.

Still shuddering, she scrubbed black slime from her face, swearing vehemently between coughs. It was several moments before she realised that she and Ashurek were now standing on the fleshy surface.

'Let's get off here,' she said brusquely. She could still feel the rabid corruption gnawing at the soles of her feet.

But Ashurek, seeming untouched by it, replied, 'We can't get off. Look around . . .' She did so and saw that the darkness was not absolute. She could see Ashurek quite clearly, and that the spongy, nauseous mass of the swamp extended in all directions, though vanishing into opaque darkness after a few hundred yards. The only landmark was an indistinguishable black shape far ahead of them. They seemed to be trapped inside a dark drum, standing precariously on a skin that vibrated with malice.

'Oh, ye gods,' she muttered. She tried to move, but each step sent aches of evil shooting through her legs.

'I was lucky,' Ashurek grinned humourlessly. 'I bounced to my feet when I landed. Obviously the swamp did not want me. Are you all right?'

'I'm fine,' Calorn snapped in answer. 'But there are dreadful things in this morass. I can still feel them.'

'The Regions are formed of evil, as I warned,' Ashurek said thornily, half to himself. 'The Serpent designed them cleverly, to contain everything man might fear . . . or lust after.' He pointed to the black landmark and said, 'We'll make for there, for a start.'

They began to walk, the fleshy surface bouncing slightly at each step. Calorn gritted her teeth and tried to ignore the sadistic hints of horror knifing into her feet. Her glance flickered everywhere, to either side, behind and above them,

as she tried to take in everything she could about this unknown Region.

'Look,' she said suddenly. 'Up there.'

He stopped, although she carried on walking, reluctant to
stand still on the evil marsh.

'What?'

'The tunnel back to H'tebhmella. Can't you see it, like a
faint half-closed eye?'

Then Ashurek understood. The Dark Regions had seemed
cavelike to him before, as if they were everywhere enclosed
by a low roof of rock. Now he realised that the 'roof' was
the other side of the Blue Plane. Instead of lying upon the
surface, the Dark Regions hung suspended from it, gravity
inverted. So they had fallen from the mouth of the tunnel
and landed upon the ground, and now their escape route was
some forty feet above their heads. As Calorn observed, the
faint light emanating from it glowed in the roof-rock like a
sorrowful eye.

He cursed to himself, then, catching her up, muttered,
'We'll worry about our escape later. Let's find Silvren first.'

Calorn brushed her long red-brown hair back from her
face and smiled to show that it would take a good deal more
to daunt her. She was eager to know how he planned to find
Silvren, but the restless glitter of his eyes made her realise it
was probably unwise to ask.

Again he felt himself grinning like a skull. The blackness
of the Dark Regions matched exactly the blackness of his
mood; it was as though the grin was a challenge, daring them
to offer some additional evil which might destroy his resolve.

Abruptly the challenge was answered.

Something grey flapped over their heads, uttering an echoing squawk. Ashurek recoiled. In an instant the creature had
brought back to him, in exquisite detail, all the suffering of
his time in the Dark Regions, which had so broken his spirit
that he had agreed to go and take the Egg-Stone from Miril.
He remembered – the nightmare expansion of time that
made him think he had been there for weeks, the insidious,
subtle tortures, the grinning faces of the Shana. The feel of

the place was the softness of rotten flesh and the hardness of petrified bone. And the smell – punctuated by the acrid stenches of decay and every foulness, the smell was the stomach-turning tang of metal and the dusty, timeless odour of a crypt. The very ground seemed to emanate despair.

And he remembered that Silvren had been imprisoned here for months and months.

The grey creature flew over again, close to their heads, uttering a cry that was both mocking and desolate. Ashurek walked faster, as if that could suppress his anguish at the familiarity of the cry which he had heard so often during his internment in the Dark Regions, and which still haunted his nightmares.

In spite of their increased speed, they seemed to be no closer to the dark edifice. It was as though the shape was slowly edging away from them. And now Calorn seemed hardly able to take her eyes off it; colours were crawling across its unnameable surface – muddy blues, a parody of the pure H'tebhmellian colours – that dissolved when she stared straight at them.

She also began to notice the clamminess of the atmosphere, as though the air was the exact temperature of blood, and had not been freshened by any breeze for centuries.

Her eyes grew more accustomed to the darkness and now, in the swamp and on the shapeless landmark, she could identify ashen-greys, browns and sick ochre colours, all tainted with a blue like that of bruised skin. Nothing was true black. Even the colours of the Dark Regions were corrupt.

When she saw movement on the swamp ahead of them, she thought she was hallucinating. She blinked until her eyes hurt, but she was not mistaken: several pale figures were moving ponderously across their path, like a herd of cows.

She touched Ashurek's arm and whispered, 'Have you seen their like before?'

'I don't know. I won't know unless we take a closer look,' he replied, his voice like iron.

'Is that wise? I think we should lie low until they pass.'

'No. Coming voluntarily into the Dark Regions was unwise; the creatures may be dangerous, but they may also be our only hope.' Even as he finished speaking he was striding across the fleshy marsh towards them. Swallowing ruefully, Calorn made after him. Whatever Ashurek understood about the Dark Regions, he felt there was no time to explain to her, his uninvited companion.

Now Ashurek and she were almost upon the strange beasts, and both of them recoiled at the sight. Even Ashurek had never seen their like before. Their torsos and heads were human but they walked like cattle, each upon six human legs. They had no arms. Their skin was sickly pale and their faces were sombre, with closed eyes and mouths open as if frozen in mid-cry. Occasionally one would utter a groan, but otherwise they were silent.

Ashurek confronted them and called, 'Hail, creatures of the Worm!'

The pale beings slowed and milled from side to side at the sound of his voice, but they showed no more intelligence than animals. Ashurek cursed inwardly and was about to stride past them, when from the shadows behind them another creature reared up as if from nowhere.

It was bovine in form and had evidently been moving on all fours among the others. Now it stood upright with its front feet dangling awkwardly across its chest. In one split hoof it held a short stick. Its head was a grotesque parody of a cow's with glaring red eyes and a crooked, drooling mouth.

'Who are you?' it bellowed.

'Ashurek of Gorethria. And who are you?'

'I am called Exhal.'

'And you are not, apparently, one of the Shana.'

'No, not I!' the creature roared angrily, revealing sharp teeth more like a wolf's than a cow's. 'No demon I. I am but one of their sorry subjects.'

Ashurek thought the beast looked anything but sorry or subjected. He said, 'And what are these creatures with you?'

'You should know them!' Exhal growled, pushing them aside to walk stiffly forward. He towered over Ashurek, who reached – for the tenth time – for the non-existent sword at his side. 'Gorethria –' he formed the word awkwardly, 'that is in the upper world, the round world where we can never go. I have heard of it. What do you want here, man of the round Earth?'

'I've come to take someone home,' Ashurek answered. 'You can tell me where to find her.'

'What?' the creature roared. Calorn put her hands over her ears involuntarily. 'I, a mere creature of the Worm? Why should I know? The Shana keep all the live prisoners.'

Ashurek saw, from the corner of his eye, something flap through the air and settle on the ground just to the side of them. He ignored it and said, 'Then where are the Shana, O Exhal?'

'Ashurek of Gorethria,' the beast answered, its voice rife with envy and its long white belly heaving, 'you descend from your round world with utmost ease and come to us – we who can never escape this pit – to insult and mock us with your good fortune, then ask our help?'

Ashurek gave a laugh of bitter irony and his eyes glittered with verdant fire as he replied, 'You think me fortunate? Then I cannot begin to comprehend your misery, Exhal. To direct someone to the den of the Shana would not normally be construed as "help". However—' he stood his ground as the ghastly ox-creature made a threatening lunge of its head, 'however, I have no choice. I must go there, and a few words from you would end this useless conversation.'

The beast's eyes glowed like light shining through a film of blood. It craned its bovine head forward and Ashurek felt the heat of its breath. Its teeth glistened with saliva.

'And what – what do I receive in return? That's the way the Shana work, is it not? A bargain – a bargain, isn't that it? Find me a way out of this pit – a way to the upper world, where animals can feed on grass and sleep at night, and are not cursed by a cognizant brain – show me the way, and I will take you to the stinking demons myself.'

'I cannot do that. You would have to pass through the Blue Plane, and you would not survive,' said Ashurek simply. He observed that the six-legged human-cattle had edged round and surrounded him and Calorn, and were now swaying their heads from side to side. He noticed something else even stranger about them then: they were impossible to count. There could have been ten or a hundred or a thousand for all the sense he could make of their number. He tried to ignore them and concentrate on Exhal, who was hissing as if he had been struck.

'You stinking spawn of hell! Then I will kill you – though it will be a poor fight, since you are unarmed!'

'I warn you, Exhal,' said Ashurek with calm assurance. 'I am no ordinary mortal. I know the Shana. There is much they want of me – therefore they may be more willing to help me than you realise.'

The creature hissed again and drew back.

'There is your answer, then. Call one. Have me punished. Then see if you can pay their price.'

At this point a new voice broke in; the speaker sounded as if he had been listening in amused silence for some time.

'Oh, Exhal, do tell them. I can't bear any more of your ridiculous prevarication.' The voice had a metallic rasp to it that sickened the ears. Ashurek and Calorn turned to see the grey flapping thing that had screeched above their heads sitting near them. Calorn backed away instantly and Ashurek found himself struggling to keep his ground.

The aura of horror that emanated from it was far stronger than that of Exhal, although it did not seem so physically threatening. It was about the size of an eagle, though it barely resembled a bird. A framework of grotesque bones was covered in a loose grey skin that stretched between its limbs to form wings. Its head bore a crest of flesh and its forward-facing, owlish eyes, above a hooked beak, gave it a human look. Its face was bitter as iron, yet the horror of it was more than physical.

'Have you been properly introduced to Exhal?' the grey being continued. 'He is a herdsman. He herds the souls of humans across the plains of hell. So they say. Small wonder he is so cheerless, eh?'

'He—' Ashurek heard Calorn gasp.

'Go back to your masters, Limir,' Exhal bellowed. 'Leave the humans to me – I will finish them, the Earth-dwelling scum!'

The bird-creature stretched its wings and its voice cut the atmosphere like wire through cheese.

'You cretinous ox, Exhal. Can I believe my ears? Leave them to you? I have been tolerant of you – your self-interest, insubordination, whining talk of Earth – because the Shana considered you a good herdsman. But other herdsmen can be found.'

The ox-creature shrank back slightly with the instinct of long fear, but its voice was loud with rebellion.

'You've mocked and humiliated me for the last time, Limir. Do not think to threaten me; the two humans are mine.'

'By the three eyes of the Serpent, yours, are they?' Limir exclaimed with gleeful sarcasm. 'You think I haven't waited for this moment, or one like it? You think I would miss this opportunity just to satisfy your whims? Now your stupidity has gone beyond my wildest imaginings. Move aside. Take your herd somewhere else, before I destroy you.'

'I said, do not think to threaten me,' Exhal answered, his gruff voice suddenly sinister. 'My human herd are loyal to me. I will open their eyes.'

This apparently meaningless threat had a devastating effect on Limir. The grim bird whirled into the air, screeching like the clashing of bronze claws.

'Another herdsman will be found!' it cried, swooping down onto Exhal's head. Whatever counter-attack the bovine beast had planned he was too slow-witted to carry out. His eyes red with fear and anger, he stood like an ill-formed statue while Limir sank claws and beak into his neck. Grey blood rivered down the white neck and belly.

About them the six-legged creatures milled in panic, though their mask-like faces remained unchanged. Then they seemed to find a mutual direction and were running away, uttering their heart-tearing groans.

Ashurek and Calorn exchanged a glance and moved as one; she seized the short stick that Exhal had dropped, he lunged forward and dragged Limir off Exhal and thrust him down into the swamp. Together they set upon Limir, Ashurek holding the creature down and Calorn striking its malformed head again and again, possessed by a loathing and bloodlust she had never felt before.

But Limir refused to die. He thrashed in the Gorethrian's grasp as if the blows were a mere irritation, his vicious talons and iron beak drawing blood from both their hands. Finally Calorn knelt bodily on the beast and pressed the stick across its thin gnarled throat.

'Break its neck!' she cried to Ashurek, her voice, as in a nightmare, rasping from her throat in a reluctant whisper. 'Kill it!'

His face was full of the same murderous revulsion that she was feeling as he clasped his hands about the bird's wiry neck. Then Exhal lumbered forward, knocking Calorn – by clumsiness, not design – off Limir and into the swamp. He thrust one hoof into Limir's belly, staggering and hopping to keep his balance. The air was full of screams – Limir's, Exhal's bellows, and Calorn seemed to be screaming herself, long, deep, silent screams of fear and anger as she fought the swamp, fought to get near to the hellish bird and attack it again.

Then Ashurek was swaying to his feet, gasping, 'It's done. I've broken its neck.'

Calorn dragged herself out of the black swamp, staring at the body of Limir which lay, harmless and pathetic, like a rain-rotted sack before them. The bloodlust had faded but she seemed to be staring at the emotion as if it was a real object physically retreating from her. She was shaking with disgust at the sight. She was no stranger to conflict, and she had killed before, but only from necessity, swiftly and with sombre respect for her defeated adversary. She had never – never – felt that sickening, sensual surrender to desire for blood and death before; she knew that if she ever felt it again, it would be time to end her own life.

'This place corrupts,' she said, and Ashurek nodded, not needing to ask what she meant.

Exhal had dropped onto all fours and was uttering soft, deep coughs that shook his whole body and sent drops of grey blood flying into the air. But, it seemed, he was not too badly injured. After a minute he ambled forward and faced the two humans.

'Come then, Ashurek of Gorethria. I will take you,' he said almost meekly.

'You've had a change of heart?' Ashurek said, surprised.

'A bargain, a bargain. Escape from this pit may be impossible – but at least Limir's death makes my existence here more bearable. For that I have to thank you, humans of the Round World,' Exhal said gruffly.

'You know where Silvren is, then?' Ashurek asked with renewed urgency.

'Of course. I am the herdsman. I know each and every prisoner – for most of them, eventually, join my herd.'

Ashurek heard Calorn breathe something like, 'How horrible.' Her comment angered him. The implications of the herdsman's words were, indeed, too terrible to contemplate – he did not need anyone to confirm and accentuate the nebulous swirling of horror within him.

Now the human herd were slowly wandering back towards them with the obtuse curiosity of cattle. Eyes blind, mouths open in continual silent screams, it was as if they were utterly directionless, yet desperately seeking something. Even the way they held their pale, cruelly malformed bodies was pathetic. Tears came to Calorn's eyes; she no longer felt curious, or revolted, or afraid of them. Only their misery, tangible as the warm, slow breath of cattle in the 'real' world, touched her. If only she could embrace their despair, comfort it in some way – but the evil of the Dark Regions was too powerful to allow expression of any feeling that was not cruel and base.

As the herd approached, Ashurek said, 'Come on, then,'

and began to stride across the marsh ahead of them. Calorn caught up with him. She had the ability – a very useful one – to dismiss complicating issues from her mind and concentrate on vital, immediate matters. But Ashurek tended to brood. He was deeply disturbed by the six-legged human-beasts. What had Exhal meant, 'I will open their eyes'? In what way was that a threat, serious enough for Limir to try to kill him?

Exhal unhurriedly rounded up his herd and then followed, snorting and shaking his heavy head from time to time, as an animal tries to rid itself of pain it does not understand. Ashurek was heading for the dark landmark again, but this time – with the ox-creature to guide them – they were rapidly drawing closer to it. It was roughly like a broad obelisk, but with its angles rounded off shapelessly. Brown smokes wreathed it. As they reached it they found it was completely blank and featureless and rubbery to the touch, like the swamp.

'Show us the way,' he said as Exhal caught them up.

'Have you no patience, Ashurek of Gorethria?' the beast grunted, raising itself on its hind legs and once more clutching the stick it had retrieved from Calorn.

'We don't have much time.'

'Don't you? I have for ever,' Exhal replied savagely. He began jabbing at the wall with the stick, searching back and forth along it. Eventually the stick slid half-way into the wall. Then Exhal thrust a hoof in just below it, and seemed to be struggling to force open a slit in the rubbery surface. His head and heaving shoulders disappeared into the wall and they could see the elastic opening stretched tautly around him, straining to close shut again.

Ashurek saw Calorn gritting her teeth, obviously afraid and revolted by the idea of forcing through the black rubbery wall. But he never again doubted her bravery after she unhesitatingly approached it and pushed her way through after Exhal without saying a word.

He followed, pushing his arms and shoulders into the reluctant substance, and leaving the eerie groans of the human herd behind him; then he was inside the wall. For a few long, nightmare seconds he could not see or breathe. He flailed desperately, feeling he was trapped in the gullet of some gigantic beast. Then, at last, he fell from the slit in the other side of the wall and found himself beside Exhal and Calorn.

They were in a cavern in which a malevolent, pale light shone through writhing steam. All was blue, like cyanosed skin, and there was a scent in the air so sweet it was a nauseous mockery of cleanliness.

The cavern stretched as far as the eye could see, its floor sloping downwards and covered with a honeycomb maze of hollows and pits.

'I must leave you here, lest my herd wander away and lose themselves,' the ox-creature said. 'Take yonder tunnel,' he pointed with his stick to a pit from which a purplish light glowed, merging with the blue, 'keep to the ridges between hollows, don't fall into the wrong one.' Then Exhal was pushing his huge body through the wall again.

Calorn called, 'We thank you, Exhal,' but she did not think he heard.

Ashurek set out onto the 'honeycomb' on hands and knees, finding the ridges as slippery and treacherous as a living mucous membrane. The hollows on either side yawned down into apparently endless, vertical tunnels, all glowing and steaming eerily with sickly bluish light. Each led, he realised, to a different part of the Dark Regions. The pit towards which they were heading was some two hundred yards out, if distance could be measured in that strange, logic-mocking place. The wall behind them seemed to have disappeared and been replaced by another stretch of the honeycomb. Above them only bluish-white steam could be seen.

Both of them slipped several times, and were shaking with the exertion of staying on the soapy ridges by the time they reached the pit. Like the others it went down almost vertically, winding out of sight.

'There's only one way down,' said Calorn.

'Yes,' said Ashurek. And he let himself slither off the

ridge and down into the tunnel, bouncing against its soft sides as he fell. She watched him for a second before launching herself into the hole.

Instead of the sensation of falling she had anticipated, there was something worse: a strangely still, grey blankness in her mind. Her limbs felt so light and bloodless that the sensation was unbearable, and she was twisting her hands together and writhing and groaning like a child in fever.

Had she been unconscious? Hours or days could have passed when she found herself lying still on a dark crumbly surface. She had no idea where she was. She could have been a newborn child for all she knew or remembered.

Someone was holding her arms, pulling her upright like a rag doll. She coughed and instinctively tried to find some strength in her limbs.

'Calorn.' Ashurek was saying, 'Come on, we're there. You'll be all right.' Her eyes focused on him. Memory returned like splinters of black slate piercing her brain. He looked shaken, almost grey, and she knew that only sheer determination had kept his sense of purpose intact through the disorientating tunnel.

They were in a landscape of soft black rock, with a gritty path stretching ahead and rows of squat, roundish hillocks on either side. There was a ceiling of darkness only a few feet above their heads, creating a sense of inescapable claustrophobia, and there was just enough dim light to make out their surroundings.

'I was here, once,' Ashurek said distantly. 'They keep the prisoners here.' He made to walk down the path, then paused. 'When we find Silvren, she may be very ill – thin . . .' he tailed off and Calorn knew he was not telling her, but trying to prepare himself for what he might find.

There were no demons or other creatures of the Serpent about, but despairing cries and moans issued from many of the dark mounds. Calorn ran to the nearest and peered into the grim cell within it. It was no more than a roughly-made roundish burrow in the mound with a transparent membrane stretched across the entrance. There was just room for a human to lie inside, like a bee grub within its honeycomb cell. The man lying there was skeleton-thin, skin and hair the same dull grey. Calorn tore at the membrane, but could not break through.

She went to the next cell, and the next, and on the other side of the path Ashurek was doing the same, calling, 'Silvren! Silvren!'

In almost every dark, fleshy cell a prisoner lay, thin, tormented and aged by the Shana's treatment, some weeping and shouting in desperation, some slumped unconscious, some staring blankly out and muttering to themselves.

It took Calorn every ounce of her self-control not to scream and run from such cruelty, but for Ashurek it was even worse. He had never realised the Shana had so many prisoners. In his time here, he had thought himself totally alone. The prisoners were all unaware of each other's existence and could not even seek comfort from each other. He ran on, fighting desperate terror, shouting, 'Silvren! Silvren!'

While Calorn slowed down in her search, disheartened. For even if Silvren were here, somewhere, in this apparently endless labyrinth of cells, would Ashurek even recognise her? Would she hear him? Panic began to swamp her – she who was renowned for her calmness and tenacity – and she could see the same thing happening to Ashurek. She ran to keep up with him, lest they lose each other and all hope of escape – all hope of everything.

Then, all at once, a figure was coming towards them, clear to see because she was dressed in white. Ashurek and Calorn halted in the centre of the path, watching and waiting. The figure was slender and upright and walking with steady, assured steps. Her long, dark-gold hair was glossy, her skin clear and showing no sign of ill-health or ill-treatment whatsoever.

She came up to Ashurek and the two stared at each other, lost in amazement.

'Silvren? It is you?' Ashurek said hesitantly. She was

wide-eyed, but seemed at the same time aloof and emotionless. It was hard to believe she was not imprisoned, not ill.

'Yes. I heard you calling . . . I . . .' Then suddenly she fell forward into his arms and was clinging on to him, shuddering as tears of relief and misery poured from her soul. It was, indeed, his Silvren.

'I thought you were an illusion sent by the Shana,' he said, so relieved to find her he could hardly speak.

'I thought that of you,' she sobbed, 'but, oh, you are real.'

Calorn tactfully distanced herself and kept a lookout for the approach of any demon or other creature, but she could still hear their conversation.

'You look well,' he said. 'Are you all right?'

'Yes. The Shana have not treated me badly. I have been lucky. Oh, Ashurek,' she wept.

'Listen, I don't know how we are going to escape from this pit, but I have something that may—'

'Escape?' Silvren pulled back from him, suddenly confused. 'Ashurek, how did you get down here? Have you gone mad? It must be a dream—'

'Silvren, it's all right. We came through from the Blue Plane. Calorn guided me – she works for the H'tebhmellians.'

'Oh – H'tebhmella,' Silvren gasped, as though a memory had revived which caused her intense guilt and pain. 'You found your way there, then – at last?'

'Yes,' said Ashurek, smiling, suddenly feeling confident that somehow it would be possible to outwit the Shana and escape. 'With my two companions, Estarinel and Medrian – we eventually reached the Blue Plane.'

But Silvren did not seem overjoyed.

'Then why are you here? What do you mean – you came through?' she questioned, understandably – Ashurek thought – puzzled and distressed.

'The Dark Regions hang from the opposite side of the Blue Plane,' he began to explain gently. 'I thought you must know – you gave me the first clue when you appeared to me and said that this hell-hole was blue, not black.'

'I don't remember,' she said miserably. 'I remember speaking to Estarinel, warning him about Arlenmia . . . oh, Arlenmia . . . but that was before . . . Oh, alas for H'tebhmella . . .'

'It's just one more cruel trick of the Serpent,' Ashurek said. At this Silvren visibly winced as if under an unbearable burden of grief and despair – something he had never seen her do. He realised that although she seemed lucid and physically well, no one could be unaffected by the nightmare confusion that was induced just by being in the Dark Regions. Perhaps her once irrepressible spirit had been crushed by the Shana – it was no worse than he should have expected. At least she was alive, and sane, and now he must take her out of this appalling domain before it was too late.

Not realising, yet, that it was already too late.

He pulled Silvren to his side and called, 'Calorn! We'd better make a move. Have you seen anything?'

'There don't seem to be any Shana-creatures about,' she replied with a grin. 'I think I've found the beginning of a way back.'

'What does she mean?' Silvren asked with distress in her voice. 'I used to try to escape. It's impossible. Oh, Ashurek – how are you going to get back?'

'Three of us are far stronger than one,' he said reassuringly. 'Come on, let's follow Calorn – somehow we will escape.'

He began to walk along the dull, gritty path behind the chestnut-haired woman who was continually looking this way and that, sensing which way to go. But as he led Silvren along, he felt her growing more and more tense at his side.

Suddenly she jerked away from him and stood as if rooted in the corrupt ground, crying, 'No!' She was trembling violently. 'I can't go. I can't ever—'

Ashurek turned and held her, saying, 'It's all right. I'm with you now. Trust me, Silvren, we'll soon be out of this accursed Region.' But she pulled back again, and he saw that the clear light in her beloved eyes had been replaced by something so desolate that he could not look into them.

'No – you don't understand – I can't go there – I can't go back to Earth. I'm—' she faltered. Her shuddering stilled,

99

like the last tremor of a dying bird. 'Oh, my love, why did you come here? You were safe. I was content.'

A terrible, cold sense of foreboding came over him as she spoke those strange words. Content – in the Dark Regions? He did not know what she could mean – except that whatever the Shana had done to her, it was something far more devastating than physical torment or insanity.

'Beloved, no need to fear the Shana now,' he said quietly. 'You must come.'

'No,' she repeated, as if the word was a protection against madness. 'No. I have to stay here.'

Calorn came forward suddenly and grasped Silvren's hands, trying to instil her with her own clear courage.

'Who says so? Only the Shana – and they are not here. Please come – we need you to help us.'

'Don't speak to me as if I were a child!' Silvren flared. '*I* say I can't leave – do you think I don't know what I'm saying? I don't want to stay – oh, ye gods, I don't want to – but I have to, for all our sakes.'

'What have they done to you?' Ashurek breathed.

'Go back without me. Go quickly, before the Shana come – leave me!' Her voice was fervent with the force of her will; she really did mean Ashurek to go back without her. And because he had always trusted her judgement, and because of the love and anguish he felt for her, he had to know why before he rescued her against her wishes.

'Have they taken away your sorcery?'

She stared up at him, her eyes clear but lightless, like shaded water.

'No, though it is weak and I cannot use it here,' she sighed, 'that burden still clings to me.'

'Then, Silvren, what? I don't understand you.'

'They have taught me,' she said, as if stricken by horror, not of the Shana, but of herself, 'a fundamental truth about myself. I am evil. For the sake of the Earth, I cannot return there – I've already done too much harm.'

'What are you saying?' Ashurek said between gritted teeth, anger and desperation seething darkly in his face.

'It's true. They haven't turned my brain. They just explained it to me and I understood – it's my fault that Arlenmia came to this Earth, my fault the Egg-Stone has wreaked its havoc and may be unleashed again. Because of my evil, the Serpent will win.'

'Because – how can you believe that? You've spent all your life fighting it.'

'That's just it,' Silvren replied, her face glowing with an acid light as if the sickness of her soul was concentrated there. 'I had no right to fight it. The Serpent was here before us – it will outlive us. Trying to find a way to slay it was arrogance. Just desire for power – do you understand? I was arrogant, ambitious – evil. And my sorcery is just the outward manifestation of that evil' – she repeated the word as if it was a venom with which to kill herself – 'not the power for good I thought I was shaping it to be. Not the beautiful and magic future of the Earth. Just evil.' She slumped in his arms, stricken by the agony of bearing this terrible knowledge about herself.

Ashurek was numbed, so deeply shocked that his rage and sorrow seemed to be a bottomless pit into which he was falling, falling. He thought he had prepared himself for the worst, that she would be weakened by torture, lack of food, the nightmarish torments of the Shana – dejected and hopeless of spirit. He had never, in his worst phantasms, foreseen that she would be so racked by self-loathing, destroyed by a simple lie.

The Shana were cunning. They always found the sharpest weapon to use against the victim.

'It's a lie, Silvren—' the words struggled up past the iron in his throat. 'A lie, invented by Diheg-El to break your will.'

'No, I know it's true,' she responded, emptily but with unshakeable conviction. 'I'll tell you how I know. It's because I felt – feel – jealous of Arlenmia's power over the Shana, because she can control them and doesn't fear them. And that's because she's more evil than they are. And I wanted that power! And I – and I loved her. And we are both entrenched in wickedness. It's proof. I am a danger to the world as long as I still have my sorcery. So I can't go to the Blue Plane, not with this taint of sickness on me. Do you see? The only help I can give anyone now is to stay here.'

Ashurek stared at her, feeling his heart torn into fragments, unable to find any voice for the screaming torment within him. Silvren looked back and knew what he was feeling. Tears fell from her eyes because there was nothing she could do to help him.

'I'm sorry, Ashurek,' she said, adding with hopeless irrelevance, 'I don't mind it here – they don't mistreat me. No, don't touch me again,' she said, seeming to shrink back into herself. 'I can't bear it. Please leave.'

Ashurek made a grim decision then. He had never before gone against Silvren's judgement, never questioned what she thought was right or tried to submit her will to his. If she truly believed the Shana's lie, and continued to believe it after they were safe on the Blue Plane, she might never forgive him. But he could not leave her here.

'Lead on, Calorn,' he said, and he gripped Silvren's shoulders and pushed her on in front of him.

She fought him, really fought. But her sobs of despair were for her own supposed evil, and inside she was fighting herself, not him. Gritting his teeth he twisted one of her arms behind her back and frog-marched her after Calorn, showing no mercy when she stumbled or gasped with pain.

And he prayed that she would one day forgive him.

It was with a rush of relief that Calorn heard Ashurek say, 'Lead on.' Instantly she set forth along the path between the grim mounds, following the course she had tentatively plotted. But the Dark Regions were constructed in an illogical way, unlike any world or dimension she had ever encountered before. Planes tilted and intersected with other planes, all incomplete, with no definite boundaries. Larger areas were contained within smaller areas. And all slid and changed position in relation to everything else, as if the Dark Regions consisted of a mass of restless amoebae. It would seem a prisoner could walk amid the ghastly cell-mounds for ever; although she could strongly sense paths leading out of the prison-area, they were invisible.

She tried to maintain calm confidence. But fear was growing that her skills would prove useless. The Dark Regions were treacherous and could turn a correctly chosen path into a wrong one in a second.

And now, she could not even find the base of the invisible path that she knew led out of this terrible area.

Unless—

She almost broke into a run, Ashurek and Silvren following.

'Here,' she said, indicating the cell mound that had drawn her strongly. 'We have to climb up it.'

'I'll go first – you help Silvren up to me,' Ashurek said. Silvren had stopped struggling and was quiet and pale, as though she had also given up the fight against her own despair and shame.

Calorn helped Silvren, who crawled up the steep side of the mound like a puppet. Ashurek lifted her up to stand beside him, then Calorn swallowed her own repulsion at the evil, fleshy feel of the mound and scrambled up its side.

As she reached the top, the unseen path became visible at last, a brownish, steep bridge curving up and out of sight. The ceiling of darkness seemed to have receded.

Relieved, she leapt to her feet, only to be blasted by an explosion of silver fire. She was flung off the mound and slammed into the ground below where she lay winded for a few seconds. Then she painfully crawled back up the steep side, dazed by the sudden light.

As she regained the flattish top of the mound, she saw Ashurek's tall figure silhouetted against the glow which she now perceived to come from a being standing in front of him. She moved round to get a better look, and saw that the creature was human in form, perfect in proportion, asexual, with a broad, grinning face. It was naked and its skin shone like purest silver.

She might have known the Shana could appear at will – watching out for them had been useless.

And beside the demon – oh, horrible, impossible – the hellish bird Limir was hopping gently up and down as if with suppressed glee.

And behind them, coming ponderously down the narrow walkway, were the pale forms of Exhal and his herd.

She came forward to stand beside Ashurek and Silvren, facing the demon bravely although its aura filled her with revulsion, as though her very eyeballs were racked by nausea.

'Prince Ashurek of Gorethria,' the silver figure was saying, the words oozing sibilantly from its red mouth. 'I am privileged. My name is Ahag-Ga.'

'I don't give a damn who you are,' Ashurek hissed. 'You've destroyed her – she's useless to you now. Let us pass.' Calorn was astonished at the contempt with which Ashurek addressed the Shanin, but she realised that his anger must have long ago gone deeper than fear.

Petulantly, the demon responded by suffusing them with a crackling argent light. The light was pure pain. Calorn staggered back, coughing, but Ashurek and Silvren stood their ground like two steel blades until the demon-power bled away.

'Just a small reminder to show respect to those with power,' Ahag-Ga grinned. 'Forgive me, Prince Ashurek, *I* did not destroy your sorceress. That was the work of Diheg-El, with the encouragement of Meheg-Ba. However, as you will observe, those two venerable Shana are not here. They are at large on the Earth, with Siregh-Ma, so I am fortunate indeed in being the one to welcome you.'

Ashurek perceived at once, from the wry jealousy permeating the demon's mocking tone, that it was subordinate to Meheg-Ba and Diheg-El. But that did not make it any less dangerous.

'Indeed, it would go badly for you if your superiors returned and found you had let us escape,' he said acidly. The demon's mouth stretched in a red hiss of fury and it did not

104

notice the deft movement of Ashurek's hand as he drew a small phial from a pocket.

'My so-called "superiors",' Ahag-Ga sneered, 'will, on the contrary, be more than delighted to find their lost Prince imprisoned here. However, I am not in the slightest degree interested in their petty bickerings over you and the sorceress. There is another score to be settled.'

At this Limir bounced in visible glee, cackling with the chilling menace of a harpy.

The demon continued, 'It has come to my notice that on your way through the Dark Regions, you attempted what would, on Earth, be termed a brutal murder. The fact that your attempt failed is immaterial.'

'We tried our hardest!' Calorn blazed, angered by the demon's mockery. 'I can see no reason for Limir to return to life after what we did to him, except that he is too evil to find peace in death!' She took a step towards the dreadful bird. 'You would be dead a thousand times over if I had my way.'

'You amuse me,' said Limir. 'It was an excellent joke, feigning death at your hands, but all jokes must be paid for eventually.'

'I believe the penalty for murder, in many of the civilised countries on Earth, is execution,' Ahag-Ga went on, grinning horribly. 'But here in the Dark Regions we can offer many more terrible fates. Eternal ones if we choose, eh, Exhal?'

The huge ox-creature said nothing, just glared balefully at them all.

'You can see,' said the demon, 'I am in no position to release you – even if I wanted to, to spite my – er – "superiors". Justice must be done.'

Ashurek gazed steadily at the demon as he raised his hand. The small phial was glowing with a pale golden light. It was the phial that Setrel had given them, claiming that the powder within had some power against evil.

'Silvren,' he said, 'does this substance have any power that you can see?'

'Yes, yes it does,' she said, her expression transformed as

105

though she was remembering the beauty of her sorcery before the Shana had contrived to corrupt it. 'Where did you get it? I can't see how—'

But the hissing of the demon and the metallic screeching of Limir drowned her voice. Both looked furious, like blood-streaked ghouls in their anger, as Ashurek held the phial out towards them like a weapon.

'I know not how much damage this powder could do to you or to your Regions,' he said. 'Will you take the chance, or will you let us go?'

'Aha, a challenge!' cried the demon, while Limir took off and circled menacingly over their heads. 'I will take a chance. Let us fight, Prince of Gorethria!'

Swiftly Ashurek drew the stopper from the phial and cast a pinch of the powder into the air. It formed a glittering gold curtain around Silvren, Calorn and himself, dazzling in the darkness. A feeling of protective warmth came from it, though it also seemed insubstantial, for it was formed only of soft motes of light. Moving forward with the 'curtain' around him like a shield, Ashurek bent – like a man turning into a gale – to face the demon's power.

Grinning, Ahag-Ga slowly began to raise its arms and silver fire crackled out to meet the gold. Ashurek felt Silvren mustering what little sorcery she could to help him, though that feeling was suffocated as he began to sense the mounting of distant powers.

It was suddenly as if he was standing below a dark, forbidding mountain range whose sides were scarred by ancient battles and among whose desolate peaks birds like Limir screeched forlornly. And on the highest peak, as if from a domain of evil gods, a dread power was accumulating. All the ancient anger of the Serpent, all the jealousy and vile power of demons, the blood-lust of Gorethria, the leering insanity of those who had bargained with demons – all were swirling into a thunderous sphere of power.

He was quite alone below the dark thunder of the mountain range, laughing with hunger – waiting for that dark, dread sphere to roll heavily down towards him. And now the cumulus of power was approaching, gathering wisps of evil as it rolled, growing ever larger and more terrible, like all the thunder and violence the world had ever known. And part of him desired that power, lusted for its terrible might to enter and overtake him. It was the fire that had driven his ancestors to conquer their Empire. It was the malevolent fever of the Egg-Stone and the gross, infinite energy of the Serpent; it was the calling of the dark blood within him.

And it was everything he had given up for Silvren's sake . . .

Beside him, though as unaware of him as he was of her, Calorn was struggling in a different way. Ahag-Ga was on the point of possessing her.

'It is a most simple bargain,' the demon was saying. 'I can grant your freedom instantly – you will find yourself back on Earth, relieved of this pain. All I require is that you summon me from time to time, give me some small assistance . . .'

The silver aura was swimming in front of Calorn's eyes, filling her with an unbearable sensation of pressure. Ashurek and Silvren had, for her, ceased to exist. All she knew was that if she only surrendered to the darkness, to the distant thrumming of a membrane stretched like an ear drum across the universe, her pain would be relieved. The membrane would burst. She could go to sleep.

'Help me,' she whispered.

The demon grinned. It knew she was appealing not to Ashurek, but to itself for help. It held her balanced on one hand, the Gorethrian on the other, and both were about to break. The curtain was weakening.

It only needed Ashurek to say yes to the dark and terrible power he so obviously desired. Say yes, yes!

Say yes – Ashurek seemed to see his father upon the dark mountain, and he was speaking. *Ashurek, would you fail me again? Take your power – it is your birthright.*

Father! he cried as the thunderous sphere rolled inevitably towards him. Let the power be mine – so that I can set right all the harm Meshurek did. He stretched his arms wide, laughing exultantly as he welcomed the evil cumulus of power

107

as his own. No conflict, no bitter torment within him now – why had he not known before that this was his appointed destiny?

Suddenly there was a woman between him and the power, standing in its path. He did not recognise her, but she was slender with eyes, skin and long hair different shades of deep gold.

'I don't care,' she was saying. 'The truth is – I cannot stand to be alone any longer. I can't stand it. Can you?'

'Silvren!' he screamed as the dark sphere swallowed her. 'No! No!'

Calorn did not hear Ashurek's cries, for she too was shouting in protest. From some unstoppable source within her, logic came forth to fight the demon's illogic.

'What Earth?' she cried. 'My Earth is not your Earth – which would you send me to?' And thinking of her own world, she then remembered H'tebhmeila. A red fire ignited in all her muscles – the fire of who she was, what she believed in. It gave her the strength to thrash away from the demon's evil. Wrenching herself backwards, she collided with Ashurek, then half-fell to the ground.

In unison they shouted, 'No!'

The last of the gold light and the last of the argent lightning crackled away together. Ashurek and Calorn slowly returned to the grim reality of the Dark Regions. The remainder of the powder in the phial was grey and lightless. Ahag-Ga had defeated its energy, but the Shanin's own power was also spent, and it had failed to overcome Ashurek or Calorn. A stalemate had been reached.

'I maintained the power as long as I could,' Silvren said softly into the silence. 'I'm sorry.' Ashurek looked round at her, relief flooding him as he realised that her destruction by the dark sphere had been an illusion – a figment of his own tortured imagination.

'You saved us,' he said. 'We could not have resisted without your help.'

'The powder is useless now,' Ahag-Ga's voice tore at the atmosphere like a saw. It folded its arms and its mouth stretched into a red sneer. 'So is she, though that is nothing new. Saved, but to undergo your trial and accept your sentence!'

'You are bluffing, Ahag-Ga,' said Ashurek. 'You have exhausted your strength fighting us. You have no more power now than we do.'

'That is hardly important,' replied the demon gleefully, 'when I have so much help to hand . . .' it extended an arm and Ashurek was aware of an awful silver glow on the periphery of his vision. He and Calorn looked round and saw, encircling the mound, some thirty demons. All were hissing and laughing with anticipation, awaiting the next move in the scene being enacted above them.

'Oh, but don't you think one or two would have been enough, Ahag-Ga?' exclaimed Limir. 'This argument is so entertaining, I would hate them to be too frightened to continue it!'

Ahag-Ga nodded and laughed maliciously.

'Now, back to business. Limir, bring Exhal forward.'

The evil grey bird flapped the few yards along the narrow walkway to where Exhal was standing and pecked and worried at him, in a way that made Calorn shudder, until he reluctantly ambled forward. His red eyes rolled wildly as he came, and his tongue lolled from side to side over his wolfish teeth.

'The prime witness to your appalling act,' said Ahag-Ga to Ashurek and Calorn. 'Exhal, tell all of us assembled here the violence you saw perpetrated upon poor Limir.'

The huge ox-creature hesitated for several seconds, breathing heavily as if about to explode with rage.

'They – Limir tried—' he stammered gutturally.

He did not know what to say. Limir had tried to kill him – the two humans had tried to save him. But now Limir was still alive – they had failed him, the betrayers!

'They did indeed try to murder Limir!' he roared. 'They deserve their fate.'

But Ahag-Ga turned a sinister red smile upon the huge beast.

109

'Exhal, my friend,' it said solemnly. 'Is that all you have to say?' The herdsman gave a nod. 'Perhaps you should think again. A confession at this stage might help your case.'

Exhal's great frame visibly rocked with fury and sudden fear.

'Case?' he managed to growl.

'Your long-standing dissatisfaction with your lot and insubordination to your superiors is well known. You have frequently insulted Limir – your dislike of that noble bird is no secret. And we know that you actually gave help to the two humans.' There were mocking murmurs of 'Shame!' from the Shana below. 'It is becoming obvious that you are as guilty as they. What say you, Limir?'

'I have to confess that Exhal did in fact play an active part in my attempted murder,' said the hell-bird with a leer that chilled Calorn's blood. 'He stuck a hoof in my stomach while Prince Ashurek broke my neck. My neck still hurts,' Limir added pettishly.

'So, fellow Shana,' Ahag-Ga roared, 'do you find the herdsman Exhal guilty?'

'Oh, yes, yes indeed,' the assembled demons muttered, looking at each other and laughing as if something fascinating and amusing was happening.

'Carry out the sentence, Limir,' said Ahag-Ga.

As Limir rose into the air, screeching metallically, Exhal began to roar, 'Traitors! Betrayers, all of you! I was your herdsman – where will you find another? And you – humans of the round Earth – you pretended to help me – you accepted my help when all the time you were betraying and mocking me – your bargains are more hollow and worthless than the Shana's! Betrayers!'

Limir circled him, allowing the outburst to continue, enjoying the herdsman's pain.

'Traitors! Scum! Now you are all going to pay! Who is loyal to me but my herd?' He pulled himself up to his full height and awkwardly stretched out his front feet, brandishing the short stick. Words, slow and deep and awkward-sounding came from his throat. But they were as powerful and unstoppable as a lava flow.

If it was possible for a demon to blanch, Ahag-Ga did. Below them, the glow of the Shana flickered and lost strength, and they were turning to one another, making exclamations of astonishment and fear. Limir was screaming in rage, but could not drown Exhal's voice.

Along the walkway, the human herd were swaying and groaning and shaking their heads.

'Limir!' Ahag-Ga cried. 'Shut him up!'

Just as when they had met Exhal out on the black marsh, Limir descended like a lead arrow on the ox-beast. The attack was so vicious that grey blood spurted everywhere, spattering Ashurek, Calorn and Silvren. Exhal staggered, struggling for life, still groaning out the terrible words. By the time he fell, his head was half-severed.

His body shook the mound as it toppled, then rolled off and hit the ground below.

But the words continued.

Ahag-Ga, Limir and Calorn all looked round wildly to see who was speaking them, and saw that Ashurek was now staring at the six-legged human-creatures, standing as rigid as a tree blackened and hardened by fire. He had picked up the short stick and the words of Exhal's spell came with strength and assurance from his mouth.

'Do something! Stop him!' Ahag-Ga appealed to the fellow demons standing below him. But half of them had disappeared already, and the others were backing away, their skin dull with fear. 'Limir—'

'It's too late,' said Limir, flopping onto the mound like an empty sack.

And the human herd opened their eyes. Not all of them, for only Exhal could have opened all their eyes, but enough.

Ashurek looked at Ahag-Ga. The rest of the demons had gone.

'Now you will let us go,' he said.

Never had he seen such dismay on the face of a demon. It made it look almost human. He had no idea what harm the opening of the herd's eyes could cause, but the extreme fear of Ahag-Ga and Limir was real enough.

'Yes,' said Ahag-Ga. 'You had better go – but not her.' It pointed at Silvren.

'You have no choice,' said Ashurek, angered.

But before he could usher Silvren forward, she said, 'I have a choice. I told you, I have to stay here. Don't make me explain again, it hurts too much.'

'Silvren, come on! I told you it was all a lie of the Shana's – you'll see that as soon as we reach the Blue Plane!' Ashurek cried in distress, for he could see the determination in her eyes.

'No,' she said.

'If you don't leave her, I will send an emanation of darkness through to the Blue Plane after you which will taint it for all time,' said the demon flatly and with no trace of its former mockery. It was also terrified of the punishment it would receive when Diheg-El and Meheg-Ba returned and found Silvren gone, Calorn realised.

'Can it do that?' Ashurek asked Silvren disbelievingly.

'Yes, it can. Its loss of power won't last much longer – you'd better go.'

'Ashurek, the humans are starting to close their eyes again,' said Calorn. 'Hurry, before it's too late.'

'Go without me, please,' Silvren implored. 'For the sake of the Blue Plane, if nothing else.' She took one of his hands and kissed it, but he could not bring himself to kiss her in return; he felt too cold, destroyed. How could a kiss bring him or her any comfort?

'I will still carry on the Quest,' he said dully. She nodded, giving no indication of whether or not she still wanted him to – and she had set him upon it in the first place.

Then Ashurek started to walk up the narrow brownish bridge that curved upwards from the top of the mound. Calorn tried to give Silvren a smile of encouragement before she followed, but failed. Ahag-Ga had closed its hands on Silvren's shoulders and Limir was squatting possessively in front of her, and Calorn was glad Ashurek had not seen that.

They had to squeeze past each of the pale human-cattle in turn, and their progress was slow. Most of them had their eyes shut again, and their faces were unchanged – pale and sombre as death-masks. They swayed and groaned faintly, oblivious of Ashurek and Calorn, oblivious that their herdsman lay dead below.

'Ashurek, how did you know the words of that spell – whatever it was?' she called to him.

'How did I know?' he said sharply, glancing round. 'The words were written in Exhal's eyes!'

She shrugged and bent her mind to finding the rest of the way out of the Dark Regions. The walkway was growing steeper and it was a struggle to climb it and negotiate their way past the herd. As they passed the stragglers, Calorn noticed that two still had their eyes open. The eyes were fully human, alert, intelligent – seeming not to belong in the witless, sorrowful faces. Shivering, she passed them by, but noticed that Ashurek had begun to climb much faster as if he had been deeply affected by the eyes. Now she could barely keep up with him.

Just ahead the bridge vanished into darkness, and she dreaded losing sight of him before she knew what lay ahead.

A rank breeze began to moan around them, thick with swirling particles. Calorn strained to reach Ashurek, but she could not catch her breath. She was choking on the dense air, becoming sick and faint. He was out of sight – then, suddenly, it no longer mattered. The breeze became a roaring wind which bore them both off the bridge and away into darkness.

They were hurtling at inestimable speed through a void. Ashurek uttered a despairing cry as his last chance of returning to Silvren was torn from him. Now he could not breathe, and unconsciousness – or death – was tugging his mind into its dark flow. He fought it desperately, for each time the darkness submerged him, he was again confronted by the horror of those eyes – the eyes of the two human-cattle, which he had recognised as those of his sister Orkesh and his brother Meshurek.

113

5

'I was alive here'

A FIGURE drifted through Estarinel's dreams, a girl whose
silver-fair hair obscured her face as she leaned over an
ancient, hand-bound volume of illuminations. His sister,
Arlena. Strange that she had so loved books, when in all
other ways she had been adventurous, outgoing and wild.
She would have set off on the Quest brave and laughing, like
Calorn . . . He remembered how they used to race their
horses, or how she used to ride over the rim of the valley to
greet him, her silver hair flying and her eyes full of laughter.
Then there was Lothwyn, dark-haired and quiet, so like their
father. It seemed he had hardly known them, for both had
used few words and devoted themselves with quiet affection
to their work; his father to the sheep and lambs, Lothwyn to
her weaving. Then he dreamed of his mother, leaning on a
fence outside the house and watching, with her clear amber
eyes, the mares and foals she had so lovingly tended. Ah,
the horses, they were gone too. Memories of love and affection and contentedness drifted through his mind, as if he was
saying goodbye to them.

Yet there was no pain in the dream. The tranquillising
power of tears and exhaustion had helped him to accept, for
the time being, the loss. As he slowly drifted out of sleep he
felt heavy as lead but calm, as if he had just recovered from
a long illness. The faint golden light of dawn was shimmering
through the window. Medrian lay curled against his shoulder,
her hair spread like glossy black silk across his chest. She,
above all, had saved him from insanity.

He gently wrapped his arms around her and kissed her

head, trying not to wake her. Images of their journey drifted across his memory, seeming distant and enigmatic as dreams. How he had killed a man, before he even had time for doubt, to save her on Hrannekh Ol. And how after that time, and after the battle with Arlenmia's nemale mercenaries, she had spoken to him – reached out to him from the strange cold darkness of her soul – to try and lessen his pain. Or had she been trying to show him a way to be as callous as she was, so that she could be sure he would have the strength to complete the Quest? It was as though she had seen straight through him from the start, seeing his growing fondness for her . . . and at every opportunity had tried to warn him away. Everything she had said and done – the time Arlenmia had stabbed her in the neck, and her sinister horse had died instead – should have made him think she was some sort of fiend, less than human, a creature of the Serpent. But no. Instead he had fallen in love with her.

She had said she could only function by not feeling anything, and he had observed how she encased her being in ice, numbing herself against all emotion. Anything that threatened to dissolve that protective casing, like an offer of affection, caused her acute distress. He knew she would have been happier if he could have been hostile to her, or at least cool and uninvolved. But he could not – it was totally against his nature. And besides, he had always sensed that behind her coldness she was crying, crying for help . . . Did it hurt her even more to be offered that help, when she knew she could not accept it?

He wished he understood her. He wished he knew why last night she had been colder to him than ever, then changed so suddenly, going completely against everything she had tried to make him think she was. Something had broken within her . . . Oh, Medrian, Medrian, is it possible I have harmed you by caring for you? If so, forgive me. You've haunted me since I met you . . .

More memories. Medrian, commanding a demon to depart as if she was its master, chasing a sinister black horse away as though it was death come to claim her, Medrian in Gastada's castle, horribly tortured—

That recollection made him start, pull her protectively closer to him. She woke up then and looked at him, and for once he was able to hold her gaze without feeling fear. There was an expression in her face and dark grey eyes that he had never seen before, a sort of tenuous serenity.

'If I had a wish,' she said, 'I would like to stay here for ever.'

'So would I,' he replied softly.

But as it is, she thought, these few hours will have to be enough . . . enough for my whole life. Oh, what have I done? I may have made it impossible for the Quest ever to be completed. I tried, I did try . . . but I am human. And perhaps I've condemned the world to hell, because I wasn't strong enough to resist the need for happiness. I'm a fool, I don't know what I've done. But I don't care. Whatever else M'gulfn can do, it can never deprive me of these few hours.

She kissed him with tenderness he would not have believed her capable of a few weeks earlier.

'Estarinel,' she began softly, 'no one ever saw anything in me worth loving before. I still don't know what you see. I tried so hard to make you dislike me – that was for a reason which I can't tell you, but which you'll eventually know and understand. It was important, but all the same, I just didn't try hard enough—' she swallowed, trying to steady her voice.

'Medrian—' Estarinel began, but she silenced him.

'Please listen, while I'm still able to say it. It's not your fault. You did as I asked. It was my strength that failed . . . but I'm glad. I didn't realise until last night that I loved you, or that I was even capable of love. This is the only good moment I've ever had in my life, can you understand that? Because of you . . .'

'Then I'm glad too,' he said very quietly, dreading what he was sure she would say next.

'But now I must face the fact that I may have doomed the Quest to failure. My fault, not yours, as I said . . . but there is some hope left, and I swear it is our only hope – and it

116

depends on you as well. I have to ask you something very difficult.'

'Go on,' he prompted gently, seeing how anxious she was about his reaction.

'When we leave Forluin, and especially when we leave H'tebhmella,' she said, willing herself not to avoid his eyes, 'things must be exactly as they were before, as if we hardly know each other. You must try to forget that you loved me – because I will not have any choice.' He said nothing. She forced herself to continue. 'But if you do really love me—'

'You know I do,' he whispered, stroking her hair.

'I have something even worse to say. The time may come when I ask you to do something that seems terrible; know that it is not without good reason. You must give me your word that you will comply and not protest – I do not ask this lightly. Please promise these things – the Quest will fail otherwise.'

'Medrian, Medrian,' he sighed. 'It's all right. I give you my word. What choice do I have? Perhaps the Quest is doomed anyway, but without you I could never have continued it, and I will never, never knowingly let you down . . .' After a minute he felt her relax in his arms.

'I know,' she whispered. 'How could I doubt you?'

'Is that why you came with me, to make sure I didn't lose my nerve?' he asked with a smile.

'Only partly,' she answered honestly. 'There were many reasons, some I didn't even know about . . . listen, don't let us think of the future now. We still have a few hours in Forluin.'

And it was mercifully easy, Estarinel found, to forget her ominous words and the chilling promise he had had to make, just for the time being. But at the same time a new strength began to grow in him. She had saved him from despair and madness, and surely he owed her something in return – at least to help make the future less black than she expected it to be. She had helped him bear the loss of his family – and now there was almost no one left, he became determined

117

that he would not lose her also. That would be a loss beyond bearing.

Falin noticed, later that morning, how much better Estarinel seemed. Not happy, but he had a tranquil resignation about him. Wryly Falin realised that he and Medrian were more to each other than just companions on a journey. Obviously Medrian's apparent coldness was deceptive and she had been able to comfort and help him after all; but Falin still wondered if Estarinel was making a mistake in trusting her. Or, he thought, do I just resent the fact that a stranger could console him when I couldn't?

As they ate breakfast he apologised for the poor quality of the bread; much of their farmland had been ruined. Medrian replied that all the same, it was the best bread she had ever tasted, and she smiled at him; the effect was like spring sunshine after a long winter, lighting up her face with warmth of character that made him think he really had been wrong about her.

It was still quite early and there were only a few people about in the village. The sun was warming the air and coaxing soft colours from the stone walls of the cottages. Estarinel waited until there was a lull in village activity and went back up to the long stone barn to take a last look at his family.

Falin and Medrian walked up with him, and waited outside. But as he went in, a terrible memory of the previous evening gripped Medrian like a steel hand on her throat. She staggered, reaching out to the barn wall to steady herself. How could she have forgotten! The perfect, undecaying bodies – the hideous evil of the Worm – she struggled with herself, turning her back on Falin so he could not see the pain in her face.

There was no need to say anything to Estarinel, she decided. It was only a feeling, after all, probably unfounded – no need to cause him further pain by revealing something that might only exist in her imagination. That decision made, she tried to put it from her mind.

'Medrian, are you all right?' Falin asked.

Long years of practice enabled her to make her face quite emotionless as she turned round and said, 'Will the bodies be buried?'

Falin started at the unexpected, almost callous, question.

'No, no,' he answered thickly, 'there's an Elder who cares for the dead – every village has one. The bodies are brushed with powders and herbs that keep them whole. They stay in the place of rest – we normally use a much smaller building – for at least a year. Then they are taken to a certain hill in sunlight, and they turn to dust – return to the Earth and sky. But there's usually just a few of the very old – not like this—'

'I see,' she said shortly. He stared at her, mistrust welling up again. She was an enigma – she frightened him. He was glad when Estarinel reappeared, because he had the illogical feeling that the darkness of her eyes would consume him if he stayed alone with her for much longer.

As they began to walk down the grassy slope back towards the cottage, he decided to speak before his uneasiness about Medrian made him reverse the decision he had come to the night before.

'E'rinel, I've got something to ask you. I thought very carefully about it last night, and—' he suddenly found himself unable to explain why he felt so strongly that he wanted to take his friend's place on the Quest. He just said, 'Let me go instead of you.'

Estarinel and Medrian both stopped and stared at him. Medrian's eyes widened and a thrill of grim hope made her catch her breath. That could be the answer, she thought. Falin doesn't like me; it would be easy, so easy to make him hate me. Estarinel and I could part here, now, and save all that doubt and pain – but even as she thought it, she knew it was impossible.

'Oh, Falin,' Estarinel sighed, placing his hands on his friend's shoulders. 'I understand – I know it's hard to stay here, and watch me go away again. I would feel the same. But I have to go – I was chosen in the first place, and even though it was a random choice at the time, it was a final one.

119

I set out on the Quest, and I have to finish it.' He shook his head sadly. 'I know I shouldn't have come back – oh, Falin, I'm sorry if I've made things so much harder for you. But you are needed here.'

Falin nodded with grim acceptance.

'I think I knew you'd say that,' he smiled sadly. 'There may not be much hope for Forluin, but while you are on your journey, you can be sure we'll be doing everything possible to fight the Serpent here as well. That I swear.'

They went back into the cottage, but there did not seem to be much left to say, and soon Estarinel began to feel it was best if they said goodbye and began the long walk back to Trevilith Woods.

So they said their farewells, and Estarinel added, 'Give my love to Lili, when you see her – oh, no, don't,' he said regretfully. 'It's better that she doesn't know I've been back. I don't think anyone but you has seen me – so don't tell anyone, not even her.'

Falin nodded, knowing it would be painful to be unable to tell her – and that Lilithea would be deeply hurt if she ever found out.

'Fare you well,' he said, and he and Estarinel embraced like brothers who would never see each other again. Then Falin placed a hand on Medrian's shoulder and looked into her eyes and said, 'Take care of him for me.' She smiled faintly and nodded.

'Fare you well also,' Estarinel said. He took Medrian's hand and Falin stood at the corner of his aunt's cottage, watching them walk from the edge of the village, across a meadow, and into the cover of trees until he could no longer see them.

Then he went into the living-room and sat still for a long time, so shaken he was unable to think or feel anything. Eventually, still numb, he dragged himself from the cottage to join the others going about their farming work, trying to convince himself that nothing had happened.

Estarinel went by a different route back to Trevilith Woods, avoiding even a distant glimpse of the Bowl Valley.

A lone bird was calling sadly, like a bell tolling, as they trudged between the trees. Medrian was silent, and seemed very calm, almost sleepy. But she kept looking round at the trees and sky and earth as if they were the last things she would ever see.

'It is still beautiful, even now,' Estarinel said. 'There's a spirit in this land that cannot easily be destroyed.'

'And in its people,' Medrian said with a gentle smile. 'Especially in its people.'

Now they were at the place in the woods where the Entrance Point would intercept them. They stood waiting calmly, but when it appeared, a distant cloud of blue light floating slowly towards them, Medrian turned to Estarinel and hugged him fervently.

'Oh, forgive me for the future,' she cried, almost in tears. 'Remember that I do love you, even if I can't tell you again. This has meant so much to me . . . I have hope for you, if not for myself. For myself, I wish only for peace . . .'

He returned the embrace, kissing her dark hair, not knowing what to say. The Entrance Point was almost upon them and he suddenly felt terrible regret that they had to go through and continue the Quest, that time would not stand still for them. Hand in hand they prepared to step into the void, but just before they did so, Medrian looked at him with a radiant light in her face he had never seen before and probably would never see again. She had finally found words to express what she felt.

'I was alive here,' she said.

Even as Ashurek and Calorn spun through blackness, Calorn was trying desperately to orientate herself. Upwards – the malevolent gale was bearing them upwards. With increased dread she realised that they were about to be expelled from the Dark Regions. She gagged with the effort of calling out a warning to Ashurek, but she could not make a sound.

Particles battered them like earth and stones caught in a hurricane. They were forced at painful speed through a moist fleshy tube, then through some dense, evil substance, like liquefied rubber. Gasping for breath they emerged from it and were flung through air and then against rock. Calorn caught the briefest of glimpses of an infinite, flat, black swamp some forty feet below before the dark wind thrust them upwards into a fistula of rock.

They were in the passage that led to H'tebhmella. Probably without the dark energy to lift them through the air they would never have regained it, but now that power also seemed intent on destroying them. It was forcing them through the narrow tunnel at agonising speed, and they were helpless to slow down. The rock tore at their limbs and hands, ripped their clothing and abraded their skin. Calorn lost consciousness long before they were expelled, like battered dolls thrown into the air by a child, onto the surface of H'tebhmella.

She did not know how long they lay there before they were discovered; almost at once, it seemed, someone was bathing her face with sweet, cool water. With unspeakable relief she gulped in clean air, and opened her eyes to find Filitha, a dark-haired H'tebhmellian woman, bending over her in concern. Slowly her eyes focused on the gentle faces, pale robes and silken hair of several more H'tebhmellians, thronged around the pillar of rock which contained the tunnel from the Dark Regions. Ashurek was already on his feet. Beside him stood the Lady herself; she seemed to be questioning him, but he only shook his head gravely in reply.

Calorn pulled herself to her feet with Filitha's help. The Blue Plane's healing power seemed to act most swiftly on those in greatest need, and already the ache of her bruises was fading.

'Ashurek, are you all right?' she asked urgently. His clothes, like her own, were torn and blood-soaked, and he looked as exhausted and stricken as she felt. With relief she saw that H'tebhmella's energy was swiftly restoring him, but he did not answer her, and the look in his eyes was so distant and so grim that she recoiled. She felt the pillar of rock pressing into her back, Filitha's hand on her arm. The

H'tebhmellians were all gazing at her and Ashurek in silent curiosity; among them she saw Estarinel and Medrian, equally perplexed.

Into the eerie silence the Lady said quietly, 'Ashurek, Calorn, do you feel well enough to offer me some explanation of what has occurred?'

Recovering her self-possession, Calorn began, 'Yes, my Lady, I—' but trailed off as she saw the Lady's expression. It was not gentle; it was stern, and sternness in that pure face shone forth with crystal clarity. It unnerved her more than Ashurek's severe silence. She muttered, 'Do you really need to ask?'

There was a terrible light in the Lady's eyes, as clear as diamond and as hard and precise. Her tall form seemed to be clad in a mantle of icy light. 'I realise that your purpose was to rescue Silvren. The miracle is that you have returned with relatively little harm to yourselves and H'tebhmella. Ashurek, I had thought I could place trust in you. I can hardly believe I was so wrong. I understand why you felt compelled to go, but surely you must have known that the task was utterly impossible. Why then did you attempt it?'

Still Ashurek did not speak, as if pain and misery had gone too deep within him for words.

'You have put the Blue Plane at terrible risk,' the Lady went on, her voice ringing like a steel bell. 'I think you do not appreciate just how great the danger was. The Shana might have sent a destructive power after you which would have damaged H'tebhmella for all time, and your passage through the Plane would have made it possible. Did you not perceive it? Does it mean nothing to you?' The adamancy of her visage was daunting, but Ashurek only glowered back, the pain in his verdant eyes equally formidable.

'I will not expel you from the Blue Plane. You will be permitted to remain until the Quest departs, but under sufferance, and only because the Quest is so essential. I see you are not repentant. Ashurek, will you not tell me what befell?' There was a beseeching echo in these last words, but the Gorethrian still did not respond. As if her words were no more than cobwebs destroyed by rain, he gave her one last baleful look, then strode away. The H'tebhmellians fell back to let him pass, and he was soon out of sight among the rocks.

The Lady turned to Calorn. 'I hardly need to ask – it is clearly readable in your eyes that you were fully aware of how dangerous and wrong your actions were. And yet, instead of trying to stop him, you used the very skills on which the Quest depends to help him. You put in jeopardy not only your life and his, but the very future of the Earth. Calorn, I trusted your judgement implicitly! What did you hope to achieve?'

Calorn felt she was facing a cold and pure wind that must surely destroy her inferior substance, destroy the loathsome part of her which had lusted for Limir's death. But somehow she held the fragments of herself together and replied with all the warmth and honesty in her soul, 'My Lady, you know the answer. I am human. Perhaps I have more idealism than sense. I could not have stopped Ashurek, but with my help, I believed we had a chance. Without me, he would have found his way there anyway, and he would have been killed!' The Lady nodded gravely, waiting for her to continue. Suddenly tears sprang into Calorn's eyes as she added, 'My Lady, the rescue was so nearly successful . . .'

Gently, the Lady prompted her, 'I think you should tell us exactly what happened.'

Fighting the excruciating revulsion and misery with which the memory of those events filled her, Calorn did so. Estarinel and Medrian listened in appalled silence.

'It was Silvren's own decision not to come back,' Calorn concluded at length. 'The Shana have done something terrible to her. They have convinced her that she is evil, and must never again taint the Blue Plane or the Earth with her presence. Do you wonder that Ashurek has nothing to say to you after that?'

The Lady's clear grey eyes were now shining with distilled grief. 'Ah, Calorn, I cannot fully express the sorrow I feel for Silvren's plight. Yet you have proved that the time for her rescue is not yet ripe. Until the Serpent dies, no short-cuts can be taken. Do you understand why I am angry?'

'Yes, my Lady,' Calorn answered. 'Yet – I know that I would do the same again. Therefore I feel that I should resign from your service.'

The Lady did not reply at once. She placed a hand on Calorn's shoulder, her face suddenly gentle. 'Dear one, there is much doubt and obduracy mixed in you, but I will not, cannot expel you from my service. I cannot even adjure you to act only on my instructions in future, because it is your very independence of mind that makes you so valuable to us.'

Calorn held the Lady's clear gaze and responded, 'Then it is my only desire to continue to serve you.'

'That is well. No amount of words can undo what is done, so I shall not speak of this again. Come now, and rest.'

The Lady began to walk away, the other women of the Blue Plane following. Estarinel and Medrian hung back until Calorn caught them up, and the three walked along together, some distance behind the H'tebhmellians.

'Calorn, are you sure you're all right?' Estarinel asked. She nodded, giving a rueful smile. 'I can't believe Ashurek tried to do something so insanely dangerous.'

'Can't you? I thought you knew him by now,' Medrian put in quietly.

'Yes, it was insane, I suppose,' Calorn sighed. 'And I'm extremely worried about him. You can imagine how he's feeling.'

'But the Lady was right,' Estarinel said. 'What have Silvren and Medrian said all along? The evil must be torn out at its roots. How could there be any hope of rescuing Silvren? Did Ashurek think the Quest ended at that – if he had brought her back safely, would he have stopped there? Perhaps he would have been content to let the Serpent win. He didn't scruple to put H'tebhmella at risk!'

'He has learned,' said Calorn eventually. 'He has said that he will continue the Quest. But Silvren sent him upon it, and now that she has lost her resolve, he . . .'

'He only has his own bitterness and desire for revenge to motivate him,' said Medrian, looking at the ground. 'I don't think he has learned anything. I think he has lost too much. Haven't we all?' She gave Estarinel a brief, compassionate glance.

'Well, I suppose you're right,' Calorn said. 'I know we should not have gone. But I still believe we had no choice.'

'No choice?' Estarinel exclaimed. 'What about H'tebhmella? If the Blue Plane had been maimed, what would any of us have had left? Ashurek has achieved nothing except to inflict more pain on Silvren and himself. He'll destroy everything if he goes on like this.'

Calorn looked at him in surprise. 'I thought – well, I thought you'd be rather more sympathetic to him.'

'Why do you care?' Medrian enquired acidly. 'The Worm must be destroyed. Nothing else matters – nothing.' And she hung her head as if she only half-believed her own words.

Sighing to herself, Calorn left them and went to seek Filitha's company instead. She did not want to be alone with memories of the Dark Regions, for although her body was healing rapidly, her soul was still weeping raw from the sickness of that place.

The Lady was true to her word; she reproached neither Ashurek nor Calorn any further over the matter. But there was no need; the awesome purity of her anger was not easily forgotten. It hung over the Plane like an intangible mantle of diamond, and nothing seemed quite the same.

Ashurek doggedly avoided company, rejecting Filitha's and Estarinel's attempts to talk to him with calm but uncompromising moroseness.

'I don't know why you're worried about him,' Medrian said to Estarinel. Several hours had passed by and they were alone in a secluded hollow by a waterfall. 'Has he shown a ghost of concern about your family?'

Estarinel shook his head, sighing. 'I wouldn't expect him

to. It's not that. I'm thinking of the Quest: perhaps he feels unable to continue, after all.'

'No. He won't fail us in that.' She slipped her hand through his arm. 'I'm convinced of it, Estarinel. Don't worry.' It's the least of my worries, she thought with a shiver of dread.

'I wonder how much longer we have to wait?' he murmured.

'Not long. Not long,' Medrian replied with quiet, sinister conviction.

A rich indigo twilight enfolded them. Soft blue-green moss sparkled beneath their feet, and all around them stood trees like columns of violet glass. Nearby, the stream slid musically towards the lake; no other sound disturbed H'tebhmella's calm. Motes of light were drifting like dandelion spores across the dark blue sky, each as distant and awesome as a star, yet as warm and comforting as a candle lit to welcome an exhausted traveller.

'The Quest can't begin soon enough,' Estarinel said, half to himself. 'Yet how hard it will be to leave here.' He turned to embrace Medrian, but she moved stiffly out of his grasp.

'Estarinel, I told you that when we left Forluin, things must be as they were,' she stated, turning her back on him. She was thinking, I must be strong, I must end it before M'gulfn ends it for me—

Her inner struggle was evident in the taut lines of her neck and shoulders, and Estarinel's longing to understand her turned like a knife in his heart. But he knew that anything he said or did would only make her conflict harder. He did not reply, just stood gazing at her, and suddenly, in total contradiction of what she had just said, she turned to him and put her arms round his neck and kissed him with a passion that was more desperate than his.

I have no strength left at all, she cried inwardly. Because of my weakness the Quest will fail, and knowing this, still I cannot help myself.

Estarinel was woken by someone calling his name, distantly, but as he surfaced from sleep and sat up on the soft moss, he thought he must have imagined it.

And Medrian had gone.

The H'tebhmellian sky had returned to a clear, pale blue and all seemed calm, but he felt suddenly anxious. He stood up, looking about him. He must have been asleep for several hours; he wondered how long ago she had wandered off alone. Saddened, he knelt on the stream's bank for a while, drinking of the cool water and splashing his face and neck. After a minute he heard his name called again, closer now, and presently the H'tebhmellian woman, Filitha, approached him through the trees.

'There you are, E'rinel,' she said. Her eyes were deep blue, and azure light swirled around her. 'The Lady asked me to find you. You must come with me to the Cavern of Communication. There is news of the Silver Staff.'

He was on his feet at once. She began to lead him towards a bridge, a mere strand of sapphire arching over the glassy lake.

'Have you seen Medrian?' he asked.

'Yes, she was walking alone on the far side of the lake earlier,' Filitha answered. 'Calorn has gone to fetch her.'

Estarinel thought, I have been trying to deny what Medrian said to me, but in my heart I know she's right. Already she is drifting away from me.

A few minutes later Estarinel was standing in a cavern within the root of a tall rock pinnacle. It was roughly dome-shaped inside, its surface made up of mirrored planes that reflected all shades of blue, indigo and silver. The effect was eerie and he was glad that he was not there alone; the cave was filled by a throng of H'tebhmellians. But they were all silent, and it was like being surrounded by pale sentient jewels rather than human beings. He saw Calorn and Ashurek standing together and made his way over to them. He looked anxiously about him but could see no sign of Medrian and eventually asked where she was.

'She refused to come with us,' Calorn replied.

128

'Did she say why? She knows how important this is.'

'Perhaps that's why she preferred not to witness it,' Calorn said, noticing his look of distress. 'It's understandable; don't worry about her, I think she wanted to be alone for a while, that's all.'

'Yes . . . I'm sure you're right,' Estarinel responded faintly. He was startled at how anxious he felt, as if the air of expectancy within the cavern was itself being mirrored and multiplied by the faceted walls.

The Lady was standing in the centre of the cave. Before her was a perfectly smooth, circular plinth of rock, which was waist-high and barely the width of her two hands in diameter. Estarinel was at the front of the throng and could see that the surface was mercury-smooth and reflective as glass; he was reminded uncannily of Arlenmia's mirrors.

At the apex of the dome was another perfectly circular mirror. Reflections danced back and forth in the air between the two, like a language of light too fast for any human to understand. The Lady watched this flickering for several minutes; it was only because he could see it reflected in her agate-grey eyes that he knew he was not imagining it.

Beside him Calorn and Ashurek watched with equal tension. Ashurek had not spoken a word or even acknowledged him; his eyes were less intense as though his grief and anger were becoming more and more deeply buried within him. But this only served to make his tall, dark figure appear more dangerous.

Now the Lady placed her hands on the glassy stone surface and looked up towards the roof of the cavern. The flickering light became clearly visible, like rippling water caught by sunlight. Faster and faster it danced until a form could be discerned within it; delineated by faint white shadow lines, a face hung in the air above the plinth.

Its mouth moved, and some of the H'tebhmellians gasped, but Estarinel could hear nothing of what it appeared to be saying. The visage was perhaps that of an elderly man with long, pale hair; it was too blurred to be recognisable, except that, to Estarinel, it clearly had no eyes.

129

He began to feel dizzy. No one around him seemed affected, but suddenly an unreasoning fear was choking him. His
vision became grey as if a mist had suddenly filled the cavern.
He could no longer see the faceted walls, or the people
around him, the Lady or the face: all was blotted out by
canescence. Through this fog he saw layer upon layer of
some translucent stuff like red glass. Behind it grey figures
moved. They were faceless, yet they stared straight through
him; they were powerful, yet without conscience. Inhumanity
radiated from them like death. Then in a second vision
overlaid on the first he saw a needle-thin streak of silver. It
was not resting on anything, but neither was it floating or
flying: it simply *was*. Around it he sensed a vast darkness,
the crushing infinity of the universe. Against this blackness
countless stars were arrayed, but although they were mere
points of light, they were not the tranquil, frosty flowers seen
from Earth. He was aware of each one as an inferno of
incomprehensible size and power; no human could draw near
to these spheres of blazing energy without being obliterated,
consumed to a tiny ash, which might as well never have
existed. What he was witnessing was beyond the minute
scope of human experience. It reduced him to less than
nothing. And across the immeasurable lightless wastes that
lay between the stars, swelling waves of invisible energy
ebbed and flowed. Here the needle of silver danced, at one
with the great arcs of power yet seeming to mock their
strength. Now many long grey arms stretched up towards it
as if from another dimension, fingertips straining to touch it,
to coax it. It lent itself to their touch, compliant yet seeming
to laugh with the vast, silent amusement of a god.
    Estarinel's perception changed, his awareness became
gigantic, as if the universe itself were not large enough to
contain him; he was soaring through darkness as if round
and round the inside of a dark ball. Then the ball split and
fell away, and beyond was a sun of such awesome size and
brightness that his mind reeled; he felt he was falling towards
it and yet would take years to reach its inescapable fiery
heart. But then he realised that he was not in fact moving;

that the fire was only a dim golden radiance; that it was not vast, but tiny. It filled his vision because it was very close to his face.

He was standing like a granite monolith on a perfectly flat, colourless plain, but the ground itself was moving, carrying him away from the small, glowing sphere. Now at a great distance he saw insubstantial grey beings bearing before them the long Staff of silver. It seemed the only reality in this strange vision. Of their own volition, Staff and sphere touched; the sphere faded and was gone, but the Staff was glowing joyously, vibrating, filling the universe with emanations of power. Estarinel shared in its exuberant strength, felt joy in its mystery and wild triumph as if the Serpent was already dead. But the feeling was momentary. The grey figures and the silver entity were so far away that he could barely see them.

And now Medrian was at his elbow, and he was flooded by the emotion that she was experiencing: terror so absolute that it was more than fear, because fear at least contains some hope of survival. What Medrian radiated was utter desolation.

He looked at her and she whispered, 'Not me. Not me. Where is she?'

She looked round at him for a second, then pulled away from him and was gone. He stumbled forward, trying to reach her, and found himself on his hands and knees in snow, suddenly physically freezing cold and more alone than he had felt even at the edge of his parents' devastated farm.

He must have cried out then; instantly, he was back in the cave. He was startled to find that he was still on his feet, but Filitha and Calorn were supporting him and everyone was looking at him.

'Are you all right?' Calorn asked.

'Medrian – where's Medrian?'

'She didn't come in, I told you.'

'She was here—' he put a hand to his forehead and tried to re-orientate himself. 'I'm sorry – I felt ill for a minute. I am all right, really.'

131

But the Lady was looking at him very gravely from the other side of the stone plinth. The ghostly face and dancing lights had gone.

'Estarinel, did you hear what the Guardian said?' she asked.

'No – I saw him, but I heard nothing,' he replied.

'Only I and the few H'tebhmellians who have been in constant contact with the Guardians through this cavern understood what he had to say, but I thought, from your reaction, that you heard him also.'

'No,' he shook his head. 'I half-fainted – that's all I know.'

Yet as the Lady began to speak, he found he knew exactly what she was going to say, and he could not erase the image of the grey figures and Medrian's terror from his mind.

'Then, if you are well, I will repeat what the Guardians have told me. There is good news: they have succeeded in their mission to capture the lost positive energy within the Silver Staff. They are within the domain of the Staff and guarding it until the Quester arrives to take it.' She was addressing everyone within the cavern, but now she moved towards Calorn, Ashurek and Estarinel and lowered her voice so that only they could hear. Around them the H'tebhmellian women began to murmur quietly to each other, a sound as sweet as the soft chiming of crystal.

'Now, perhaps you already know this, but I want you to be aware that only one person is permitted to go after the Staff and to bear and wield it. That person is to be Estarinel.' The Forluinishman betrayed no reaction, but a flame ignited in Ashurek's eyes. 'Calorn's purpose is to guide you into the domain. Then you will be alone, and your journey will be quite unpredictable. But understand this: it will be a route pre-planned by the Silver Staff itself, designed purely to test your worthiness to use it. It is the nature of the Staff; the Guardians can do nothing to prevent you undergoing these tests. They may be dangerous and you may fail. That is what I meant when I said the journey to fetch the Staff would be perilous.'

The Lady spoke more bluntly than was her usual way, and Estarinel was grateful that he had been forewarned by Calorn.

He began to speak, but Ashurek suddenly interrupted, 'Wait. Estarinel seems unwell. My Lady, I believe it would be better if I went upon this dangerous path.'

Estarinel looked at the Gorethrian and saw an unmistakably avid green fire burning in his eyes. He felt horribly chilled by it. He wished more than anything that Ashurek could go instead of him; with his long experience of fighting the supernatural, his fearless determination, he seemed the only obvious choice. Yet, with grief, rage and vengefulness burning within him, the idea of the Silver Staff in his hands was a terrifying one.

But how powerful against the Serpent he would be.

The Forluinishman began to speak in support of Ashurek's suggestion, but stopped himself. Am I becoming as callous as the Guardians themselves? Would I stoop so low as to use a friend's despair as a weapon to unleash against the Serpent? That makes me a user, a manipulator, no better than those grey beings . . . sick with himself, he waited for the Lady's response.

'No,' she said, facing Ashurek calmly. 'Estarinel is not unwell, and the choice cannot be remade.'

'For what reason? The tests of the Silver Staff will not daunt me; I am merely being realistic in believing that I have the greatest chance of succeeding in the mission.' His voice was dangerously quiet; he seemed too controlled after what he had endured.

'The tests may not be what you imagine. It is required that the Quester be "clear of purpose".'

'What does that mean?'

'Clear of the purpose for which the Staff is to be used . . . not for some secondary purpose, not a vengeful one,' stated the Lady. 'And in addition, there is another factor which makes it preferable that you do not wield such a weapon.'

'The Egg-Stone?' enquired Ashurek.

'Yes. No one may so much as touch it without being

133

affected in some way. We do not know how much it may have harmed you.'

'In other words, the Silver Staff could become another Egg-Stone in my hands?'

'Yes, it may be so. It cannot be risked,' she replied.

'I see you are adamant. I will not press the point,' conceded the Gorethrian with a very sardonic smile. Estarinel and Calorn were both privately surprised that he had given in so easily; they did not know whether to feel relieved or alarmed.

'Thank you,' said the Lady. 'Believe me, Estarinel stands the greatest chance of success, and the Quest consists of three people, not just one. Now we will speak of the arrangements for the journey; *The Star of Filmoriel* lies ready to sail—'

'We will sail immediately?' asked Estarinel, both relief and tension mounting in him at the realisation. Around them the H'tebhmellians began to sing a haunting air sometimes sung in Forluin; here, the mirrored walls of the cavern reflected the clear, crystal-like voices of the H'tebhmellians until the song became quite unearthly. It was exquisite, seeming to distil the beauty and tranquillity of the Blue Plane into the core of Estarinel's heart. He did not know how he could bear to leave.

'Yes,' replied the Lady gently. 'The Silver Staff is ready; you are all restored to health. There is nothing else to stand between you and the last part of the Quest.'

The Star of Filmoriel was just as they remembered her: a small, graceful ship of pale wood with a mythical beast's face on the tall figurehead. White stars gleamed on the three thin, sail-less masts as she bobbed gently in the clear, blue lake. Estarinel felt a tightness in his throat when he recalled how they had left her, stranded like a dead swan on the White Plane. No thanks to us that she is here now, he thought.

They were approaching her across a craggy shore of blue-green rock. Behind them a great stalk of rock rose up, spreading at its summit into a flat expanse on which crystalline

134

trees grew and strange, lovely animals grazed. Across the clear lake other such rock formations stood rooted, some mushroom-shaped, some taking more fantastic forms. The beauty of the Blue Plane had lost none of the initial impact it had had on Estarinel, and was now more poignant because he felt sure he was seeing it for the last time.

With him were Medrian and the Lady of H'tebhmella. Before them walked Ashurek, Calorn, and Filitha. A group of H'tebhmellians were already waiting by the *Star* to bid them farewell. They had made her ready, and were now waiting by the lowered gangplank for the four travellers to go aboard.

The four were all now similarly clad in H'tebhmellian travelling gear: breeches, long boots, belted jackets and heavy cloaks, which were all of neutral colours, fawn, russet, mushroom- and slate-grey. The material was stout as linen yet as soft and warm as wool. In the hold were all the provisions they needed, including clothing and equipment suited to the Arctic weather they would eventually have to face. There was nothing to wait for, nothing to say except farewell.

Estarinel felt he had been on the Blue Plane – which he had longed all his life to see – an age, yet now it was suddenly slipping away from him. Time had begun to turn swiftly beneath his feet; he tried to return his mind to the Quest, but still the pain of loss gripped him. It startled him that, having endured so much pain, he still had the capacity to feel more. He looked at Medrian; her face, though she tried hard to let no expression appear on it, betrayed a terrible fear and strain that immediately made him forget his own feelings.

'The blessing of H'tebhmella be upon you,' said the Lady, facing the three companions. 'Ashurek, remember that Silvren acted always from love of the world, not vengefulness.' The Gorethrian's eyes narrowed a little, but he held her gaze and his demeanour contained a distant but sincere respect. He said nothing but bowed gravely to her, then mounted the gangplank and went aboard. Calorn followed him, having exchanged a solemn salute and a speaking look with the Lady. Both were obviously eager to be away, and Estarinel felt infected by their restlessness; to delay in the Blue Plane was pointless.

The Lady turned to him and said, 'E'rinel, I am so sorry about your family.'

'There was a lot I wanted to ask you,' he said softly. 'Angry, futile questions: hasn't the Serpent done enough to Forluin? Why did Ashurek act as he did? And Silvren – is there no limit to M'gulfn's cruelty? But I know the answer well enough. Of course there's no limit; it will go to every length it knows to torment and defeat us. In accepting that, I understand that rage and vengeful grief are useless – impotent, broken weapons. The only answer is to stop it. Go forth and put an end to it . . .'

'You have changed,' the Lady said.

'Yes – I'm beginning to sound like Medrian,' he said with a faint smile.

And like Medrian, he is beginning to lose himself, the Lady thought. He retains his Forluinish love and compassion. But how wary he has become . . .

'Can I be right in thinking that you have lost your trust in H'tebhmella?' she asked unexpectedly. He glanced at her uncomfortably as if she had hit on a truth he had wished to conceal.

'I have no real trust left in anything,' he admitted hesitantly.

'Not even in me?' she persisted.

He thought how distant, how unhuman she seemed, despite her closeness. 'How can we be sure you want to help us – that we are not just being used to free H'tebhmella from the Dark Regions? Who or what dare I trust? You want to save the Blue Plane, not the Earth,' he said flatly.

'Estarinel, the Blue Plane *is* the Earth!' she replied earnestly. 'In what way are they separate? Do you think I do not long to rend the Serpent, to rid the Earth and universe of its abominable presence in one supreme act of cleansing? But I am powerless to do so. It was born with the Earth as we were. We fear each other yet the laws of our creation prevent us from entering each other's domains. So, yes, in a way you are being used to achieve what we cannot. And we are being used in our turn. Perhaps the chain has no end, or circles upon itself. But there is another way of looking at it, which is that we need you as much as you need us. If not more. Are not Forluin, H'tebhmella and the Earth worth saving?'

'Yes . . . whatever the cost,' he murmured. 'It is a strange feeling to accept that you are no longer an individual but an instrument to save others . . . It is another reality.'

'In understanding that, you come closer to understanding Medrian,' the Lady said, almost in a whisper. He gave her a sharp, questioning glance, but she only added, 'Fare you well, and remember, I am never so far away as you imagine.' She kissed his forehead and, as if in a trance, he turned from her and walked onto the smooth, pale deck of the *Star*.

Now Medrian and the Lady spoke softly together, their voices drifting up like smoke, only half-heard.

'I could not have stayed here,' Medrian said. She sounded too calm, her terror too deeply suppressed. 'Even here, and free, the space it leaves is a gaping hole that fills my whole universe. I have one future, one only, and there can be no alternatives and no escape routes; that I have always known. I'll take my responsibility and go.'

'I wish I could be with you, but I cannot, not while – it drives me away, even me,' murmured the Lady, her eyes filled with tears like rain.

'This is now my past, and ahead is only weary night. The dark vortex. Still . . .' she made a small, shrugging movement of her shoulders. 'I wish to thank you for allowing me a glimpse of another life . . .'

The Lady, white-clad and with the soft blue glowing from her, embraced her closely. 'There's nothing I can say. Your misery is mine, as is the misery of E'rinel and Ashurek and Silvren . . . all who suffer under the Serpent. Go on now. Bless you.'

Medrian looked up at the ship and as Estarinel caught her

eye it was as if someone had sung a high, jarring note; from her eyes a breath of disharmony touched the Blue Plane. She hurried up the gangplank as if desperate to remove that discord from H'tebhmella.

Their leave-taking thus finished, Calorn called to the two water-dwelling horses harnessed to the ship. Their great shoulders and quarters moved, gleaming like sea-washed boulders, and the ship began to glide forward. They swam willingly, raising and lowering their long, fine muzzles into the water as they went.

Looking back to the shore, they saw the Lady raising her hand to bid farewell. She was as still, as lovely and enigmatic as a pale tree silvered by moonlight; from her fingers a shaft of blue light fell on the *Star*'s figurehead and the ship leaped in response like a brave and willing horse.

The *Star* cut through the clear waters of H'tebhmella for several minutes before they noticed the waters clouding. The pinnacles of blue rock seemed foggy and distant, the sky low and dark. Waves began to heave beneath them, tugging at the small ship. The two great sea-dwelling horses were confused for a moment but swam on.

The open sea was all around them, a disc of grey, heaving mercury. The world seemed very claustrophobic and dim, and the Blue Plane untouchable now that they had returned through the Exit Point. Estarinel clutched the rail, feeling a sudden, terrible panic; there was so much he could have said to the Lady – so much he should have said to Medrian. But time had tricked him, it was too late.

The sea seemed to be turning upon them, growling. A storm crawled towards them, slow and violent and malicious, like the storm that had swept them into the White Plane. The clouds seemed low enough to touch, spitting Serpent-coloured lightning. The waves, like billowing, filthy silk, began to drag the ship faster and faster through the oily atmosphere. A foul wind caught at their faces.

Standing at the prow between Estarinel and Ashurek,

Calorn was the first to speak. 'What appalling weather! Is your Earth always as bad as this?'

'Yes,' was Ashurek's brief response.

Calorn was determined to make some attempt to lighten the mood of gloom that had descended, but before she could continue, there was a movement behind her, and Estarinel cried, 'Medrian!'

The dark-haired woman had stumbled forward apparently with every intention of throwing herself off the ship. Only the rail had stopped her and she now hung over it as if losing consciousness.

Calorn rushed to help Estarinel pull her back onto the deck.

'Does she get seasick?' she asked.

'No – no, it's not that . . .' Medrian was a dead weight in his arms, yet she was not unconscious. Her face was grey, her eyes wide and staring. Her breath was slow and so laboured that every exhalation sounded like a groan. Then she blinked, and her visage twisted with a mixture of pain and revulsion. With a remarkable burst of strength she pulled away from Estarinel, ran blindly down the steps from the fo'c'sle to the main deck, then fell to her knees and began to scratch at the smooth planks with her fingernails. She struggled to catch her breath and began to utter low, hoarse screams, which were horrible to hear.

'Medrian! Medrian, what's wrong?' Estarinel cried. He followed and tried to pull her to her feet. She writhed in his arms like a mad puppet fighting itself, and her fingers were bloody.

'Leave me! Leave me! Leave me!' she shrieked.

'We must get her below – Calorn, help me!' said the Forluinishman, holding grimly onto her.

They carried her to one of the aft cabins and laid her on the bunk. Calorn lit a lamp, which swung wildly from the ceiling as the ship tossed in the storm, filling the cabin with a sweet, starry light. But the Alaakian woman's face was ghastly as she writhed on the bunk in some terrible, private distress that Estarinel felt powerless to comfort.

'Has this happened to her before?' Calorn asked, observing his helplessness and anxiety.

'No. But I think she knew it was going to happen. That's why she was so afraid before we left H'tebhmella,' he said, hanging onto one of her hands and watching her, his own face drained of colour.

'Stay with her. I'll bring some wine, it will restore her. Don't look so worried!' Calorn left the cabin. Estarinel was grateful for her practicality, but it did nothing to reassure him. Medrian wrenched her hand away from his and began to claw at her hair, drawing it in a black tangle over her grey, distorted face.

Now there was rage in her expression, battling with the horror.

'Damn you! Damn you! Don't try me, you'll lose!' she cried out. 'It will be as it was before. I am not yours!'

Estarinel started at these words, yet she did not seem to be addressing him. 'Medrian – Medrian, it's all right, I'm with you,' he said. But she was locked in some private hell and could not hear him.

The cabin door opened. Ashurek entered and looked down at her prostrate form. 'She's not ill,' he said. 'She's fighting something.'

'That's obvious,' retorted Estarinel, glaring up at him. 'Well, is there anything we can do for her?'

'Alas, no, my friend,' the Gorethrian answered, sitting on the end of the bunk. 'She can only help herself.'

'A knife, a knife,' Medrian muttered. Then, her face livid as if she was furious at Estarinel's lack of response, she propped herself on her elbows and stared at him. 'A knife, give me a knife.'

'I haven't got one. Why, Medrian?' he said, startled by this request.

'A dagger, a blade, anything,' she hissed.

'The H'tebhmellians gave us no weapons. There were none on the Blue Plane, if you remember,' Ashurek said coolly.

'Something sharp – anything. It's essential,' she repeated, her voice weak but irrefusable.

140

'Lie down – try to rest,' Estarinel implored her without success. Then, alarmed, 'Ashurek, what in the name of all the gods are you doing?'

He was removing from around his neck the chain on which the Egg-Stone had once hung. The clasp was an ingenious Gorethrian device designed to prevent theft; anyone attempting to remove the chain without knowing the correct method of undoing it would find a poisoned blade in his thumb. Death followed in seconds.

Ashurek carefully sprung the tiny blade and handed it to Medrian. Estarinel stared at him aghast.

'It has held no poison for many years,' Ashurek said to her. 'It is not dangerous.'

She took the chain with its vicious clasp gratefully; the risk of poisoning meant nothing to her. Then she pulled back her sleeve and began methodically to inflict shallow cuts on her inner forearm.

Estarinel leaped forward to stop her with a cry of horror; Ashurek stayed him, his hands on the Forluinishman's shoulder.

'Have you gone mad? Don't you know she tried to throw herself off the ship? She's trying to kill herself!'

'No – not now,' Ashurek replied calmly. 'She needs the pain to regain her self-control. Leave her alone – she knows what she's doing.'

Estarinel saw, horribly, that his companion was right.

'I can't watch,' he muttered.

'Then go on deck – I'll stay with her.' But neither could Estarinel leave her. He slumped on a seat in the corner of the cabin, barely noticing when Calorn brought a flask of reviving H'tebhmellian wine.

Ashurek was proved right. With every cut Medrian's dreadful struggle was diminished. When her whole forearm was bloody and her face white with the pain, she became calm at last and gave the clasp back to Ashurek.

'Thank you,' she said stiffly. Then Estarinel came forward with some bandages that Calorn had brought, and she allowed him to bind her arm. But she would not look at him, and he knew that it was Ashurek who had given her the help she needed, not himself. She sipped some wine then lay back on the bunk, so pale that she might have been dead.

'She will soon recover,' said Ashurek, seeing how ashen-faced Estarinel was. 'I'll sit with her.'

Sighing bitterly, Estarinel left the cabin, and wandered across the deck. Calorn, who was waiting outside, approached and asked concernedly, 'What's wrong with Medrian?'

'I don't know. For some reason she can't tell us,' he replied, his voice strained with anxiety. 'Ashurek seems to have more perception of what she's enduring than I have, and so is better able to help her . . . I think it's something –' he shook his head, and Calorn felt moved by his pain, 'something that doesn't bear thinking about.'

'You love her very much, don't you?' she asked gently.

'It doesn't make any difference. I would still care about her.'

Calorn was silent for a while. Then she said, 'When I saw the evil of the Dark Regions, how effortlessly it corrupts all that it touches, I was filled with anger – determination to do anything that will help recompense you and destroy it.'

'Do you always keep your concern for others – never yourself?'

She shrugged. 'I am a mercenary, a soldier who serves others. I have nothing left for myself. But this is the way I've chosen to live – therefore I am content. Does that make sense?'

'Yes, I think so.'

'I also know that people can be destroyed by caring too much . . . but nothing I say will stop you, will it?'

'No. I am not free to make that choice.'

'Come on,' she said, smiling. 'I must take up my duties; someone has to navigate. You can assist me. I think night is drawing on and this storm won't help us find our bearings.'

Estarinel helped her to set up navigational equipment upon the fo'c'sle. The deck tipped beneath their feet and waves broke over them, but the H'tebhmellian cloaks were sturdy and waterproof. As it grew darker, the diamond radiance shining on the masts gave them light to work by.

'Now, all we need is a sight of the stars. Meanwhile, I think we should retreat to a cabin and have something to eat,' Calorn suggested cheerfully.

They were making their way across the deck when the door of Medrian's cabin opened and she emerged. The wind swept her hair back from her face and she looked very pale under *The Star of Filmoriel*'s lights. She made to walk straight past them, but Estarinel stopped her and said, 'Medrian? Are you feeling better?'

She looked at him, perfectly composed.

'Yes. It won't happen again, I assure you.' She was as cold as the distant stranger he had first met at the House of Rede; it was as though all they had been through together was obliterated. The darkness had returned to her eyes, making them seem like grey and black caverns full of shadow. He felt like shouting in protest, No! I won't let this happen to you! But at the same time he felt so cold that he could not say anything at all.

'Estarinel,' she added, 'remember what I told you. I meant it. It must be as it was before.' Then she went on her way and stood alone at the prow, staring out into the bitter storm. Estarinel tried to swallow his unbearable emotions for her sake; he knew that even those few words were more than she could afford to offer him.

143

6

The Domain of the Silver Staff

THE STORM abated during the night. The travellers emerged
from their cabins at dawn and saw that the clouds had curled
back to reveal patches of colourless, rain-washed sky. The
ship's violent pitching of the night before had subsided to a
gentle rolling motion as she glided with the swell of the
waves. On the horizon before them, the sun was rising like
a giant pearl behind gauzy layers of cloud.

Calorn climbed up to the fo'c'sle deck, tying her cloak and
disentangling her long chestnut hair from the hood as she
went. She took a deep breath of the cold, salty air, and
leaned over by the figurehead to check that the sea-horses
were well. They were swimming with unrelenting strength,
unaffected by the storm. She gave them a shout of encouragement and they shook their delicate, tapering heads in response.

Making a check of her navigational equipment, she found
that only a slight adjustment to their course was necessary.
This done, she stood looking out across the milky grey ocean,
one hand on the figurehead's slim neck.

After a few minutes Ashurek and Medrian joined her on
the deck. Medrian looked ghastly. Calorn thought she had
never seen a face so white that had not belonged to a corpse;
even Medrian's lips were waxen. Her expression had a frozen
look to it, as if all ability to express emotion had been leached
out and her features petrified. But the intense darkness of
Ashurek's visage did not make Calorn any less uneasy. She
looked about for Estarinel, but could not see him.

'Well, do you know where we are?' Ashurek asked shortly.

'Yes,' she said, relaxing into a smile. 'We are on course. Look, I'll show you.' She pulled a map out of her belt and unfolded it, doing her best to flatten out the creases. Their destination was a small Northern country on the West coast of Tearn called Pheigrad.

'Here is our goal,' she said, pointing to a small bay on the map. 'And we are here . . . about four day's sailing will bring us in to land.'

Estarinel came up to join them, carrying slabs of dark, rich bread and flasks of H'tebhmellian wine. He distributed this breakfast among them without speaking. Calorn noticed that he looked pale and exhausted, as if he had emerged on the far side of grief completely numb. He did not meet the eyes of Medrian or Ashurek, and it was the first time he had greeted Calorn herself without a glimmer of warmth. She looked enquiringly at him but he just stared at her blankly for a second, then looked away.

'Four days?' Ashurek was saying. 'Can we be there no sooner?'

'Possibly, if the tides are in our favour. I've made a realistic estimate. And we could have landed two weeks or two months away. We've been lucky.'

'It's still four days in which the Worm may thwart us,' Ashurek answered with unrelenting pessimism. Calorn had to bite back an exasperated retort; there was no use in antagonising him. He went on, 'And once we have landed, how much further then?'

'The entrance to the domain of the Silver Staff is about thirty miles inland from the bay,' said Calorn. 'So, however fast you can walk thirty miles.'

'That depends upon the country. We will hope there's not a mountain barrier between us and our destination!'

'The map shows it to be easy country.'

'The map? Have you made no reconnaissance visit to this part of Tearn?'

'No, I have not,' Calorn replied. 'I have never been on this Earth before. But, you see, my particular skill is a very instinctive one; prior knowledge of a place is no advantage, in fact, it is often quite the opposite, so don't let my lack of geographical knowledge trouble you. I take it you don't know this part of Tearn?'

'No, I don't. It's on the whole a dreary continent,' Ashurek said acidly, 'so I doubt that Pheigrad is any different.'

Calorn washed a mouthful of bread down with a long draught of the refreshing wine.

'I hope you believe I know what I'm doing,' she said pointedly.

'Well, how can you be so sure that the entrance to the Silver Staff's domain is where you claim it to be?' He gave her a hard, sceptical stare.

'I know where the entrance is. I know it as surely as a compass knows where North is. It's as though I have an internal lodestone which never leads me astray. Ashurek,' she added softly, 'I don't know how you can doubt me, after . . .' She trailed off and the memory of how she had unerringly found the way into the Dark Regions returned vividly to him.

'Aye,' he assented grimly. 'You're right, I have every reason to trust you.' They stood in silence for a time as they ate their meal, but presently the Gorethrian spoke again.

'There's something else I can't feel easy about. The Lady said that the knowledge of the Silver Staff had been kept upon the Blue Plane, so that M'gulfn would not find out about it. But now, here we are upon Earth, with the knowledge, so, does the Serpent yet know also?'

'I – I don't know,' said Calorn, startled by this thought. 'I hadn't considered it. But the Lady must have been aware of the possibilities; she would not have misled us. I am sure that the Serpent could not possibly know.'

'Are you?' Ashurek turned his back on her, squinting at the hazy white sun. 'Someone must be able to tell us for certain. Someone must know . . .'

He turned round, very slowly, and fixed his eyes on the pale Alaakian woman.

'Medrian,' he said. 'For some reason, at which I will not even hazard a guess, you seem to have a more intimate knowledge of the Serpent's ways and whims than the rest of us. You had better let us know the worst: does the Serpent know about the Silver Staff? And if so, what will it do?'

Only Estarinel did not look at her. He seemed intent on the Western horizon, where leaden clouds were already accumulating, threatening another storm.

Medrian seemed to find it as easy to speak as a marble statue might have done. The way she looked at Ashurek and the stiff, minimal parting of her lips made Calorn feel like telling him to leave her alone.

'That I cannot answer,' Medrian uttered.

'Cannot, or will not?' said Ashurek, giving her a sharp glance of puzzlement and suspicion, which she ignored. He turned away to look out at the sea again. Calorn began to explain, in her lively way, something about her particular navigation skills, and then to comment upon the weather. Presently, however, she got the distinct impression that none of them, even Estarinel, was really listening to her. She trailed off with a self-mocking grin and leaned against the rail, a breeze tangling her hair as she looked sideways at the Forluinishman. She had never before seen him so numbed and resigned to misery. Even defeated by it. Previously he had always fought against such defeat; she prayed that this was not the beginning of the self-destruction that she had foreseen.

After a while he turned and spoke to Medrian.

'You'd better try to eat more than that,' he said in a quiet, gentle tone. 'We all need as much strength as we can get.' She glanced at him and at the piece of bread still in her hand. And she nodded, and forced herself to finish it.

By mid-morning, the storm threatening in the West had overtaken them and was forcing *The Star of Filmoriel* forward at wild speed, like a hare before the fangs of a great hound. It was as if the Serpent, far from being afraid of them, was dragging them eagerly towards itself.

For the next four days, storm after storm broke over them

but never drove them off course. The horses glided with the current, barely having to exert themselves by swimming. Their reins remained knotted around the figurehead because there was no need to guide them. Calorn was pleasantly surprised by this apparent good fortune at first; after a day she began to think it sinister. But she did not voice this thought, which was probably already uppermost in the minds of her three gloomy companions. Again and again she had to remind herself not to become involved with them but to keep her mind upon her own role. She knew that the best help she could give them was to remain cheerful and practical – no hardship, as that was her nature.

The Serpent threatened, but it did not strike. On the fourth afternoon the storms subsided and they sailed across a small bay towards a dull shore glimmering under discoloured white daylight. Around the *Star* the waves swelled like mountains of jade with nets of light breaking over them.

Under Calorn's direction the horses brought the ship to anchor by a narrow, pale shingle beach. Beyond were sand dunes and low, grey hills. Easy country, as the map had indicated. The travellers completed the packing of food and clothing for removal from the *Star*; presently they were ready to disembark with packs strapped to their backs beneath their hooded cloaks. Calorn had only a small pack, as she would not be going to the Arctic with them. She and Ashurek lowered the gangplank and they all waded through the tide to the shore.

Calorn had explained to them that *The Star of Filmoriel* would wait for her until the search for the Silver Staff was over. Then the ship would take her back to the Blue Plane, while the others continued Northwards towards the Arctic. There was also something she had not mentioned – which the Lady herself had mentioned only so briefly that it might have been forgotten – which she hoped would be a pleasant surprise to them, and proof that she could guide them with absolute accuracy.

A few seabirds were circling above the delicate ship, curious. There was no other sign of life. As they crunched

148

across the narrow beach the sky darkened and a cloudburst drenched them, streaming down the folds of their cloaks and dancing in a mist above the sand. Calorn looked round at them with a despairing grin, and led them along a path that wound inland between the sand dunes. Estarinel turned for a last look at the ship to see that she was already veiled by rain, only the firefly lights atop her masts still visible.

Beneath their feet sand and stone gave way to wiry grass. The ground rose gradually, presenting a vista of featureless low hills that offered no shelter. Pulling their heavy cloaks around them they plodded on, resigned to the weather.

After they had walked for about an hour the country grew more rugged and they followed rock-strewn paths winding between steep hillsides covered with rough grass. Once Ashurek noticed four goats staring at them from a high vantage point; the rain had lessened somewhat, and he could see that they were wearing bells. So, he thought, the country is not uninhabited after all.

Eventually the rain dwindled to drizzle and the landscape was besilvered by the sun filtering through the clouds. The land became richer and there were trees ahead, glittering in the drenched, silver light. Calorn led them into this forest, turning round to say enigmatically that there was not much further to go.

Within the trees the light had a different, softer quality. Evening was imminent, and shadows lay like pools of dark water around the grey tree trunks. Even the long, blade-shaped leaves were grey, as if cut out of slate or hammered iron. They formed clusters from which hung bunches of large round berries, some amber-coloured, some the dark red of clotted blood. All gleamed and dripped with gelatinous-looking rainwater.

Presently Calorn slowed her pace and began to look about her. Then she led them off to the left along a thin, overgrown track and out into a small clearing. Medrian, Ashurek and Estarinel stopped in surprise: there, in the gloom, stood three horses. They gleamed in the dark silver light, their heads up and their ears pricked at the humans' approach.

Behind them flickered an elusive blue glow. There was something uncanny, mystical and dreamlike in that moment; the feeling persisted as Estarinel walked slowly forward and touched the smooth, rain-dampened coat of his stallion, Shaell. Beside him stood Ashurek's fiery mare, Vixata, and the horse they had taken from Arlenmia, Taery Jasmena.

'Now will you believe that I know my job as your guide?' Calorn asked with a grin.

'I never doubted it, but to find our horses with such ease—' Estarinel began, then broke off as he saw the source of the eerie blue glow. There was a H'tebhmellian on the far side of the clearing. Seeing them, she began to glide forward, the light floating round her, her beautiful features sombre and one white hand outstretched.

It was Neyrwin, the H'tebhmellian whom they had first seen in the castle of Gastada. She had drifted past them in that evil place, giving Estarinel, who had been near death, the strength to escape. Later they had learned that she had been dispatched by the Lady to recover their horses.

'Greetings, Neyrwin,' Calorn called. 'I'm so glad to find you here.'

'We are well met this hour,' the H'tebhmellian responded. Her voice was faint and there was something insubstantial about her form, as if she had been diminished by an extended period on Earth.

'Did you find the horses easily?'

'I travelled a great many leagues, but I found them at last. For their own comfort I had to remove their saddles, which I could not carry, but I have their bridles. They are in good health, as you see. I brought them here at a leisurely pace.'

Estarinel saw an extraordinary vision then, of the H'tebhmellian drifting across the miles of Tearnian soil like an unearthly spore of light, and the three horses, bridleless, following quietly like lambs following their mother. Shaell nuzzled at his arm and he reached up to slap the great silver-brown stallion on the neck, delighted to see him again.

'Hello, old friend,' he whispered. 'I thought we'd parted for good.'

'Calorn, I will not wait for you here,' Neyrwin continued. 'We were not meant to dwell long upon the Earth, and I am exhausted. *The Star of Filmoriel* will give me rest, so I will wait aboard her.'

'As you will. I thought you looked – fragile, somehow,' Calorn said, sounding concerned. 'Must you wait for me – can't you find an Entrance Point?'

'No, my strength is so diminished that I cannot find one quickly.'

'But the Lady said that you could find one at will.' Calorn seemed so worried that Ashurek began to sense something ominous.

Neyrwin began to drift past them, her lovely face unlit by the tranquillity and hope that was normally intrinsic to any H'tebhmellian. She looked like a figure made of frost, as if even a breath would be enough to dissolve her. 'The Lady did not know . . . I must tell her.'

'Know what? What do you mean?' asked Ashurek, starting to follow her.

'My purpose was not only to recover your horses, but to observe the state of the Earth and tell her what I saw.'

'Well, what did you see?'

She pivoted slowly to face him. 'It is nothing you do not already know. This world is more deeply in the Serpent's power than we of H'tebhmella had understood. In Excarith, where all seemed peaceful and normal, I sensed it – in the weather and in the earth. As I passed through Guldarktal, it was more evident in the desolation all round. The sky was sulphurous and the ground black with ruin. I saw nothing that lived except one grey, lumbering beast of the Serpent, which did not flee as I passed but sat watching me from a desecrated hillside, keening as if my presence were an abomination to it. As I passed through the countries between Guldarktal and here, although they were not desolate, I could still feel the Worm's growing power. I saw more of its beasts. Everywhere I saw people living in fear of them. I saw them stricken by illness and by famine, instilled with terror by even a simple storm. All along my way I saw them bending

151

to worship the Serpent in hopes of appeasing its wrath. This reality has bled my strength from me in tears, even as Filitha wept when she saw Forluin.'

'But what—' Ashurek started, but Neyrwin was drifting away again. She needed to be aboard the *Star* before she grew any weaker. He rejoined the others, abstractedly caressing Vixata's head as she nudged him for attention.

'Worshipping!' he exclaimed. 'Worshipping the Serpent? Such a thing is unheard of! To my knowledge, few have acknowledged that M'gulfn even exists, let alone made obeisance to it.' Out of the corner of his eye he saw Medrian walk away to the edge of the clearing and begin to collect wood for a fire. Estarinel and Calorn looked uneasily at him.

'It indicates that things have grown worse here, even since you have been on the Blue Plane,' Calorn said quietly.

'Yes. What else could we have expected?' the Gorethrian said bitterly. 'Come, let us make a camp.'

'This is as good a place as any,' Calorn agreed with what cheerfulness she could muster. 'Medrian's building the fire. Let's help her light it and have a meal. Estarinel, we will not set off until the morning. It's not far now, and we will be the better for a night's sleep.'

They camped at the edge of the clearing, where the closely woven branches afforded shelter if it started to rain again. Presently the fire was blazing red and yellow, deceptively merry against the iron-grey shadows of the forest. The heat drew steam from their cloaks as they ate a meal of H'tebhmellian bread and wine. The horses slept standing, close together for warmth and company. When they had finished eating, Ashurek got up to check that the beasts were sound – or to be alone with his thoughts. Medrian stretched out by the fire and fell asleep; Calorn moved round to sit by Estarinel.

She prodded the fire, sending up a shower of sparks into the thick woodsmoke.

'I think I've told you all I can about the Silver Staff,' she said, so that only he could hear. 'Just a few miles from here is the path that will lead you to its domain. I'll set you upon it and then you will be alone and at the Staff's mercy.' He was silent, so she went on, 'Estarinel? You've been so quiet, so preoccupied since Medrian was ill . . . I'm concerned about you. Are you sure you feel well enough to go?'

He looked startled at this. 'Yes, of course I do,' he answered with the ghost of a smile. 'Nothing that has happened has given me any thought of turning aside from the Quest. Each of the terrible things I've seen or experienced has made me more and more certain that the Quest is the only answer. It's as though something has been trying to teach me that lesson over and over again. Don't think I'm too demoralised to go after the Silver Staff; far from it, it's my only thought and hope at the moment. That's probably making me seem preoccupied as much as anything.'

'I'm glad to hear that. I was worried. If you can focus your mind upon the Staff and nothing else, you will win.'

'Yes, I know. I have taken some of your advice to heart, you see,' he answered with a touch of his old warmth.

'When you three first came to the Blue Plane, for all you had much to be unhappy about, you seemed very close to each other – even Ashurek. Now you seem miles apart . . .'

'You're observant,' was all Estarinel said.

'Well, it is nothing to do with me, I know.' She sighed reflectively. 'I have to keep reminding myself that mercenaries are not supposed to become involved. I have always needed to feel in control of whatever situation I am in, and I usually have been. But you three make me feel somehow powerless . . .' she shook her head. 'It's something I can't define. It's like wanting to chase away the darkness, but knowing I can't. And this help with the Silver Staff is all I can give you.'

'That's all right,' he said, clasping her hand for a moment. 'Calorn, it's enough.'

When dawn came they rekindled the fire and partook of a silent breakfast. Even in daylight the forest still seemed colourless, though the early sun drew glittering points of white and silver from the grass and the beaten-metal foliage of the trees, while the strange amber berries shone like jewels. A breeze carried the sweet, fresh smell of rain; there was no sense of the Serpent's presence such as Neyrwin had described. Vixata wandered across the clearing and began to chew Shaell's tail. The scene took on a homely familiarity for Estarinel, so that he could almost have imagined himself in Forluin. The imminent search for the Silver Staff seemed so distant and unreal that he did not feel even the slightest pang of apprehension. Calmly, he checked Shaell over and fastened the buckles of his bridle.

Calorn was to borrow the palfrey, Taery Jasmena. He was an unearthly looking stallion, finely built and beautiful with a coat like blue-green silk and a golden mane and tail. Medrian was busy with him now, picking up his feet and running her hands over his legs for any sign of injury. Meanwhile Calorn slipped the bridle over his head. She and Estarinel would both have to ride bareback.

In only a few minutes they were mounted and ready to leave. Both were travelling light, without cloaks, and Estarinel had only a small pouch of provisions strapped to his belt. Even at this moment of departure there was little communication between him and his two companions. They stood waiting for him to leave, but Medrian's eyes were downcast and she stood like a wax figure, gripping her cut forearm with the other hand as though it still hurt. She looked ill, white and hollow-cheeked. Ashurek was looking straight at Estarinel as if he wanted to give some words of encouragement, but felt unable to do so. Instead, his green eyes seemed to contain terrible warnings against the consequences of Estarinel's failure.

'Would that I could go instead – or come with you,' Ashurek muttered.

'I'll do my utmost. I can promise no more,' Estarinel replied quietly. Then he turned Shaell to ride away.

'Fare you well,' the Gorethrian's voice followed him.

154

Calorn led the way through the forest for several miles. Taery Jasmena danced as he went, starting at every real or imagined sound. Estarinel's silver-brown, heavily built beast followed sedately at a high-stepping walk, his usual willing, good-spirited self. The trees grew closer and closer together while the ground between them was choked with bushes, fallen logs and grey-green ferns whose fronds were bent and glistening with dew. Calorn was having difficulty in restraining her exuberant mount to a walk, and only the thickness of the undergrowth prevented him from bolting.

'It seems this beast is not content with being an odd colour,' she called over her shoulder. 'It has to behave in an eccentric manner as well!' Estarinel grinned despite himself, and began to tell her of the remarkable leap Taery had made over a huge wall when they had been evading Gastada's army in Excarith. This passed the time and served to keep him in his calm, detached frame of mind.

He thought nothing of it when Calorn turned off the already narrow, overgrown track into an even thinner one which disappeared into a mass of bushes. She made Taery forge straight into the tangle of waxy, dark green leaves. Estarinel followed, the branches yielding against Shaell's massive shoulders. Within the bushes he had a strange sensation of being under water; an emerald-coloured ocean that was full of ever-changing light and shadow. Around them the rustling of the foliage sounded like the movement of great, slow sea currents. The leaves brushed against his face and body, pulling at him, letting him pass only with great reluctance. He could not see where he was going. Only the occasional glimpse of Taery's tail ahead, like a golden flag, and the faint gleam of the path, kept him on course.

'There must be an easier way than this!' he called. 'Is it much further?'

'Estarinel, we are there!' Calorn replied.

'What – you mean that this is the domain?'

'Yes.' They came at last to a clearing, like a small cave, and Calorn halted. 'I am permitted to take you a little way into the domain.'

'But – I thought we were still in the forest. I have no feeling of being other than on Earth . . . Are you sure?'

'Yes. Why, what were you expecting?'

'Something sudden – like an Entrance Point.'

'Ah, no,' Calorn said, smiling. 'This is all it is.'

'Did you find the path easily?'

'More easily than I'd expected,' she said casually, leaving Estarinel mystified as to how she had found it at all. 'Now I think it's best that we part ways here. Look, the bushes are thinner now and you can see the path clearly.' She pointed and he saw the track like a faint silver thread winding on into the green shadows of the undergrowth. He made to dismount, but she said, 'No, you must ride.'

'Why? I don't want to take Shaell into danger unnecessarily.'

'You won't. But he may be able to find the way when you cannot,' Calorn answered enigmatically.

'Well, I'll be glad of his companionship,' he said.

'Yes, you will,' she smiled and again he felt grateful for her bright spirit, the courage she made him feel. They clasped hands and then she reined Taery back and gave a friendly salute. 'I'll return to the camp now. I don't know how long you'll be in this domain, but I will know when you return, and I'll come to meet you. Now, you must go. Don't turn aside, whatever happens.'

He nodded and returned the salute. 'Farewell, Calorn.'

Then he turned Shaell and sent him into a walk. But they had only gone a couple of strides when he saw a weird figure on the other side of the leafy 'cave'. It was roughly human in shape, about four feet high, thin and shapeless like a clay figure made by a child. Its face was a featureless blank. On its head bristled a crest of long white spines, and as he watched it plucked one of these out and threw it, like a spear, at Calorn.

Estarinel looked round in alarm and saw the spine pierce her eye and bury its length in her head. Her hand came up to grasp it and she fell forward onto Taery's neck with a dreadful groan. Blood was pouring from the eye socket; her limbs jerked spasmodically, then flopped into the limpness of death. Taery threw up his head, snorting with fear. Then he wheeled and bore Calorn's body out of sight among the bushes.

Horrified, Estarinel urged Shaell to follow, but the usually amenable stallion suddenly became recalcitrant. He side-stepped and set his head against the bit, determinedly facing forwards along the path. As Estarinel struggled with him, he saw the little shapeless figure running away in that direction. Enraged, he let Shaell have his head and gave chase. But the bushes were still dense and the tangled foliage hampered them. In seconds the murderer was out of sight.

'Damn you!' Estarinel screamed. 'I'll find you, don't doubt it!' He pulled Shaell back to a walk. He was gasping with shock and disbelief. Torn between going back to Calorn or pursuing the murderer, he made another abortive attempt to turn Shaell. His horse continued stubbornly along the path. And it was as if he could hear Calorn's voice nearby, saying again, 'Don't turn aside, whatever happens.'

'Whatever happens,' he repeated. He put a hand up to his face and felt tears there. In the midst of his outrage and grief, a thought came to him.

This was the first of the Silver Staff's tests.

What kind of entity would commit a bloody murder just to test someone's 'clearness of purpose'?

He shuddered. Suddenly he saw the Silver Staff as he had seen it in his vision in the Cavern of Communication: something of vast, dwarfing power. Without conscience. He knew then that he did not want the thing, did not even want to go one step nearer to it. But what choice did he have? Perhaps this was another test in itself.

Knowing he could do nothing to save Calorn, he went grimly on.

The undergrowth gradually thinned out, but it did not grow any lighter. The atmosphere was now a deep liquid blue and still had that strange under-water quality. He knew for certain that he was no longer in the forest, where it had been early morning. There was a pungent, fresh smell in the

157

air, like wild currant. Around him the bushes swayed like seaweed, tugged by a breeze he could not feel. Anger and horror burned in him as he rode, mingled with uncertainty. Perhaps he had failed the first test. Perhaps he should have left Shaell and followed Taery on foot. How was he to know? He had never imagined that there would be 'tests' of this sort . . .

Shaell jogged on with his great brown neck arched and his ears pricked, impervious to the tormented thoughts of his rider. Estarinel felt that if the stallion could speak, he would have said, 'Trust me.' He seemed to know instinctively that he must follow the gleaming path.

Abruptly, the undergrowth came to an end. They emerged into a deep blue night; there was a star-sprayed sky above them, a wide, undulating plain below. The path shone with a faint radiance under Shaell's hooves.

For a moment Calorn was forgotten. The landscape was vast and empty, with an aura of mystery about it. The arching sky had a wildness that drew him towards itself while remaining unobtainable. The forlorn, barren beauty of the plain caught in Estarinel's throat and he urged Shaell into a gallop.

The stallion leapt forward eagerly and Estarinel gave him his head, not guiding him, drinking the soul-rending wild emptiness of the sky; there was space, space, blue and grey and star-filled, eternal and untouchable, drawing him on and on. There was none of the suffocating sense of malicious evil that emanated from the Serpent M'gulfn, none of the tranquil perfection of the Blue Plane. There was infinity – vast, supreme, uncaring infinity, and Shaell was a mere spark galloping through it.

Estarinel knew then that this was the domain of the Silver Staff, that here was the vastness that could crush the Serpent as a man crushes a fly, and never notice its passing.

Shaell galloped on tirelessly, as if the breath of the stars filled him as it did his rider.

But the glorious night did not last. After an immeasurable length of time, there was a strange dawn. First a blazing light rimmed the horizon, and presently a small white-hot sun curved swiftly into the sky, only to station itself directly overhead. There it remained, burning down upon a landscape of glaring white stone and sand. Soon it was unbearably, blindingly hot.

Shaell jogged on nobly, apparently unaffected by the heat. Estarinel could no longer see the path; soon, all he could see was whiteness as the blazing light burned into his eyes. Transient greens and purples burst across his vision as he squinted against the brightness.

Perhaps the heat was an illusion, he thought, but its effects on him were real enough. There was no shade and no water to be found anywhere. The white desert surrounded them, endless and unchanging. The horse walked on steadily, but after a few hours the weird, motionless sun began to take its toll of Estarinel. His head ached and burned. Even squeezing his eyes shut could not keep out that white-hot light. He began to feel ill, dehydrated.

What sort of test was this?

Soon fever took hold of him. Voices whispered to him; his body felt burnt out and swollen to twice its size. He fell forward onto Shaell's neck, exhausted. Consciousness came and went, distorted by a nightmare delirium. Again and again he thought he was with Calorn in the clearing, seeing the strange, shapeless being just in time and averting the fatal spine from its target. Again and again he saw her ride off alive, only to remember that in reality she was dead. And so the dream would repeat itself, as if he could change the past by the strength of his thoughts, and the pain of the sun on his head and back became the pain of Calorn's death and his yearning to have saved her. They were indistinguishable.

Eventually the vision subsided. Now all he could see was greyness, smooth and flat and somehow terrifying. In his delirium he became obsessed with the idea of getting Shaell out of the sun. Yet another part of his brain was aware that he was unconscious, helpless, and that his desperate struggles to save his horse were taking place only in his mind. He tried

159

to cry out, to fight his helplessness, but even his cries, loud and real to himself, existed only in the fevered dream.

He opened his eyes. He was lying on the ground near a small, circular stone hut. He must have slid from Shaell's back while unconscious; now there was no sign of his horse. It was unlike Shaell not to have stayed by him; surely he had not gone on, riderless? He remembered a previous time when he had regained consciousness, desperately ill and with a fiercely hot sun beating down on him. Then Arlenmia had 'rescued' him. The thought of her filled him with reasonless terror; she must not find me, he thought, and staggered to his feet.

The stone hut was the only solid thing in the hostile desert. He stumbled forward and collapsed against the door. For a moment he had a memory of Medrian pretending to faint against the door of Skord's house; he could hear Skord's voice saying, 'Those of Forluin are harmless . . . those of Forluin are harmless . . .' over and over.

Now he was inside the hut. It was just a small round room, empty but for a wooden pallet with a straw mattress. There was a water pump set in the floor. At the sight of it, his desperate need for water brought him back to reality for long enough to kneel down, work the handle and feel the cold, clear water flowing over his burning head, pouring down his parched throat. He gasped with relief. Then, looking up, he had a bizarre hallucination.

The path was gleaming like a snail track across the floor of the hut. Following it, Shaell trotted in through the door, across the room – and straight through the solid stone wall opposite. It was as if either he or the wall had no substance.

He was gone. The path had disappeared. Still in the grip of sunstroke, Estarinel staggered to the bed and collapsed into a feverish, dream-plagued stupor.

Looking down at him was the formless brownish figure that had murdered Calorn. He cried out and struggled to rise, but could not move. It was featureless, yet it had a voice.

'I am the shape of your fear,' it said. And as he watched,

160

it raised its arms and absorbed them, like the processes of an amoeba, into its body. Its form elongated, its head gelled into a different shape. For a second it formed itself into a perfect effigy of the Worm. Then it became humanoid again, though squat and gnomelike. It pulled one of the white spines from its head and held the point against Estarinel's throat.

'No pain. Understand,' it said.

But it did not kill him; it replaced the spine upon its head. 'What is real here is chiefly what you believe,' it said. Then it bent forward and rose upon four equine legs, metamorphosing into a nightmare horse. And as Estarinel stared at it, it seemed to dissipate into the air.

Other visions followed, ones he had seen before, but now promising an understanding that had always remained out of his grasp before. There was red glass, layer upon layer, and behind it moved inhuman grey figures that paralysed him with dread. He longed to flee but knew he must approach them. And as he went slowly forwards, the red glass shattered and dissolved and behind it stood Silvren.

'The House of Rede will be the last to fall,' she said.

'No!' he exclaimed.

'Yes.' She took his arm and turned him round. They were standing at the edge of a vast, glittering expanse of snow. Very distant from them was a figure, but he could see quite clearly that it was Arlenmia, standing with her arms raised to a towering edifice of blue and green ice. 'Her vision is false. Damn her, she was my friend!' Silvren said. And then she was not Silvren, but Calorn, brave, laughing, alive, uninjured. She raised a hand to point across the snow, but before he could speak she had vanished. And now it was Medrian beside him, one white hand raised, her terrifying dark eyes fixed on his face.

'There is something I have not told you,' she whispered. 'Know that it is not without good reason.' And then he was running, floundering through the snow, and Medrian was gone, and he was weeping, searching desperately for something he had lost. He had searched for years, it seemed, before he found the dead bird lying in the snow. And at last he understood . . .

Estarinel awoke violently and sat up, gasping. The visions and the understanding were lost immediately; what had seemed profound in the dream was now no more than a fevered delusion. He shook his head, realising that it no longer ached. He was still in the hut. Experimentally he sat up, finding that he felt weak but clear-headed and well. The fever had abated at last.

He stood up, wondering how long he had been lying on the pallet, and if time had the same meaning in this domain as it did on Earth. He had a long drink from the pump, then gazed around the room. He had an uncanny sensation that something was out of place. Then he started in incredulous dismay.

The door by which he had entered had vanished.

The hut was a stone cell with no escape.

Estarinel rushed to the one window, which was a mere slit, impossible to climb out of. The white desert glared back at him. Panic ran through him. His fingers gripped the edge of the window-slit, spasmed, while he cast his eyes frantically over the stone ceiling and the hard, sandy floor. There was no gap, no weakness anywhere, to offer him hope. Dread of being trapped threatened to suffocate him; he shut his eyes, trying to force himself to calm thought.

This was another test . . . but with what purpose? To test his ingenuity in escaping? Or to see whether he could withstand the simple fear of being enclosed?

He ran his hands over the wall where the door had been. It was solid. He rested his forehead against the cool grey-white stone, thinking, 'If I escape, I will only be out in the desert again . . . that's almost worse than being in here.'

Then he remembered. Calorn had said that Shaell might be able to find the way when Estarinel could not. And the shape-changing being of his nightmare had said, 'What is real here is chiefly what you believe.' He remembered the strange illusion that the silvery path had lain across the floor

162

of the hut, and that Shaell had followed it, melting through the opposite wall like a phantom.

At once he crossed to the place where Shaell had vanished and pressed his hands against the stone. And in that moment, such was his conviction that he was not going to remain a moment longer imprisoned in the hut, that he could feel not stone, but smooth wood beneath his fingers; and his right hand was lifting a heavy latch; and although he still could not see the door, he was suddenly outside the hut.

Long fronds of grass, shimmering with pollen, reached to his waist. He was in a narrow, overgrown lane between tall hawthorn hedges, sweet with the scent of tall, white-flowered weeds. Relief that he was not back in the white desert flooded him. He had not realised how weak he had been feeling until the fresh, summery air swept the remains of the fever from him.

Looking back, he saw that the hut had vanished. He felt no surprise at this. He felt calm now, resolute. Time enough to grieve for Calorn later; for now, he must regard her death only as another aspect of the evil against which he must win the Silver Staff. He set off along the lane.

Slanting afternoon sunlight delineated each grass stem with light and turned the pollen dust to a golden haze. He might have been somewhere in Tearn or even in Forluin. Soon the hedge on his right-hand side grew so low that he could see over it into a patchwork of fields stretching to a clear-cut, blue horizon. The sweet smell of new-mown hay was in the air.

On the far side of the hedge he saw a stream winding through the meadow. He climbed through the hawthorn and knelt down on the grassy bank to drink. The water was cold and crystal clear; if this domain was an illusion, he could only wonder that it seemed so real.

When he stood up again, to his amazement, he saw his horse grazing in the next field.

'Shaell!' he cried out, running to the next hedge and fighting his way through a gap. The great silver-brown stallion threw up his head eagerly. Yet he did not come towards his master. He turned his head the other way, as if there was an equally strong call from the other side.

'Shaell!' Estarinel called again. He began to walk towards the horse, wondering what was wrong. Shaell pranced on the spot, turning this way and that. 'Come on!' The stallion's ears flickered, but still he disobeyed the call.

Then Estarinel noticed another horse beyond Shaell, a dun-coloured, ill-formed beast whose shape rippled and fluctuated as though seen through water. No, not a horse: the shape-changing creature that had killed Calorn. Its appearance when he was ill had not been a nightmare. It was cavorting and rearing, somehow luring the stallion away from Estarinel.

Again he called. But the shape-changer had begun to canter away. Shaell glanced back once at his master, and promptly followed the creature at full gallop. Estarinel groaned despairingly as he watched his horse, head high and tail streaming like a bronze banner, disappearing towards the skyline.

He pursued at a run, but his way was hampered by the hedges over which Shaell could sail easily. He soon lost sight of the stallion. When he emerged at last onto a broad sweep of grass that stretched to the skyline, Shaell was a good half-mile ahead. The skyline looked remarkably close; it was then that Estarinel discerned that they were on top of a cliff. As he drew closer and could still see no land or sea beyond the edge he realised that it must be extremely high. Now Shaell was galloping up and down along the edge of the precipice, and the shape-changer was nowhere to be seen.

'Shaell!' Estarinel gasped, out of breath. There was still nothing beyond the cliff but the perfect blue arch of the sky. Then, to his horror, he saw his horse canter straight at the edge, lower his head, and leap downwards off it as if jumping no more than a small drop.

With a burst of speed Estarinel gained the cliff-edge and flung himself onto the ground to peer over it. Surely Shaell had fallen to his death. Then he stared at what was below, incredulous.

He had come to the edge of the world.

The 'cliff' was a sheer rock wall dropping away into infinity. Above him, before him, below him, was a blue void. There was no sign of Shaell, not even a speck still falling below.

'By the Worm,' Estarinel groaned, putting his head in his hands. Not content with the murder of Calorn, the Silver Staff had to stoop to the gratuitous killing of his horse. Filled with outrage, he jumped to his feet and shouted, 'What kind of test is this? You've gone too far!'

'It is the ultimate test. We have all failed it,' said a voice behind him. Starting violently, he spun round, almost losing his balance on the cliff edge. There were a number of people around him, gazing at him, slowly converging on him. There were men and women of diverse ages, clad in all manner of strange garments. They all seemed to be of different places, different times, certainly not of his world. He could not believe they were real. Yet the woman who had spoken seemed substantial enough.

She had yellow skin and dark, almond-shaped eyes. Her dark hair was in a wild tangle and she was wearing a long jellaba of purple and black that spread out like butterfly wings when she opened her arms. It was dusty, threadbare in places. Yes, she must be real.

'What do you mean? Who are you?' Estarinel said. He was trembling; he felt he must look mad to them. But they showed no consternation at his appearance. He realised that he looked the same as they did; the same tangled hair and despairing eyes.

'Who we are matters no more than who you are,' said the woman. Beside her was a blond man in bronze armour, an old man in a bottle-green robe, a knight clad in a tabard of tarnished gold, with a long drooping moustache, a plump woman in dark blue velvet with her brown hair in two long braids . . . He counted twenty people in all. And as they surrounded him he felt their sympathy, their sorrow, their despair. They offered him no threat. He was one of them. They were accepting him, showing that they understood and shared his misery . . .

165

'Wait,' he said, stepping backwards to avoid the woman in purple's touch. 'I don't understand you. What do you mean, the ultimate test?'

'We saw what happened to your horse. The shape-changer drove it over the edge. When they murdered my love, I was steadfast; I thought, I have passed this test. What more can they do? Nothing, I thought. But I was wrong.'

'You mean – you were all seeking the Silver Staff?'

'Yes, all,' said the blond man. 'And here we have all failed. To think we began as rivals, each with our separate need for the Staff, each thinking his own need more desperate than anyone else's. Each arrogantly imagining that he could pass the tests! Well, here we are humbled.'

'Here the Silver Staff mocks our arrogance and our cowardice,' the woman said. 'Now come, walk and talk with us. Whatever you have suffered, we understand. Some of us will have suffered more. And we all understand your failure now. We do not condemn you. The Staff may, but we do not. We are no longer rivals.'

'No, we are comrades,' said the blond man.

'Companions against the Silver Staff, which has made us suffer. Companions in our sorrow.' She took Estarinel's arm but he resisted and stood still. He felt dizzy. Their gentle sympathy and talk of failure were confusing him. He felt that if he mingled with them, went with them, he would go mad.

'You were all searching,' he said, waving at the edge of the cliff, 'but when each of you arrived here, no one dared—'

'Yes, exactly,' said the woman. 'Well, would you have the courage?'

He looked out over the giddying void, the sheer wall of rock, the nothingness beneath. The thought of jumping filled him with a sickening, numbing dread against which he closed his eyes, and clenched his hands until the nails bit into his palms.

'Don't look,' she said. 'It's all right. We all know how it feels. No one blames you . . .'

He wondered which of them had been there the longest, why they had each been seeking the Silver Staff, but he could

166

not bring himself to ask. They were too ordinary, too human. They made him want to weep. He did not want to hear their stories and their needs.

'Why do you stay here?' he asked. 'If you can't go on, why not go back?'

'What is there to go back for?' said the woman, and the others murmured agreement.

'Better that those we have failed think us dead, than that we return empty-handed,' said the knight with the long moustache morbidly.

'So we wait here . . . to comfort such as you.'

'Let me alone – I need to think,' said Estarinel, but the woman continued to hang onto his arm.

'No, you mustn't be alone – you might go mad.'

'Nevertheless . . .' he shook her hand off, pushed past the others, and ran fifty yards along the cliff-top. He stood there, swaying, aware of those strange, lost people wandering towards him again. He must decide what to do before they reached him and his sympathy for them made him want to stay and help . . .

'Clear of purpose.'

Another test.

And again he remembered Calorn's advice: 'Do not turn aside.' And that Shaell would know the way when he did not. 'What is real here is chiefly what you believe . . .' Shaell had jumped, showing him the way.

Bravery did not come into his decision. Despair drove him. He had no other choice. He closed his eyes so that he could not see the breath-stopping sheerness of the cliff wall, nor the dizzying blue void, and made a running dive into the sky.

7

The Past and the Future

CALORN WAS in fact, very much alive, and knew nothing of the realistic illusion that Estarinel had seen. She watched him ride away and then turned the impatient Taery Jasmena back into the bushes, never suspecting that something unusual had appeared to happen. Nor did she see the shape-changer.

She returned to the camp. Medrian was close to the fire, her hands clasped round her knees, as if she was freezing cold and had all but given up hope of ever getting warm. Ashurek, meanwhile, was bridling his mare Vixata.

Calorn greeted him, jumping from Taery's back.

'Where are you going?' she asked. He glanced at her, unsmiling.

'You realise, of course, that we are all unarmed,' he said. 'I do not intend to continue any further without a good sword at my side.'

'Where do you hope to find weaponry?'

He vaulted onto Vixata's back and answered, 'We passed some belled goats on our way from the coast. There is certain to be a village or even a town nearby.'

'Wait,' Calorn said, unfolding one of her maps. 'This shows a spot to the South-West of here. It could be a village, even though it's unnamed on the map. They may not have a swordsmith, though.'

'They'll have something.'

'And how do you propose to purchase or barter for these weapons?' Ashurek did not reply, and she suddenly recalled that he was a figure of fear in Tearn. She was chilled by the idea, and felt obscurely sorry for the people who were soon

168

to encounter him. 'Do you not want either of us to come with you?'

'No,' he replied simply, 'I am going alone.' He took the map from Calorn and tucked it through his belt. As he did so he felt in a pocket the glass phial which Setrel had given them and which had helped him and Calorn in the Dark Regions. He took it out and threw it to her. 'Here, have this damned thing. I don't want to see it again.' He nudged Vixata into a trot.

'Well, be careful,' she advised lamely, watching his figure dwindle into the forest. She looked at the phial, which was still two-thirds full of pale gold powder. She was not sure that it was wise for the three of them to separate, but there was no dissuading Ashurek once he had decided to do something. He had a point, it would be better not to continue unarmed.

'There is the question of hunting, after all,' Calorn said, half to herself and half to Medrian. 'The longer you can live on game and save more of your provisions for the Arctic, the better. Talking of which, I used to improvise an excellent bow when I was younger. If I still have the knack, and if this wood's whippy enough . . .' She was moving along the edge of the clearing, reaching up to test the resilience of the branches. 'It won't be very accurate, but it will do its job. We could have rabbit for supper. You know how to use a bow and arrow, do you? Medrian?'

There was no reply, so Calorn looked round at her. She was sitting perfectly still with her knees drawn up, her chin resting on them, her dark hair spread across the mushroom-grey material of her jacket. Her eyes were very wide but so dark that for a second, Calorn got the horrible impression that the sockets were empty. She was still as pallid as wax and looked as if she had fallen into a trance from staring at the fire.

'Medrian, you haven't been well since we left the Blue Plane,' said Calorn. 'How can you hope to finish the Quest in this state?'

How can you hope to finish the Quest? said a taunting voice inside Medrian.

'And how can any of us help you, if you won't tell us what's wrong?' Calorn continued, feeling at once concerned and exasperated.

Let them help you, urged the voice gently. Within her a struggle took place even as she remained quite impassive to Calorn's eyes. Something was insidiously encouraging her to let in some kind of emotion – to snap at Calorn, to give way to self-pity, anger, anything. To surrender. Medrian fought strenuously to suppress these dangerous impulses. After a moment she was able to look at Calorn and speak, her voice steady but as dry as a dead leaf with the effort.

'There's nothing wrong with me, and no one can help me,' she said contradictorily. 'I can't speak of it. Please don't question me.'

'Very well . . . I won't. I'm sorry.'

'I'll help you with the bow, if you show me what to do.'

'All right.' Calorn decided it was unwise to persist with questions. She had never met anyone as stubborn, as unfathomable as Medrian; even Ashurek was not that hard to understand. Calorn was convinced that there was something very seriously wrong, and it was terrible to see her battling with it all alone. Yet Medrian remained adamant that no one could possibly help. Perhaps she was right. Calorn sighed inwardly and turned her mind to the bow. 'These branches are about the right strength. Can you find a couple of sharp stones so that we can strip off the bark?'

They seated themselves by the fire and set to work. Calorn had selected a good length for the bow and some straight twigs for arrows, which they were now stripping down to the pale, slippery wood beneath. Medrian continued to respond in monosyllables to anything Calorn said, or not at all. Calorn got the impression that she was not listening, and not even concentrating on what she was doing. At one point the stone slipped and she gashed her finger. Yet she did not seem to notice it, and carried on oblivious to the blood running over her hand.

Medrian's struggle against the Serpent was the worst it had ever been. She had acutely dreaded returning from H'tebhmella to Earth, knowing that as soon as she did so the Worm's mind – or that cognizant part of its being that resembled a mind – would resume its place within her own. But if she had known just how horrific that experience was actually going to be, she felt that she would never, ever have had the courage to leave the Blue Plane.

She had stood on the deck of *The Star of Filmoriel*, watching the gleaming blue lake drift by on either side, her whole body held rigid against the apprehension that gripped her. She felt her freedom leaking away like a glistening, precious raindrop that was becoming pear-shaped, stretching and stretching yet taking for ever to fall . . . She had the illusion that time itself was elongating so that every second was twice as long as the last and her freedom would surely never be stolen from her . . .

Then she saw the sea turn grey. And in a split second the Worm was back. She thought she had been ready, braced grimly for the shock. But nothing could have prepared her for this; as it plunged raging into her skull, the 'wall' she had so painstakingly built to protect herself was demolished. She was defenceless. Grey, scaly, writhing, it filled her senses and her thoughts; every nerve-ending in her body felt swollen as if her own form had suddenly become gross, Worm-like. There was a leaden weight pressing down on her skull. She was struggling, choking, retching, as if her lungs were full of viscid smoke.

The Serpent's giant, unhuman emotions swamped her as she stood helpless on the deck of the *Star*. She was shrinking before that vista of desolation and anguish, until her own mind was no more than a tiny, wounded thing, like a bird with broken wings, fluttering helplessly against the leaden mass that was crushing her.

She was suffocating in its rage and its hate. Hate, over-whelming in its intensity, like a tearing scream that reverberated along an infinite grey tunnel from the past and continued into the future, tormented, inconsolable, unceasing. There

171

was nothing else. No hope, no future, only mindless, colourless hate made into a physical thing from which she shrank, weeping with revulsion.

She could not stand it.

Mindlessly, desperate to escape into death, she was suddenly running like a madwoman towards the side of the ship. The sea lurched up towards her, promising to swallow her into blissful oblivion— Then the rail caught her across the stomach, and she hung there, utterly unable to move.

However unbearable this nightmare was, there could be no simple escape into death. The Serpent would not let her die. It was laughing at her efforts.

Two tiny, black thoughts came into her mind, as wretched and frail as crushed feathers. One was: how have I lived with this all my life? And the other was: if only I had killed myself in Forluin, while I had the chance . . .

She had no awareness of Estarinel pulling her back onto the deck. She only knew that she was fighting something, as desperately and ineffectually as a drowning man fighting a freezing cold sea. The Serpent had what it wanted: it had control of her, and now it would begin to take revenge for all the wrongs she had perpetrated against it over the years.

But Medrian had not spent all those years defying M'gulfn for nothing. Somewhere in her being her iron determination remained intact, like a small, clear voice calling in the centre of a storm. It told her that she needed something to anchor her to reality: physical pain.

It was black despair that gave her enough fragile control to ask Ashurek for something sharp. Grimly, she held on to that control as if she was clinging to the edge of a precipice by her fingers, her whole body spasmed by a tremor of exertion. And slowly, the simple, blissful pain of the blade incising her flesh brought her back to herself and forced the Serpent back, inch by inch.

It was so hard, harder than it had ever been before. The further back she forced it, the more viciously it fought. But the excruciating pain of her arm kept her will whole. Gradually she became reaccustomed to the horror of the

Worm's being; every gruesome aspect of its amorphous, monstrous psyche became once more familiar to her. Strange, that familiarity . . . she had never been aware of it before. Neither had she realised how deeply ingrained was the feeling of icy coldness that now permeated her brain, slowly numbing her emotions. Fear, revulsion, desire for escape were all frozen until her mind resembled an Arctic wilderness. M'gulfn was separate from her; the mental wall, like a great glacier, had been rebuilt against it. As long as she felt nothing, the Serpent could not touch her.

But her control was more fragile than it had been before they had gone to the Blue Plane. She could feel the Worm writhing against the wall, shattering holes in it and lunging at her with its malevolent thoughts. It was a constant battle to keep the barrier intact, one which eroded her strength and exhausted her mentally and physically.

Why was it so much harder?

It would have been better if she had never gone to H'tebhmella, let alone Forluin. That blissful, tormenting experience of freedom had affected her more deeply than she had feared. Emotion had always been the danger, and now, thanks to her insane surrender to it, the self-containment that sustained her whole existence had been damaged. It was almost the same as surrendering to M'gulfn.

I knew this would happen, she thought. I knew – and still I did not take heed! I might as well have given in to M'gulfn in Alaak, and never begun the Quest . . .

But there was something else. The Serpent was angry with her. Its anger was as devastating as its hate, and that alone kept it lashing at her when ordinarily it would have subsided into a sullen torpor.

It was the personal quality of its anger that revolted her. Sometimes it left her so sickened that she had to use all her will to fight the impulse to wrap her arms round her head and scream with despair. There was only one way she could define the emotion: jealousy.

Now, as she sat by the fire with Calorn, the struggle continued. She was grateful to have the bow to work on, because it helped to concentrate her mind, but she could feel the tremor in her hands, and kept finding herself staring at them as if they did not belong to her – oscillating white things outlined by evil red firelight. She knew how strained and ill she must look to the others; perhaps they thought she was losing her mind. There was nothing she could do about it. At least Estarinel was respecting her need to be left alone – she dared not spare a single thought for him – but Calorn's warmth and concern made her feel there was a black abyss yawning at her feet, and it would be easiest to jump screaming into the darkness . . .

She could not deny it. She was losing her self-control. Every day it grew more tenuous, as if she was clinging to a glacier that was gradually slipping away from her. Her whole body ached with the cold, but she dared not let go. Had she been able to acknowledge any emotion, she would have found that she was terrified.

Even when she slept, she was continually haunted by phantasms and could find no peace. She and the Serpent shared each other's dreams. Then they did not fight, but seemed to drift together through torpid nightmares, sometimes towards some grey thing that filled her with dread of ever reaching it; sometimes towards a small, bright-eyed, brown and gold creature, which was the embodiment of life but which filled the Serpent with such loathing that it flooded Medrian too. These nightmares were worse than the waking conflict.

Now that its initial fury had subsided, it spoke to her. It did not use words as such, yet the meaning of its thoughts was as sharp and precise as a snake's fangs, curved and glutinous with venom, striking repeatedly into her brain.

How dare you? it said. *How dare you go to that place where you knew I could not follow? The part of me that lives in you was left in limbo. Limbo, vile nothingness. For that I cannot let you go unpunished, Medrian. And for denying me, for hiding your thoughts, for setting out upon this evil Quest, you must be punished also.*

'And how will you punish me?' Medrian asked it.

174

By defeating you. By possessing you, the Worm answered simply. *By whatever means will hurt you the most. Hosts have rebelled against me before; you are not the first. But none has prevailed.*

'I know,' she said. She had the miserable stories of all those hosts imprinted on her memory.

Then be warned. Do not continue this foolishness, my Medrian. I know that you went to that place with the most evil intent. Now you are keeping something from me . . .

Medrian knew that M'gulfn meant the Silver Staff. So far she had succeeded in shielding its mind from knowledge of the Staff. Although Ashurek had voiced the fear that it must know already, in fact it did not, thanks solely to Medrian's dogged efforts. But it was aware that she was hiding something, and that was very dangerous. It made M'gulfn angrier, more persistent in its vicious attacks on her defences.

I must know what it is. You will reveal it to me eventually, have no doubt.

'There is nothing to know.'

But there is. What is it, Medrian, what is it? You must tell me . . . But she remained silent, cloaking her thoughts in a mantle of ice. M'gulfn's tone became soft, petulant, edged with bitter jealousy. *I cannot permit you to go anywhere without me, Medrian. You should not have gone – you had no right. I will never forgive you. I see something in your mind . . . I see that you have dared to turn away from me. You have steadfastly refused me, yet you have dared to share your soul with some wretched human, while I was in that void. I will not allow your attention elsewhere, my Medrian, I will not tolerate it.*

'I am not yours,' she reiterated faintly. She could not bear its possessiveness, it made her writhe.

I could have taken another host, M'gulfn said unexpectedly. *I need not have waited while you were away, betraying me . . . How could you have continued your evil Quest then? Yes, I should have taken another host.*

'Don't be stupid, you could not have done,' she said, feeling weary. It continued to taunt her in the same vein, but she knew that even the all-powerful Serpent could not choose a new host on a whim. For some reason it was closely tied to its hosts, keeping them alive into extreme old age and only then reluctantly letting them die. She sensed that it found the transition from its old host to a new one very unpleasant, if not actually painful. Worse: it attached itself to its host like an incubus, in a grotesque parody of human affection. She had never had any fear – or hope – that it would not be waiting for her when they left the Blue Plane.

I grow tired of you turning away from me. Tired of you not listening . . .

'I am listening. You give me no choice.'

You listen to them. When they offer you help, I feel you yearning towards them, longing to betray me. Why don't you let them help you, my Medrian? Why not stop fighting me? You must be very tired. You want to weep . . . why not surrender? I will not hurt you . . .

Medrian stubbornly ignored this transparent cajoling. Unexpectedly – its moods never were predictable – it became angry again.

I will make you listen to me, Medrian. I will make you surrender and let me into your thoughts. It would cause you pain, would it not, if one of your human friends were to die? That woman by you, for instance . . .

'No – you must not!' She could always distinguish between its hollow threats and genuine ones; appalled, she realised that it really meant to cause Calorn's death. 'You cannot. I won't allow it.'

You will have no choice. I will kill her. No . . . I will make you kill her. That will be even better. You doubt that I can? It was laughing, its mockery reverberating through her skull so that she craved to put her hands over her ears in a futile attempt to block it out. It laughed and spoke to her at the same time, its wordless voice at once very loud and very quiet, as if she was suffering the distorted perceptions of a fever. She felt that she was going mad beneath the onslaught of its will, inexorably mutating into a puppet controlled by M'gulfn.

'You can't make me do anything,' she whispered faintly, striving not to lose her determination. But the Serpent continued to laugh.

Ashurek rode at a hell-driven pace. His mare, Vixata, was lightly built but deceptively fast and strong; she was a brilliant copper-gold in colour and her mane and tail danced on the wind like white fire. Her nostrils were scarlet and sweat creamed on her neck, but still she galloped as if filled with tireless manic energy.

He was out of the forest now and heading South-West, crossing a hilly terrain of silver-green grass, dotted here and there with outcrops of granite and ash-brown copses. Ashurek's grey cloak billowed out behind him but the hood was pulled well down to conceal his dark, baleful face. His mood was very grim, images of Silvren, Meshurek and Orkesh arrayed like a grisly backdrop to his doom-laden thoughts.

His route was taking him towards the coast, some miles South of where *The Star of Filmoriel* lay. He could smell salt borne on a cold wind from the sea and he could see the silver line of water glittering on the horizon. Sheep and goats grazing ahead of him scattered as he approached. Now he saw the roofs of a small village set in a dip at the sea's edge. He pulled Vixata to a walk and climbed a hill to get a better view.

It was a sprawling settlement of simple, wattle and daub dwellings with greyish-yellow thatched roofs. Many of them were surrounded by enclosures full of poultry and pigs. He looked for something that might be a smithy. All he could see was a long, two-storeyed building constructed incongruously of stone with a red tile roof, which was broken by a number of turrets. It was almost on the shore and it looked new and out of place.

His gaze moved beyond to the sea. The view was obscured by the village but he could discern the masts of several large ships lying anchored along the shore in front of the stone manor.

Ashurek was mystified. He would have expected to see fishing vessels near such a village, but what possible use could they have for ships of war? He rode down the hillside and skirted the village, determined to take a closer look. The hill flattened out and the grass gave way to a rust-brown, fissured rock, dark with seawater and patterned with pools. The rock fell away into deep, calm water, so forming a natural harbour. Ashurek turned Vixata along the edge towards the village and she picked her way surefootedly over the rough ground. Fifty yards further on, a wooden quay jutted out above the water and along this lay four great, three-masted caravels.

They were obviously Tearnian in construction, strong, solid and cumbersome. Yet the design of the ships was Gorethrian. He rode slowly along the quay, Vixata's hooves echoing dully on the planks. There were some men at work on the nearest vessel, applying a recognisably Gorethrian device to the hull.

Ashurek halted Vixata and stared. Ghosts of the past thronged round him and he felt chilled by apprehension. Somewhere a wisp of thought passed through his mind: 'This is the Serpent's doing.'

A man standing on the quay came walking towards him, saluting. He was middle-aged and thin, with weather-darkened skin and pale grey eyes that had a glazed look to them.

'Sir?' the man called, sounding uncertain. 'We, er, we have nearly completed the first device, perhaps you would care to inspect the work, er, I hope it will meet with your approval, although—' he broke off as he reached Ashurek and stared him full in the face. A mixture of shock and confusion transformed the man's visage. He backed away, then turned and ran along the quay. Ashurek watched him draw level with the turreted stone building, run up the wide path that led from the quay to the door, and disappear inside. Then he rode after at a walk, conscious of the other men on the quay and the ship staring at him as he passed. He ignored them.

He came to the main entrance to the manor, which was a

great double door standing open. Within he could see a lofty, bare stone hall with another pair of doors at the far side, and the poor cottages of the village beyond that. He halted Vixata on the white flagstones of the path, and immediately the thin man came hurrying out of the building and approached him.

'My, er, my master requests that you tell me your name and business, er – er – Sir,' he stammered.

'Tell him that my name is Prince Ashurek of Gorethria, and that I will state my business to him in person only.'

The man flew back into the hall. A minute or so elapsed. He came out again but hurried straight past Ashurek without looking at him, evidently having been ordered to return to his work. Ashurek waited and presently another figure emerged.

It was a Gorethrian. A very familiar face, one he had not seen for five years or more. The shock of recognition was intense, unpleasant. Ashurek felt himself caught in a dull spiral of foreboding, winding inexorably towards a pre-destined fate, almost as though he was about to relive something that had already happened.

The figure was Karadrek. He had been Ashurek's General, his second-in-command, throughout the years when Ashurek had been High Commander of the Gorethrian Forces.

'Prince Ashurek. Your Highness. This is – this is – unexpected,' said Karadrek, by way of understatement. (Evidently the man had mistaken Ashurek for him at first glance.) He was tall and thin and his purple-brown skin was darker than Ashurek's, almost black. His face was hawk-like and his pale green eyes had a keen, malevolent look to them. He was wearing black robes embellished with purple and gold brocade and Ashurek noted that his missing hand had been replaced by an artificial one encased in a matching glove.

It was Ashurek who had severed that missing hand.

'I thought you were dead, Karadrek,' he said quietly.

'You hoped,' said Karadrek in a brittle tone, 'but I am not.' And he smiled, a humourless, predatory smile. Ashurek slid off Vixata's back and pulled back his hood.

'Well, what in the name of the Serpent are you doing here?'

179

he asked, keeping his voice level and devoid of emotion.

'I would ask the same of you,' was the cold, grinning reply. 'You can bring your mare through to the other side of the hall and tether her, if you please, your Highness. Then we can talk. Isn't she the mare you took when you . . . ah . . . disappeared?'

'The very same.' They walked through the doors, across the bare hall, and out into the village. Ashurek tethered Vixata to a post and gazed around at the wattle and daub dwellings which were surrounded by a maze of muddy tracks. The air was thick with the smell of animals, mingled with another, more sinister aroma. 'Vixata is not so young now, but still fit . . .'

'Why are you dressed in mourning?' Karadrek asked unexpectedly, his voice sharp.

'What?' Ashurek exclaimed. Then he realised that Karadrek was referring to his grey, H'tebhmellian cloak. Gorethrians always wore vivid colours: black, red, gold, green, purple. Grey was reserved for mourning only. He was about to say that he had merely adopted a Tearnian style of dress; instead, he replied grimly, 'I have much to mourn, Karadrek.'

'Yes . . . I can believe it,' was the callous response. They were speaking Gorethrian, a language which Ashurek had avoided using for years. 'Tell me, your Highness, how did you know I was here? Why have you come?'

Ashurek wondered how to reply. There were too many unanswered questions; the cold, calculating part of him that was intrinsic to his Gorethrian mentality told him to proceed with utmost caution.

'I did not know that you were here. My purpose is very simple; I need weaponry, good quality swords and knives.'

An equal amount of calculation seemed to be taking place in Karadrek's mind. He must have wondered what Ashurek needed with such weapons, and why he was unarmed at the moment, but he tried to conceal his curiosity.

'I have an excellent store of arms . . .' he replied impassively. 'Why do you need them?'

'It is too long a story to explain, General Karadrek. I do

not intend to try; however . . . I might make the effort, if only you will explain to me how you came to be here.'

They stood and looked at each other, Karadrek smiling like a lizard. Ashurek had a strange feeling of unreality, of detachment and sour resignation. The desire to murder Karadrek had lain dormant in him for a long time; now he found himself reconsidering the reasons for that desire.

Karadrek had urged Ashurek to usurp his brother Meshurek and take the Gorethrian throne. But having no desire to be Emperor, Ashurek had refused, and Karadrek had never forgiven him. Later Karadrek had been corrupted by contact with the Egg-Stone and he had conspired with the demon, Meheg-Ba, to disgrace Ashurek by massacring the Drishians. Ashurek had burned to take revenge for that atrocious, irremediable act. Often he thought what a fool he had been only to have cut off Karadrek's left hand, and not to have executed him. Afterwards Karadrek had disappeared, and most had thought him dead.

Now, here he was, inexplicably in a remote part of Tearn, building warships . . .

'Yes, perhaps I can make you understand. Follow me,' Karadrek said thoughtfully, beckoning him to the side of the hall and up a sweeping stone staircase. 'Prince Ashurek, your Highness, I know that we have had our differences in the past; yet now I am suddenly happy that you have come here! I feel sure that if you will only bear with me, you will appreciate what I am doing, and why . . .'

Shades of Arlenmia, Ashurek thought darkly. They entered a room that took up half the top floor of the manor. Here were arms enough to equip the caravels moored along the quay.

'A token of my goodwill, your Highness,' said Karadrek in his dry, reserved tone of voice. 'I no longer bear you any grudge; surely this meeting is fortuitous, and a sign that we should forget the enmities of long ago? Take whatever weapons you require.'

'What do you require in return?'

'I think you have paid me already. By giving me renewed hope.'

Ashurek gave him a candid look and calmly selected three good steel swords with scabbards and three knives. There was a limit to how much they could carry; he decided also to take two axes and a crossbow, and leave it at that. Karadrek watched with sardonically raised eyebrows, no doubt wondering where – and who – his two companions were.

Ashurek strapped a sword at his hip, and put the rest of the weapons into a saddlebag, which he took outside and placed near Vixata, ready for when they left.

'You built this manor?' he asked of Karadrek, indicating the sweep of the red roof with its pointed, Gorethrian-style turrets.

'Aye,' Karadrek chuckled. 'It's not much of a village to be master of, is it? A few Tearnian peasants hardly compare with the imperial Gorethrian Army, but they have their uses. Within this manor I have my smithy and weaponry, my chandler and shipyard, living quarters for myself and my servants . . . all very basic, I fear, but it serves its purpose.'

'Which is?'

'Ah, as sharp as ever you were, your Highness.'

'I'm curious, naturally. How long have you been here?'

'Four years, thereabouts.' He was leading Ashurek along a wide, flagged way – the only one there was amid the mud – that led from the manor, up a gentle slope through the centre of the village, and to a modest, square hut. Ashurek was aware of the villagers staring at them as they passed. All had paused in their work and were solemnly saluting Karadrek. He noticed the uniformly glazed, fishlike glare of their eyes, the slow, plastic way they moved; a familiar anger kindled within him.

Ashurek stopped and gripped Karadrek's arm.

'Let us cease these deceitful civilities, Karadrek,' he said, and the other looked suddenly discomfited by the cold green fire burning in the Gorethrian Prince's eyes. He had seen it many times before, and it had always boded ill. 'The atrocities in Drish were perpetrated with a demon's help. I believe you must have escaped with a demon's help also. And once they have their claws in a human, they do not easily relinquish their hold. Tell me the truth; are you working with the Shana now?'

'Of course!' Karadrek hissed, his pale eyes flashing. 'How else? Tell me, how else? Do you not work with them?'

'No!' Ashurek exclaimed vehemently. He felt like striking Karadrek; only the shameful memory of how recently he *had* bargained with a demon stopped him. 'I was in their power once, as you know. But I forsook that evil, although it cost me dear.'

'More fool you,' Karadrek said coldly. 'Prince Ashurek, listen to me; there was no other way I could achieve what I wanted. I could not stay with the army, they hated me for what had happened. I saw that thanks to you fleeing – thanks to Meshurek's inept rule! – the Empire was falling apart. My only hope was to disappear and to hide. After long months of travelling I came to this godforsaken village where I knew I would never be discovered. Here I decided what to do.'

Ashurek listened to this with growing despair. Karadrek, as he had feared, was in the grip of at least one Shanin, perhaps more.

'The villagers were not happy at my arrival,' he continued. 'They loathe Gorethrians upon the West coast almost as much as upon the East. I should not have been surprised, of course. They nearly killed me, then imprisoned me, then tried to murder me again. Meheg-Ba could not help me, because he was with Meshurek. But he instructed me in how to summon another demon to my aid. The villagers have been no trouble since . . .'

'I'm sure they haven't,' Ashurek whispered, feeling sick with fury at the plight of the villagers, whose dull apathy was a clear sign of the Shana's influence.

'The Shanin gave me power, made sure I was acknowledged as their master and then advised me upon what to do. I had the villagers build me this manor, and the quay, and then I started them upon the ships. Soon they will form my army and navy.'

Karadrek paused, smiling like a hyena. The men and women were gazing at him; all looked thin, wretched, eaten by a fear they had forgotten how to fight. The demons pretended to create power, but all they could truly bring was decay. It was as though the villagers felt that the sight of Ashurek had put a seal upon their fate.

The sense of the Serpent and its minions came strongly to Ashurek then. Neyrwin had been right. Tearn was sliding ever more deeply into its power, and Karadrek was just another instrument in its design.

'Your army? What do you mean?' Ashurek asked, trying to suppress his emotions and sound genuinely curious. One of the Shana's effects upon their human slaves was to erode their perceptiveness and judgement, rendering them unstable and dangerous, yet strangely naïve.

'I am going to sail back to Gorethria. Home! I hate it here; I wish to go home,' said Karadrek, pulling at his gloved hand with his living one. 'I hear Shalekahh is racked by strife over who is now rightfully in power, while the Empire falls about their ears. I shall end all that. I, and my army, and the Shanin, and the Amphisbaena. We will put it all to rights, and I will rule. What say you to that, your Highness?'

Karadrek's eyes were glittering palely with manic ambition. Ashurek took in the meaning of what he had said, reflecting bitterly that his second-in-command had not changed, merely become more transparent.

'You always . . . wanted that power, didn't you?' he said carefully.

'By the gods! You should know it, Prince Ashurek! Did I not advise you, plead with you to take the throne? I wanted the power for *you*, not myself! My loyalty was always to you!' was the impassioned response. He tugged at Ashurek's arm, now drawing him into the doorway of the hut. An extraordinary scent met them, sweet yet redolent of mindless, malevolent power. A lambent glow danced on the ceiling and walls like a reflection of rhythmically moving water.

'Now come in here and look,' Karadrek said.

There were several men and women in the hut, kneeling erect with their arms dangling at their sides, their eyes glassy as they stared unblinking at a strange creature.

'This is the Amphisbaena,' Karadrek whispered. It sprawled on a dais in the centre of a hut, a two-headed, tentacled creature twice the size of an ox. Ashurek stared at it with a mixture of repulsion and amazement. It was extraordinarily beautiful: its heads were long and slender, eyeless, forever questing the air, while its smooth tentacles were perpetually curling and intertwining with an underwater grace. It was pure white and luminous, but waves of colour, consisting of masses of blue, red and green spots, swept continually along its skin. The pulsing rhythm was hypnotic, beautiful, fatally entrancing.

Ashurek realised that this was a temple and the people around him were worshipping the eerie beast. He felt an intense longing to join them, as if something was pushing his knees to the ground. Disgust flooded him and he lurched away from Karadrek and out of the hut.

'What is wrong?' said Karadrek's soft, dry voice beside him.

'Explain to me what that thing is,' he said tightly.

'It is the Amphisbaena. The Shanin gave it to me.'

'It is a creature of the Serpent.'

'Why do you sound so concerned? You helped the demons yourself. You carried the Egg-Stone. This is only another stage in the same plan.'

'But they are worshipping it! It has rendered them mindless! Karadrek, as evil as Gorethria was, it was ever our way to give our opponents a fair fighting chance. This is nothing of the sort. This is unfair. It's appalling, horrific.'

Karadrek shrugged. 'Times have changed. Let me explain. The demon is too busy to be with me all the time. Therefore I was given the Amphisbaena, which inspires fear and obeisance. Through the beast I control them.' Seeing Ashurek's expression of loathing, he added, 'It may not be the Gorethrian way, but it is expedient. When the ships are ready, I

185

will set sail – the villagers to crew the ships, the Shanin to help us, the Amphisbaena to create the fear and loyalty we need to enable us to take power in Shalekahh . . . but your Highness, listen, there is more! You are here now! I know that Meshurek is dead; the demon told me. This means that you are now rightfully Emperor!' Karadrek said this as if it were a revelation, the culmination of his dreams.

'Aye. That's correct,' Ashurek said drily.

'But – but – does it mean nothing to you? Why have you not gone back to claim the throne? Perhaps you have been unable to find a way,' he speculated wildly, carried away by his ambitious dreams. 'But you have found me now – I have a way, I have laid it all out before you, I am offering it to you! It's as though it was predestined, and I did not know it! Oh, I have hope, real hope, that you are changing your point of view; after all, it is not too late. Why else should we have met like this?'

Ashurek looked at Karadrek in astonishment.

'I cannot believe this. Are you saying that after making all these careful plans for yourself, you would relinquish your power to me? Even after what has transpired between us?'

'Yes!' Karadrek exclaimed, the burning of his eyes making him look more hawklike than ever. 'It was the only thing I ever wanted. You as Emperor. This is what my plan has been missing. You, Prince Ashurek.'

He realised then that Karadrek was sincere. The man was a born second-in-command, he thought ironically, and then he understood that the betrayal and the atrocities in Drish had originated out of his bitter disappointment at Ashurek's stubborn refusal to usurp Meshurek. Nurtured by the Shana, of course.

Ashurek stood very still, watching the black swirling of baneful emotions within himself as if they were physical realities, while everything else had ceased to exist. Vaguely, as if from a great distance, he saw men and women filing out of the temple-hut, and others moving woodenly in to take their turn at worshipping the creature of the Serpent. This is sick, he was thinking. He saw his sister die screaming on his blade and his brother falling towards a red-hot lava crust, and they were screaming and falling for ever. This is hell, and Miril is dead.

Once, long ago, he had felt love, respect, and comradeship for Karadrek. Such feelings could never be totally eradicated.

'Well, your Highness?' A voice at his side roused him from his black thoughts. 'What say you?'

'This,' Ashurek said quietly. 'Your plan is madness. It is a delusion.'

'What do you mean?' Karadrek's tone was guarded, as if he could not countenance a refusal. 'You cannot – you must not make a hasty decision—'

'I never coveted the throne. I want it even less now. I never want to return to Gorethria again.'

Karadrek glowered at him, angry and disbelieving. 'I thought – I thought Meshurek's demise would have brought you to your senses, made you see that I had been right from the beginning.' His voice rose and there was grief mingled with his fury. 'I was always loyal to you! The most faithful of your Generals! I saw that Meshurek was unfit to rule and that for Gorethria's sake, you should have taken the throne. Even in Drish, I did what I did for your sake, because compassion had overcome your judgement, and the Drishians would have made fools of us all! Everything I did was for you and for Gorethria. And in reward for my pains, I get – this!' He held up the artificial hand in its brocaded glove, brandishing it like an accusation of treason. 'And the loss of the Empire. And exile to this forsaken hole. I hold you to blame, Prince Ashurek. I always acted for Gorethria. You only ever acted for yourself!'

'Perhaps you are right. Gorethria's collapse is more my fault than anyone's; I do not deny my guilt. But then,' Ashurek's voice was level and his eyes were dangerous, 'I had come to understand that Gorethria is evil. She deserves everything that is happening to her. Perhaps she even deserves you and the Amphisbaena.'

'You're talking like a fool!'

'I don't expect you to understand. But try to believe this;

187

your plan to take power in Shalekahh is a delusion, because the demon is not helping you; it is using you.'

'That is nonsense! I summoned it; it works for me!'

'You sound exactly like Meshurek,' Ashurek sighed.

'You compare me with your brother?' Karadrek exclaimed contemptuously. 'He was an idiot!'

'Those who summon demons are often very intelligent men, not realising how foolish they have been until it is too late. My brother summoned Meheg-Ba to increase his power. It seemed a clever idea to him. But the Shanin gave him nothing. It used him and it leached everything from him, even his reason. It was pathetic beyond the reach of grief.' Ashurek could not quite keep the feeling out of his voice. 'I see the same thing happening to you. It began the moment you craved the power of the Egg-Stone, and spoke with Meheg-Ba. You can never hope to fulfil your dreams. The demon will use you to continue extending the Serpent's chaos over the Earth, and when it has reduced you to a husk it will imprison you in the Dark Regions. Just as it did with Meshurek.'

'You're lying!' said Karadrek lamely, his eyes glassy with fear.

'It is the simple truth.'

'How can I escape it?' he cried, his hand closing like an iron claw on Ashurek's arm. Ashurek was taken aback. He had not expected this sudden, desperate plea for help. But before he could take advantage of it, Karadrek drew back, his eyes hard again. 'No,' he said. 'I forget how you have betrayed your country. I cannot trust you, your Highness. So if you will not agree to help, you must be forced. This is what the demon would advise.' He gestured with his gloved hand and Ashurek put his hand on his sword hilt, sensing the movement of men behind him. 'More than that, it is your duty. You owe it to Gorethria and to me!'

Without warning Ashurek drew his sword and swung round, slashing the arm of a villager. The others, who had been poised to capture him, fell back out of his range. All looked terrified and he knew they would not dare to approach him again.

Immediately Karadrek drew his own blade, shouting angrily at the villagers not to be such cowardly fools.

'Prince Ashurek, please don't make it necessary for me to kill you,' he said, his expression desperate. 'We need you.'

But Ashurek only shook his head, his mouth set in a grim line. 'It matters not whether you listen to me or not, General Karadrek,' he said so faintly that Karadrek did not catch the words. 'There's only one way for you to be rid of the Shanin . . .'

He and Karadrek began to circle one another; both were highly skilled swordsmen, having had the finest training the Gorethrian Army could provide. They had often fought each other before, though only in mock combat. Their blades clashed and they began to move into the familiar rhythm of sword-play.

Ashurek knew it was likely to be a long drawn out fight, and one he did not relish. Then he noticed that Karadrek was muttering as he fought, and he recognised the ancient Gorethrian tongue; Karadrek was summoning the demon. As always the words filled him with a cold, strength-sapping horror, as though something was exerting a terrible pressure on his skull, and his mouth was full of cobwebs—

As soon as the demon materialised, Ashurek knew that he would be disarmed and bound in an instant. He had evaded the Shana once too often; they certainly would not permit him to escape again. He could not let the summoning be completed, and he knew there was only one way to prevent it.

The air shimmered and groaned. Animals were squealing in fear and stampeding around their enclosures, sensing the evil aura before the humans did. There was a moment of pressure so intense that it seemed the very atmosphere would fracture – and a perfect, leering silver figure stepped out of nowhere.

Ashurek saw an opening and lunged desperately at Karadrek's stomach. It was a risk – he could have miscalculated and impaled himself on Karadrek's sword. But he did not. His weapon met its mark and drove up into his compatriot's heart. Karadrek, eyes and mouth gaping with shock, slid slowly off the blade with a soft rasping noise and lay dead, blood welling over his chest.

The demon, roaring with rage, was sucked back to its own Region.

Ashurek leaned on his sword, staring at Karadrek's body. Now he had killed again; the blood of a former friend was added to that of his family. He felt stained from head to foot, as damnable as the Serpent itself. He was cursing silently, bitterly. Karadrek had had to die; a demon could only be banished by the death of the summoner. That was the bitter lesson he had learned with Meshurek. But this knowledge was no consolation to him at all. It did not make him feel any less stricken, less black with guilt.

Slowly he cleaned his blade and resheathed it.

'That was not for myself,' he murmured. 'That was for the Drishians, General Karadrek.'

He turned and made for his horse, oblivious to the men and women standing around him, staring. A man came running up to him, the thin, nervous one who had first spoken to him on the quay.

'Sir – sir, what's happened, what does this mean?' he cried.

'It's over. Your master is dead and the demon will trouble you no more. You won't have to sail to Gorethria; in fact I'd advise you to burn those caravels,' Ashurek said brusquely, brushing his hand away. But the man caught hold of his cloak and followed him.

'But, sir—' he persisted, looking more distressed than ever. 'The – the—' he waved a hand at the temple-hut. Angered, Ashurek stopped and looked back.

Even as he turned, there were shouts of terror from within the hut. Seconds later the Amphisbaena came undulating out of the entrance, its heads wagging blindly in the air, the colours pulsing rapidly along its form. Its two mouths were gaping wide, revealing not teeth, but powerful ridges of muscle designed to crush and suck the flesh from its prey. They glistened crimson with the blood of those who had been worshipping it.

He should have realised. Karadrek – or the demon – had had some control over the creature. Now it was unrestrained, directionless – except for its Serpent-given need to destroy.

Shouting a warning, Ashurek sprinted towards it. But the villagers did not even move. At the sight of it the fear left their eyes and they became ensorcelled, some dropping to their knees and some prostrating themselves in the mud. It was among them at once, crushing their limbs, torsos, heads in its merciless mouth. Some groaned as they died, and some made no sound at all.

By the time Ashurek reached it, some fifteen of them were dead. With an unearthly howl of battle-lust he unsheathed his sword. It rang discordantly as it curved through the air. He held it two-handed, bringing it down onto one of the Amphisbaena's necks and hacking at it until the head fell with strings of flesh and viscid blood whipping after it. The Amphisbaena began to make a dreadful keening noise which made Ashurek long to drop the sword and block his ears. The remaining head wove back and forth, its jaws opening and closing. He could see the rippling of the muscle ridges and he knew that once the mouth closed upon his arm or leg, he would never prise himself out of that deadly grip. The waves of colour beat frantically along its body and its tentacles were entwining themselves around his ankles. He almost lost his balance, extricating his feet just in time. He swung the sword and caught the Amphisbaena across the side of the head; it screamed like a child and lurched towards him, the colours of its skin changing madly. Ashurek struck again, chopping repeatedly at its neck. Its blood spattered him. It is not going to die, he thought. Then, all at once, it was over. The Amphisbaena's second head was severed, and as the creature subsided lifeless to the ground its whole body flashed black, then pale luminous green. The tentacles continued to jerk convulsively for several seconds.

Ashurek stood back with the creature's milky blood running down his face like tears. He scrubbed the stuff away, gasping with a mixture of exertion and horror at the preventable deaths of those poor men and women.

191

The creature's strange body lay before him in a smooth, pale mound, the lovely hypnotic colours gone. Around him the rest of the villagers seemed to be returning to their senses. Some were weeping, some were clinging to each other. But still they all seemed afraid to approach him.

As he turned away, still wiping the slimy blood from his face, the thin man was in front of him again, staring at him accusingly.

'This is all your fault,' the man uttered, his voice tremulous. 'What are we to do now?'

'The Amphisbaena is dead,' Ashurek said, feeling aggravated and exhausted.

'You don't understand. You damnable Gorethrians! At least the other one was protecting us; in return for our help, we had the Amphisbaena to worship, so that the Serpent would not vent its wrath upon us. We had enough to eat. Our master was not cruel. Now what do we have? Many of us are dead and the rest have nothing to worship, no one to protect us. The – the creatures that roam about in the hills will come down to prey upon us and our livestock, and we will starve or be killed—'

'Then arm yourselves,' said Ashurek curtly, pointing to the stone manor. He put the saddlebag of weapons over Vixata's back and vaulted on. She began to dance, unsettled by the weird events in the village. 'You can't defeat evil by worshipping it. Fight!'

He sent Vixata into a canter and the man jumped out of his way, unnerved by the viridian gleam of Ashurek's eyes, startling against his dark face.

The other villagers shrank back as the fiery mare passed, their gaze following the rider out of the village and across the hillside beyond as if they were too stunned to do anything but stare at him.

Ashurek made Vixata gallop, his head lowered against the wind which was stinging his eyes like acid. 'How many – how many more deaths must I cause before the Serpent is satisfied?' he was thinking, his mind raw with fresh pain.

Karadrek had been an agent of the Serpent, a bringer of

192

evil like Arlenmia and Gastada. And like himself, Ashurek thought. If Karadrek deserved death then I am infinitely more deserving. My guilt is so much greater than his . . .

Karadrek had never known any way of life except unquestioning loyalty to Gorethria, and belief in her absolute supremacy. Was he to blame for that, or for becoming yet another wretched victim of M'gulfn? What is blame, what is evil? Ashurek wondered.

Ashurek believed himself to be evil. Yet Silvren believed the same thing of herself, wrongly but just as unshakeably. But the infamy of what the Shana had done to her was far greater than any corruption she could think herself guilty of . . . the idea of 'evil' became meaningless . . . the more Ashurek tried to analyse right and wrong, the more senseless everything seemed, fading into a formless, indecipherable chaos like a swirling fog in which demons gibbered.

His brother. His sister. His once-loyal General . . . their eyes seemed to stare accusingly out of that fog, out of the terrible bodies in which they were imprisoned in hell. *The more you fight the Worm, the more you aid it*, they seemed to be saying. And, *fight it or surrender to it, it is all the same. If you fight, you will destroy everything . . . surrender, and the Earth is doomed anyway* . . . And then, contradictorily, *Help us. Avenge us. You must destroy the world to give us release.*

Ashurek screamed as he rode, his voice lost on the wind. He felt that he was rushing headlong into a black destiny, had been rushing into it since birth, and all attempts to avert it were but painful delusions. He must accept his fate, because to resist it brought only torment, not escape . . .

Vixata was tiring, and it was nearly dark. He felt no desire to return to the relative comfort of the camp; instead he slept under an outcrop of rock, without food or a fire, as if daring some beast of M'gulfn to come and kill him. The keen, cold loneliness of the night seemed to match the torture of his soul, and so excise the pain to some extent.

By the morning he felt calm, but his character had settled into a deeper grimness. It seemed the inevitable culmination of the renewed anguish, which had been stirred by his abortive excursion into the Dark Regions. It was as though he had accepted his guilt and his doom; if it was a form of madness, he was not aware of it.

He faced the new day with an untroubled, black resolve.

'Very well,' he thought. 'If I can only defeat M'gulfn by destroying everything and everyone else as well – so be it.'

8

Children of the Worm

SILVREN LAY in the Dark Regions, staring at the inside of the cell in which she was imprisoned. It was no more than a round burrow, a little longer than her body and about three feet in diameter, so that she had just enough room to turn over. The surface was soft and smooth, like flesh about to go rotten, and mottled with sickly browns and blues. Across the open end, at her feet, was a transparent, impenetrable membrane. She had no wish to look through it; beyond were only lumpish mounds containing more cells. And sometimes there were grisly creatures with odd numbers of legs meandering about, cackling, or there might be one or two demons, leering mockingly at her. So she never looked out.

She wished she could get used to the smell of the Dark Regions. It was a metallic stench of corruption, which instilled horror and wretchedness into the bravest of souls. She could not remember when she had last eaten, but felt that she could not have stomached food anyway, with that stench in her throat.

The Shana used to feed her . . . before Ashurek came. It must have been food somehow brought from Earth, because it had been untainted and edible. And they had not confined her, nor subjected her to anything beyond the simple torment of just being in the Dark Regions. Meheg-Ba and Diheg-El had been almost pleasant in their way, making her see that she was evil, and therefore better off out of harm's way.

Yes, yes, she thought, closing her eyes. Out of harm's way.

But after Ashurek had tried to rescue her, the Shana had

not been so kind. She had not actually seen Meheg-Ba or Diheg-El, only Ahag-Ga, who had imprisoned her – for her own good, it said – so that she might contemplate her evil. Since then – it might have been yesterday, or ten years ago, for time was utterly meaningless here – she had lain in the cell, barely sleeping, gazing upon the abhorrent form that was her self. She felt that the fleshy walls of the cell were only an extension of her evil, and that they stretched out from her in every direction, an infinite, bloated liver in which she lay cocooned like a maggot.

Often she wondered why she had not gone mad, but then, perhaps she had, without knowing.

Trying to remember her life before the Dark Regions was like poking about in an old wound. It filled her with a raw, shivering ache and made her want to writhe and squeeze her eyes shut and moan with black depression. Yet she was unable to resist inflicting that silvery, razor-sharp torment on herself. Again and again she saw Athrainy, her land, which she had loved and been forced to forsake. A country of stark, imposing beauty; sweeping hills of granite and silver-grey grass, great trees with bronze-purple foliage, a people whose hair, skin and eyes were different shades of deep gold. And, with anguish, she thought of her mother. Widowed young and burdened by many responsibilities, Silvren had been the only joy in her life.

This is evil, child. Evil.

But Silvren had been possessed of a strange power, unwanted, unpredictable and dangerous. At first it had manifested itself as no more than a golden electricity that sometimes crackled about her face and hands, disturbing, but not frightening. But as she grew older it began to take a more terrible form, a force that could splinter a tree or tear a field from end to end with a careless thought. Silvren was a gentle and loving girl who dreaded harming anything, so the knowledge that she was involuntarily placing those around her in danger, and causing her mother anxiety, was unbearable.

'Child, you are frightening me,' her mother had said

harshly. 'Why do you do these things? Either it stops – or you will have to leave.'

Silvren, devastated, had hung on to her mother's arm, pleading with her. 'Please don't say that. I can't help it, truly. I'd do anything to be rid of the power—'

But her mother had pushed her away, made intransigent by incomprehension and fear. 'This is evil, child. Evil! What have I done to deserve this – my only daughter, a witch?'

And in the end, Silvren had left. Barely sixteen, lonely and wretchedly homesick, she had boarded a ship bound for the House of Rede, desperate to find an answer.

Eldor and Dritha had greeted her like a daughter, explaining gently that her power was not evil, rather, she was a sorceress born. 'But this is very strange to us, for there is no sorcery upon this Earth,' Eldor had said. 'The Serpent and its servants are the only beings able to wield such power. Now, there may be a time when the Serpent is no more, and then sorcerers will exist freely . . . but for now, I cannot explain why you have this power. My dear, it seems that you have been born out of your time, and I know no easy remedy for it.' He had given her a choice. To stay at the House of Rede for as long as she wished, or to be sent to another world in another dimension, where there was a School of Sorcery at which she could learn not just to control the power, but to wield it as a full Sorceress. 'The difficulty is that if you return to Earth as a Sorceress you will possess at least equal power to a demon, and you may well be in great danger because of it. It is the opposite to the Shana's power, therefore they will fear and hate you.'

'I'm not afraid,' Silvren had answered resolutely. 'I would like to go to the School of Sorcery. But one day I will come back, because I love this world, and I feel sure this power was given to me to fight the Serpent M'gulfn.'

In the Dark Regions, Silvren moaned and squirmed in her trance of memory. The School had been her home for ten years, the happiest of her life; how carefree and innocent she had been, walking arm-in-arm with Arlenmia, how trusting and unsuspecting. 'Your world means a great deal to you, doesn't it?' Arlenmia would say. 'Tell me again about the Serpent M'gulfn . . .' and Silvren would confide everything to her as they walked in the exquisite gardens surrounding the fantastical, scintillating buildings of the School.

Never dreaming how bitterly she would one day regret these confidences.

Even now, she recalled vividly the brilliance of Arlenmia's hooded eyes, the charismatic intensity of her low voice. 'And are you certain the Serpent is evil?' she asked once.

'Oh, yes – wholly diabolic!' Silvren replied fervently. 'It hates the world and would like to dominate it and destroy all life.'

'Silvren, I don't doubt you,' Arlenmia reassured her. 'It's only that I am hesitant to judge between good and evil. It's not that I have no standards, but I believe that such vast forces as the Serpent and the Shana you describe have such a different standard of good and evil that it is barely comprehensible to us. And unless we try to free ourselves of human ideals and encompass cosmic ones, we will never be truly powerful.' It was not the first time that Arlenmia had spoken in this way, but Silvren still listened in wonder as she went on, 'I have always believed that life must surely evolve onto a higher plane than this miserable mortality, and why do we possess sorcerous powers, if not to effect that change? Why mess about healing a wound here, an illness there, while life continues in the same wretched way all around us? It's such a waste – when these skills should be used to effect a profound and radical healing of the whole world. All worlds.'

Silvren was astonished at this. 'I thought I was idealistic, but you put me to shame. How do you hope to achieve these things?'

'Dear heart, I don't know. That is why I am here, the same as you, to learn. It seems that your world is in just such a state of change as I believe is necessary for life to evolve to higher levels. This Serpent cannot just be "fought". Either it must be destroyed utterly, or it must reign supreme. But the transition is what is causing human suffering; most likely, on a cosmic scale, no cruelty is intended at all.'

198

'Your words seem to make sense, but I can't accept them. The Serpent intends great evil, and it must be destroyed.'

'Silvren, I do believe you. In fact . . . when you return there, would you let me come with you? I think you are going to need my help.'

'Oh, do you mean it?' Silvren exclaimed. 'If only you would, it would mean everything to me. I am going to be so alone, otherwise.' She had been overjoyed, sincerely believing that Arlenmia meant to help her – what agonising guilt there was in the memory of that naïve, blind trust. Silvren writhed in her cell, but the train of recollection continued, relentlessly.

Distraught at not being considered a true Sorceress, Arlenmia had half-devastated Ikonus and fled to Silvren's world. Oh, what a fool I was, she groaned to herself, taking so long to realise where she'd gone. If only I'd found her sooner . . .

When Silvren finally discovered Arlenmia in Belhadra she had already established herself in the Glass City. Silvren confronted her amid the shining towers, still outraged at what had happened to Ikonus. Yet she greeted Silvren like a long-lost sister, her face vivid with genuine affection and delight. She had never meant any harm to Ikonus, she said, it was a terrible mistake, an accident that she deeply regretted. Could Silvren not forgive her? And at last, swayed by her warmth and sincerity, Silvren relented.

'But if it was truly an accident, you should not have fled. And why have you come here?' Silvren demanded, her suspicions not wholly assuaged.

'Dear one, did I not agree to come to this Earth with you? This is not quite how I planned it, but Ikonus is in the past, and we are here together now.' She was leading Silvren into her strange, metallic house.

'You mean you still want to help me?' Silvren exclaimed, thrown off-balance.

'Yes, of course I do,' Arlenmia smiled. 'And I have already created us the perfect stronghold. Mirrors are my medium – have you any idea how much power a whole City of Glass gives me?'

'But this is not your City – you can't just—'

'Oh, what does that matter? Silvren, we are speaking of saving your Earth, and all life on it. Borrowing the Glass City is just one of several means to that end. Now, are you going to come here and work with me, or not?'

'I suppose so,' Silvren said, finding it impossible to remain angry with her. She knew that although Arlenmia's ideals tended to operate on a plane beyond good and evil, her intentions were noble. 'You must think I'm very ungrateful, when you've done so much already, and I can only sit here asking suspicious questions.'

Arlenmia smiled. 'Now you sound like my Silvren again. I have also recruited us some helpers. I must say they were singularly rude and unhelpful when I first met them, but they were easy enough to master, and they are going to be exceedingly useful. Let me show you: but come into the courtyard. I don't like them in the house.' Mystified, Silvren followed Arlenmia outside. There was an oval mirror set into one of the walls – presumably for this purpose – and Arlenmia stood before it, sketching a few runes over its surface with practised ease. The mirror darkened, and Silvren suddenly felt afraid.

Out of it stepped two demons, shining with a pungent light, crackling with malice.

Silvren did not know she was running away until she went headlong into a wall. Stunned, she sank to her knees and hid her head, like a terrified child, while a golden, protective lightning danced around her without her willing it. Distantly, she heard Arlenmia's voice saying impatiently, 'Oh, go back – yes, go – I'll send for you later.'

A moment later Arlenmia was pulling her to her feet. 'Silvren, whatever is the matter? It's all right, I've sent them away.'

'By the gods, Arlenmia, don't you know what they are? They are the Shana, the demons I told you about – they are evil, they will possess you.'

'Try to calm down. Come, I'll get you some wine.' Arlenmia led her back inside her house, and Silvren swallowed

200

the wine and sat clutching the goblet with white fingers.

'Don't you understand? You cannot – cannot work with those vile creatures. Oh, I'm sorry if I didn't explain this to you – I thought I had—'

'Silvren, I don't know what you are so frightened of. They are only like children, really.'

Silvren stared at Arlenmia in amazement. 'You mean it. You really are not afraid of them, are you? You called two together – and you just asked them to go, and they obeyed.' She gave a shuddering sigh and closed her eyes. 'I had no idea you were so powerful.'

'You flatter me. I'm sure that you could control them as easily.'

'No. I might fight one on equal terms – but not more – and they would never obey me. Oh, Arlenmia. If only I had come after you as soon as you left! I would never have let you do this.'

'Don't worry. I will order them to obey you as well.'

'No! You don't understand,' Silvren gasped, her eyes flying open. 'You must not work with them at all. They are evil – the Serpent's creatures. You cannot use them to fight against the Serpent.'

There was a long, strange silence. Sometimes, afterwards, Silvren felt that that silence had somehow got inside her soul, so that whenever she was alone, or not thinking about anything else, it would rise to the surface and envelop her like a cool, glassy void. And after a long time, Arlenmia's soft words would filter into that emptiness – like her mother whispering, *This is evil, child. Evil* – as shocking as the first time they were uttered: 'We are not fighting against the Serpent.'

'What?' Silvren said, not trusting her ears.

'Dear heart, I did bear in mind everything you said. But I have done much learning of my own since coming here. This Serpent is of such great power that it would be futile to resist it. What we must do is join our power to it, and so increase it. The chaos it causes – which you call "evil" – is only the by-product of the transformation that it will eventually effect

201

over the Earth. It will be swifter, less painful, if we help it. We must recruit as many as possible to this belief – because those who believe and understand will escape death and ascend to that higher level of being, which is truth and beauty—' Arlenmia continued to talk of the Serpent in this vein for several minutes, but Silvren was so shocked that she barely took any of it in. All she knew was that Arlenmia believed what she was saying, and it was completely beyond her power to persuade her that she was disastrously wrong.

Before Arlenmia had finished, she was sitting with her head in her hands, her golden hair covering her face, so blank with horror and culpability that she could not even weep.

'Oh, what have I done?' she muttered.

'Silvren, don't be a fool! I know you've never agreed with my ideas, but now I have a chance to prove that I am right. Give me a chance, at least.'

'A chance? By the gods, Arlenmia, the Worm is infernally evil! I don't know how to make you understand! I beg of you, don't do this; go away, go home, anything.'

'After I have found what I have been searching for all my life? A genuine, godlike being with the power to transform life? Oh! Silvren, you are a milk and water idealist! You want to help your Earth, but you don't want to change it. Would you plant new flowers in a bed without pulling out last year's rotten ones, and the weeds too?'

Silvren stared at her, wild-eyed. 'This is fanaticism. Delusion,' she whispered.

Arlenmia seemed stunned, as if she could not quite believe that Silvren was serious. Eventually she said, very sadly, 'So you are not going to help me, after all?'

'Never. Never, until you see that you are wrong. I shall do everything in my power to stop you.'

'Silvren, I don't want our friendship to end like this. Please, don't make me—' But Silvren had turned sharply away and was walking to the door. 'Where are you going?'

'I don't know. I'm leaving. Are you going to stop me?'

'No,' said Arlenmia. Suddenly her expression became one of icy rage. 'Silvren, I warn you, if you insist on fighting me – I will send one of those demons after you.' Silvren froze in the doorway. 'I mean it. No one is going to prevent me from pursuing my plan. No one.'

'I don't care,' Silvren replied with equal adamancy. 'Someone has got to.'

That was how the nightmare began. From that day she was hounded across Tearn by the Shanin, Diheg-El, and other eldritch creatures of the Worm. Protecting herself against them placed a great strain on her sorcery, leaving her nothing with which to fight Arlenmia and M'gulfn. She became an outcast, unable to seek anyone's company without putting them in terrible danger from her pursuers. The years eroded her resilient spirit until all she knew for certain was that she must go to the Blue Plane; only there could she be safe from the demon, and find advice and help. But time and again she failed to find an Entrance Point, and at last, wearied beyond endurance by her struggles against the Shana, and desperately lonely, she was certain that her strength was about to fail.

It was then, on a dark and damp night when she was not even sure where she was, that she opened a tavern door and saw a Gorethrian, clad in black war gear, sitting alone. His brooding, handsome face scarcely betrayed that he was a loathed and feared figure the world over. But Silvren knew who he was at once, and to her witch-sight the Egg-Stone was like an orb of white-hot lead at his throat.

And from then on, Ashurek's history was hers, until Diheg-El captured her at last.

What was it about evil people, she wondered in her cell, that fascinated her and drew her to them? Either it was that she was evil herself, or else, in her arrogance, she deluded herself that she could redeem them. Fighting the Shana, destroying the Serpent . . . all had been a delusion. In her blind, arrogant belief that she was 'good', she had brought nothing but evil to the world. Everything that I most dreaded to be, I now know that I am . . .

There was movement at the end of her cell; the transparent membrane was being peeled away. Argent hands seized her ankles and she was dragged out onto the gritty, discoloured path that ran between the cell mounds. She was pulled roughly to her feet and found herself standing, swaying and disorientated, in the grasp of Diheg-El. In front of her, Meheg-Ba was reprimanding a third Shanin.

'Did we not make it clear to you, Ahag-Ga, that she was not to be treated as an ordinary prisoner? Look how thin she has become. For this infernal incompetence, I am going to send you on a dreary errand to Earth. You are required to go and destroy the so-called House of Rede.'

'That's hardly a punishment at all,' sneered Diheg-El, 'in the face of your crimes. Ashurek here and you let him escape! And now this mishandling of Lady Silvren, my sorceress. She is not to imagine that she is a prisoner. She is to understand,' the demon grinned, 'that she is one of us. Please accept my apologies, my Lady, I hope you have not been too uncomfortable.'

'I think she looks bored. Don't you think she looks bored, Diheg-El?' Meheg-Ba mused. Silvren had grown so used to them that they hardly frightened her any more.

'Oh, there is nothing more terrible than boredom,' Diheg-El said. 'We will have to find you an occupation, my sorceress, to keep you busy while we are on Earth again. Otherwise you will begin to bore us, and that is dangerous.' She did not have the energy to reply.

'Yes, they are dull when they no longer argue, aren't they?' Meheg-Ba agreed. 'Well, we need a new herdsman, since Exhal was destroyed. I'm sure she will do the job admirably.'

'I agree. It's not good for her to lie about doing nothing,' said Diheg-El, laughing sibilantly. 'We might as well take you up to the plain now, because all of us, including this fool Ahag-Ga, have to answer our summons to Earth. Come along. You will enjoy the job, sorceress.'

Presently Silvren found herself alone on an infinite, rubbery swamp without much idea of how she had got there. In the darkness shapes were moving, converging on her, but she stood still and watched them, completely without fear or any other emotion. Soon she was surrounded by creatures which had human heads and torsos but which walked horizontally on six human legs. Their faces were like tragic paper masks stretched over their skulls, with closed eyes and open mouths. They swayed from side to side and groaned as they sought her, blindly, without knowing why. She felt no revulsion for them, only pity. She stretched out her hands to touch their faces and feel their warm, moist breath.

'Oh, I am not like the Shana, I am like you,' she said. 'Soon I will die and join you, and then I will be more human and less evil than I am now. Oh, I wish you could open your eyes, so that I could know I am not the only human soul here. You opened your eyes for Ashurek, don't you remember?'

Yes, we remember, the human cattle seemed to say.

'Someone loved me enough to brave this terrible place for my sake. Isn't that strange? But it is true.'

We want to open our eyes, said the souls. *We would open our eyes for you, if you tell us to.*

'I don't know the right words.'

Evil only triumphs where there is no love. We are dead and damned, but you are alive and loved. You can free us, if only you will find a way to open our eyes.

Silvren had a flash of insight then – the insight that may come in the deepest despair or madness – that what she had come to believe of herself might only be opinion, not truth. She still believed it, but here were these poor trapped souls seeing her as the only being in the Dark Regions who was not evil, but their only hope. Who was she to prove them wrong?

The herd of pathetic creatures was now her responsibility. In a way it was an actual relief to turn her thoughts from herself to others; she felt somehow cleansed by it. In those moments as she stood on the swamp with the herd milling wretchedly around her, she saw the Dark Regions in a different way, not as a place of nightmare terror, but as somewhere sterile and self-defeating, an ultimately impotent weapon.

'I'm not frightened any more,' she said, feeling this to be a revelation. 'Do you think it's possible to become so inured to horror and fear that you emerge on the other side, whole? Even when that horror was of yourself? I only know that you are more in need of help than I.'

You are our herdsman. The herdsman always knows the words, the human-cattle sighed in response.

'Don't even think of it,' scraped a harsh metallic voice nearby; Silvren looked round and saw, squatting on the back of one of her creatures, the hellish aviform parody, Limir.

'There, I've finished. Four arrows should be enough,' Calorn said, some time later. They had strung the makeshift bow with some twine, which Calorn had in her pack, and made arrows by sharpening and notching the straight twigs. They had discovered that the tough leaves of the strange trees could be cut up to make adequate flights. Calorn experimentally shot a couple of arrows into a tree trunk and said, 'Hm. Not bad. It'll do. Do you want to try it?'

She held out the bow to Medrian. *Yes. Yes, take the bow. Wait until she turns away. Then* . . . Medrian struggled against the persuasive thoughts, and the illogical feeling that if she only killed Calorn, all her pain would cease.

'No. No, I don't,' she said hurriedly.

'Oh – all right,' Calorn said, giving her a curious glance. 'Come on, then, let's hunt.'

They found a part of the forest where the undergrowth was thin and the trees widely spaced. There was a good population of rabbits here, lop-eared, silver-grey creatures as big as hares. Calorn waited while Medrian worked her way round in a half-circle to flush the animals out and towards her. Skilfully, she picked off three and walked over to gather them up. Then, wondering where Medrian had got to, she looked about for her. Eventually Calorn spotted her, standing like a figure carved out of alabaster between two tall trees.

If you think that you can avoid killing the human merely

by forgoing a weapon, then you are mistaken, murmured the Worm, its thoughts stabbing like poisoned spikes into Medrian's brain. *A weapon is not necessary. I can make you kill her without even touching her.*

'I do not believe you,' Medrian replied intractably.

I will make you believe me. Look at that creature . . .

'No. No!' She resisted desperately, but she felt her self-control slipping away, like jagged lumps of ice sliding through her hands. There was a large rabbit just a few feet from her, sitting on its haunches, staring at her. The Serpent forced her head round and up until she was looking straight at it.

'No. Do not do this . . . please,' she begged, struggling to move. But the Serpent's will held her like a vice.

And Calorn, watching from a distance, witnessed something extraordinary and horrible.

She saw Medrian standing as rigid as stone, and she saw the rabbit in front of her, motionless but for the twitching of its long, colourless whiskers. At first she thought that it must have frozen in fear, and that Medrian was planning to catch it. But there was something unnatural, eldritch in her stance and expression. Her face seemed to be glowing faintly with a ghastly, acidic light and her eyes had glazed over with a bluish cast.

Calorn suddenly felt cold and sick with the same kind of fear she had experienced in the Dark Regions.

As she watched, the animal wilted under Medrian's intense, preternatural gaze. Trembling, uttering tiny screeches of fear, it keeled over, kicked a few times, and lay dead.

The hideous light faded from Medrian's visage and she put her hands up to her face, visibly shaking.

'Medrian – whatever is the matter?' Calorn cried, starting towards her.

'Don't – don't come near me,' she exclaimed, turning her head away and putting out a hand as if to ward her off. 'Go back to the camp – I'll follow in a while.'

Calorn did as she said. It was not like her to abandon someone who was in obvious distress so lightly, and she could not excuse herself for turning and almost running away. It

207

was an illogical, uncontrollable fear, made the worse for being inspired not by some ghastly creature of the Dark Regions – but by someone she counted as a friend.

When she reached the fire she had to force herself to stop and not flee any further. She went and leaned against Taery Jasmena, breathing hard as his warmth and solidity slowly eased the chill in her heart.

She did not even want to think about what she had just seen.

A few minutes later Medrian rejoined her, now perfectly composed. She went up to Calorn, but avoided her eyes; she looked ordinary again, human, frail and exhausted. Her lips parted and she murmured, 'I'm sorry.'

'But – that rabbit—' Calorn exclaimed, unable to stop herself.

'I know,' Medrian said dully. Then, after a few seconds' pause, 'Please don't tell the others.'

'I won't. There doesn't seem to be any point.'

'No. There isn't. We had better skin those rabbits.'

The Serpent was raging at Medrian, but she felt distanced from it. Its attempt to prove its supremacy, by killing the rabbit, had disgusted her to the core. An animal was bad enough; the idea that she could be forced into a similar, grisly murder of Calorn appalled her. So sick with revulsion had she been that from somewhere she had found a hidden reserve of strength: the very anger and despair the Serpent had caused, she had used as a weapon against it. She had resisted it, and she had won.

Now it was wailing its frustration and rage, but for the time being it could not touch her. The effort required to control her for those few moments had tired it, as well as her. She remembered an occasion when she had bent its will to hers: when Ashurek had summoned a demon which had then refused to return to the Dark Regions. She had made M'gulfn order it to depart. The Serpent had never forgiven her for that. Even after Gastada had tortured her in the most horrendous way, it did not feel that justice had been done . . .

'Oh, be quiet,' she murmured to it, like a mother chiding a truculent child. Unexpectedly it ceased struggling and railing at her. Its sudden silence was ominous.

Darkness fell, and Ashurek had not returned. They roasted and ate a rabbit, then decided upon a watch rota. But as Medrian made to wrap herself in her cloak and sleep, Calorn said, 'What's that?'

'What?' Medrian sat up and peered across the clearing, which was illuminated by the eerie red glow of the fire. In the grey and black shadows, barely discernible, stood a black horse. It was an ugly beast, too long in the back and with a pinched, ill-tempered look to its head. Even in the gloom its eyes shone bright blue.

'Ye gods,' Medrian breathed.

'Oh, it's just a horse. It's a nasty-looking creature, though. I wonder what it's doing here.'

'Never mind. We've got to drive it off.' Medrian climbed to her feet and, never taking her eyes off it, backed into the trees and began pulling down hefty branches and shoving them into the fire. 'Help me. We need brands to frighten it away.'

'What about my bow and arrow?'

'No use, you'd only wound it. It would hardly feel anything. It is a creature of the Serpent, you see.'

'But we can frighten it?'

'Yes,' Medrian actually smiled, though without humour. 'They are not very clever beasts.'

'We'll work in relays; one of us fires the brands, while the other drives it off.'

'Yes, I'll go first.'

Medrian advanced across the clearing, swinging a branch with a great plume of fire spitting on its end. The horse snorted and bared its teeth, edging uncertainly backwards. The fire ran down towards her hands and began to burn her, but she continued threatening the beast until she was forced to drop the branch. Then Calorn took her place, yelling as

209

she lunged at the horse, making ghostly streaks of fire hang in the air. Near the fire, the palfrey was whinnying with fear, but he was tethered and could not bolt.

Medrian advanced again, and the black creature was retreating among the trees now. 'Go! I no longer have any need of you!' she was muttering through clenched teeth. She had gone quite a long way into the forest when she heard Calorn, back at the camp fire, give a yell of astonishment and pain. She ran back towards her, and saw another creature of the Serpent.

It resembled a great white bear, but there was a sinuous quality to its movements which also suggested an ape. Its thick pelt gave off a rank, musty stench and its eyes were the same searing blue as the horse's. It had crept up silently behind Calorn, so that she had only sensed it at the last moment. She had swung round so that the mighty swipe which it had aimed at her head had glanced off her shoulder. Her cloak protected her, but she felt the sharpness of its long sabre-shaped claws through the material.

She and Medrian swung their flaming branches at it, but it was not to be so easily cowed as the horse. It dipped its head from side to side, something between a growl and a roar emitting from its red, carnivorous mouth. It rose on its hindlegs, sniffing at the smoke and heat, irritated by it. It lumbered forward, losing its balance, and then lunged at the two women with its forepaws. Medrian saw the curved, vicious claws flash past her face and she felt the branch jerked from her grasp. The bear's muzzle was close to her, the rows of flesh-tearing ivory teeth shining with saliva, its breath foul and steamy on her cheeks. She stumbled backwards, pulling Calorn with her to the other side of the fire.

Now she knew the reason for the Worm's silence. It had decided to defeat her physically instead of mentally. The creatures would incapacitate or even capture her, and kill Calorn.

'By heaven,' Calorn hissed. 'There's more – look!' Nebulous white shapes were moving amid the trees, converging on the clearing. The stench of the bears filled the air. Taery

210

Jasmena reared frantically. The picket to which he was tethered came out of the ground, and he bolted into the forest. But the creatures ignored him.

'Are these – creatures of the Serpent as well?' Calorn asked, trying to keep her voice steady.

'Yes.' Medrian pulled another branch out of the fire and swung it back and forth before the bear's head, so that it followed the movement with its eyes as if becoming hypnotised. Then it growled and snapped at the flame, whimpering as it burnt its mouth. 'Have you got the bow and arrow to hand? These things are not as impervious as the horse.'

Now the other bears were moving into the clearing. Calorn counted seven. Muscles rippled under their shaggy pelts as they ambled forwards; they were magnificent creatures in their way, but the monkey-like fluidity of their gait marked them as unnatural. There was something horribly wrong, misformed, about them. And the mindless glare of their cyan eyes repulsed her like the acid light of demons.

Picking up her weapon she carefully took aim at the bear which was menacing Medrian. The first arrow thudded into its throat and made it pause and howl with rage. The next found its eye but still it remained on its feet. It staggered and the third shot missed, but the fourth also hit its head and at last it toppled heavily onto its side and died, grey blood oozing from its wounds.

But now the other bears were upon them, growling, striking out with their steel-daggered paws. Medrian and Calorn were trapped by the fire, which was waning. They only had one decent brand left, and that was burning down rapidly as Medrian swung it at the bears' noses, making them rear back in irritation. Calorn tried to retrieve her arrows, ducking as a bear swung its claws at her head, using the dead creature's body as a shield.

It was hopeless. She could not stand and fire arrows one way, because that made her vulnerable to the beasts behind and to the side of her. The fire would die before long, and what little protection it afforded them would be lost. If only they had swords, spears, anything! She saw Medrian dodge

211

and stagger as a blow caught her shoulder. They did not stand a chance. Exhaustion would fell them after a few hours, and then the bears would cease their toying and close in—

Calorn felt the moist, rank breath on her neck too late. There was a flash of white in the corner of her eyes – more sensed than seen – and she felt a stinging blow across the back of her head. Claws raked through her hair as the ground raced up to meet her. She lay helpless, the weight of the bear's paw pressing into her back, its muzzle snuffling hotly over her shoulders.

'Medrian! Medrian!' she croaked. Perhaps she had not called loud enough; her ears were ringing, giving the eerie illusion that all was silent. The moment extended, and she became acutely aware of tiny details, as if she had all the time in the world to contemplate them; red sparks floating from the fire, dazzling against the night; something hard, like a stone, digging painfully into her ribs. Against the crushing darkness, she sucked in half a breath and gasped with all her strength, 'Medrian!'

Still there was no reply. She had also fallen, or – Calorn writhed in denial of a sudden, horrible illusion that Medrian was not lying on the grass at all, but standing beyond the circle of bears, watching, smiling, far more the Serpent's child than they.

9

'At the Staff's mercy'

ESTARINEL WAS falling, falling through blue infinity. For a
time, following the initial shock of the leap, he could not
breathe at all. Now, as he grew accustomed to the sickening
sensation, he began to draw in uneven, convulsive breaths.
The cliff-face was a sandy-brown blue as he plummeted, the
sky changeless, impassive. After what seemed an age – it
was only a few seconds – he became convinced that he was
doomed to fall for ever. A helpless terror swamped him. He
writhed as he fell, fighting what was impossible to resist.

But his movement only served to send him spinning in
towards the perpendicular face. He felt his hand scrape
against it, and for a split second saw it clearly: ancient brown
rock, textured with cracks and fissures that ran vertically as
if in mockery of his swift descent. Every muscle in his body
was clenched, his jaws rigid, as he fell with ever-increasing
velocity, now spinning out of control.

The first blow as he bounced against the cliff-face was
painful, dealing a shuddering blow that reverberated agonis-
ingly through his bones. He stretched out his arms to avoid
the second, only to be sent in a somersaulting arc. Helpless,
he wrapped his arms round his head, awaiting the next
collision in a fog of numb anticipation.

It came, jarring and bruising him. Again and again, he
bounced against the merciless face, limp as a rag doll. It was
a long nightmare of mindless pain before he began to realise
that he was no longer falling through empty space. The
physical discomfort was continuous as he was buffeted by
the rocky surface, but now it seemed to be curving away

213

from the vertical, arcing under him to receive his bruised body and reduce the speed of his fall. Gradually he found that he was no longer rebounding off the surface, but rolling over and over. The pain lessened, the shocks eased. Yes, he was rolling . . . the movement became fluid, almost soothing. All his muscles relaxed, a blissful sensation. The descent slowed as the ground curved up to cradle him, bringing him to a gentle rest, like a parent first chastising, then comforting, an errant child.

Estarinel lay still. Slowly, very slowly, the pains stabbing through his body subsided. Aching, exhausted, disorientated, he remained prostrate for a long time, unable to open his eyes or think. The relief of being on horizontal ground was indescribable. He wanted nothing to detract from that simple pleasure. In his mind's eye he saw the expanse of sandy rock criss-crossed by fissures, the perfect blue sky overhead; they were supremely beautiful in their starkness.

Surely he should be dead after such a fall, or at least severely injured. But the Silver Staff had its own rules. It might not be above cold-blooded murder, but it obviously did not wish him dead yet.

He opened his eyes, only to have another shock.

He was not lying on the surface he had envisaged. Instead, he was on a lawn of short, scurfy grass. Before him was a raised area like a burial mound. Atop the mound was a squat, black tower. It was a malicious-looking building that immediately instilled him with intense depression. Twin suns glared down at the scene, bathing it in a sickly, greenish light. It was a bald, desolate, forsaken place and he loathed it instinctively.

He sat up, trying to rub some life back into his spasmed limbs. He took a piece of H'tebhmellian bread from his pouch and forced himself to eat it. It seemed to restore his strength and spirit somewhat; weary, but determined to face whatever else the Silver Staff had to offer, he walked towards the malevolent tower.

As he climbed the mound, a figure rushed past him. With astonishment he saw that it was the almond-eyed woman.

Her black and purple garment streamed out behind her like the wings of a giant moth as she ran and her hair was like a tattered pennant. She gained the tower and entered through a black, studded door that shut behind her with a great clang.

She must have found the courage to jump after all, he thought. So, now he had at least one rival in his quest for the Silver Staff, and she might easily prove more worthy than him, her need more pressing, her world facing something even more horrendous than the Worm . . .

Trying to put these thoughts aside, he grasped the iron ring in the door and pushed it open.

He was in darkness. After a moment his eyes became accustomed to it and he saw that he was at the foot of a spiral staircase, the edge of each step glistening faintly in the gloom. He began to climb, feeling along the wall on his left.

He went cautiously. The tower felt as malevolent within as without, and the stairway was steep, uneven and claustrophobic. He could not suppress a sense of dread that the stairs might crumble beneath him, or that some fell creature was stalking down to meet him—

There was something. Padding noiselessly down the steps towards him, a huge white bear with glaring cyan eyes, its wet-fanged jaws gaping like a snake's.

Estarinel froze. Before he even had a chance to defend himself, it was upon him – and gone, past or through him, as if it had no substance at all. He swung round, and for an instant he thought he saw Calorn and Medrian, and knew it was they who were in danger from the bear, not him.

The images were gone; it must be another trick to confuse him. He turned with determined forbearance and continued upwards.

Abruptly the steps ended, but not in a void: they led to a small black door. He pushed it open and hesitantly entered the dark chamber beyond.

For several seconds he could see nothing. Then something happened; imperceptibly his awareness changed and he found himself in another place, another time. Forluin. And he was a younger self, not just recalling an experience but actually reliving it, with no awareness of the Serpent or the Silver Staff, the happy innocent he had once been.

He was walking through a wood with Falin and his younger sister, Lothwyn. There was rich, green grass beneath their feet, scintillating with rainbow colours from a recent shower of rain. Silver-gold sunlight filtered through the trees so that the leaves shone every shade of translucent green in a complex unfathomable pattern, like layer upon layer of gleaming lace. The sweet smell of wet grass and soil pervaded the air. They were laughing, because Falin was recounting how a goat had got into their kitchen that morning and begun to eat his mother's best cider apples, and how she had chased it round and round the table in a vain effort to shoo it out . . . his description had them helpless with laughter. And they were laughing because they were together – Lothwyn between him and Falin, arm-in-arm with them both – and because the morning was beautiful, and they were alive, and walking through it.

Then they came upon a gazelle, lying injured across their path. It must have put its foot down a rabbit warren and broken its leg. It lay helpless, gazing up at them with a huge, liquid, brown eye.

'I'll run and fetch Lilithea. She'll know what to do,' said Falin. So Estarinel and Lothwyn knelt by the creature, doing their best to quiet it, and waited. Presently Falin and Lilithea came hurrying along the grassy path towards them, Lilithea carrying her sack of healing herbs and ointments.

Lilithea bent to examine the gazelle, her rich bronze-brown hair falling forward to conceal her delicate face. She whispered gently to the animal, smoothing its russet coat with calming hands until its breathing slowed. Then she straightened up and said, 'I can do nothing for it. It has broken its leg in two places. Even if I make it a sling to stand in, so that it can't run about, it still would not heal. It would only suffer great pain.'

'Oh, poor thing!' exclaimed Lothwyn. Lilithea reached into her sack and took out a short bow and a small, sharp arrow. Estarinel saw what she meant to do. Her expression was resolute, but the rosy colour had drained out of her cheeks and her hands were unsteady.

He took the bow and arrow from her and said, 'I'll do it, Lili.'

'Straight into its eye. Don't hesitate,' she said. Lothwyn hid her face against Falin's arm. Lilithea gently held the gazelle still while Estarinel did as she said, and destroyed it.

Then he handed the bow back to her while her large, dark eyes held his face, shining with a mixture of sorrow and gratitude.

'Thank you,' she said quietly. 'I can't bear doing that.'

'I could not have done it at all!' Falin exclaimed feelingly.

'Well, we had better bury the poor creature,' said Estarinel, putting an arm around Lothwyn, who was struggling not to cry. And they went among the trees, and found a place to dig, and with that the scene ended.

Estarinel was back in the dark chamber. He raised a hand and rubbed his forehead to bring himself back to the present. That had not been a memory, not a dream; he had actually relived something that had taken place several years before, something he had hardly given a thought to for a very long time. He wondered what it meant. Surely it could not be a test?

He shook his head. There was a tightness in his throat. Time had numbed the pain of remembering how Forluin had been before the Worm came. Now it had been brought back to him so vividly that the old agony reawakened. He kept thinking of Lilithea; at least she is still alive, he thought – or will even she and Falin fall victim to M'gulfn before much longer?

He crossed the chamber, his hands outstretched like a blind man. He found another door, another stone staircase winding upwards – and at the top of that, another room as dark as the first. He entered, closing his eyes.

Again, he was somewhere different.

Rain lashed down onto burnt, rotting timbers inside a half-ruined building of decayed stone. The roof was open to the sky, admitting a miserable twilight choked with wet ash and the smell of decay: the smell of the Worm. Ominous creakings filled the house as if it were still in the process of collapsing. Estarinel was kneeling on the floor, shivering from the rain on his back, sickened by the ash that was all that was left wherever the Serpent had been in Forluin—

The house was horrifyingly familiar. It was his house – his family's farmhouse – and he was aware that although this was not a memory it was nevertheless a real event that he was now observing like a disembodied watcher in a dream.

There was a faint cry – a woman calling for help. It sounded like someone he knew, it sounded like his mother—

There was a sound of light, running feet, two voices raised in panic. And now he could see two slender, rain-soaked figures bending over a shambles of timber.

'Mother, Mother,' they were crying. They were his sisters, Arlena, Lothwyn.

'The wall fell on me, I couldn't move in time.' At the sound of his mother's voice, Estarinel cried out and tried to crawl forward. But although he could see, hear and feel, he could not move, could not make himself heard. Because he was not really there.

His sisters, weeping pitifully, were trying to drag away the timbers that buried their mother.

'We can't move it, Mother, it's no good—'

'Get out!' his mother cried. 'Go on, the whole house is falling in. Save yourselves – go on, my loves, please!'

For the Lady's sake, can't you hear me? Can't you see me? Estarinel screamed soundlessly, his powerlessness agony to him. Rain and ash and the Serpent's sickness poured down upon him as he watched his sisters bending over their buried mother, weeping. And as they struggled ineffectually with the timbers, the rest of the wall collapsed and his sisters, coughing and crying out, were submerged in stone and smoking wood.

He could still see Lothwyn, but she cried no more, nor moved. Her hair was spread out like a splash of dark water across the rubble. And of Arlena and his mother he could only see – hands. Three white hands sticking out of the

218

rubble, limp, graceful, sculptural, as if frozen in different gestures of description. Like strange trees growing on a bizarre, desolate landscape.

Misery and impotent rage flooded him as he cursed the Serpent, struggling like a madman against the nightmare paralysis. Indeed, he was insane in those moments of horror and grief.

Then the house was spinning around him, time whirling forwards. He was looking down into the Bowl Valley, seeing it submerged in grey venom, and somewhere through a thick fog he could hear Medrian saying, '. . . it'll kill you . . . it'll kill you . . .' and then 'I'm sorry . . . sorry . . .'

When he came round inside the dark tower he was lying on the floor, shaking convulsively. It took him a long time to remember where he was, what he was supposed to be doing. He sat up, his knees bent, his head on his arms. How could the Silver Staff have such insight, such power, as to show him a scene which could destroy him? What he had seen was undeniably real, undoubtably the actual death of his mother and sisters. It was unbearable. Of all he had been through, this was the worst. Unbearable.

Calorn had told him that the tests would be arduous and even unfair. But this was cruel, worse than cruel, monstrous, ghoulish in its callous extremity. The Silver Staff was a pitiless entity. He loathed it. It was no better than the Serpent.

He gave up then. He felt that he, Medrian and Ashurek had been tricked; so had Calorn, and so had even the H'tebhmellians. They should have known that there was nothing that could help them against the Serpent. And something had given them false hope, in order to mock and torment them further. Desolate, he surrendered to the darkness, wishing only to die.

When he felt something sharp against his hand, he did not even start, let alone try to escape it. It felt like a claw . . . a bird's claws, closing on one of his fingers. And a soft, sweet voice, so faint that he might have imagined it, said, 'This is not the whole reality. I am not yet destroyed, only lost. If you would find hope, you must look for it . . .'

He sat very still, feeling that if he moved the creature would vanish. But she disappeared anyway, as if she had been no more than a wisp of darkness. Then he got to his feet, thinking, however hard this is, it is only another test. I can and I will withstand it. And he walked calmly across the room until he found the door, and continued up the next twisting section of steps to the topmost chamber.

As before, it was totally dark. But this time no vision came to claim him. He could see lights flickering in the darkness, ghostly and elusive, and a soft breeze full of malice was sighing past his face. He felt cold, instilled with a dread that was at once illogical and paralysing, as in a bad dream. But he had already endured so much that he felt strangely detached from his own fear, and stood calmly waiting for something to emerge from the weird gloom.

The light grew brighter; pale candlelight illuminated the round, plain chamber, filling its recesses with dancing shadows. On the far side a tall figure, concealed from head to foot in what appeared to be a shroud, was holding a huge candelabrum and lighting each wick with a taper. In the centre of the room lay a woman: she who had been on the cliff-top, and who had rushed into the tower ahead of Estarinel.

She was dead.

She lay on her back, her eyes staring sightlessly into the air, the purple and black jellaba draped in folds around her thin form. Her throat had been torn out. From her chin to her collarbone was a mass of torn flesh, glistening with dark red, congealed blood.

To the left of her stood a huge wolf. Its glowing eyes were fixed on Estarinel and its tongue lolled over its great fangs, dripping bloodied saliva onto the floor.

On the right side stood a child of about three, blond and rosy and innocent. His huge wondering eyes were also intent upon the Forluinishman.

'Now, your final test,' said the shrouded figure in a toneless, off-hand voice. 'This woman, as you see, has been savagely killed.'

'Nothing you do would surprise me now,' Estarinel whispered, his voice bitter with disgust.

'All we require is that you correctly identify the murderer so that they may be justly executed. The wolf,' the figure moved a hand to indicate, 'or the child?'

'You're mad!' Estarinel exclaimed, feeling exasperated, weary with despair.

'You must choose. Otherwise you will have failed.'

'This is a trick. It must be the wolf, mustn't it? But that is too obvious . . . so knowing that, and knowing the child would therefore be chosen, perhaps it is the wolf after all.'

'Just so,' said the grey figure.

'And if I choose rightly, the murderer will be executed?'

'Yes.'

'What if I choose wrongly?'

'Then you will suffer the same fate as this woman, and be used to test the next one who passes through this tower.'

'But you know – you *know* – that I cannot choose the child!'

'Choose as you will,' was the impassive reply.

'Very well, I'll tell who it is!' cried Estarinel furiously. '*I* am the murderer! If not for me, this test would not have been set up! Stop this evil charade – stop it now!'

The grey one uttered a noise which sounded suspiciously like a laugh.

'You have answered well,' it said.

'What?'

'I said, you have answered correctly. You have passed the final test. No one is going to be executed; it was, as you said, a charade. A philosophical riddle. To test your wits.' And as the figure spoke, the child moved, its limbs elongating, its rosy skin becoming fawn-coloured. And the woman sat up from the floor, and stretched out her arms, and transformed slowly into something like a rough, flexible clay figure. Meanwhile the wolf's coat flattened and its ears, muzzle and legs were absorbed into its body. Then the three shapeless beige creatures touched and melded into one roughly humanoid form. The shape-changer, which had haunted his whole

221

journey. And it turned to Estarinel and gave a deep, mocking bow. Then it rippled like a reflection created by a heat-haze, and dissolved into nothingness.

'You will follow me, please,' said the figure, oblivious to Estarinel's obvious consternation, ignoring his entreaties to be told what was going on. It raised a hand and pushed open a small, arched door. 'It is time for you to be judged.'

Estarinel had thought they were at the top of the tower; he expected to see the pale mound below, and those hideous greenish suns. But he was wrong again. They were at ground level, and before them was a sweep of rich green grass rising between an avenue of stately copper beeches, rustling ceaselessly in a summer breeze.

And at the end of the avenue, on the summit of the hill, stood a castle, a beautiful, terrible, splendid castle of red glass. It was vast, towering above them in a glory of rich, translucent blood-reds and crimsons. Sunlight poured down upon it like red gold, and snow-white pennants flew gaily upon its towers and battlements.

Estarinel knew at once that it was a place of great power. He was aware that he had often glimpsed it in moments of prescience, and the feeling of dread that those glimpses had induced was no less now.

'Follow me,' said the shrouded figure again. It began to walk briskly along the avenue towards the castle.

'I think I am owed some sort of explanation, after all I've been subjected to. Just what exactly is the idea of all this?' Estarinel persisted angrily.

The Grey One ignored him for a time, but eventually replied, 'You are owed one thing only, and that is a final examination to judge your worthiness to wield the Silver staff. You were told there would be tests. We are not bound to explain them to you.'

'Tests? Murders!' Estarinel exclaimed, trembling with an overwhelming sense of outrage at the Silver Staff's atrocities. But the shrouded one said no more. Estarinel subsided, awed by the closeness of the castle.

An oppressive sense of doom filled him at the prospect of

222

entering. Swallowing his dread, he marched determinedly through a great arched doorway after the Grey One. Within, they passed through corridors and halls of red glass. Walls, floors and ceilings were transparent and he could see into the rooms beyond, a confusing pattern of rubescent light like the gleaming facets of a garnet. There was something unnerving in the sanguine glow, beautiful though it was.

Presently he could see figures ahead, shadowy figures seen through red glass. He could feel them looking at him. They were as faceless as the shrouded one by his side, yet he sensed that they were ancient beings with narrow eyes and long, pale beards. And they were powerful, and heartless, just as he had seen them in the Cavern of Communication. Neutral, yet utterly without compassion.

They were the Guardians: the Grey Ones.

The figure at his side said, 'Wait here,' and he stopped like an automaton. They were in a many-sided room like the inside of a jewel. The Grey One continued through a doorway and mingled with the others, swiftly becoming indistinguishable from them. He could hear a murmur of voices. He waited grimly, watching the shadows moving behind the translucent glass wall. The redness of the castle seemed to be the colour of the blood staining the Guardians' hands, Calorn's and Shaell's and that of the countless other murders they were no doubt guilty of. The blood of their inhumanity swelled and ebbed in the air.

He waited what felt like hours while the Guardians talked. He could pick a few words out of the general murmur, but he could not make sense of them. The Grey Ones seemed puppet-like, distant and wooden, as if they had their reality in a plane far above his understanding. The knowledge that they were judging him filled him with revulsion.

'Don't be foolish. It is quite unnecessary.' He heard these words clearly, and strained his eyes to identify the speaker.

'I disagree. I say that he is deserving of an explanation,' another voice replied.

'With what purpose?'

'That of his better understanding! He is not a child: humans grasp more than you can possibly realise!'

'Well, you alone of us should know. But still I say it is a waste of time.'

'And I say you are wrong!' answered the second speaker. 'I must talk to him. Can you not understand, I owe him that at least?'

'No, we cannot understand this apparently – ah – human obligation. However, if it is what you wish, you may go to him. We have no reason to gainsay it.'

Estarinel saw one of the shadows moving away from the group. It glided along behind the wall and passed through the doorway towards him. This figure was massively built, cloaked from head to foot in pale robes which were steeped in the red light. It stopped in front of him and said, 'Estarinel of Forluin. The Guardians have assessed your endurance of the various tests which were laid in your path. You have been judged and found clear of purpose. You will be permitted to wield the Silver Staff.'

Estarinel experienced no thrill of victory at this speech. His apprehension subsided abruptly, but he still felt filled with bitter fury against the Guardians and the Silver Staff.

'At what cost?' he said, not expecting an answer.

'I will take you now to the Silver Staff,' said the Guardian.

'Wait,' said Estarinel, his voice low but insistent. 'I want to know the nature of this – thing I will be wielding.'

The Guardian paused, looking at him through the gauzy veil hiding his face. 'It cannot be described. When you touch it, you will know its nature.'

'I believe it to be evil.'

'No, Estarinel, it is not evil.'

'How can I believe anything the Guardians say? I will not know until I touch it, and then perhaps there will be no going back. Like the Egg-Stone,' he spat.

'No. Ah no, I swear to you it is not like the Egg-Stone,' said the Guardian, a human distress entering his deep voice.

'You swear? And the tests – the tests – if they were "set"

by the Silver Staff itself, why then do the Guardians stand in judgement on me?'

'Oh, Estarinel, how you have changed. You have suffered much,' the Grey One said sadly. He gripped the edge of the veil and slowly raised it from his head to reveal an old and noble face with a high forehead, broad nose, and clear grey eyes. He had white hair and a dishevelled white beard.

Eldor.

Estarinel was barely aware that he was backing away until he felt a wall against his back, and he was half-sobbing with a mixture of dismay and astonishment. He had one hand on his forehead as if to shield out the blood-red light.

'Eldor. Eldor. By the gods, you are one of them,' he was gasping. Eldor, the wise, kindly sage of the House of Rede. Eldor, who had advised them, helped them, told them that the Serpent must be destroyed and given them hope that it might be achieved. Who had been the one anchor-point on the insane Earth. Trusted. Completely trusted.

And now . . . Eldor revealed as a Grey One. An eyeless, heartless manipulator of destiny. A pitiless tormentor and murderer of Calorn.

On the Quest Estarinel, Ashurek and Medrian had often felt that they were being manipulated by unseen beings, tossed back and forth between the Serpent and the forces opposing it. But never, never had he dreamed that they had been used from the very outset by the one kindly being in whom they had put absolute faith.

They had been betrayed. Betrayed, he thought. And it was Lothwyn he was thinking of, his little sister and all those others who had least deserved to die, even less deserved this betrayal.

'Bastards,' he whispered. 'You bastards.'

'Estarinel,' said Eldor softly, approaching and placing one large hand on the Forluinishman's shoulder. 'I know what you are thinking. That is why I came out, and not one of the others, to try to explain . . .'

'Explain? This is explainable?'

'Yes. But please, trust me in this. I want you first to come

225

and take the Silver Staff. Then we will go outside the castle, and talk.'

'All right,' Estarinel sighed. An unnatural calm and resignation came over him, so that he felt grimly self-possessed. 'I can't judge what's right and what's wrong. I'll do as you say.'

He followed Eldor out of the room, through a mazelike arrangement of halls and staircases, and along a gleaming, geometric corridor that led to the heart of the castle. There they entered a chamber of silver light.

It blinded him at first, his eyes having become accustomed to the deep redness within the castle. Then he saw that they were in a many-sided hall that was crimson in its furthest recesses, but with a heart of pure light, like a fountain springing from a pedestal of diamond.

At the centre of the brilliance was the Silver Staff.

It was lying on a base shaped like a giant ruby. It danced before his eyes like a streak of lightning with curves of silver radiating from it. All the glory of the star-filled night through which he had first entered the domain was concentrated here, fiery, searing, and full of the promise of wild invincibility.

'Take it,' Eldor prompted gently.

Estarinel approached it hesitantly. The incandescent power of the Staff was real, dangerous, crackling white and silver with electricity. He felt waves of static dancing like fireflies against his face and hands. He outstretched his fingers to grasp the Silver Staff, braced in anticipation of a great shock-wave.

The sensation as he touched it was surpisingly gentle, yet it increased in intensity until it was as devastating as lightning. The feeling was elation. In that moment Estarinel felt that the Serpent and all the demons of the Dark Regions held no fear for him; should he but turn to them and laugh, they would retreat before him and be consumed by silver fire, blackening and crumbling and blowing away on the wind before the Staff's glory.

And the Silver Staff was speaking to him. The words were voiceless, rapid, indistinguishable, but full of humour and

226

delight, like a hundred children each singing a different song. Children, yes; the Silver Staff was a wild entity, as joyous and vital and carefree as a child. It was not evil, yet it had no concept of good. No conscience. It was simply itself: powerful, yet a total innocent.

Estarinel shared a strange fellow-feeling with it then. It seemed vulnerable in its innocence. It had been manipulated by the Guardians, and it did not even know; it, too, had been used.

It became quiescent under his touch, the flaring electricity fading until he was able to look at it without being dazzled. It lay in his hands, cool and heavy. He felt surprised at how plain it was, although he did not know what else he had expected. It was a silver rod a little under three feet long, about half an inch in diameter at one end and tapering to a needle-sharp point at the other. That was all. There was not even any kind of engraving or decoration on it to mark it as unusual. He wondered how it could be used; it certainly could not be wielded like a sword, and seemed so delicate that it would surely break before it did harm to anything.

Yet, holding it, he felt euphoric, certain of power. He sensed a spirit of comradeship with the Silver Staff; for once he was happy, assured – whole.

Eldor gave him a scabbard for it, a slim rigid tube of red leather. Estarinel strapped this round his waist and slid the Staff inside, sharp end first. A leather flap fitted over the other end so that it was completely enclosed.

'Come, then,' said Eldor. And they walked through the eerie castle of red glass until they passed under the archway to the outside. The green of the grass was brilliant, almost physical in its intensity, after Estarinel had grown so accustomed to the red light. Eldor led him some distance down the hill and sat down under one of the copper beeches, his great arms clasped round his knees. He still looked just as he had in the House of Rede – wise, kindly and human.

'So, Master Eldor,' said Estarinel, 'what are you doing here?'

'Ah, that is a long story. I think I want to tell it all in

order, Estarinel.' He spoke thoughtfully. Estarinel could feel no animosity towards him, only towards the other Guardians. 'Dritha and I were terribly worried about you. You see, we knew that the H'tebhmellian ship had not arrived on the Blue Plane, but we did not know what had happened to you. We thought that the Serpent M'gulfn had won already. It was not until I came here,' he waved a hand at the blood-red castle, 'that I heard, to my relief, that you were safe. Dritha still does not know, alas.'

'Is Dritha—'

'Dritha is also a Guardian, yes. But she chose to remain at the House of Rede to give comfort to the refugees.'

'What do you mean – refugees?'

'Ah, alas,' sighed Eldor, 'the world is falling very rapidly into the Serpent's power. A kind of anarchy is running through Tearn and Vardrav, accentuated by the crumbling of the Gorethrian Empire. Beasts of the Serpent roam freely, instilling terror and causing plagues and famines. The very elements have turned savage, the Earth erupting with new-born volcanoes, its coasts lashed by tidal waves . . . A few humans – comparatively few, by which I mean hundreds – have escaped to the House of Rede, which is safe as yet.'

'To think that when I began, I thought only Forluin was suffering . . .'

'The Serpent is possessed by an overwhelming loathing of mankind, and wishes only to cause chaos and destruction until it feels that the Earth belongs totally to itself again.'

'It seems to me,' said Estarinel, a little sharply, 'that the Guardians can only fight M'gulfn by being as cruel and callous as it is.'

'Estarinel, it gives me great sorrow to see you so embittered. But perhaps the Guardians have deserved your anger. Understand, when I try to explain their actions, I am not trying to excuse them. They were not going to say anything to you at all, but I insisted.'

'Yes, I heard you arguing.'

'And there's something else I want you to know, though I am not trying to excuse myself either: Dritha and I did not

228

know about the Silver Staff. Because we were on Earth, the other Guardians withheld the knowledge from us. I did not know about it until I came here, having been summoned to help – and they had already decided how you must be tested.'

'Well, I'll accept that it wasn't your fault. But why was it necessary—' his voice became choked with anguish, 'for Calorn to be murdered? Just – savagely, pointlessly – by that shape-changing thing. And after that, as if scratching around for what little else they could take from me, they even lured my horse over that cliff.'

'Estarinel,' said Eldor gently, 'Calorn is not dead.'

'What do you mean? I saw—'

'It was an illusion.'

'And Shaell?'

'Your horse is alive too. To him, there was no cliff, just a little drop and an inviting meadow.'

'I can't believe it. It was so *real*. And those wretched people on the cliff?'

'All illusions – or at least, only a temporary reality. They can create and destroy within certain limits, so it is easy enough to make anything seem real: deserts, paradoxical buildings, people . . . murders. I swear to you that Calorn was not killed. She rode away unharmed.'

Estarinel was silent for a few seconds, thinking this over.

'But I believed it was real! Why torment me with such illusions? Eldor, my family were killed; in that black tower, I saw it happen! It was worse than cruel. It was abominable,' he ended in a whisper. Eldor looked very sad.

'I agree. I did not approve of it, but it was only my voice against all the others. They had to be sure you could carry on not only through physical perils, but against the most absolute despair. And not just carry on blindly, but with perception and intelligence.'

'Well, I hope they were satisfied,' Estarinel muttered.

'They have no real understanding of human emotions, you see. Like a man watching the behaviour of an insect: he finds it fascinating but has no concept of how the insect may feel or suffer. They know that if you are treated in a certain way, you will react in a certain way, with anger, fear, grief, and so on. Yet they do not know how these things *feel*. In this way they are, I agree, cruel and inhuman.'

'And it was the Guardians who required these tests, wasn't it? Not the Silver Staff at all. I could tell when I touched it. It is innocent.'

'Yes, you are correct. There never have been any other questers. Those people you saw were not real. This domain is not the Silver Staff's, but brought into being by the Guardians to contain it. There is something else they would not want me to tell you, Estarinel, but I will: they do not know what the Silver Staff is. They do not understand its nature. They have used it as a vessel to contain the power which is the opposite to the Serpent's power, but they are unsure of the Staff itself. Even a little afraid. After all their pains to capture and use it, they hardly wished to give it to a mere mortal without some proof that he was worthy to bear it. That was why only one of you could come; more would have been impossible to test.'

'But why the pretence?' Estarinel exclaimed, angry again. 'The stories that thousands had sought the Staff, and that *it* insisted on the tests. Why did the Lady of H'tebhmella lie to us?'

'She did not. The Guardians lied to her.'

'They – why?'

'Because if she had thought that the tests were not inevitable, she would never have permitted them.' Eldor's words dropped like stones into a cold, dark pool. Estarinel stared at him, incredulous.

'You've confirmed everything I suspected,' he said at last. 'The Guardians are deceivers. To lie to the H'tebhmellians is – beyond contempt. It is unforgivable.'

'I agree with you,' Eldor said.

'And in spite of their heartlessness, they are yet "human" enough not to want anyone to think badly of them? Or to suspect that they are imperfect?'

'Yes, I am afraid so. When I have finished telling you about the Grey Ones, you may think even less of them than you do now,' said Eldor with a touch of irony. 'Countless ages ago, long before man evolved upon the Earth, the Guardians went to the Serpent and tore out one of its three eyes in order to reduce its powers.'

'Yes, I know – the Lady told us.'

'Then imagine the rage with which it reacted. Its power over mankind had been taken from it. It developed a hatred of man – and, indeed, of all life that was not of its own making even before such life appeared. Its malice was vast, feeding on itself continually. Do you see what this means?'

'I'm beginning to . . .'

'The very hatred which it now directs against Forluin and the rest of the world, the hatred which created the Shana, was sparked off by this act of the Guardians.'

'Ye gods! Is there any end to this?' Estarinel cried. 'Are you implying that if they had not interfered, it would have lived peacefully and left us all alone?'

'Perhaps. Or perhaps the world would have fallen into its power aeons ago. No one, not even the Grey Ones, can say what would have been. But the next thing they did was as terrible, in its way. The Serpent had created for itself the beings we call the Shana. The Guardians caused their Dark Regions to be removed from Earth, but they failed to put a constraint on where they might be situated instead. And, somehow, using their combined power and that of the Serpent, the demons played a ghoulish trick and moved the Dark Regions onto the far side of H'tebhmella. Now, the side of the Blue Plane which you have seen, is a place of exquisite healing beauty. The other side was lovelier still, beautiful beyond imagination and with a purpose that only the H'tebhmellians could truly comprehend. They have never divulged exactly what has been lost, beyond referring to it cryptically as "paradise". But when the Dark Regions were put there, they were justifiably outraged. An abominable act had been performed against them, and they blamed the Guardians for their mishandling of the Serpent. The Guardians and the H'tebhmellians have continued to work

231

together, but not without a certain resentment and mistrust.'

'That is dreadful,' Estarinel said, appalled.

'Some of us thought so too. Notably Dritha and myself. You see, the Guardians are not gods – though when men call upon the name of the gods it is no doubt with some vague concept of the Grey Ones in mind – and their function is only to enforce the rules, not to make them. To keep a balance, and maintain the universe in benign neutrality. I must tell you that we know of no gods – only great, uncognizant energies which have to be kept in check. And this the Guardians do by manipulating, using, twisting the rules – anything which achieves their end.

'Dritha and I were afraid for this Earth, however. We felt that there was something which mattered more than the balancing of distant, mindless powers. We decided to stay upon the Earth and watch over her. In doing so, in remaining in flesh and bone bodies and being in continual contact with humans, we have learned something of human values, conscience and love.' He paused for a few seconds, apparently lost in thought. 'So don't condemn us out of hand, Estarinel, as being exactly like our comrades. We were not deceiving you. We do truly care about the world.'

'I believe you, Master Eldor.'

'But the other Guardians disapproved. They tried to stop us. They said we were being foolish, sentimental. They warned us that we were breaking the rule that says we may not interfere directly with mankind. They said that the idea of a House of refuge and learning was madness, because we risked giving too much away. But we disobeyed them and lived on Earth anyway. We only watched and advised – we do not help materially or give orders – but the other Grey Ones still insisted that we were flouting the law. So they held us in contempt, treating us as outcasts and not consulting us about their schemes.'

'Except when it suited them.'

'Indeed. It suited them to use us in the Quest of the Serpent. They would not tell us about the Silver Staff, yet they needed me to help them prepare it. They have delighted

232

in alternately keeping us in the dark and using us – it is their revenge for our defiance. Dritha, as I told you, refused to answer their summons, feeling that her duty lay at the House of Rede. I would have preferred to stay there too, but I came here because I wanted to know what the Guardians were doing, and because I was concerned for you.'

Estarinel listened to this with his head bowed, thinking deeply. Presently he said, 'So Medrian, Ashurek and myself are being used to undo the Guardians' mistakes?'

'In a way. This is what I could not tell you when you first came to the House of Rede.'

'So you were using us, but being used in your turn . . . and likewise the H'tebhmellians. Next you'll tell me that the Guardians engineered the attack on Forluin so that a Forluinishman "clear of purpose" could be used to bear the Silver Staff!'

Eldor sighed remorsefully at this bitter outburst.

'Ah, no, Estarinel, even the Grey Ones are not that twisted and cruel.'

'But why could you not have told us all this at the beginning? I feel – I am sorry, Master Eldor, but I feel that even you have deceived us!'

'I swear that I have never lied to you. Only said less than I could have done. Yes, you have been used as tools in the hands of the Grey Ones, and will continue to be used so. But how would knowing this from the start have helped? How has it helped you now?'

'Perhaps it hasn't. It's made me bitter, disillusioned. But at least I am nearer the truth. I couldn't have assimilated this knowledge at the start of the Quest. But I've been through so much since then; I've changed. Now I can also be cold-hearted and manipulative. I will co-operate with these manipulators whom I loathe for their inhumanity, simply because I will go to any length – *any* – to restore my country.'

There was a new, grim depth of purpose in Estarinel's voice.

Eldor placed a hand on his shoulder; there was empathy between them, threaded through with bitter sadness, yet somehow reassuring.

233

'Will you be going back to the House of Rede now?' Estarinel asked.

'Alas, no. I am not allowed back. You see, I know about the Silver Staff now, and the Serpent would see that knowledge immediately.'

'But surely it knows by now anyway? When we were aboard the *Star*, Ashurek remarked that it must have known as soon as we re-entered Earth from the Blue Plane.'

'It will know eventually, it is true. But human thoughts are a vague muddle to it, and we hope it won't sense the actual presence of the Staff until it is too late. But that knowledge in the mind of a Guardian would be seen clearly, as through a cold, pure ether. It cannot read our thoughts as such, but I could not keep from it the awareness of the one thing that has the power to destroy it. So the Guardians say, anyway,' he sounded weary. 'I am tired of arguing with them.'

'I cannot imagine the House of Rede without you.'

'Neither can I,' said the sage. 'Now, it is time for you to go back.'

They stood up, but Estarinel faced Eldor squarely and asked, 'Is there anything else you haven't told me?'

Eldor held his gaze and said nothing, but his expression clearly said, 'Yes.'

'And I must find it out for myself when the time comes, I suppose?'

'Yes. It is so. But I will say this much: the Silver Staff is a wild force which has to be tempered by compassion. It is up to you – and Ashurek and Medrian – to discover and understand what that means. I am only a Guardian. Even if I knew what it meant myself I doubt that I could explain it to you. It's something that cannot be explained, only discovered for yourself.'

Estarinel felt something touch his elbow, and turned round to find Shaell standing behind him, ears pricked and eyes bright with health. He gasped with relief and gave the stallion a hug.

'He is unharmed and well, as I said,' Eldor smiled. 'And

did he not lead you surely along the tortuous path the Guardians had laid?'

'I've always suspected that horses have more sense than their riders,' Estarinel replied, vaulting onto Shaell's broad back. 'Fare you well, Master Eldor.'

'Fare you well. And don't let your thoughts dwell on the Grey Ones. They want to save the Earth, whatever they have done. Think only of Forluin.'

'That is all I do think of,' Estarinel replied quietly. Gathering up the reins, checking the thin red scabbard, he rode away.

Shaell cantered down the long green hill with the purple-bronze beeches swaying and rustling on both sides. Estarinel did not look back at the red glass castle or at Eldor, for fear they might have vanished. He let the stallion go where he would, trusting him to find the way back to Earth by instinct.

He did so. But it was a wild and strange ride, as if the Guardians were toying with their invented landscape and laughing gently at him. The green hill transformed into a golden beach washed by a turquoise sea, the sand foaming around Shaell's hoofs as he galloped. Then they were crossing a crystalline landscape of amethyst with weird silver creatures frozen in its depths. Caves with walls like cobwebs of gold passed them by, only to mutate into a field of giant sunflowers. It was like a dream landscape rolling past them, exquisite and confusing.

Suddenly they were crossing an undulating plain under a blue-grey, star-filled night. It was again the wild, glorious night through which they had entered the domain, as breath-taking in its emptiness and beauty as before. And for a few minutes Estarinel felt he was no longer a speck, but part of the domain's infinite night, understanding all and caring for nothing; he was one with the Silver Staff, part of a mystic, joyous dance that led along a shimmering path between the stars into eternity.

Then Shaell carried him underwater and they left the domain behind for ever. Deep green water was all around them, a scintillating mosaic of dark and light which rustled like a great forest. Gradually he became aware that it was foliage, not water. Shaell was forging his way through the dense, waxy-leaved bushes, and the path was gleaming under his hoofs. It was raining; Estarinel noticed the change in the atmosphere as it became softer and full of the scents of wood, earth and rain. The silver path faded and was gone. Without warning the bushes ended and Shaell stepped out into the grey and amber forest.

Estarinel pulled him to a halt, feeling disorientated. At once he checked that he still had the red scabbard containing the Silver Staff at his side; at least that had not been an illusion. His memories of the domain were not dreamlike, but starkly real, even those happenings which he knew to have been phantasms. He would have preferred to forget the whole thing. He felt exhausted, and very hungry; he wondered how long he had been in the domain.

He let Shaell walk on through the trees, but after a few minutes he began to feel disturbed. Eldor had assured him that Calorn was alive. And she had said that she would know when he returned, and would come to meet him. Yet there was no sign of her.

Out of nowhere an image came back to him: the monstrous, fanged white bear advancing on Medrian and Calorn. Apprehension stabbed him, and he urged his horse into a trot against the dense undergrowth.

10

Across the River

'No. MEDRIAN . . .' Calorn whispered, the last of her breath trickling from her. Her body was a mass of pain, ribs bruised, spine aching with the bear's weight, its claws four deadly points of pain across her back. And worse than that was the terrible illusion that Medrian was towering above her in the night sky, black and demon-silver like some ancient deity laughing with infinite malice. The night seemed as soft and rank as the Dark Regions, while the glowing flecks from the fire became the red eyes of imps, dancing with glee at her death.

And suddenly it was over. There was a flurry of fire in the air, sparks and ash swirling together, and she felt the bear lurch backwards and away from her. Relieved of its weight, she struggled to stand up, trembling violently and gasping with the shock.

Medrian was standing in front of her, wielding the brand with which she had forced the bear off. She was small, human, ordinary – Calorn stared at her for a moment, shaking her head. An illusion. Only an illusion.

Savage with relief, she exclaimed, 'What kept you?' She rubbed at the pain in her ribs, and her fingers closed on the object which had been sticking into them, the phial that Ashurek had thrown to her.

'Nothing. It only knocked you down for two or three seconds.' Medrian sounded surprised. The bears had withdrawn a few feet and were pacing slowly round and round the dying fire, their lips drawn back over their ivory teeth.

'It seemed like hours.' Calorn was backing towards the

237

fire, her eyes fixed on the bears, one hand reaching for another brand, but there were only smouldering logs left, nothing she could hold. She did not notice Medrian staring at the phial gleaming in her other hand.

'Calorn, let me see that.'

'What? Oh—' She handed Medrian the phial, just as one of the beasts turned towards them, its jaws gaping, its eyes mindless as death. 'Look out!' Calorn seized a red-hot lump of wood from the fire and hurled it at the creature. It hit the bear's shoulder in a shower of sparks and the beast shied back, roaring as its pelt caught alight and smouldered for several moments.

Medrian, looking at the tiny glass bottle, hardly noticed. At first she could not think what it was, why it seemed significant. Then memory came rushing back. Setrel! The village elder whom they had helped had given it to them. She remembered his words, 'A powder that can hold some sorcerous energies within it. If in peril you scatter it about you, it will repel evil creatures.' She had not given a further thought to it until this moment.

'Ashurek gave it to me—' Calorn began to explain.

But Medrian interrupted briskly, 'We have to scatter it in a circle.'

'It's no use – it had some power in the Dark Regions, but it's dead now. The demon neutralised its power.'

'But we have to try,' Medrian snapped. 'We've no other chance. I'll scatter it. Here, take the brand and follow me round to keep those creatures off. And if it does fail,' she added morosely, 'we are done for.'

With Calorn protecting her, Medrian trickled the gold powder sparingly onto the grass, working her way round in a rough circle that included the fire and a place for them to sit. She did not really believe it could help them. But by the time she completed the ring and the last of the substance was gone, she could hear a different note in the bears' voices. Their growls were louder, higher-pitched.

'Now, let us retreat and see what happens.' They withdrew to the centre of the circle, their backs to the fire. To their

238

astonishment, although the bears continued to rear up and lunge, not one of them placed a paw or muzzle over the line of powder. Then Calorn realised that although the substance had become neutral in the Dark Regions, once on Earth again it must have regained its potency. And now, like a ground mist, a faint, shimmering veil of gold hung above the ring. It was very much fainter than the dazzling curtain of light-motes Calorn remembered from the Dark Regions, but it was real enough.

The bears ceased striking out and began to pace round and round the circle of aureate light. They were wailing with frustration. It was a horrible noise, but Medrian and Calorn were too euphoric with relief to care. They shook hands, and Medrian actually grinned briefly. She must have been in severe pain from the blow on her shoulder, yet she looked better now than she had done for days.

Estarinel had once told Calorn that Medrian was always more cheerful and communicative in a crisis. Some people, Calorn reflected, were like that.

'They know,' said Medrian. 'Look at them, they're furious. I'd forgotten all about that powder, I certainly never thought it would work.'

'How long will we have to stay in the circle, though?' asked Calorn, visualising being there for days, while Estarinel and Ashurek came unsuspecting through the forest only to be torn to pieces.

'I don't know. Watch them.'

The bears continued their restless vigil outside the ensorcelled ring. After a couple of hours they seemed to forget why they were there and began to fight among themselves. Presently three lay dead, and the others had wandered out of sight.

The clouds cleared and there was some colour in the sunrise, a soft rose and golden light giving warmth to the forest, coaxing browns and greens into the trees. Calorn stood up and stretched painfully.

'Oh, I'm bruised all over, and frozen stiff.' She winced as she probed the back of her head where the bear had struck her. 'Do you think it's safe to go out of the circle yet?'

Medrian did not answer. She was extremely pale, as morose and withdrawn as she had been the previous day. Calorn asked, 'Are you all right? How's your shoulder?'

'Not bad. I'll survive,' Medrian said, and there seemed to be a touch of black irony in her words. Memories fell on Calorn like a bear's paw: the rabbit keeling over under the acid glare of Medrian's eyes, the horrific illusion that she was standing untouched amid the bears, grinning pitilessly.

Trying to shake off the night's horrors, Calorn said briskly, 'Well, bears or no, I'm going to rebuild the fire so we can warm up and have some breakfast. Still no sign of Ashurek. And Estarinel must still be in the domain. I wonder where Taery's got to?'

She stepped out of the circle.

The undergrowth would not allow Shaell to proceed faster than a walk; the impossibility of hurrying only increased Estarinel's state of alarm. He pressed on against the hampering trees and bushes, filled not with panic, but with a grim mixture of anger and despair. If Calorn was dead – if Eldor had lied – then the Silver Staff itself must be a lie, all their hopes proved false.

Then he saw the corpse. A shaggy white bear lying across his path, its limbs folded at awkward angles. A stench rose from it, redolent of the Worm's venom. The usually imperturbable stallion whickered with fear as he edged past, sweating.

Estarinel felt dislocated. Time had gone by. He was too late. He would come to the camp and they would be lying dead. Medrian, Calorn, even Ashurek.

It could not be.

The high-pitched squeal of a frightened horse rang out nearby, sending shock through him like an ice-cold spear. Shaell whinnied in response. Ahead, where the path became clearer, Estarinel saw Taery Jasmena. Riderless, roaming loose, confirming his worst fears.

240

It could be. The Worm had caught up with them at last, and revenged itself thoroughly.

Numb with fury, but totally self-possessed, Estarinel caught the palfrey and urged the two horses along the path. Presently he came out into a clearing, and there were two more bear corpses, locked together, bloodied, their mouths savagely agape even in death. And near them was Calorn.

Alive. Alive!

From staring at the bears, she looked up at him, and her expression became one of utter joy. 'Estarinel!' she called out. 'Oh, I'm so glad to see you! I would have met you, but I was trying to catch Taery, and then I came across these bodies – but are you all right? What happened? Did you find—' but as she was speaking he jumped off Shaell, ran over to her, and hugged her so hard that she could not breathe.

'What was that for?' she gasped, laughing.

'For being alive,' he smiled. 'Just for being alive.'

As they rode back towards the camp, Calorn explained about the black horse, the bears, and Setrel's powder. 'When we came out of the circle next morning, there was no sign of the creatures. Ashurek came back in the afternoon – safe, but I think something had happened to him; he won't speak of it, but I can tell. We anticipated another attack last night, so we built a good fire and stayed within the circle, now armed, thanks to Ashurek. But nothing happened. Thank the Lady. This afternoon I decided to come and look for Taery, and as I was doing that I sensed you'd returned from the domain, so I was on my way to meet you – but I kept finding these bear corpses along the way. Horrible.' She shuddered, then grinned to make light of it. 'But it's over. And you found the Silver Staff; I knew you would.' Seeing his exhaustion and the veiled pain in his eyes, she constrained herself from questioning him.

'How long have I been away?' he asked.

'About two and a half days.'

'Is that all? It seemed . . . I don't know. And Medrian is all right, is she?'

'Oh – about the same,' Calorn said as casually as she could, but Estarinel had noticed the involuntary lowering of her eyes, and knew something was wrong.

They reached the camp, where several bears lay dead about the clearing. Even woodsmoke could not quite mask the odour rising from the corpses. Ashurek came forward to greet them, but Medrian hung back in the edge of the trees, as pallid as bone. Calorn went over to her, and Estarinel heard her say, 'The bears – all through the wood, they're lying dead, torn to bits by their fellows. Whatever made them turn on each other like that?'

And he heard Medrian reply, her voice low but very clear, 'Hate. All the children of the Worm hate each other.'

As Estarinel dismounted, Ashurek said, 'Well, what luck did you have?'

'I've got the Silver Staff,' Estarinel answered quietly. Ashurek clapped him on the shoulder and grinned, but there was no warmth in the expression; rather, it was sinister. Medrian was now collecting wood for the fire, apparently unwilling even to greet him.

'Medrian specifically said that she did not want to see the Staff,' Ashurek told him. 'I don't know why. However, I am eager to view this wondrous weapon.'

'I am eager to eat and sleep,' Estarinel replied with a sigh. But he unfastened the top of the red scabbard and drew out the long, thin Silver Staff for Ashurek to inspect. The Gorethrian took it from him and studied it, turning it this way and that and weighing it in his palms.

He noted its plainness, and that it was as sharp and apparently without strength as a needle. He could not imagine how it was to be held and used as a weapon, because it had no kind of handle or grip. Still, the Egg-Stone itself had been no more than a tiny gem . . . Gradually he began to sense the power that the Staff contained. Like the rumbling of a great volcano many miles distant, just below the level of hearing, he could feel it reverberating through his bones.

And at once a strange and bloody vision arrayed itself across his mind, a terrible map of the future; in that moment, he felt he understood the Staff's function and how it related to his own prescience of doom.

When the Staff touched the Serpent, the meeting of the two opposite energies would cause a cataclysm that would destroy the Earth.

So, the Quest is hopeless after all, Ashurek thought. I never really thought otherwise– but now I know why. I see hope in Estarinel's eyes, for all he is so tired; he has touched the Silver Staff and found faith that it is a cleansing weapon which will restore Forluin. Alas for Estarinel and for his country! And alas for Silvren and for my brother and sister . . . I will never know if they find peace or eternal torment. All I know is that my dreams of rescuing them were in vain. The forces that gave us the Silver Staff do not care; the Earth is expendable, as long as the Serpent is destroyed and their wretched balance restored.

Ashurek thrust the Staff back into Estarinel's hands and turned abruptly away, his cloak swirling out behind him.

'Ashurek, what's wrong?' the Forluinishman called after him. He looked questioningly at Calorn, but she was only able to shake her head.

'I don't know what is the matter with him, Estarinel.'

'And Medrian does not even want to look at it!' He slid the Silver Staff back into its scabbard, feeling dismayed. He had thought that Medrian and Ashurek might express some relief at his safe return, a degree of optimism at the retrieval of the weapon. Evidently it was safer not to expect anything. He recalled the coldness he had felt when he had first told them about the Worm's attack on Forluin, and neither had betrayed any reaction at all.

Calorn seemed to know what he was thinking, and took his arm. 'You need to eat and rest. Come and sit by the fire, and have some H'tebhmellian wine.'

Later, when they had eaten supper, Calorn cautiously asked Estarinel to relate what he had been through. He hesitated and Ashurek said, 'Only tell us if you wish to.'

'I don't really want to talk about it,' said Estarinel, 'but there are certain things I must tell you . . . about the Guardians and Eldor.' So he began his account, speaking quietly and glossing over the more painful events. But the others could tell from the tone of his voice and from what he left unsaid that his experiences had been terrible. When he came to explain about Eldor, however, he told them everything.

'And the Guardians lied – they *lied* – to the Lady of the Blue Plane. How do we know what other lies they have told? Even Eldor, whom we trusted . . .' he finished. He looked pale and drawn, even in the firelight. Calorn glanced at Medrian, who was staring expressionlessly at the fire, and Ashurek, whose green eyes were burning with a dangerous brilliance. Calorn herself felt shocked.

'Then I have misled you . . . told you things that were false . . . because of those lies,' she whispered. 'To deceive the H'tebhmellians in that way is unspeakable!'

'Yes, it is,' said Estarinel, his voice stronger and steadier now. 'Medrian? Ashurek? Have you nothing to say? You don't even seem surprised at what I've told you. Perhaps you knew these things already.' It sounded like an accusation.

'No, I did not know,' Ashurek replied. 'But neither am I surprised, my friend; I always knew that we were being manipulated and deceived. This is only a clearer explanation of it. You are right to be so dismayed and horrified – I share your feelings.' And if only you knew, thought Ashurek, of the Guardians' ultimate deception: the false hope of the Silver Staff. But he had vowed not to tell the others. If they knew, they might want to stop the Quest, and he could not risk that.

'Medrian?' said Estarinel.

'My opinion is the same as Ashurek's,' she said in a dull tone. 'It doesn't really matter. This knowledge is unpleasant, but it makes no difference to the Quest; we must forget it and go on.'

'The world is unpleasant and unfair; good and evil are not always easy to differentiate. The terms can be meaningless,' said Ashurek.

Estarinel stared at him, his normally gentle eyes glittering. 'For once I think I agree with you. Don't mistake me, I still intend to save Forluin. Nothing else matters now.'

There was tension between them, like a shell of black glass which was vibrating under such incredible pressure that it must surely fracture and implode, revealing what lay beyond: a writhing grey sky which was at the same time the Serpent M'gulfn, dwarfing the Earth with its unassailable, heartless omnipotence. It was oblivious to them, yet at the same time it seemed to mock them, its laughter utterly devoid of humour, vast and diabolic. Its insanity enclosed them like a prison of wire and thorns, binding them helpless, terrified and humiliated before it. And they saw a bird fall from the sky, dead, like a tiny black cinder.

Estarinel closed his hand over the top of the Silver Staff, willing it to reassure him. But the confidence and wild joy with which it had first filled him were gone. Perhaps they had just been illusions within the Guardians' domain. Gradually the vision faded. He could hear the horses grazing, the fire crackling, leaves stirring in a gust of wind . . . even a mouse running through the undergrowth. The moment was vivid and fragile. Then the faint, musty stench of the Serpent's creatures came to him and in his mind he was suddenly running and running under the powerful delusion that escape was possible – only to find that he was running towards Falin's house, and the Worm was in front of him, lying on the ruins, staring at him—

'So, Eldor said that the Serpent would not know about the Silver Staff at once,' Ashurek said, breaking his reverie. 'But now the thing is actually on Earth, how soon will M'gulfn realise? Medrian?'

Medrian wondered how to answer. M'gulfn need never know, as long as she could mask the knowledge within her own mind. But she could not tell Ashurek that, and at the same time she could hear the Serpent whispering, insistently,

*There is something that I must know you must tell me what it
is you must you will . . .*

'It is my guess,' she said carefully, 'that the Worm will not
know until we are close enough for it to sense it.'

'How close is that?'

'I don't know. Perhaps the weapon protects itself.'

'And what will happen when the Serpent does know?'

'It will be frightened. Very angry. It will do its best to
destroy us and it will probably succeed. This speculation is
pointless, Ashurek.'

'Aye,' he agreed, sighing. And now he began to see the
Quest even more clearly. Surely all that was required was
for the Staff to touch the Serpent. All they had to do was
stay alive until they reached M'gulfn, or, better still, it came
looking for them; it did not matter if it attacked them – as
long as Staff and Serpent met – because they were all going
to perish anyway.

Doubts began to assail him. He was hiding this knowledge
from the others. He had withheld certain truths from his
family in the past, thinking to protect them, and they had all
died as a result. Perhaps there was another way . . .

No. As Meshurek and Karadrek had had to die, so must
the Worm – whatever the cost. Sometimes the need for the
destruction of evil outweighed the desirability of sparing
what was good.

And yet . . .

He wrapped himself in his cloak, willing sleep to obliterate
these black thoughts from his mind. Calorn also curled up
and was asleep in minutes. She had her worries, but knew
they were as nothing compared with her companions'
troubles. It moved her unbearably to see how haunted each
of them was. She welcomed somnolence.

Although they were safe within the circle of Setrel's powder, they still had a watch rota and Medrian was keeping the
first vigil.

'Why don't you go to sleep?' she said to Estarinel, who
was still sitting up and looking abstractedly into the fire. The
desire to be free of the Worm, free to communicate with

246

him, was intense; it weakened her in a way she could ill afford. She added in the same cold, flat tone, 'You look exhausted. Are you all right?'

'Yes, of course,' he murmured. His longing just to hold her, to share her misery even if he could not alleviate it, was so extreme as to be painful. He found it ever more difficult to watch her struggling alone. Gently, he said, 'Medrian, we have a weapon now. Does it give you no hope at all?'

Her reaction was unexpected. She visibly recoiled and a deadly expression came over her face.

'Don't speak of it!' she hissed. She was trembling and looked so stricken that he made to get up and go to her, but within a few seconds she had regained her composure. She held out a hand as if unconsciously warning him not to come any closer, and said calmly, 'Estarinel, I beg of you never to speak of the – the weapon to me. I don't want to hear mention of it and I especially do not want to see it. Is that clear?'

'Yes,' he replied, knowing better than to ask why. He stood up and went over to Shaell, thinking, I can do nothing to help her; I must think only of Forluin. He stroked the satiny neck of his horse and the great head with its bold and kindly eye. This was the one creature that had seemed sane and real to him in the worst moments of the Quest. All the gentility, faithfulness and love that were missing from the world – everything that he was fighting to save – seemed to be embodied in Shaell. And he thought, I must help her. To lose her would be a loss beyond bearing. Then he lay down beside the fire and went straight to sleep, too exhausted to dream.

Morning came, and they were all ready to commence their journey. The remains of the fire had been obliterated, their packs shouldered, and there was nothing else to do but say goodbye to Calorn.

There had been some discussion about the horses, but eventually it was concluded that they could only ride so far

North; sooner or later they would have to abandon the animals somewhere on the cold Tundra. This seemed an unnecessary cruelty when the three travellers could manage quite adequately – if more slowly – on foot, so it had been agreed that Calorn would take the horses aboard *The Star of Filmoriel*, and thence back to the Blue Plane. Estarinel in particular was adamant that he did not want his stallion to undergo any further hardship. Ashurek eventually conceded that Vixata was rather old to endure the cold weather of the North.

There was now only one way for them to reach the Arctic, which was to plod Northwards across the vast Tundra until it joined the frozen Arctic ocean. It was a long and daunting journey, but it had to be faced. Even the H'tebhmellians had only limited means of controlling the Entrance Points which might otherwise have shortened the way. They had compasses and maps, and Ashurek had planned a route, although he feared the maps were too inaccurate to be of any real value. They would have to take the country as they found it.

'My task to help you find the Staff is over, so I must leave you,' Calorn said with a cheerfulness she did not feel. 'I don't know what to say. It seems fatuous to wish you "good luck" – but I do, anyway. And I hope I see you again.' She clasped Medrian's hand, and there was a tenuous comradeship between them, tempered by Medrian's coldness and Calorn's mixed sorrow for her and fear of her. Then she went to shake hands with Estarinel and found herself embracing him with tears in her eyes.

'I'm going to miss you,' he said.

'Please take care of yourself,' was all she managed in response. He had changed even in the short time she had known him; she was still afraid that he was in danger of being destroyed by everything he had endured, and the feeling made her want to weep. She pulled abruptly away from him and went up to Ashurek.

The Gorethrian looked at her for some time without speaking. Then he placed his hands on her shoulders and kissed her forehead, a Gorethrian gesture of love and respect that he had not bestowed on anyone for years.

'I wish to thank you for your steadfastness in the Dark Regions. Even though we did not succeed, it wasn't for want of courage on your part.'

Calorn bit her lip and said, very softly so that only he could hear, 'I have something to confess. I deluded myself into believing that I really wanted to come with you to the end of the Quest, if only you would permit me. Now I realise that I cannot – I dare not. It is very hard to discover that you are not as brave as you thought you were.' She did not add that it was Medrian who had inspired this dread in her.

'Calorn, you must not doubt your courage; it is not bravery that's required on this Quest. It is desperation. There is one simple reason why you cannot come with us, which is that you do not share our despair.'

'Yes. I appreciate that,' she acquiesced.

'Go back to the Blue Plane with Neyrwin. If you can, return to your own world.'

'I could not do that! The Lady of H'tebhmella may still need my services,' she exclaimed. Then her expression changed. 'Wait . . . this is a warning, isn't it? That even the Blue Plane may not be safe?'

'Who knows? It is only conjecture on my part.'

'Well, I am not yet so devoid of nerve that I would put my own safety before my duty! But I will tell the Lady all that Eldor said to Estarinel. She may see a meaning in it that we can't perceive.'

Ashurek looked at her a moment longer; then he took his hands from her shoulders and said, 'Farewell, Calorn.'

She forced a smile onto her clear, valiant face. 'Fare you well, all of you. I will see you again.' She gave special emphasis to the last words and then she turned away and vaulted onto Taery Jasmena's back. She gathered up the reins of the other two horses, gave a brief, fierce salute with a clenched fist, and turned to ride away into the forest.

They watched her disappearing through the trees, an upright, cloaked figure, her long hair glowing copper-red in the translucent early light. On one side of the blue-green palfrey Estarinel's noble brown stallion walked sedately, and on the other side Vixata danced along with her head high, shards of golden fire flying from her mane. Presently they were out of sight.

Then it seemed that all warmth, colour and life had left with Calorn and the horses; Medrian, Ashurek and Estarinel each felt a discomforting sense of emptiness. They were together, yet each of them was alone. It was as if they were suspended in a hostile vacuum, black and white and utterly cold, like the pitiless depths of space. But there was also a clearness in the feeling, the sense of a new beginning.

'Now,' said Ashurek with uncanny eagerness, 'now the Quest of the Serpent truly begins.'

They walked through the forest for a day before it gave way to a terrain of folded hills. The trees washed between the ridges in long fingers of shadow, so that when they had climbed a good way and looked back, the forest resembled a still, grey tarn in the distance. Silver-green grass spilled over the uplands, constantly ruffled by the wind so that gleaming argent snakes appeared to glide and slither over the ridges. The sky was a clear, pale blue with layers of cloud drifting along the horizon, soaking up an aureate glow as the sun set. At intervals throughout each day swollen grey clouds edged with white tore across the sky, melding into a grim, thunderous mass. Then the companions would glance apprehensively skywards, fearing Serpent-sent storms. But the clouds always broke apart like scum on clear water and dispersed in trailing strands, precipitating nothing worse than a few drops of rain.

The ground had been forced up and folded into tortuous ripples across which there was no easy path. The ridges were not too steep to be crossed on foot, but the constant toiling up one slope and down the next was tiring and monotonous. It took them three days to cross a distance that would only have taken two had it been flatter. On the fourth day they saw with relief that the ridges softened into different country ahead: undulating grasslands sweeping towards a chain of hills that lay along the horizon like sleeping turtles, scaled with celadon and amber. They would be walking uphill, but at least the incline was steady.

By the fifth day they were amid the hills, plodding on at a steady pace which enabled them to cover at least ten leagues a day. Sometimes there were great outcrops of fuscous granite to scramble over. But mostly they walked on star-shaped, springy tufts of pale grass, while around them lay drifts of rust-coloured bracken. Here and there were clumps of tall evergreens crowned with clouds of dark needles. There was no shortage of small game to sustain them on their way, and often they found bushes bearing plump nuts or dark, sweet berries, growing alongside running water. But they saw no signs of human habitation; the North of Tearn (perhaps with Gastada's help) had long been thinly populated.

It was over sixty days since they had first met and set out from the House of Rede – although it seemed much longer, their experiences having made time seem confused and paradoxical, as in a dream. At the South Pole it had been the beginning of the dark season; by now Dritha would be experiencing the depths of lightless winter. But here, in the North, it was late summer. The further they went, the longer the sun would hang above the horizon like a basket of fire, eventually not setting at all. But one thing Ashurek dreaded was that if anything should delay them – which, knowing the M'gulfn's wiles, seemed inevitable – the light season would slip by them and they would have to confront the Serpent in darkness.

The pockets of trees became more frequent, eventually running together, like tributaries flowing into a lake, to form a great forest within a valley. The trees were widely spaced and lofty, their straight red-brown trunks soaring for hundreds of feet up to a remote ceiling of smoky-grey foliage. Through it the sky gleamed like a mosaic. The floor was carpeted with tawny needles from which a sharp fragrance broke at every footfall. And in the distant tree-tops they could hear unseen birds calling to each other, their peculiar keening, ponderous squawks echoing like the cries of the bereaved.

Estarinel, Medrian and Ashurek traversed the forest for several days. The going was easy, and there was plenty of timber from which they could make a fire each night. They always kept a watch rota. Although they no longer had Setrel's sorcerous powder, they were well armed now – but nothing worse than a fox and a few squirrels came to trouble them. Only the haunting bird-cries made them wish they were out of the otherwise friendly forest. At first merely weird, presently the desolate calls began to scour their nerves, so that they were always waiting with apprehension for the next. Each sounded more like a wail of pain than the last, harsh and dissonant with a heart-chilling falling note at the end . . .

When at last they saw the end of the forest ahead, they lost their forbearance and completed the last half-mile at a run. With overwhelming relief they burst out of the trees and gained the clear country ahead. But Ashurek, ever cautious, drew his sword at once and said, 'If the Serpent meant to hound us out of that forest, it has succeeded; we'd better be alert for any trap it may have set us out here.'

'Or perhaps we are all suffering from over-active imaginations,' Medrian said tersely. 'Not all dubious creatures, birds or otherwise, are the Serpent's personal property.'

'Yet,' said Ashurek.

But nothing sinister awaited them, only more of the undulating wolds, clad in crisp bracken and pale green grass. They walked on, the days differentiated by the changing aspects of the country around them, the rising and falling of hills and the ever-metamorphosing sky.

The weather was very changeable: at times the sky was a thin, pale blue, while the sun radiated enough summery heat to make travelling uncomfortable. At others a wild, rainy wind blew from the North, carrying the distant taste of imminent winter.

Sometimes Estarinel felt caught up by the sky, as if he was

252

hypnotised, oblivious to his companions and even to the rhythm of his own feet on the ground. The clouds drifted in an endless dance across the heavens, now moving as softly as docile white mares, now racing along on the wind like taut, blue-black sails – like ships in another, unimaginably vast dimension. Then, again, they would be oyster-grey, dense and utterly still, until a stormy silver-gold light began to infiltrate them, like branching veins in negative. Then the clouds would soften, like clots of cream, to let diaphanous nets of light fall onto the horizon. And as the sun set the stratus would scatter and stream out in all directions, now gold-edged purple against the hyaline, rose-and-amethyst sky. And Estarinel had the illusion that the clouds were about to bear him with them to some wild, mysterious other-world, that nothing else mattered or even existed – that he was seeing the far side of the Blue Plane.

He would have to drag himself back to Earth at these times and force himself to concentrate on the mundane reality of the journey.

Gradually the highlands became more rugged. The tall evergreens grew everywhere – albeit on a small scale compared to the great forest – and the grass grew even sparser and more wiry. Jagged layers of dull, brownish rock thrust through the topsoil, jutted intimidatingly out of hillsides. Ahead they could see a line of crags silhouetted against the sky. Often now they had to climb rather than walk; Ashurek had long ago given up on the map, which had nowhere near enough detail to guide them round natural obstacles and dangers.

They crossed a flat, stony gorge with trees leaning like gnarled goblins out of the ragged walls on either side. They paused to drink and fill their leather flasks from the ice-cold, foaming stream, jumped it at its narrowest point, and climbed up the far side. Now the line of crags confronted them like a wall stretching from West to East; to proceed North they faced a long and hard climb.

It took them two days to ascend the worst of the scar.

Nowhere was it utterly sheer or impassable, but it was an exhausting climb, dangerous at times. They felt they had been a lifetime on the mottled, damp rock, scrambling for footholds with shale sliding away beneath their feet, the unforgiving ridges of rock cold and gritty under their spasmed fingers. They spent one night sheltered in a cleft while the wind screamed through the crags like a banshee. On the second night they hauled themselves onto the top of the scar, bruised, sore and gasping for breath.

Before them, shining coldly under the light of two opalescent moons, lay an unwelcoming vista of diorite. They camped under a tor, some ill-nourished conifers to their right providing enough fuel for a small fire. They sat round it, willing its meagre heat to ease the aching of their limbs. If any of them spoke, it was only to discuss the practicalities of the journey; it seemed that no amount of travelling could lessen the distance between them.

Noting the grim faces of his companions, Estarinel thought, 'If we each have so little hope, why are we carrying on?' But he did not care to answer the question; he simply made himself as comfortable as he could on the rock and went to sleep. Analysis only caused him pain, and there was a limit to how much anyone could suffer before the mind began to defend itself. At present he felt numb, as though there was a lump of granite lodged somewhere between his throat and his heart. He had experienced this numbness before, after the Serpent's initial attack on Forluin. It had stayed with him throughout much of the voyage from Forluin to the House of Rede. He dreamed about that voyage now: he was on a ship with Falin, Arlena, Edrien and Luatha, seeing their faces before him as clearly as if they were really there. In the dream they were laughing and merry as if the attack had never happened; their being in mid-ocean seemed without logic. But Estarinel felt that they had lost Medrian somewhere along the way, and was pleading with them to turn the ship round and look for her, but the others only continued to smile as if they had not heard him. Frantic, he tried to say, 'We must go back and find her; if I don't find

254

her, you will all die.' But in the way of nightmares, he could not speak.

Ashurek, meanwhile, kept the first watch. He studied the vista before him, an expanse of pale rock flecked with mica and quartz which glistened with a greenish cast in the moonlight. It was scored and seamed by the weather, stepped into many different levels, and littered with tumbled rocks. Here and there tors rose in improbable, top-heavy shapes, which gave a ghostly voice to every breath of wind. In the distance he could see the glitter of porphyritic crystal.

He looked up at the two milk-white moons cruising impassively through swift-moving wisps of cloud. Shapes were moving across them: first in ones and twos, then in whole flocks, flying creatures were streaming Northwards across the sky. They were just tiny silhouettes – oddly primeval in shape, though that may have been a trick of the light – so he had no way of judging how big they were. They went by in silence, eventually trailing off to a few stragglers. Ashurek found his hand resting without reason on his sword hilt, as his eyes followed the last of them towards the skyline.

A chill, rainy morning came and they went on. Medrian walked ahead of the others, her face set against the North wind, as intransigent as the visage of a statue chiselled from quartz. She trod surefootedly over the rough surface, leaping cracks or scaling great blocks of the greenish diorite as lightly as if she was really on another plane. It was as though she was running away from something and towards it at the same time, which, in a way, she was.

Great nodules of white and purple crystal became ever more frequent along their way, while the rock changed imperceptibly from green-grey to shining black. Another day's travel brought them to a river. Long before they reached it, they could hear it rushing volubly along its course. The sun came out as they slithered over the black basalt and came in sight of a torrent some thirty yards wide, scintillating like a liquid aquamarine as it raced down a series of rapids. The far bank gleamed like jet and was clad in ebony trees

255

against which the blue-green water and diamond-white foam were the more startling.

'We could waste days trying to make a detour round this,' said Ashurek, having to raise his voice to be heard. 'I suggest we find a way across.'

The thunderous current looked forbidding and impassable. They scouted along the bank and came to a great step where the torrent – running from East to West – leapt the edge in spirals of liquid glass to crash into a haze of vapour some twenty feet below them. Just before the lip of the waterfall the water pooled and slowed a little, and there were rocks shining just below the surface.

'We can wade it here,' Ashurek said, sounding so adamant that Estarinel decided not to voice his doubts. They each removed their boots and cloaks to give them more freedom of movement, rolling them and strapping them onto their packs.

Estarinel went first, lowering himself down the slippy bank into the water. It surged around his knees, ice-cold, its muscular force almost overbalancing him. Cautiously, he edged out onto the lip of the fall. Once he had got used to the current and learned to lean into it, it was not so bad. He glanced down at the water flowing glassily over his feet as he slowly felt his way from one rock to the next. He was conscious of the cloud of spray on his left, could feel the moisture on his face, but he did not look over the edge.

Behind him came Medrian, wading with steady, resolute strides, and then Ashurek.

Ashurek was half-way across when he saw Estarinel clamber out on the far bank, dripping and visibly exhausted. The first half was not so hard, but after that the freezing water and the exertion of keeping a foothold against the current began to take their toll. Battling against the tremor in his limbs, Ashurek went determinedly on.

Suddenly Medrian came to a standstill in front of him. He caught her up and shouted, 'In the name of all the demons, don't stop! Take my arm if you must, but keep going.'

She did not reply, but turned slowly, with the ease of a joint being wrenched from its socket, to confront him.

'What—' Ashurek began, but shock left the words in his throat. Her face. He had seen her look ill before, but now her face was exactly like that of a corpse. The skin was like discoloured ivory, glowing with a faint acid light, and her eyes had a cyan glaze. Her mouth was open as if in a silent groan and now her hands were coming at him, long and white and gnarled like a bird's talons.

She was trying to push him over the edge of the waterfall. His feet slid on the rock as he fought desperately to retain his balance, conscious of the drop behind him, the strong yearning of the current to bear him over and fling him onto the rocks below. He seized Medrian's arms above the elbow and grappled with her, as much to save her as himself.

Estarinel saw what was happening from the bank, and struck out into the water again, concerned and puzzled.

There was something inhuman in the strength with which Medrian doggedly resisted Ashurek, edging him towards the drop. He felt himself weakened by the kind of revulsion with which the Shana filled him, so that he was gasping for breath, braced for the plunge which now seemed inevitable.

When she suddenly released him, he nearly fell anyway, from surprise. Her face lost the sick light, her eyes closed, her hands fell limply to her sides. He thought she was about to faint (and ever afterwards wondered if he would have bothered to save her if she had) but she did not. She turned and marched, like a clockwork figure, along the lip. Estarinel came out to meet her and guide her to the bank, although she hardly seemed to need or even notice his help.

By the time Ashurek had dragged himself onto the dark, faceted basalt, shivering and cursing, Estarinel was there alone.

'Where is she?' Ashurek demanded. Estarinel thought he had seen him look angry before, and now realised he had not.

'She ran past me into the trees, I couldn't stop her.'

257

Ashurek dragged his boots onto his wet feet and strode off into the carbon-black forest. Estarinel hurried to catch up with him.

'Ashurek, I couldn't make out what was happening,' he said. 'I thought at first she'd got into difficulties and you were trying to help her, but . . .'

'It did not look quite so innocent, I suppose,' said Ashurek, looking right and left through the trees as he walked purposefully on. 'She was trying to kill me.'

'What?'

'I repeat, her intention was to push me over the waterfall and so kill me. She nearly succeeded.'

'But you must be mistaken!' Estarinel exclaimed.

Ashurek stopped and faced him, his verdant eyes blazing, his tone as controlled and menacing as a surgical instrument. 'That is one mistake no one, not even you, could have made. If you had seen her face – it was not her own. It was demonic.'

'But why should she want to kill you?'

'Why has she waited so long to try, is a more pertinent question,' said Ashurek, striding on again. 'I should have known.'

'You don't still believe that she hates you, surely?'

'I explained to you, a long time ago, about Gorethria and Alaak. Such deep-rooted loathing may be suppressed for a time, but never lost. Don't misunderstand, I don't resent her hatred. I think it is perfectly natural and I don't hold her to blame in the slightest degree. But I think it is only part of something much worse. She cannot be permitted to jeopardise the Quest.'

'What do you mean to do?' said Estarinel, his voice apprehensive and guarded. He could not allow any harm to come to Medrian.

'I don't know. Talk to her,' Ashurek said ominously, 'for a start. I've suffered her deceptions and her precious silence for long enough. Cast your mind back. Remember when *The Star of Filmoriel* was being carried towards the Roseate Fire? The sea-horses were just starting to pull us clear. Medrian promptly jumped into the sea and unharnessed them, so that we were conveniently swept onto the White Plane.'

'A misjudgement . . .'

'You think so? And what of the time she lured us from the cover of a forest so that Gastada's crows could get at us?'

'Neither of us were forced to follow her,' Estarinel said stubbornly.

'Then perhaps you'll have a simple explanation of how it was possible for her to be stabbed in the neck, and her horse to die instead. Or how she dismissed the demon Siregh-Ma, apparently just by muttering at it? Or how she knows so much about the psychology of the Serpent? Or why she refuses to say a word about herself?'

'If you're implying that she's in league with the Serpent— By the Lady, that's an appalling accusation!'

'Yes, it is. Well, what other answer do you have?'

'But you're remembering isolated incidents, forgetting all the rest of the time when she worked with us!'

'You have a point,' said the Gorethrian drily. 'M'gulfn must have slipped up in sending an only partially adept dissembler.'

Now Estarinel began to feel angry. 'When she dismissed that demon – however she did it – she saved us from it! You can't have forgotten how horribly Gastada tortured her – the Serpent would not do that to one of its own.'

'You're wrong there. It treats its friends as nicely as its enemies.'

'Then you should feel sorry for her,' Estarinel said sharply, and all at once Ashurek's expression changed from anger to a distant, unreadable kind of bitterness.

'In a way, I do,' he replied quietly. 'But that is no reason for risking the Quest.'

Estarinel was remembering the times Medrian had obliquely warned him not to put implicit trust in her. 'You may be most cruelly betrayed,' she had said. And, 'Half of me wants the Serpent destroyed, but half of me is in its

259

power.' But he was not about to add weight to Ashurek's case by repeating these chilling words.

He said, 'She was different in Forluin. Completely different. She . . . Ashurek, she has no loyalty to M'gulfn. I would stake my life on it.'

'It is possible to work for a cause without feeling loyalty to it. Can you also swear that you believe she has no connection with the Serpent whatever?'

Estarinel was silent. Then he shook his head. He said, 'But surely the Lady of H'tebhmella would not have let her come, if her presence really did put the Quest in danger?'

'How do we know? The Grey Ones lied to the H'tebhmellians. Who knows what other lies have been told? There may be no limit to it . . . Don't you remember how vaguely the Lady answered certain very specific questions? Perhaps she had not the gall to actually lie, but truths have been hidden from us, nevertheless.'

They saw Medrian ahead, standing by a tree. She had put her cloak and her boots back on and appeared to be waiting for them, her head bowed and her arms clasped across her stomach.

'Don't be harsh with her, Ashurek,' Estarinel said.

'I will do whatever the continuance of the Quest requires,' was the unbending, metallic response.

Thousands of miles away, at the Southernmost tip of Morrenland, Benra was running – staggering, rather – along a cliff-top. Benra was a neman; a human of a third, asexual gender which sometimes occurred in Northern Tearn. The neman was close on seven feet tall and from its shoulders two pairs of arms sprouted, one above the other. Its skin and hair were the same shade of gleaming golden-bronze, and it was naked except for straps that held its sword, shield, axe and knife. Normally there was a kind of beauty in Benra's sombre features and its symmetrical, long-limbed form, but now its face was streaked with dirt and blood, and it was

260

sprinting back and forth along the cliff-edge like a gangling marionette.

'What ails you, good sir?' said a voice. The neman turned, gasping raggedly through contorted lips, to see an old man, clad in a soiled cream-coloured robe. His skin was a dull yellow, like old brass, and he was almost bald but for a stiff wisp of grey hair. His eyes were as pale as milk.

'Ships – why are there no ships?' demanded Benra, waving a hand at the ocean below the chalk cliff.

'Alas, they have all gone,' said the old man impassively.

'They can't have done! I must get to the House of Rede!'

'Good sir, you sound demented. Be calm, I pray you. Every ship that was seaworthy has already departed for the House of Rede.'

'This cannot be – I must fulfil my mission!'

'I also wished to go to the House of Rede, but I could not, because no one asked me to go with them. Tell me, friend, if you were to find a way there, would you take me with you?'

'Yes, yes, of course,' Benra muttered abstractedly. 'What are you babbling about – how can we get there without a ship?'

'There might be a way, if you will only tell me why you need to go there.'

'What?' Perhaps the old man was a dotard, but the neman was too crazed with fear and desperation to care. It needed to tell someone; the words began to tumble over one another. 'I am Benra, formerly of Sphraina, now in the service of Setrel, the village Elder of Morthemcote in Excarith. Excarith was beset by an army of walking corpses, but Ashurek of Gorethria came to our aid and vanquished them – but then he and his two companions vanished – so Setrel sent me South to tell Eldor that Ashurek and the others were lost, and to relate the terrible things that had happened to Excarith, and whatever else I saw on my way—'

'Now who's babbling?' muttered the old man with a gap-toothed grin, but Benra paid no heed.

'– and on my way here I have seen terrible things, I have

261

seen people stricken with a plague but walking about, mad with fever – this in Belhadra – complaining that the great Sorceress to whom they paid tribute had left them to the mercy of the Worm, and I saw people bent in postures of obscene worship of the Worm, trying to appease it in their terror. When they tried to make me join them I ran, but then I was trapped for three days in a fell storm, which spat red lightning at me whenever I tried to emerge from my shelter. When it abated and I came out, there were creatures of the Worm roaming the lands; I was attacked by some vile thing, like a great bald dog with too many mouths. I slew it, but there were more, things that seemed to have heaved themselves up from the sea, things that were ill mockeries of true animals . . . and I have run the rest of the way, all through Tearn to Morrenland, forgetting to eat and sleep. But the worst thing—' Benra gripped the old man's arm, eyes wild. 'The most horrible thing is that a demon has been following me.'

'A demon?' said the old man as if he thought Benra was mad.

'You don't believe me? You've never seen one, I can tell.'

'No, I've never *seen* one.'

'They – they pretend a human form, but they crackle with a silver light, like lightning. Their mouths are red, their eyes shine like coins. And they – they – do you not know how it is never to have feared anything in particular, and then to find Fear standing at your side, laughing, giggling at you? It is not the fear of death, or even of pain . . . but fear of Fear itself. I must get to the House of Rede before it catches up with me.'

Benra's face was blanched under the golden tint of its skin, and now it was gripping the old man, involuntarily, with three of its four hands.

'You're a neman!' The old man exclaimed. The surprise and disgust in his voice seemed to hit Benra like a whiplash.

'Yes,' said Benra, withdrawing its hands. 'I thought you had noticed.'

'No. I'm blind, you see.'

'And I did not perceive it, any more than I recognised you as a Sphrainian,' Benra said, a long-buried bitterness surfacing in its voice. 'I must apologise.'

'What are you then, a mercenary?'

'Yes. In Excarith's pay, as I said. An exile, like my siblings.' The old man was backing away, and the expression of disdain on his face began to anger Benra beyond reason. Benra should have realised by the colour of his skin (although faded with age) and the familiar accent, that the old man was a Sphrainian. But the neman had been too distressed to notice.

In Sphraina, the third sex was regarded with hatred and suspicion. Every woman with child dreaded to bear one, and if she did it would be left out to die. But few actually did die, because they were hardy, and there were groups of nemen who would take in and raise the abandoned ones. Most nemen chose self-inflicted exile rather than remain within a society that hated them, and because they were tall and strong and four-armed, most became mercenaries. As such they ceased to be despised and became respected as formidable fighters, highly valued by their paymasters.

But confronted with the scorn of this Sphrainian man, frail and rheumy though he was, Benra felt the old humiliations of its childhood reawaken.

'I suppose now that you know what I am, you will refuse to travel with me anyway,' it said.

'I want to go to the House of Rede. I'm afraid we must travel together, albeit under sufferance,' said the man with exaggerated distaste in his voice.

'So here we stand, supposedly countrymen, on a white cliff almost on the edge of the world, with drooling beasts and demons closing in on us, from which the rest of the world has fled already, leaving us trapped by a shipless ocean,' Benra exclaimed furiously, 'and still you can think only of the disgust you feel for nemen?'

'I can't help it. I'm old, I can't change my ways. No, don't touch me!' The man cringed as Benra gripped his shoulders and arms with all four hands.

'This world is decaying before our eyes! We might be the last two people left alive! Yet still you cling to the old, irrational hatreds!'

'You're out of your mind! Don't hurt me—'

'Yes, I am out of my mind. I'd like to see the human who can be chased by a demon and stay sane. I am human, you see, just like you, born of a man and woman as you were.'

The old man was shaking in Benra's hands as if racked by a convulsion. No, he was laughing. Astonished, Benra stared into the grinning red mouth, suddenly aware – too late – that the old man was changing. Before Benra's eyes the robe fell away like wet paper and the yellow skin split and curled back from the man's torso like a rind. Benra recoiled, stunned and nauseated. Wet gleams of silver showed through the cracks, like the new skin of a snake as it discards its old one. Gradually the moist figure eased out of the rind and there stood the demon – the one Benra had been fleeing – glistening argent, a laugh hissing from its blood-red mouth. The skin of the old man lay on the ground in a heap of leathery flesh, the face, horribly, still intact.

'I am Ahag-Ga,' said the demon.

'Why are you chasing me?' stammered Benra, retaining a trace of oddly cold reason through the enveloping fear. 'Why?'

'Why not?' the Shanin leered.

'I wish you would kill me quickly, and not torment me,' Benra said. 'What do you want?'

'I have what I want, my dear neman,' Ahag-Ga replied. 'Someone commissioned me to go to the House of Rede. Alas, due to the peculiar laws governing my actions, I cannot go there unless I am legitimately invited by a human.'

'And I—'

'Yes, while I was disguised as the old man, you said you would take me with you! By the way, your description of me was very pretty. I am flattered. "Fear of Fear"! Very eloquent.'

'Oh, Setrel, forgive me,' Benra groaned, falling to its knees, feeling a terrible pressure like a metal vice on its head.

'Demon, tell me, why did you pretend to be a Sphrainian?'

'Oh, you were so touchy, I simply could not resist baiting you. It was a rare delight,' said Ahag-Ga. 'Well, I am sorry that your errand for Setrel has been such a waste of time – for you, I mean, not for me. Incidentally, Ashurek is not lost. Would that he were. I have particular reason to dislike him. Still, that doesn't concern you any longer. Stand up, my dear neman.'

Benra did so, now glassy-eyed and almost completely in the Shanin's power.

'It is time to go to the House of Rede. Thank you for asking.'

'We still have no ship,' Benra said woodenly.

'That's all right. I don't need one. All I require is you.'

'I don't want to serve you. I would rather die,' the neman whispered.

'Would you? Oh, all right.' The demon shrugged, then in a swift movement it seized Benra's shoulder with one hand, and with the other rent the neman's belly so that the vitals spilled out in a red gush.

A few minutes later the demon, Ahag-Ga, was trotting towards the ocean, wearing the guise of Benra.

11

The Mathematician

This has gone too far, my Medrian, said the Serpent.

'Let me alone. Don't speak to me. You will never weaken me like that again,' she replied, hugging herself against the mole-black, icy pain in her head.

But I will. Like that and worse. Again and again until you surrender. Again and again until the two humans die by your own hand. And until you tell me about the weapon, and until you give up this pitiful Quest. Again and again and again and . . .

'No. Damn you,' she whispered.

You are becoming very weak. There is a limit even to your stubbornness, my Medrian, and you know that in only a short time you will be able to tolerate this pain no longer. Accept this.

'No,' she croaked. But she knew that M'gulfn was right. Her dreadful battle against it had continued without relief since the night of the bears, all across the hills and through the forests and over the crags and the rock-bed and the river . . . and all the time she had deluded herself that she had it in check.

Ever since she had first learnt to suppress M'gulfn, when she was very young, she had had confidence in that control. She had never considered that the Serpent could so determinedly begin to erode it, chipping at her wall of ice and iron day after day until it was hardly stronger than a sheet of frost about to shatter.

Perhaps M'gulfn had never been this afraid before.

She had put absolute faith in her ability to operate independently of the Worm. Now the unthinkable was in view: her imminent capitulation. Her faith in herself was gone. She had turned with the Serpent raging in her and tried to push Ashurek to his death. He had seen the corpse-light in her face. She had nothing left to fight with.

This pain, this humiliation, said the Serpent as if it was reading her thoughts – had she even lost that now? – *are the inevitable results of trying to fight me. You have chosen a hard way to learn this. Only let me into your heart, and you will find release.* Its thoughts were blunt, almost soothing.

'Release! Just as all your other hosts found it?' she replied. 'Their agony was worse than mine, because they found no way to resist it! You think, having come this far, I would condemn generations more to this unspeakable abuse?'

You will always be my favourite, the Serpent mused, like a benevolent old man misunderstanding what was being said to him. But it understood well enough. It was mocking her.

Then Medrian made a decision, and managed to stop herself running. Calmly, despite her violent trembling, she put her boots and cloak back on and ran her fingers through her hair to tidy it. And she stood and waited until she saw Ashurek and Estarinel coming through the trees.

She was going to tell them everything.

It had always been her intention to wait until the very end of the Quest, but that was no longer possible. At least now they would understand her strange behaviour and her purpose. And then, even if the Serpent conquered her completely, they would understand what was happening, and they would be able to bind her and take her with them like a prisoner, and so defend themselves from its power in her.

'Medrian!' Estarinel called as he reached her. 'Are you all right?'

'I'm sure she is more than all right,' said Ashurek brusquely, laying a long-fingered, dark hand on her shoulder. His gaze knifed into her, but she did not look up at him. Estarinel's heart went out to her; he had never seen her look more alone. 'Medrian, do you deny that you made a fair attempt to murder me just now?'

267

'No,' she muttered.

'Might we be permitted to hear some sort of explanation?'

Medrian, as Ashurek had expected, remained silent. 'Listen to me,' he went on, softly menacing, 'we have borne with your silence thus far, just as you requested when we first met. That was one thing. But attempts to sabotage the Quest are quite another; you've no right to expect them to go unremarked. Indeed, you have forfeited your right to keep your motives secret. Do I make myself clear?'

She nodded. Her lips parted and she drew in an uneven breath.

'Well?'

'Ashurek—' Estarinel began, unable to forget how Medrian had almost implored him not to question her, as if questions could impale her flesh like barbs, and answering would make her bleed to death from those tears. But Ashurek only waved a hand to quiet him.

'You can begin by telling us who you are.'

Her eyes flew open, agate-grey and black, rimmed with darkness.

'Yes,' she whispered, staring at him. 'I want to tell you. It was never my intention—'

No, screamed the Serpent. *You know that you are not permitted to speak of this.*

Medrian froze in mid-sentence, no breath passing through her waxen lips. Her eyes turned glassy.

'Go on,' said Ashurek, gripping her shoulder. A thin moaning noise came from her throat and she slid from his grasp and fell like a stone to the ground. At once Estarinel knelt by her and lifted her head; her eyes were wide but she was unconscious. Swiftly he removed her pack and loosened her jacket.

'Just like Skord,' Ashurek observed. 'She tried to speak, and something stopped her. Or she inflicted this trance on herself, to avoid having to explain . . .' Estarinel was cradling Medrian in his arms so that her head rested back against his shoulder. He felt how weak and rapid the pulse in her throat was.

268

'Will you pass me some water?' he said. Ashurek took a leather flask from Medrian's pack and handed it to him. Estarinel began to bathe her face.

'You were able to break through Skord's trance,' said Ashurek.

Estarinel stared at him, aghast. 'Don't even think of it!'

'But this is important, far more important than Skord. Estarinel, whatever Medrian is concealing, it is vital for us to know. You have a very particular technique of hypnotism.'

'That technique is only supposed to be used for the purpose of healing,' said Estarinel grimly. 'I should never have hypnotised Skord. It was wrong. After what happened to him, I swore I would never risk misusing the art again. Especially not on Medrian.'

'Even though the risk of not doing so may be greater?'

'No! Ashurek, I will not do it under any circumstances. Don't ask me again.'

'Very well. What do you suggest instead?'

'I suggest that you just leave her alone!' Estarinel blazed. 'I never really believed you were evil, Ashurek, but I am beginning to have my doubts.'

The Gorethrian sighed and turned away, his cloak swinging behind him. He leaned against a nearby tree and stood glaring down at Medrian, his lean arms folded.

Presently she began to recover. Her eyes fell shut and some colour came into her cheeks. Estarinel got her to drink some water, and she began to breathe evenly.

'Yes, it is cold, isn't it?' she murmured. He bent his head to hear her, but she seemed to be talking to herself. 'I am not yours, but I am hers, and the more you hate her the more she will give me healing. You have not destroyed the wall yet. It is colder than you know . . .'

She awoke with a start and looked up in confusion at Estarinel. In one sinuous movement she drew herself out of his arms and stood up.

'Now what?' said Ashurek, looking levelly at her.

'What do you mean?' she said.

269

'I hope you are not about to conveniently forget everything that has just transpired. I still require an answer.'

'Then I must disappoint you,' said Medrian curtly, picking up her pack. 'I wanted to say something, but as you have observed, I cannot.'

'In that case, don't assume that we can still risk you coming with us.'

'How do you propose to stop me?'

'I don't know,' Ashurek said. 'As you have the enviable talent of receiving fatal wounds without dying, I may have to think of something else.'

'Understand,' she said softly, lowering her eyes, 'I never had any intention of harming you. I apologise for what happened. But I must come, Ashurek. I swear that you have no hope of finishing the Quest without me.'

'And less hope of finishing it *with* you, apparently.'

'Ashurek, let her alone and let us carry on,' said Estarinel. 'We all need to eat and rest by a good fire. Let's forget all this and find somewhere to camp.'

'Very well; I will say no more about it for the time being. But I will be watching you, Medrian – and be warned, I will see this matter resolved before ever we set foot in the Arctic.'

They spent one night in the dark forest with the sound of the river, although in the distance, echoing as though they were near it in a great cave. In the morning they moved on. The forest gave way to a barren terrain of rock which changed gently from black to bitter brown to russet as they crossed it. The ground became flatter, the trees sparser and more stunted. Now the cold, which before had only come to them in biting gusts of wind, became constant and they knew that the true Tundra was not far ahead.

They marched on for several more days, during which their isolation from each other grew more acute. It was as if the air between them was threaded through with black wires of tension which both bonded them together and kept them apart. Medrian became totally withdrawn and barely spoke

270

at all to either of them. Since the return to Earth she had become so thin that it seemed impossible that she could walk such a distance every day. It was as though something had sucked from her the last remnant of the healing strength with which the Blue Plane had imbued her; the way she still carried on was unnatural. With her gaunt, white face and dark eyes, Estarinel, if he caught a sideways glimpse of her, often got the horrible impression of a walking skeleton, animated by some unknown, demonic purpose.

Almost as distressing was the way Ashurek kept her under observation, like some silent, omniscient shade disguised as a bird of prey.

Estarinel had no real fear that Ashurek actually meant to harm Medrian; but sometimes he wondered if he should be more worried. He thought he had got to know Ashurek quite well, but now he was realising that he hardly knew him at all. Perhaps he should not be so sure that the Gorethrian's behaviour would be predictable or even reliable.

Also, he could not be certain that whatever madness had induced Medrian to attempt Ashurek's murder would not possess her again. So he found himself watching them both, not with Ashurek's suspicion, but with the love he had come to feel for both of them like a perpetual cold ache in his chest. And the invisible wires thickened and tightened about them like a bizarre, meshed cage that might exist in the Dark Regions.

Sometimes, in the darkest moments of the night, Estarinel would rest his hand on top of the Silver Staff and find that it brought him a kind of peace. Its intrinsic innocence and power would flow into him so that he felt reassured, purposeful, free from doubt and pain. But the mood was transient; as soon as he stopped touching the Staff the sense of calm strength would elude him, not to be recaptured. So he viewed it as a false feeling. He could place no reliance on it, and soon came to touch the Staff as little as possible, lest it prove as treacherous and addictive as a euphoric drug.

In a cold blue morning they crossed an area of copper-coloured rock, patterned with concentric indigo circles. The terrain had a rough look, dotted with windblown trees and with grass and hardy plants growing in every crevice. The rock blended gradually to pale red as they walked, and presently the landscape through which they were travelling became unearthly. The stone beneath their feet changed to a delicate, clear pink, rising all around them in strange, lacy formations like coral. It was fascinating to look at, but hard to traverse because it yielded nothing from which they could make a fire.

After a couple of days, they began to see unusual forms of vegetation. They were huge pitcher-shaped plants, the height of a man, with gaping green mouths angled towards the sun. They had a smooth, sculptural kind of beauty. There were others like fleshy obelisks with silver-blue streamers blowing from them like a maiden's hair, making an eerie and lovely sight. Another sort lay along the ground like a flower basket, exuding a sticky substance like nectar. This attracted insects and rodents inside the plant, where they were trapped and absorbed. The pitchers, too, contained a bright yellow fluid in which lay the half-digested remains of birds and flies; and the streamers of the maidenhairs were tangled with sparrows, bats and even owls. Around the base of their stems lived armoured insects the size of lobsters, scavenging whatever bits of flesh the plants dropped.

The three travellers soon learned to keep well clear of the carnivorous flora.

The Tundra, which they had previously dreaded reaching, now seemed an enticing prospect compared with this exquisite, venomous landscape. As they went on the plants grew thicker around them, and soon the coral-pink silica was streaked with the decaying remains of ones that had died. Apparently they survived better singly. Where there were too many they seemed to spring up and fade with great rapidity.

It was on the fourth evening, just as the sun set, that they saw an end to the poisonous vegetation. Relieved, they hurried past a clump of the maidenhairs – only to find themselves on the shore of a strange lake. It was about a mile to the other shore, but on either side it stretched as far as the eye could see. However, it appeared to be only a few inches deep. A flat, sandy-gold floor gleamed just under the clear water, and dotted everywhere were clusters of cushion-shaped stones. In the distance a mist curled up from the water.

'It looks shallow,' said Estarinel. 'Can we wade it?'

'I hope so,' Ashurek replied. 'The sooner we can be away from these plants, the happier I shall be. But we must be cautious. The floor of the lake could be quicksand.' He knelt on the rock and put a hand in the water, but jerked it out at once with a curse. 'It's hot – boiling!'

Estarinel tested it himself and found that Ashurek was not exaggerating. 'It must be some sort of volcanic spring,' he said. 'Look – you can see it bubbling in places. That mist on the water must be steam.'

'Well, we can't wade it, that's certain. We'll have to find a way round. But I suggest we wait until morning now – at least this part of the shore is free of decomposing vegetation.' So they rested by the lake, although none of them slept much; the rock-cushions in the lake glowed with eerie phosphorescence, and the night seemed filled with the sighing and groaning of spectres.

Ashurek woke violently from a restless doze and sat up with the knowledge that something was wrong. Overnight more of the fleshy plants had sprung up in a half-circle round them, enclosing them at the lake's edge. The sound they had heard all night had been the creaking of their rapid growth. Even as he watched, the silver-blue streamers were curling away from the plump stems, and fluttering on the North wind, fragile and moist like the antennae of newly-emerged butterflies.

Ashurek woke Estarinel and Medrian, who looked at the throng of vegetation with alarm. They were trapped, and their only escape route now appeared to be across the boiling lake.

'Unless we can hack a way through them,' said Ashurek. They all stood up and strapped their packs on, but as Medrian

273

was tying her cloak, a streamer whipped out and clung to her hand. She did not make a sound. Worse, it seemed for a second to have paralysed her. Ashurek swiftly drew out his knife and severed the silver-blue ribbon, then prised the remaining piece off her hand. It peeled off reluctantly, leaving a line of needle-like stings in the reddened flesh.

Estarinel inspected her hand and felt her forehead on which an ice-cold sweat had broken out. He could feel her trembling.

'Don't let those streamers touch you,' she managed to say through chattering teeth. 'More than one will kill you.'

'I must get these stings out of your hand,' Estarinel said.

'Not now, there isn't time. I'm all right. All it needs is for the wind to change, and they will all blow this way – do you see?'

'She's right. And the wind is changing: it's dropped,' said Ashurek. He held up the knife, and they saw that the cutting edge had been eaten away by the acid in the plant. 'We are being driven,' he added grimly.

They were already on the very edge of the shore, and it would only take one gust from the South to sweep the venomous, stinging ribbons all around them. Ashurek said quickly, 'Our boots should protect us from the heat somewhat. Follow me.'

One stride took him into the scalding water, and the next to the nearest of the stone formations in the lake. He balanced there precariously for a moment, then took two splashing steps to the next. He gritted his teeth as the scalding heat began to penetrate his boots. Medrian and Estarinel followed.

In daylight, the stones gleamed with brilliant patterns of green and purple, magenta and blue. They protruded from the water in rounded lobes like lithops, broader at the top than at the base. When Ashurek felt their springy resilience under his feet, he realised that they were not stones at all, but living things. He hoped they were not malevolent cousins of those on land.

In the middle of the lake the water was not clear, but

swirled and bubbled like a cauldron, thick with crusts of garishly coloured bacteria. A sulphurous miasma hung over the surface, and the bed of the lake slipped and sank when they trod on it. Fortunately, the cushionlike pads grew more thickly there, so that they did not have to step in the seething water so often. Sometimes Ashurek felt himself skid on their silky, marbled surfaces. He managed to keep his feet, however; he could not afford to fall. Even Medrian, who was feeling ill from the poison in her hand, found the energy to run and leap across the morass without faltering.

The growths began to thin out, and the far shore was within reach at last. They had been crossing the springs for what seemed for ever, although it was only about twenty minutes. There was a gap between the last of the pads and the shore, and they had to splash through the water for six or seven strides before gaining solid ground at last. Once safe, the pain continued to throb through their feet and ankles like hot knives for several minutes before abating. Medrian collapsed at once, trembling convulsively.

They were on another stretch of the coral-pink rock, but there were no carnivorous succulents apparent on this side. It seemed they were out of danger for the time being, and Ashurek only hoped that there were no more volcanic springs to be negotiated. Perhaps it was his imagination, but the lithops-like growths appeared to be drifting and regrouping on the lake. He said, 'We'd better not delay here.'

Estarinel was attending to Medrian's hand, painstakingly drawing out each of the tiny stings. He dressed it with a herbal cream which he had brought from the Blue Plane, and made her drink some of the reviving H'tebhmellian wine.

'I feel better now, can we go on?' she said, although she was still shaking and her hands felt icy.

'It will take a while for the venom to leave your system, and it will make you feel worse if you try to move about,' Estarinel said. But Medrian got unsteadily to her feet.

'Ashurek is right, we should distance ourselves from this lake,' she said. 'I probably look worse than I feel.' It was pointless arguing with both of them, and it would be good to get away from the hot stench of sulphur. Estarinel packed the herbs away and the three resumed their walk over the rock.

There seemed to be no immediate menace on this side, and nothing followed them from the lake. Soon they found themselves on the beginning of the Tundra; there was grass beneath their feet and the roseate rock now showed itself only in reef-like formations breaking through the ground here and there. The country all around them was flat and featureless.

Medrian had omitted to tell them that the plant's poison had been enough to kill her. But the Serpent did not want her to die. At present its will alone was keeping her alive, as it had done on several occasions previously. However, it did not protect her from enduring the discomfort of the venom working its slow way through her body; that was another weapon which M'gulfn could use to break down her resistance. But there was still the paradox that made physical pain a two-edged sword: the Serpent liked her to suffer, but when she did it always seemed distant from her, so that she was better able to resist it. Sometimes she wondered if M'gulfn actually feared her pain.

But while her mental fight was eased, her body was being racked by intolerable discomfort. The burning of her head and the cold heaviness in her back and limbs were not eased by resting, so she thought she might as well walk, pretending as best she could that she was well.

Before long the poison clouded her mind, and she forgot how to stop walking.

She occasionally heard Estarinel, at her side, ask if she was all right or suggest that it was time they rested, but through the vague haze of her delirium he seemed unreal, like a white shadow. By rights she should be dead, or at least unable to move, and yet she trudged on like one of Gastada's re-animated corpses. She wondered if this was how it felt to die. How weird, to watch herself die and yet still be alive at the end of it, as if nothing had happened. M'gulfn's sadism was infinitely inventive, but she could not find the strength to hate it. A strange delusion took her then; the memories of other hosts came thronging back to her, and she became convinced that she was the Morrenish woman whom the Serpent had forced to walk, with broken limbs and a mortal wound in her guts, the thousands of miles from the Arctic to Morrenland. That woman's agony and humiliation were joined to her own, and somewhere she could feel the Serpent laughing at her unendurable anguish. Around her the Tundra lay like her own desolation made physical, the whole of the terrible dark future under the Worm's power reduced to a single flake of bone on which she was doomed to crawl for ever.

Come to me then, all of you. I do not fear you. If you want to come to me, do so. It will please me to observe your shame when I have stripped your arrogance from you. Don't you know I can crush you on a whim? Ah, your pride amuses me . . .

'For the Lady's sake, Medrian, will you stop?' It was Ashurek's voice and he was in front of her, physically restraining her from walking any further. 'It's nearly dark. What is the matter with you?'

She looked dazed, as if she did not know where she was. She allowed herself to be sat down by a fire that they made from scrubby, furze-like bushes, but she did not speak and, to Estarinel's increasing concern, refused to eat anything.

'The poison is doing this to her,' he said to Ashurek. 'She will burn herself out. She must be made to rest.'

'I think it's more than the poison,' Ashurek said.

That night Estarinel slept badly, and he was certain that Medrian had not slept at all. Before dawn he must have dropped off, because he woke with a sudden jolt and sat up to find that Medrian was nowhere in sight. He woke Ashurek.

'I only hope she has gone North,' the Gorethrian said drily. 'If not, we have no chance of finding her. I for one have no intention of scanning all the points of the compass for her.'

They were on the Tundra proper now. It stretched out around them in all directions, unrelieved by hills or trees, but with a stark beauty of its own. It was carpeted with tough, dark grass and emerald green moss, starred with tiny white and yellow flowers. As Estarinel and Ashurek walked, the mild wind from the South swung round to the North again, and they could taste snow on the air. They wrapped their cloaks round them and pulled on the thick gloves the H'tebhmellians had provided.

All day they walked, and were forced to stop when night fell. Estarinel was so distressed by their failure to find Medrian that he barely noticed Ashurek's own morose mood. They roasted a hare over their furze fire and then slept as best they could, waking and walking on long before dawn.

'Perhaps we have passed her in the dark,' Estarinel said.

Ashurek was intent upon the compass, a flake of clear rock crystal beneath which a shining needle floated on a silvery liquid, enclosed in gold. 'It's possible,' he said.

'Don't you care?' Estarinel exclaimed.

'Whether I care or not is not going to help us find her,' Ashurek replied. 'We cannot risk turning aside or back, it would be pointless. The important thing is that we have the Silver Staff. We must continue the Quest.'

As they went on the sky became clotted with dense iron-grey clouds and snow began to swirl around them. They could see barely a few yards ahead in the gloom. Within Estarinel rose the awful knowledge that their search for Medrian could easily prove futile. Perhaps desperation tricked his eyes into seeing what he wanted; for a moment, it seemed that the horizon was illuminated by a ghastly, stormy light against which a small figure was staggering along in silhouette.

He broke into a run, leaving Ashurek behind, calling Medrian's name. There was no reply, no sound except the mournful sighing of the wind. He felt eerily alone in the snow-filled twilight, oppressed and dwarfed by the freezing wastes that lay ahead. A horrible moment of disorientation

278

came upon him in which he did not know where he was or who he was. There was a bird fluttering and falling on a cold wind which seemed to blow right through his soul, and he was falling too, like a fleck of ash. A voice near him, yet very far away, murmured, 'You must find me. Without me you are incomplete. While I am lost, you are lost. Remember . . .' and such a profound sense of emptiness clawed at his throat that he cried out and grasped the top of the Silver Staff.

Immediately he was on firm ground again. Preternatural calmness filled him like a silver light which also flickered and played over the Tundra and the clouds, leading him on with a gentle sureness, as if the Lady of H'tebhmella herself was at his side. He was drifting over the snow-crusted turf like a mote of light, not needing to look, simply knowing exactly where—

All at once he came back to himself and nearly fell over a small, cloaked form, ice-frosted darkness like the Tundra itself.

'Ashurek! Ashurek, I've found her!' Estarinel yelled.

Medrian was lying on a bed of heather, evidently having walked and walked until she had collapsed from total exhaustion. She was unconscious and her heartbeat and breathing were erratic. Her white skin had taken on a morbid blue-grey cast and, to Estarinel's consternation, she seemed close to death.

'How fortunate,' said Ashurek without inflexion.

Estarinel made her as comfortable as he could while Ashurek gathered enough scrub for a decent fire. Medrian's breathing became steadier, but she remained unconscious. Even the breaking of certain aromatic herbs under her nose did not revive her. Estarinel took off his cloak and wrapped it over her own, holding her curled up against him so that she would take some heat from his body.

'I don't know what more to do for her,' he said, distressed. 'If only I had Lilithea's skill . . . I fear that even rest won't be enough to heal her.'

'Estarinel,' came Ashurek's voice from the other side of

the fire, thin and distant, 'we do not have time for her to rest.'

'What do you mean?'

'We cannot afford to delay waiting for her to recover. Every day we lose jeopardises the Quest. There's nothing you or I can do for her; she will have to help herself.'

Estarinel was stunned by these words, by Ashurek's stony, matter-of-fact tone. He looked up and exclaimed, 'How can you be so callous! After we've travelled all this way together – been more than companions to each other. I even thought you understood her in a way I did not. And now you are unmoved by her suffering – you can sit there and say, "Let her help herself."'

'I am not being callous,' Ashurek replied with a touch of anger. 'It's obvious to me that only she *can* help herself. I've come to understand that much about her.'

'Once, perhaps – but not now, she's so ill! Ashurek, she hasn't got the strength. It's up to us to help her.'

'I repeat, there is nothing we can do. If she does not recover, we must leave her behind.'

An incredulous silence greeted these words. Eventually Estarinel said, very quietly, 'You've gone mad. To think I refused to believe any evil of you, thinking that my own judgement was surer than hearsay. How wrong could I be! No one could speak as you are doing – no one could be so devoid of pity, and not be utterly evil.'

'You are entitled to that opinion. I never tried to make you think otherwise. But Medrian . . . let me put it this way: how would your countrymen feel if they knew you had betrayed Forluin in order to take care of one of the Serpent's own?'

'That's a despicable thing to say,' Estarinel whispered.

'Yes. I did not expect you to be overjoyed. But think on it. Remember how she was at the river? Remember our conversation?'

'I remember a good deal of unfounded speculation.'

'If you think it unfounded, you are deluding yourself. How do you think the Serpent has known every step we've taken? How has it put so many traps in our way? How will it find out about the Silver Staff and how will it eventually thwart us? Because it has sent one of its minions on this Quest. Perhaps Medrian is a glib deceiver, or perhaps she is an unwilling ally; whichever is quite unimportant. She is unquestionably in M'gulfn's power. You must see it. We cannot afford to let her betray us any further.'

'Betray us!' Estarinel cried. 'How is she going to betray us, unconscious? For the Lady's sake, Ashurek, she's dying!'

'Estarinel, did you hear what I said? One way or the other, the Quest will fail unless we leave her behind,' Ashurek responded intractably.

'Even if you're right,' the Forluinishman said softly, 'even if you are right, I still cannot leave her. By the gods! Do you think she means any less to me than Silvren means to you?'

At this Ashurek looked up, and his eyes blazed like a sudden fire shining through two verdant jewels. Estarinel saw that he had struck a chord. All at once Ashurek's cold obduracy began to fill him with dread.

'Then your love may cost us everything,' Ashurek said.

'You are wrong. You must be—'

'Strange as it may seem, I was once accused of being compassionate. I was told that it was a weakness, a killing weakness. Since then I've come to see that that is true. I always thought that the Serpent was an unintelligent beast, but if it can cause the Quest to fail through your pity for Medrian, then its devious subtlety leaves me gasping.' There was a ghoulish humour in Ashurek's voice which made Estarinel shudder. But at the same time he sounded chillingly sane. 'Listen to me. Your love for her is as hopeless as mine is for Silvren. I have had to accept that; now you must also.'

Medrian had been drifting slowly back to consciousness for several minutes and these words began to filter into her hazy mind as she lay there, lacking any power to speak or move.

'Why hopeless?' Estarinel demanded.

Ashurek paused.

'I had resolved not to say this, but as nothing else will convince you— None of us have long to live, my friend. Do

281

you think that two powers such as the Serpent and the Silver Staff can meet without causing a cataclysm? They are vast, opposing powers. When they touch, the Earth will be annihilated along with the Serpent.'

'Who told you this?'

'No one. It is the only logical end. Naturally the Guardians neglected to mention it. It is their ultimate deception.'

Recalling all that had transpired with the Grey Ones, Estarinel found himself believing this without effort. 'And I thought they had already reached their limit,' he murmured. 'There must be another answer.'

'Such as what? To let the Serpent live? Then the world would fall into its power. We might all live then, it's true. Eternal life on a world more desolate than hell! How would you like that for Forluin?'

Estarinel remembered Silvren's description of the Earth under M'gulfn's power: 'a bloated sac which can never expel its poison'. And he remembered the terrible glimpses he had had of Arlenmia's vision, figures in a frozen landscape, bent in never-ending worship of the Worm . . .

'How long have you known that the Quest would have this end?' he asked, his throat dry.

'From the moment I first saw the Silver Staff.'

'And you said nothing – and carried on – knowing this?' 'Yes.'

'And this – this is what you want, is it?' Ashurek did not reply. Realisation dawned on Estarinel. 'By the Worm, I believe it is. You would be happy to destroy everything! You don't even want to look for another way.'

'It will be a good and cleansing act.'

'Do you know that you sound like Arlenmia?' Estarinel said incredulously. 'What is this – a purging of all your crimes? Or retribution against whatever made you commit them?'

'Both,' said Ashurek with chilling thoughtfulness. 'Both. You are more perceptive than I had realised.'

'This is insane! Why must the world pay for your guilt? What about those things which are worth saving?'

'What is worth saving? Forluin? One tiny island. I thought the Worm's attack had torn away the illusion that an idyllic existence is any nation's birthright.'

'Birthright? You don't understand!' Estarinel replied furiously. 'We worked hard for what we had. We gave our love, we gave everything—'

'All the same, no thief stops to consider whether his victim worked hard for his fortune or inherited it. The world is utterly unjust, fate utterly disinterested.'

'Yes, I've learned that much, but there's no reason for us to tolerate that injustice. If something is worth fighting for, how can you so easily turn round and say the fight is too hard, so let it all perish, instead?'

'You misunderstand,' said Ashurek with a mixture of anger and pain. 'Far from it being easy, it has been a hard and bitter struggle to accept that the only answer is for the Earth to die with the Serpent. I'm not asking you to accept it, I am telling you that it is inevitable.'

'Something must have happened to make you believe this. You weren't like this before.'

'I told you: the Silver Staff.'

'No. There must have been something else,' Estarinel insisted. Ashurek remained silent. 'You were always so determined to rescue Silvren. Calorn told us what happened. Why can't you try again?'

He thought Ashurek was not going to answer. Flurries of snow blew around them, catching the firelight. Beyond that small circle of warmth all was flat, dark and desolate, as though the world had already ended. Presently the Gorethrian said, 'The Shana have corrupted Silvren. They have made her believe that she is evil. That belief has devastated her. She refused to leave the Dark Regions because she felt her presence would taint the Blue Plane and Earth – yes, I know it is appalling, but she may never be able to conquer that belief. It will be her doom – the Serpent need not even touch her now: the seed is planted, and she will destroy herself. There is something else too, equally terrible.

'I told you of how my sister Orkesh and my brother

283

Meshurek died by my hand. I thought them dead and at peace. But in the Dark Regions I saw them. They were imprisoned in ghastly bodies, doomed to wander the hideous swamps like cattle. The Shana possess their souls. Their misery in that hell is something no human can comprehend—' his voice was gruff with revulsion and outrage and he had to struggle to continue. 'They will never know release until the Dark Regions are destroyed.'

'That's terrible – I had no idea,' Estarinel breathed.

'Of course not. I did not even tell Calorn. And then . . . in Pheigrad, while you were fetching the Silver Staff, I met a man named Karadrek. He used to be my second-in-command when I was High Commander. He too had been corrupted by the Shana, but only because of me. Because I had betrayed both Gorethria and the world itself, and the results of my betrayal were spreading outwards like ripples on a pond.

'Karadrek, too, died on my sword. No doubt he stalks the Dark Regions in torment also. But my meeting with him was as if pre-ordained – another manipulation, if you like – and through it I saw that I was doomed to be a destroyer and must fulfil that destiny. The ultimate destruction of the Earth is the culmination of my doom. Only then will the Serpent and the Grey Ones cease their sport with all of us.'

Estarinel made to reply, but no sound emerged.

'Alas, I am not insane, Estarinel. Would that I were.'

'The Planes—'

'The Planes, the Dark Regions, everything will cease to exist. This world is too lost in evil to be redeemed.'

'That's not true! Ashurek, listen – at least we must think of what other ways there may be, before abandoning ourselves to this doom—'

'Please, desist. It is pointless. You are only trying to cling to life, which is quite understandable. But now you must learn to let it go. Miril is lost, hope has been proved false. This is the dark heart of the reality behind Eldor's kind words and the Lady's gentleness and Silvren's wretched optimism.'

'I still think you're wrong,' Estarinel said quietly, fearing that Ashurek was very much right.

'Then I must warn you: if you have any thought of giving up the Quest I will simply take the Silver Staff and go on alone.'

'You would have to kill me first.'

'Yes,' said Ashurek flatly, looking at him. 'Yes, I know.'

'Ye gods. You would . . .'

'Estarinel, I can no longer afford to let love or pity compromise my purpose. I loved my brother and sister, and look what became of them. If I seem cruel, it is because I have come to understand that compassion is just another false hope – a tool of the Serpent.'

High above them, the wind seemed to be filled with faint sounds, eldritch moans with a heart-turning, falling note at the end. Shapes were dancing in the darkness, eye-deceiving; sometimes they seemed to be birds, at others no more than whirling eddies of snow.

'Well, now I really believe one thing,' Estarinel said. 'You are quite capable of leaving Medrian behind.'

'We must leave her. There is no question of it.'

Medrian was struggling to open her eyes or move, but her eyelids were weighted with lead and her hands felt like dead things. She had to speak to Ashurek – had to – but the Serpent kept her mouth sealed, as if she was a naughty child to be locked in an attic. She fought against it, but she knew she was losing.

'Then, Ashurek, you had better murder both Medrian and me,' Estarinel said. 'And you might as well do it now, to spare us any further suffering.'

Ashurek stood up.

Medrian battled to lift her eyelids, to speak. The poison had all but left her body now, but she was physically exhausted, a shell, which M'gulfn could crush easily. Yes, she had lost; the Serpent could now take her over at any time, and was only delaying in order to delude her that the fight was not quite done, and so mock her more thoroughly. She could feel wings in the air – wings like knives – they might spare her but they would not spare Estarinel and Ashurek—

The Gorethrian paused, looking down at Medrian and

Estarinel. His eyes burned like green acid. Then he turned and began to walk slowly away.

Medrian opened her mouth and croaked, 'Creatures – coming. They will kill . . .'

'Medrian?' Estarinel said, unable to make out what she was saying. 'Are you awake? Don't try to speak.'

At last she felt the sluggish blood begin to quicken in her veins, and found herself able to move and open her eyes. She flexed her rigid limbs and said rather more lucidly, 'No, I'm all right. We mustn't stay here any longer.'

'You can't think of moving yet,' Estarinel said gently. 'You don't realise how ill you've been.'

'I was only cold. I'm warm now,' she murmured. 'Where is Ashurek?'

'I don't know,' Estarinel sighed. 'Have you been conscious very long? Did you hear what he was saying?'

'Yes. I heard,' she said noncommittally.

'I only wish I could believe he's gone mad. But I don't think he has.'

'We must find him.' She tried to stand up, but Estarinel restrained her.

'I'm sure he'll come back, Medrian. You should have something to eat and then try to sleep; I'll build up the fire—'

'No, we're not safe here,' she persisted. 'I'm not delirious; there are creatures flying above the clouds, and they will attack us before long. Can't you hear them?'

Estarinel became aware of the thin, eerie moans high above them. He looked up but could see nothing but feathers of snow drifting down. 'They sound like those awful birds that drove us out of the forest that time.'

'They are the same. They've been sent after us by the Serpent. I should have realised earlier.'

'Are you sure? Then I should warn Ashurek, but I'm not leaving you alone here.'

'It's all right. Help me up.'

'Listen to me: when I say that you need rest, I mean that you are putting your life in danger if you try to go on so soon,' Estarinel said severely. 'You've been unwell since we came from the Blue Plane; perhaps you don't recall what happened to you, but after that plant stung you, you walked for two days almost without stopping, until you collapsed. It's a miracle we found you, and that you're still alive. I won't let you risk—'

'Estarinel,' she interrupted softly, her voice as unearthly as the keening of the creatures above, 'I am not in danger of dying. Please believe me. We are at greater risk if we stay here. The fire will draw them. We must go.'

There was something compelling in her voice, faint as it was. When she made to stand up he found himself helping her, everything that Ashurek had said about her like a fresh wound in his mind.

'Here, have your cloak and give me my pack – and the crossbow,' she said. Then she began to walk with stiff, unsteady steps across the dark plain. She did not refuse to lean on Estarinel's arm when he offered it. Her face was still deathlike and her limbs as frail as wax. He could only wonder at her resilience; it was as though despair ran in her veins like an ichor in place of blood.

The cries above them grew louder, rising and falling on the wind like the wails of demented children. Estarinel, shuddering, drew his sword and Medrian armed the crossbow. He looked up but could see nothing, could feel only the big, cold flakes of snow settling and melting on his face. He called Ashurek's name two or three times, but there was no response. They trudged on.

'Some sort of light ahead – can you see it?' Medrian said. Along the horizon there was a faint, spectral radiance, like an oncoming storm. Then Estarinel felt the wind turn warm, and in the same moment Medrian gasped, 'Be ready – they are coming!'

A sickly, mustard-coloured glow began to creep along the underside of the clouds towards them. It illuminated the dark Tundra, clearly revealing the figure of Ashurek about half a mile away, engaged in frantic battle with a flapping, airborne object. Beyond him gleamed a vague shape resembling an amorphous mass of crystals. As Estarinel and Medrian began to hurry towards him the snow became discoloured, like flakes of flesh, turning gradually into oily rain. A branch of blood-red lightning spat at the ground near them and the gamboge sky seethed lower and lower until it seemed to be almost touching their hands.

Out of it plunged a flying thing.

It was a huge pterosaur with a wingspan of some twelve feet. Its long jaws were gaping to reveal rows of needle-like teeth as it came at them, screaming like a soul in hell. Great claws swung below its belly and its lengthy tail thrashed the air like a barbed whip. It shone with incongruously brilliant colours, black and sapphire-blue and red, and on its head was a crest resembling a shaft of vermilion bone.

Estarinel swung his sword but it pivoted round the blade with remarkable agility for its size, and lunged at him with snapping jaws. He dodged and struck at it again, but it was like fighting nothing. Its dark wings beat around his head, creaking like leather. Their pinions bore vicious, curved claws. Even as he tried to wield his blade, one of these caught on his cloak and the pterosaur was suddenly on him, folding itself around him, chewing at his throat with cold, sharp teeth. It smelled of the dead things on which it fed.

Revolted, he tried ineffectively to prise it away. He succeeded only in losing hold of his sword. Then he remembered the knife on his belt; shuddering with disgust, he felt for the haft, found it, and began to stab repeatedly at the creature's gristly belly.

It did not let him go at once. It keened, and that terrible cry right by his ear seemed to vibrate through his skull like the screech of metal on metal, and as the note fell at the end, he felt his sanity falling with it, away into a black void. Suddenly he was lying on the turf, with tiny, snow-spangled flowers pressing into his cheek.

The pterosaur was in the air, preparing to attack again. Outlined against the viscid sky with sanguine lightning dancing around it, it looked primeval and demonic. Medrian was facing it with the crossbow in her hands, a fragile and indomitable figure. Estarinel staggered to his feet and stood there swaying, hardly able to lift his sword. He knew that if it called again he would turn and run like a madman. As it plummeted, he saw that it had cornflower-blue eyes in its pinched skull. Medrian—

Something caught it in mid-flight and it turned over and over, a bundle of flapping shadows. Her arrow had found it. It hit the ground and lay there thrashing like a giant, obscene bat. More indignant than wounded, it began to whine plaintively, and above the clouds a hundred more uncanny voices were raised in response.

Estarinel gasped, 'Medrian – more will come—' but she was already running, and he caught her hand and ran with her. The clouds ballooned like a skin swollen with abscesses while lightning chased them like the giggling of demons. The Worm-sent rain had dissolved the snow leaving the Tundra blackened and slippery underfoot.

Ahead they saw the albescent shape that they had glimpsed just before the attack. Then it had appeared small, but only because it had been in the far distance. Now they were drawing nearer they saw that it was huge, like a phantom city swathed in layers of crystalline gauze.

The pterosaurs were moving within the discoloured nimbus, making the sky seem to boil. Sometimes a clawed wing-tip would break through, sending wreathes of brownish vapour into the atmosphere. It seemed to Estarinel that they were being driven, yet again, like cattle. Suddenly Ashurek appeared as if from nowhere, running straight into them. There was blood trickling down his face, but he had evidently fended off his own attacker.

'Turn back!' he shouted, pointing at the spectral mass. 'Whatever that is, we are being herded towards it. We can't let that happen again at any cost.'

'I don't think we have much choice,' said Medrian faintly, just as the clouds exploded. Vapour swirled about them and the air was suddenly thick with claws and wings and teeth. The pterosaurs were all round them, gleaming blue and red and black – bejewelled creatures with funereal wings, reeking of carrion.

They ran. It seemed that the creatures were in fact quite impartial about which direction their prey took: their sole purpose was to kill them. The diamond-bright mirage hung ahead of the three, and now they perceived that it was drifting towards them. Or rather, it appeared to be stationary while the Tundra itself rolled slowly in its direction. Crisscross patterns of transient light rippled to and fro on its glittering surface; it resembled nothing more than a many-layered, bespangled cobweb. But the three ran towards it, because they had no other hope.

The pterosaurs swooped and danced in the air, shrieking their fiendish intent. Medrian noted, as she had surmised, that they were not interested in her. She managed to retard two or three with well-placed arrows, while Estarinel and Ashurek tried to fend them off with their swords. Their efforts were as frantic, as tiring and as ineffective as a man swiping at a huge swarm of bees; the creatures swirled out of the way, only to close in again.

Estarinel was panting, his throat raw with exertion. Blood ran into his eyes from where claws and tails had caught his head. The atmosphere rustled with darkness, reverberated with metallic, primordial cries which seemed to issue from a desolate dimension where sluggish rivers crept between bald grey hills, and pterosaurs flew in silhouette against a greenish-black sky. A cold, cynical, deadly evil was enfolding them, effortlessly ending the Quest.

But now there was a white haze shimmering across their vision as the moving apparition reached them. They stumbled headlong into it, gasping for breath.

They found themselves within something like a pale fog, sparkling with motes and strands of light. The pterosaurs seemed reluctant to follow. Most of them wheeled away from the mist wall, uttering heart-stopping screams. One, however, had dropped onto Ashurek, its wings enfolding him like a grisly cloak. Medrian and Estarinel rushed to wrench it off him, but it had its claws into his cloak and its teeth in his throat. Except for its membranous wings it was everywhere as hard as gristle, almost impossible to wound more than superficially. They wrestled with it while it flapped its clawed wings at them and squawked. Estarinel seized it by the long, blood-red crest on its head and sawed desperately at its throat to no effect.

'Cut the crest itself,' Ashurek choked. Estarinel did so. To his surprise, the knife sliced through it as through meat, and the pterosaur's lifeblood began to pour from the wound, a flood of virulent scarlet such as could never issue from any natural animal. At last it relaxed its jaws, and they were able to drag it off and throw it onto the Tundra.

Ashurek coughed and gasped, pressing a hand over the wound in his neck. Blood oozed between his fingers. Estarinel expressed some concern, but Ashurek shook his head dismissively, saying, 'My thanks, but it only nipped the flesh. I wonder where the Serpent has delivered us to this time?'

They moved forward through the shining mist, which thinned and dispersed around them like the strands of a cobweb blown away on a breeze. They found themselves standing in a strange city. All around them were towers of glass: ruby, purple, amber, green and azure, shining with a rich transparent light of their own. The street on which they stood was paved with slabs of clear beryl. The Serpent-sent storm did not penetrate here: the gauzy light seemed to form a protective dome. They halted and looked around them.

The recent exertion had taken its inevitable toll of Medrian and she sank into a sitting position at the base of a heliotrope tower, her head in her hands. Estarinel asked her how she was, and offered her some wine. She took a mouthful and passed the leather flask to Ashurek, who was regarding her as sympathetically as a demon.

'Just faint. It's nothing,' she murmured. Physically, she felt numb; she was mortally ill, exhausted, but with the Worm's will vivifying her she felt she could walk or fight for ever if she had to, like an automaton, sometimes falling but always getting up again, like some awful creature of M'gulfn's that refused to die. Mentally, she felt that just one strand of herself remained, and that was certain to break and recoil into the void very soon.

She had not forgotten her pressing need to talk to Ashurek. She knew that she must do it while the last thread of herself remained unbroken. She looked up at him, but as she tried to speak, the words died. The Serpent had silenced her instantly, painlessly, like someone putting their foot on the tail of a mouse while it scrabbles, uncomprehending, to run away. *Hush. Be still, my Medrian. Rest, for in a little while you are going to tell me everything.*

There was not even any anger or frustration in its tone. Groaning, Medrian dropped her head onto her knees, and her hands fell nerveless to the ground.

It is almost over.

'Does not this city look familiar to you?' Ashurek was saying. Estarinel glanced sharply at him, the same thought in his own mind.

'It looks just like the City of Glass,' he observed.

'You should have more idea than me,' the Gorethrian remarked caustically. 'I seem to remember you saying that when Arlenmia drugged you, you saw it in this form, without the disguise she had placed over it.'

'Yes, that's true. I would swear that this *is* the City . . . but that's impossible. How could Arlenmia have found the power to move it from place to place?'

'There may be a simpler explanation,' said Ashurek very gravely. 'We may have been transported back to Belhadra.'

'Oh, by the gods, no,' Estarinel whispered, closing his eyes. Weeks of travelling towards the Arctic, only to find themselves back in the middle of Tearn? It was too appalling to be contemplated.

'Straight back to Arlenmia,' Ashurek continued, his face calmly murderous, 'who is no doubt very much wiser since the last time we met her. M'gulfn has sprung a perfect trap. Well, my friend, what say you to that?'

Estarinel only shook his head, too shocked to make any kind of comment. It was unthinkable—

'Greetings!' came a sudden voice a few yards away. Startled, they all looked round, even Medrian. 'Ah – oh dear – I seem to have forgotten your names.'

Before them stood a thin old man, about four feet tall and as white and frail as frost. He was clad in a robe that seemed to be made of sparkling white light, and there was a certain humour in his mild face. 'Goodness, if only you could see how surprised you look!' he said. 'You do recognise me, don't you?'

It was Hranna, the mathematician from the White Plane Hrannekh Ol.

12

Hrunnesh

'WHAT IN the name of the Serpent is going on?' Ashurek demanded. Hranna looked put out; his hands fluttered like moths.

'I thought you would be pleased to see me,' he said, sounding crestfallen. 'I'm rescuing you again!'

'You're what? Where is Arlenmia?'

'Who is Arlenmia?' was Hranna's response, and there followed several seconds of confused silence. The pale old man scratched his bony head while Ashurek glared at him and Estarinel and Medrian looked on in astonishment.

'Is this place the City of Glass?' Ashurek asked.

'Yes, naturally. There is only one, you know,' Hranna replied.

'We were imprisoned here some time ago by a powerful enchantress, Arlenmia. She works for the Serpent. I surmise, therefore, that either you are in league with her, or that you are some sort of apparition sent by her to trick us.'

'Forgive my – my indignation,' the mathematician exclaimed, 'but I am not in league with anyone, and I am most certainly not an apparition! I'll write out the equation which proves it, if I must. It seems that some sort of explanation is necessary.'

'Yes, it is. However, we would prefer it in words, rather than figures, if it is not too much trouble,' Ashurek said, folding his arms.

'Well, now.' Hranna beckoned and began to lead them slowly between the many-coloured hyaline towers. 'I know of the "enchantress" of whom you speak – it's just that I'm not very good with names. What has happened is this. The Glass City is a special and delicate mechanism whose purpose is to maintain the Entrance Points to the Planes. (It is not a city at all, nor is it really made of glass, of course.) Well, after this "enchantress" had ensconced herself here, disguised it with mirrors, used it for her own ends and goodness knows what else, the Grey Ones decided that they could not risk the City being misused in such a dangerous way again. So after she left—'

'She is no longer here?' Estarinel interrupted.

'No, she is not. After you three left the City, she left also, I don't know why – we have had so much to do that we cannot even begin theorising upon lesser matters just now – but suffice it to say that when she left, the Grey Ones decided to safeguard the City of Glass against another such – er – occupation? They purposed that the City should no longer reside in – in—'

'Belhadra,' Ashurek prompted.

'Belhadra, thank you, but that it should be free to move from place to place. So they commissioned us, I mean the mathematicians of the White Plane, of course, to make the necessary calculations which would transform the mechanism from a static to a randomly orbiting body. This we have done, as you see,' said the small man with a touch of pride.

'So we are not in the middle of Tearn?' Estarinel asked.

'Goodness, no. More between two dimensions, actually. Or was it five? I'm not sure. Lenarg did a lot of the work—'

'Hranna, what has this to do with us?' the Gorethrian interjected.

'Oh – oh – forgive my abstraction. The point is this. You have sent our mathematics haywire.' Hranna wagged his head with humorous but grave disapproval.

'In that case, we must beg your forgiveness,' Ashurek said acidly. 'What on Earth are you talking about?'

'Well, when you were stranded on Peradnia – Hrannekh Ol, I mean – I think I explained to you how, with our theorems, we could predict and express the Earth's future in algebraic terms.'

'Yes. You did.'

'Well, there are always new discoveries to be made. There are random factors within any calculus, but even allowing for a variable number of these, every single one of our extrapolations predicts the same thing: the release of a rather large amount of energy which would negate not only the – the – Serpent, I think you call it – but also the Earth and the Planes. We have completed only a few billion or so theorems, it's true, but it all seems rather – ah – disheartening, all the same . . .'

Ashurek and Estarinel looked at each other.

'Now,' Hranna continued, waving his thin hands enthusiastically, 'the only way that this negative prediction can be corrected is by using a tentative theory – first proposed by myself – that you are travelling upon a wrong trajectory.'

'How can that be?' Ashurek asked. 'We are heading for the Arctic. Are you saying that we should be going somewhere else instead?'

'Er – yes, I think so,' the old man replied vaguely. 'You see, the "random factor" in this case may be mathematics itself. (If we knew exactly what it was it would not be random!) We are somewhat to blame for everything that has happened to you so far, I'm afraid.'

'What?' Estarinel exclaimed.

'Is there any probability of you beginning to make sense in the near future?' Ashurek enquired pleasantly.

'I thought I was doing rather well, considering I barely speak your language. Words are so imprecise, aren't they? As I was saying, when you were stranded on Hrannekh Ol, you should have remained on the H'tebhmellian ship. It would have taken you straight to the Blue Plane. Unfortunately we did not realise until it was too late, so because of our error, you went all over the place instead. If not for us, you would not have gone to the Glass City, and the enchantress would not have left it, and the Grey Ones would not have caused it to be moved, and I would not be here now, rescuing you . . . fascinating, isn't it?' Hranna chuckled. 'This is what mathematics is all about!'

'I knew it must be about something,' Ashurek muttered.

'Well, because of increasing evidence that the theory concerning your wrong trajectory was correct, we of Peradnia concluded that something must be done. Thanks to our work with the Grey Ones, we had access to the Glass City, and the ability to move it wherever we wished, and also a limited control over the Entrance Points. We decided that it was our duty to intercept you and give you this information. It was fairly easy for us to calculate exactly where you were at any given time. Unfortunately the figures regarding those awful – flying things out there,' he gesticulated vaguely at the gauzy dome around the City, 'were only computed at the last minute, or I would have made sure that you were intercepted earlier, before you were in so much danger. My apologies.'

'You really did rescue us!' Estarinel said. 'We must thank you. Those creatures would certainly have killed us.'

'Were you asked to do this by the Guardians?' asked Ashurek.

'Goodness, no. Our work is independent, always has been. This was our own decision. The Grey Ones are no mathematicians: they throw huge quantities of energy about with quite alarming disregard for the consequences. They should employ us more often, but I'm glad they don't, because we'd never have time to work on anything else if they did.'

'Then why do you wish to help us?'

'Ah, well, we of the White Plane also desire to see this energy you call the "Serpent" negated – without the predicted annihilation of the Earth, if possible – otherwise the loss of our physics would be a most terrible, appalling waste. Oh, and so would the loss of the Earth, of course.'

'So, you are primarily concerned with preserving your wretched mathematics?'

'I'm afraid so,' Hranna admitted with a rueful smile. 'Although without the Earth, we'd have nothing to work on anyway, of course.'

'Well, that is a rare and refreshing admission. At least a selfish motive stands a chance of being an honest one,' Ashurek observed.

'I wish only that the help we offer could have been more accurately calculated. Sometimes it seems to me that the more one learns, the less one knows, proportionately speaking—'

'Might we stay on the subject of this "trajectory"?'

'Oh – of course, I'm sorry. You are going the wrong way, and I am here to help you correct your course.' He beamed at them.

'Well?' said Ashurek. 'Go on. Where should we be going?'

'Ah . . . that I don't know,' Hranna admitted, his smile fading. 'You see, it's another random factor. Or the same one. Something is missing, or off-course, or lost, or something – this is what our equations tell us. Or rather, don't tell us. I thought that *you* would know where you should be instead, and I could just deliver you there . . .'

'Then you miscalculated,' Ashurek said sourly. 'We thought we were going in the right direction. Where *could* you take us, if we had a choice?'

'Oh, anywhere. Any point on the Earth's surface. Or I can send you through to the White Plane, the Black Plane, or the Blue Plane.'

'That is very impressive. But how are we to decide? What think you, Estarinel?' Ashurek asked. As he spoke, Hranna led them into a courtyard bounded by a square structure that gleamed like a topaz. Estarinel realised with a feeling of indescribable eeriness that it was the edifice Arlenmia had used as her house. He looked down and saw, encased in the glassy slabs below his feet, a multitude of strange sea-creatures. They were scaled with delicate, silvery colours and their mouths gaped in eternal, silent screams. He stared at them. He had seen them once before, and had thought they were a hallucination; now that he realised they were real, their terrible symbolism made him feel dizzy and breathless with dread. There was Arlenmia on one side, promising eternal life in the Serpent's shadow, and there was Ashurek on the other, promising utter destruction. And in between was all the sad, sweet, fragile life of Earth, uttering a never-ending cry for help which no one could hear.

'The North Pole,' Estarinel answered in a low voice. 'I can't see any point in going anywhere else. It would save us weeks of travelling. And end the whole thing quickly.'

'But that is still the same trajectory,' Ashurek pointed out, 'the one that Hranna says is wrong.'

'I will take you wherever you wish,' the old man said. 'Of course, you are welcome to wait for us to extrapolate what in fact you should be doing, but that may take months.'

'We do not have months.'

'Then I can only advise you that some sort of educated guess is in order. Don't let me hurry you: a hasty decision could be disastrous.'

'It seems that for once we are not being manipulated,' said Ashurek slowly, 'but genuinely helped. I may be wrong, of course. Medrian, you've been silent all this time. Have you any advice to give?'

She looked at him, her eyes like shadowy caverns against her white, drawn face.

'You know as well as I what is missing, Ashurek,' she murmured tonelessly. 'But I don't know where to look, either.'

Ashurek found himself staring at her, engulfed by the bleakness of her eyes. Yes, she was M'gulfn's child, of that there could be no doubt, but at the same time there was a quality of enigma about her that sometimes – as now – seemed awesome. It was not that he hated her. It was not even that he feared her: he only feared that she would cause the Quest to fail, whether she meant to or not. It was rather that he felt sympathy for her, and that sympathy welled from somewhere dark and grim, like a scarred mountainside where the wind mourned incessantly. It was the vista of his inmost soul, which he had been forced to look on in the Dark Regions, the part of him which had driven armies to ravage other nations, Alaak among them, and which was now driving him to be the world's doom. It was Miril who had made him understand that that darkness was evil, the opposite of hope, and, whenever he looked at Medrian it was the same as gazing into that void of hopelessness. He did not want to

299

look there. Perhaps his wish to leave her behind was no more than a need to escape the darkness within himself, and as futile. He and Medrian were both starved of hope. It was Miril that they needed.

I will fade, and hide myself in darkness to mourn, and wait . . .

'We might as well go straight to the Arctic, then,' Estarinel reiterated. 'No one seems to have any better suggestions.'

Ashurek turned to him and placed a hand on his shoulder. 'I know what Hranna means. I know where we have gone wrong,' he said. Estarinel looked at him enquiringly. 'We need to find Miril. She told me that unless I find her again, the world is doomed . . . do you see what I mean?'

'Yes,' Estarinel said, this revelation dawning on him like a golden light. 'She is our only hope that the world might be saved, and not destroyed . . .'

'Just so. This is why she is called "the Hope of the World". Without her, we have none. Hranna, I am more than grateful to you for this. Tell me, do you know anything of Miril?'

'She may be a part of our calculations,' said Hranna, uncertainly, 'but "hope" is something that cannot be defined mathematically, therefore I'm afraid . . . well, I am not at all sure what you are talking about.'

'How do we go about looking for her, then?' said Estarinel. 'She could be anywhere.'

Ashurek fell silent for a while, thinking. Medrian stood a little apart from the others, her head bowed, hugging herself. Looking at her, Estarinel wished more than anything to pull her into his arms and comfort the unfathomable, private pain that she endured continually, and the knowledge that to try would only worsen her anguish turned in him like a knife.

'Darkness,' Ashurek muttered. 'She said she would wait in darkness. But she did not mean the Dark Regions. And I am sure she is nowhere on Earth, and certainly not on the White or Blue Planes. I think she is on the Black Plane.'

'Are you sure?' Estarinel said, alarmed.

'No. It is only an intuition, but a very strong one.'

'What if you are wrong? We could be trapped there. Hranna, have you no more definite advice for us?'

'Ah, alas, I have not,' the mathematician said apologetically. 'If anything, I would advise against Hrunnesh, because I cannot guarantee that you would be able to find an Exit Point. But if you feel that you must go there . . .' he shook his head worriedly, 'well, I would suggest that you must be very certain indeed before making what sounds like a rather rash move.'

'Ashurek, we cannot risk—'

'I am as certain as I can be. Hranna, please can you arrange an Entrance Point to the Black Plane?' There was something so commanding, almost menacing, in Ashurek's quiet voice that Estarinel could not blame Hranna for obeying without further argument.

'Oh – well, if you are sure – of course. I have to go inside,' he waved at the edifice that had once been Arlenmia's house, 'to arrange for the mechanism to be operated which will create the Entrance Point. I will endow it with a physical aspect so that you'll be able to see it. It will appear in the centre of this square. I will come out and signal to you when it is ready. Well, then, I must say goodbye again. I hope that if we chance to meet again, it will be in a happier time.' Hranna was hurrying away from them as he spoke, his white hands clasped and his dazzling robe floating behind him. He went into the topaz structure.

'Ashurek—' Estarinel began.

'If you are going to argue, give me the Silver Staff, and stay here.'

'No, I'll come with you,' he sighed. 'I can't be altogether certain that you are wrong. Medrian, what do you think?'

She turned slowly and looked at him with such a blank, stony expression that it seemed her soul had fled from behind her eyes. She seemed unable to speak. There were drops of cold perspiration on her white forehead, and she was swaying slightly. Estarinel caught her arm thinking that she was about to pass out.

A dull buzzing noise began in the centre of the square. It

301

was at the lowest threshold of hearing, but unpleasantly penetrating at the same time. Then dark particles appeared and swirled in the air like a swarm of great insects – headless, wingless black bees. Hranna emerged from the topaz structure, waving to indicate that the Entrance Point was ready and they should go through, quickly.

The buzzing grew louder, thrumming painfully through their skulls. Fear gripped Estarinel, and he saw the same suppressed dread on Ashurek's face. But the Gorethrian moved purposefully towards the Entrance Point.

'No,' said Medrian, suddenly resisting Estarinel's hold on her arm. Her face was glowing with a ghastly bluish-white light, and her eyes had turned cyan. 'No – not there – not to her—' and her expression was one of such absolute, abject terror that Estarinel almost let her go in shock. She began to fight him, struggling violently to escape and run.

'Come on!' Ashurek exclaimed. 'For the Lady's sake, just let her go!'

But Estarinel could not do that. Holding grimly onto her while she fought, he propelled her after Ashurek into the Entrance Point.

The particles battered them like a swarm of carbon-black locusts. The buzzing became intolerable.

And suddenly the Glass City, the noise, and the Entrance Point were gone. A raven-black silence wrapped itself around them, softly, like a wing.

They were on the Black Plane Hrunnesh. Beneath their feet there was a firm surface that felt like rock. But they could see nothing, hear nothing. At once Estarinel was convinced that they had made a terrible, irremediable mistake; a childlike fear of primitive intensity rose unbidden and ran through him like liquid fire. He hung onto Medrian like a drowning man to a rock.

Only the fact that she was still struggling against him brought him back to himself, as his concern for her subdued his own fear. Presently she stopped fighting him, but became rigid in his arms as if clenched against some terrible, imminent blow. 'No,' she rasped, her breathing convulsive, and her voice unlike itself. 'No. I hate her. Don't make me—' She uttered a deep, inhuman groan and flopped unconscious in Estarinel's arms.

'She appears to have completely lost her mind at last,' came Ashurek's voice out of the darkness. 'You should have left her behind.'

'She's passed out,' Estarinel informed him through gritted teeth. 'I can't lie her down, because I can't see what we're standing on. Coming here was the most incredible act of folly any of us could have thought of! How are we to get back to Earth?'

'Miril is here, somewhere. I know it,' Ashurek said stubbornly.

'And if you're right, how are we going to find her? Listen, what if she did not mean that she would be in a specific place, but that we should find her in times of darkness?'

'What makes you think her words had that meaning?'

'I think I saw her – no, not saw, but heard her – in Gastada's Castle. She gave me the strength – not to die, I suppose. And when I was looking for the Silver Staff, I almost gave up at one stage and she came to me and told me to carry on. Her presence was almost physical – I thought I could feel her claws as she perched on my hand. Both were times of extreme darkness, in every sense. What if we have already found her, and did not know it, and now it's too late?'

'Why did you not mention this before?'

'Because it—' Estarinel could hardly find words to frame an answer, 'it was – personal, somehow.'

'Yes. I undersand. Have you seen her at other times?' Ashurek asked, his voice level.

'Yes. In what I can only describe as visions – waking dreams. Many times. But always like something symbolic, not something real.'

'And black in colour? We have all seen Miril thus. Guiding us, reminding us to look for her. And always I tried to turn

303

aside and push her from my thoughts, despite everything she said to me. I hope it is not too late for her to forgive me.'

'But those times she came to me, do you think she was really there?' As Estarinel spoke he realised that he could see Ashurek. It was only in silhouette, with little detail discernible, but it meant that the Black Plane was not completely dark after all. 'Or was it just in my imagination?'

'I think you are capable of finding hope in the most desperate of situations. I envy you that,' Ashurek replied more gently than usual. 'I understand you, but I still believe that she is in a specific place. Because when I met her, she was not "symbolic", she was unquestionably real, vulnerable flesh and blood. And she is not really black, but tawny-gold in colour.' He paused, then continued thoughtfully, 'I believe that Miril is what Medrian is so frightened of. Miril is the antithesis of the Serpent, so any of its minions would be bound to loathe her. Thus Medrian's terror proves that Miril is on Hrunnesh, and it proves that Medrian is working for the Serpent.'

'It's still not proof enough for me to abandon her!' Estarinel answered heatedly.

'No. Well, we will see,' Ashurek said quietly. 'My eyes seem to have adjusted to this darkness. I think it is enough for us to find our way.'

Supporting Medrian between them, they began to walk slowly through the strange landscape. If there was such a thing as black light, that was what illuminated Hrunnesh. It was unlike the night of Earth. The sky had the quality of light shining through black glass, dim yet of limpid clarity.

The Plane was quite flat, its surface as smooth and glossy as jet. Out of it there rose formations like clusters of ebony crystal throwing themselves into fantastic shapes. There were arches and slender towers and minarets, plantlike forms and others which could have been taken for graceful, unearthly animals frozen in mid-stride on an alien landscape. There were even some which resembled human figures, leaning together in love or combat. But all these shapes were ambiguous. If studied for too long they reverted to faceted clusters imbued with no more than their inherent crystalline harmony.

As their eyes adapted, they saw that the Black Plane was not wholly black, either. Everywhere it shimmered with the transient hues that glide over an ink bubble, magenta and bronze and indigo. The crystals contained flashes of silver, rose and blue-green, like the colours buried within a black opal.

Hrunnesh, they observed, possessed its own extraordinary beauty.

'The Planes are supposed to be infinite,' Estarinel said pessimistically, after they had walked for a while. Medrian was walking, with help, but her face was still cyanosed and mindless with private terror.

'But I believe their infinity to be of a paradoxical sort,' said Ashurek, 'as if they somehow repeat themselves infinitely. I believe that wherever we had entered Hrannekh Ol, we would still have met Hranna and the other Peradnians, likewise H'tebhmella.'

'Then, if we do not have an infinite distance to walk, couldn't we rest for a while?' Estarinel suggested. Ashurek acquiesced, and they sat beneath a giant sable crystal which, from some angles, resembled a bizarre long-necked mammoth with its foot raised and its head turned. They ate some of the provisions which they were conserving for the Arctic, and drank a little of reviving H'tebhmellian wine. Medrian would not eat, but Estarinel got her to drink a few mouthfuls. There was a plastic stiffness about her limbs that disconcerted him; he feared for her more than ever. He expected Ashurek to insist again that they leave her behind, but the Gorethrian said nothing. Perhaps, for once, he had concluded that arguing with Estarinel was pointless.

Presently they saw something moving across the vitreous sky. It was a black globe, with the rainbow hues of oil iridescent on its surface.

'What's that?' Estarinel wondered.

'I know not, but I believe this Plane is inhabited, just as the others are,' Ashurek replied.

The sphere began to descend and drift towards them until it was only a few yards away; then it floated silently to the ground, bouncing a little as it landed, as if it was almost weightless.

Ashurek and Estarinel were on their feet, swords drawn. As they watched, the surface of the globe was broken – whilst remaining intact – by a hand. Three more hands emerged, a head, a torso – and as the figure stepped out, the skin of the globe closed elastically behind it, like an inky bubble.

A neman stood before them. Like the nemen of Earth, it was tall and lean, with four arms and a long, sombrely handsome face. Its skin, however, was the colour of glossy ebony, as was its short hair, while the tunic it wore was so dark that it reflected no light at all, and might have been a window onto starless space. It stood looking at them, its whiteless eyes glistening like coal.

'Men of Earth, why have you come to Hrunnesh?' it said. Its voice was light, rich, and emotionless.

They stared suspiciously at it and did not reply.

It said, 'Put away your swords. I have none, as you see. It is not our purpose to be warlike. That is, it has not been proved that it is.'

'They are philosophers,' Ashurek suddenly remembered, lowering his blade.

'Yes, indeed, we are philosophers,' the neman said. 'My name is Valcad. Who are you?'

'Ashurek, Medrian and Estarinel, three travellers from Earth,' the Gorethrian informed him.

'And did you come to Hrunnesh by accident or by design?'

'By design,' Ashurek said, and the neman looked surprised.

'This is wonderful,' it said, almost smiling. 'Let me take you without further delay to my fellow Hrunneshians – they will be fascinated by your arrival.'

'How did you know we were here?' asked Estarinel.

'I was airborne in my sphere of solitary thought, and I saw you,' Valcad answered simply. 'We think in isolation, you see, and then we meet together to discuss our reflections.'

306

Ashurek turned to Estarinel and said, 'I suggest that we go with the neman. I believe them to be harmless, and they may help us.'

'For once, I agree,' Estarinel said. He helped Medrian to stand up; her eyes were open but she was catatonic and seemed to have no awareness of what was happening. She walked apparently by reflex as the neman began to lead them through the forest of mineral forms.

'The others are not far from here, so our feet will be quicker than the sphere,' Valcad explained. Seeing them looking from side to side as they went, it said, 'You admire the beauty of our Plane? I know not why it is called "Black". It is all colours to me.'

'These crystals,' Estarinel said, 'some of them resemble animals or plants. Have they been sculpted by the Hrunneshians?'

'No, indeed.' The neman sounded surprised. 'They take these shapes of their own volition. Perhaps they aspire to a higher form than their own. Now, here we are.'

In front of them was a shining block of jet, about twelve feet high, which vaguely resembled a bird with its wings outstretched. They heard voices, and as they drew closer they saw that some thirty or so nemen were seated on the many ridges and facets of the block.

'But how can we know what truth is?' one of the nemen was saying. 'Men have a standpoint from which to define it, for example, "If I do not eat, I will die." But we have no such basis. Unless we find one, our reflections must be intrinsically invalid.'

'Not so,' said another. 'It is a decided advantage. Being outside any arbitrary Earthly standard of truth, we are unlimited. Ah, here is Valcad. Who are these beings with you?'

'Greetings, Pellar. Here are three humans from Earth, who have come here to study our philosophy. I believe that we may learn from them as they learn from us: we are fortunate.'

Estarinel looked at Ashurek with a touch of alarm as he

realised that Valcad had jumped to this conclusion. But Ashurek's glance seemed to say, 'Never mind.'

All the nemen came down from the crystal block and gathered around the three, evidently fascinated by their arrival. Like Valcad, the others were very tall, and there was something eerily intimidating about their darkness, and the sinuous co-ordination of their four hands. Coppery and purplish lights gleamed on their satin skins and multi-coloured flecks sparkled in their eyes, but their tunics were as black as nothingness. Some of them reached out and lightly touched the three as if trying to perceive their true natures.

'Now, come and sit with us. We welcome you,' said the one called Pellar. They all ascended the sloping 'wings' and seated themselves on the various ridges of the crystal form, with Ashurek, Estarinel and Medrian in the centre. 'Our being, as you know, is devoted to philosophising upon the Earth's existence and the nature of Man. But it is rare that humans actually seek us out, very rare indeed. Tell us, is there a specific theme that you wish to debate?'

'Yes,' said Ashurek. 'We hope you might help us find something that is lost. Do you know of the Serpent M'gulfn?' All the philosophers murmured that they did. 'Its evil is gradually strangling the world. We three intend to destroy it, but before we can do so, we must seek a certain creature.'

'Destroy it?' Pellar exclaimed, its opal-black eyes glistening. 'That would be impossible. The Serpent is the embodiment of the supreme being, a "god". Its power is the life-force of the Earth; nothing can exist without it. If you destroy it, you destroy life.'

The neman's words had such gravity, such authority, that Estarinel's heart sank; he believed Pellar in a way he had not wholly believed Ashurek or even Hranna. Now he had heard this argument from three separate sources, and its weight became irrefutable. The Guardians really did not care, and the H'tebhmellians had themselves been abysmally deceived into thinking there was hope.

'Ah, but does the Serpent actually embody "God" or just an idea of "God"?' another neman put in.

'It is the same thing, Evor,' said Pellar. 'What is any god but an idea? There is nothing higher than ideas. The Serpent is a pure idea: it is neither good nor evil, but there is nothing more powerful.'

'You are saying that we are wrong to try to slay M'gulfn?' Ashurek said sharply.

'In that you are attempting something which is utterly impossible anyway, it hardly matters. But if, in theory, you succeeded, the Earth would cease in the same instant. Do you see?' Pellar rested its chin in one of its dark hands, and looked impassively at Ashurek.

Then Valcad spoke, its rich, thoughtful voice carrying an equal authority to Pellar's. 'I have to disagree. I think there is no "God" in such a literal sense, Pellar. The Serpent is but an animal. Or perhaps it does not even exist at all. It is but a scapegoat for all the Earth's evils, so that whatever happens, men can say, "It is the Serpent's doing." ' This also rang uncomfortably true to Ashurek.

'But these three humans *believe* it exists,' said Evor. 'That is what matters. The question is, why would they set out to destroy their own belief? They are trying to destroy themselves.'

'The Serpent is a symbol of something they hate within themselves,' said Valcad.

'Just so. This is evidence of Man's intrinsic self-loathing.'

'Not so!' Pellar exclaimed. 'It is a sign of Man's intrinsic arrogance: he cannot bear the knowledge that there is any being higher than himself. So arrogant is he that he would set out to destroy God, even though it means the loss of his own life and all other life also.'

Silvren had spoken of arrogance, Ashurek recalled. It seemed to be something that the Shana had caused her particularly to despise within herself. And yet, in reality, there could be no one less arrogant, more loving, than Silvren had been. He said, 'Pellar, if we are to follow your argument to its logical conclusion, we should surrender our arrogant selves to the Serpent and prostrate ourselves in abject worship of it for ever. Is this preferable to the Earth being destroyed?'

'I know not. Perhaps it is the only cure for the pain of Man's existence,' Pellar replied. Some of the philosophers nodded in agreement, and began to talk amongst themselves.

'I disagree,' said Valcad. 'They would only be surrendering to something they loathe within themselves. Destruction would be better than that. But, as the Serpent is only a symbol, destruction is not in question. Except figuratively. They may indeed risk destroying their Selves.'

'Can I say something?' Estarinel said, his voice low with incredulous anger. 'You speak of the Serpent as if it were something hypothetical, to be proved or disproved by argument. But it is real. I have seen it. It has murdered my friends and family and it continues to murder the world over, not because it knows no better, but because it has a malevolent hatred of life. Don't tell me that it is not real and not evil!'

'We do not dismiss this point of view,' said Pellar, unmoved by this outburst. 'But everything that appears to be, must still be proved by reasoned argument. And reason shows that very little can actually be proved.'

'Then you could sit and argue for eternity, and never achieve anything!'

'Yes,' said Valcad ironically, 'that is precisely our purpose.'

'I wonder if they have proved that that is their purpose,' muttered Ashurek, but Valcad and Pellar heard him.

'This is in itself a fascinating question,' Pellar said. 'I have often proposed that we should devote time to philosophising upon our own existence, instead of men's, simply because we are not men.'

'And I disagree, because without men there would be nothing for us to philosophise upon and we would not exist,' said Valcad. 'The business of ideas is to explain the world of experience.'

'On one level. But nothing has a higher reality than ideas,' Pellar answered. 'Perhaps there is nothing higher than ourselves. Therefore we should not consider men's existence as "doers" – but our own existence as thinkers.'

310

'But men are the reflection in which we see ourselves,' said Evor.

'But what *are* we?' asked Valcad. 'In all our ponderings we have not found the identifying essence of the universe. We have achieved nothing. Perhaps that makes us nothing.'

'But our purpose is not to achieve, but to think,' Pellar said.

'We have achieved this much: the knowledge that there *is* no ultimate knowledge!' exclaimed Evor.

'We have no proof of that. Perhaps all our ponderings so far are but as a veil, concealing the highest idea of all. These humans have caused us to debate upon the Serpent M'gulfn; this may be a hint as to the direction our thoughts should take towards that end,' Pellar pronounced.

Ashurek realised that this discussion was doomed to continue indefinitely. It was becoming apparent that the Hrunneshians saw them as no more than a philosophical problem; he wondered if they were even capable of giving any material help. If not, it was time they went on their way.

'I must intervene,' he said. 'We came here with a specific problem, and we do not have an endless amount of time to spend talking about it.'

'Oh, by all means, express this problem,' Valcad said, lifting all four hands in a gracious, curving gesture.

'We seek a creature - a bird – named Miril. We believe her to be on the Black Plane. Do you know of her?'

The philosophers all looked at each other and broke into a general muttering of surprise and interest.

'Yes, we know her,' said Valcad. 'She is the mirror that we know to lie.'

Ashurek's face became baleful. He asked softly, 'What exactly do you mean by that?'

'When we look upon Miril,' Valcad replied, oblivious to Ashurek's expression, 'what we see gives the lie to the philosophical tenet which says that nothing is real until it is proved so. And, of course, almost nothing can be proved. Yet she appears to be the essence of proof that the abstract is real.'

'I don't follow you,' said Estarinel.

'Well, there are certain abstract qualities which for the sake of argument we call "hope", "goodness", "love", and so on. Such qualities may or may not exist. If they exist, they cannot be touched.'

'They are the highest of things, pure idea,' Pellar added.

'But this Miril is a paradox. She is all these things made corporeal. We look at her and what we see says, "I am real." This is, of course, impossible. Therefore we consider her a lying mirror, which is also impossible. But then, we feast upon paradox. Has this answered your question?'

'Where is she?' Ashurek almost shouted, his eyes blazing.

'She is on the other side of the Plane,' replied Pellar benignly. 'We requested her to remove herself there, because her guise of reality was undermining our philosophy, and her singing made it impossible to concentrate upon our thoughts.'

'Is it possible for us to go through to the other side and find her?' the Gorethrian persisted, his tone as controlled as a knife.

'What has this to do with your original question about the Serpent?' Pellar asked.

'I don't know. Yes, I do – she is the world's only hope of not dying with the Serpent, or continuing to live in its shadow.'

'But she is a lying hope, which is no hope at all,' Pellar replied, becoming lost in thought. Ashurek turned to Valcad.

'Will you help us or not?' he demanded desperately.

'I think we should help them, Pellar,' Valcad said. 'After all, ours is not to influence men's actions. They must act as they will, and we must merely observe and analyse.'

The other philosophers concurred enthusiastically with this viewpoint. Valcad said, 'We can take you through to the other side with relative ease, but once there, you will have to find Miril for yourselves. Some of us will come with you.'

'At last,' Ashurek said with a deep sigh. 'Thank you.'

A number of inky spheres drifted across the limpid black sky of Hrunnesh. Below them the strange mineral landscape passed by, shining with deep tones of bronze-red and violet. In the first globe were Valcad and Ashurek, and in the next were Pellar, Medrian and Estarinel. Then came Evór and five or six more of the philosophical nemen. Within, the spheres still seemed to be no more than bubbles, smoky but transparent, and apparently guided by the nemen's thoughts alone.

Presently they saw below them a great, round hole in the Plane, as uncompromisingly black as the stuff of the nemen's tunics. The spheres began to descend towards it. As they floated below its rim, there was no shifting of gravity such as they had experienced in the shafts of the White Plane; instead it was as if they had entered a vortex. The spheres were sucked at vertiginous speed into the shaft, and absolute darkness closed around them. Estarinel closed his eyes and swallowed hard, praying that it would be over soon. Pellar said matter-of-factly, 'Do not fear.'

They fell for what seemed an age. But at last their descent slowed and the spheres began to float lazily, bubble-fashion, again. Valcad informed Ashurek that they were now on the other side of Hrunnesh. However, there was not even the dimmest illumination here: all was absolute midnight black.

The philosophers caused the globes to land on an unseen surface and they emerged into a place of dark, wet stone that was always lightless. Estarinel located Ashurek by the sound of his voice and led Medrian – who was still catatonic – over to him.

'We will stay by the spheres,' said Valcad, 'while you search.'

'Have you no kind of light to guide us?' Ashurek asked.

'No, I'm afraid not. Even we cannot see on this side of Hrunnesh, so I suggest that you do not go far, and that you locate us again by voice.'

'Which direction do you suggest we try?'

'With an infinite choice, I hesitate to suggest any. However, you may hear her singing.'

'Come on,' Ashurek said to Estarinel. 'Put Medrian between us, so we don't lose each other—'

Even as he spoke a solitary, haunting, sorrowful chirp pierced the darkness, seeming to come from everywhere and nowhere at once. And Ashurek shouted, 'Miril!' and ran blindly away from the others, heedless of Estarinel shouting at him to stop, or he would be lost.

Ashurek ran headlong through impenetrable night, shouting Miril's name. Beneath his feet the uneven, wet rock jarred and tripped him every few steps. But he was oblivious to that, and even to the possibility that more dangerous drops might loom ahead. The darkness, the fear of never finding his companions again, meant nothing to him; his only thought was Miril.

At last he did miss his footing and fall. He lay half-stunned on the damp, unforgiving surface, unable to cry out or move. And somewhere in the darkness his father, the Emperor Ordek XIV, leaned over him and said, 'Most beloved of my sons, you have failed me. Through you the pride and glory of Gorethria have been debased and lost. You shall walk in shame, clothed in the ash-grey of mourning, and the portals of your motherland shall for ever be closed against you.'

'Yes, Father. It is no more than I deserve,' Ashurek answered. And he lay, purged of all motive and memory – save that of his terrible betrayal of Gorethria – waiting for death to come.

He had never realised that death sang as it came, a sweet, mourning song like that of a lost bird. The singing was all around him, clamorous and beautiful and full of tragedy.

'Ashurek,' sang a voice by his ear. 'Ashurek, do you not know me? Ah, will you ever know me?'

'Miril,' he gasped, and sat up, shaking and barely able to breathe.

'Yes, here am I,' she chirped. 'I am real, can you not see me?' And in the darkness he could see her, a small bird as

314

black as Hrunnesh, outlined by a faint silvery light. She was perched on his knee, looking at him. He could see her eyes, the eyes that had first shattered his innocence and made him understand the appalling evil of Gorethria's tyranny. He stretched out a hand until his fingertip brushed her feathered breast, and in that touch he felt the grief and agony of every country Gorethria had ravaged: every village burned, every prisoner tortured in Shalekahh's dungeons; every child orphaned and wife widowed by the wars. And behind all was the amorphous mass of power that he had glimpsed and lusted after in the Dark Regions, the soul of the Egg-Stone, which now drove him to annihilate the Earth.

'Miril, Miril,' he uttered, tears falling from his eyes like blood. 'What am I to do?'

'Beautiful was I when I guarded the Egg-Stone, beautiful as the glad day with the joy of protecting your world from it,' her sweet voice lilted, infinitely sad. 'Oh, unhappy was the day when you took the Egg-Stone from me, for all was as I forewarned: the Earth was bathed in blood and pain and the sweetest of lands was fouled and the world rushes to its sad, sick end.

'And deprived of joy, my golden feathers have withered to black, and hope has been lost, and the Worm pursues me through the darkness. Here have I mourned, and sung out my sorrow, and waited. I have waited for you, Ashurek, waited to be reunited with the Egg-Stone so that my pain may end.'

'Miril – I no longer have the Egg-Stone,' he rasped, flooded by sudden dread.

'Ah – I know, I know. For if you still had it, you would never have come looking for me. Nevertheless, it must be found and I must be reunited with it, for it is a little piece of the Worm, and as long as it exists, the Worm will never truly die.'

'It cannot be found,' Ashurek said faintly. 'It was lost in a volcano. It is gone from my life for ever.'

Miril stretched out her wings and sang in her lovely, sad tone, 'Gone from your life forever? Just to speak its name

315

is to remember its look, its feel, its power, and the agony it causes. Gone? Gone?'

'Yes, you are right!' he cried, tormented. 'But it cannot be recovered, never. You can't ask me to go looking for it—'

'Hush, be still,' she trilled softly, resting her beak on his hand like a healing jewel. 'That will not be necessary. All is not lost.'

'Is it not? Miril, slaying the Worm will mean destroying the Earth. This is the culmination of the evil through which I have worked hand-in-glove with the Serpent to corrupt the world. Perhaps M'gulfn relies upon me turning aside at the last moment and abandoning the Earth to its rule. Or perhaps it revels in the knowledge that when it dies, all other life will die too. I know not. How can you tell me that all is not lost?'

'Ah, Ashurek,' Miril sung sorrowfully. 'You have found me – but have you found me?'

'I don't know how to find you,' he admitted gruffly, forcing himself to look into her liquid, honest eye. 'Tell me.'

'I will frame the question, but you must know the answer,' said she. 'My name is more than Hope. My true name is something deeper and stronger than Hope, and when you understand what it is, then you will have found me. When first you saw me, what did you see?'

'My guilt.'

'Yes, but that was only the first step. Now you must cease to let it torment you, for who is helped by your guilt?'

'It is not supposed to help anyone,' he replied through gritted teeth.

'Then is it driving you to put right what you have done wrong? Ah, no, it drives you to destroy, for you believe that only an ultimate fire can burn out your guilt, relieve your torment.'

'Yes. That is what I believe,' he forced himself, bitterly, to admit.

Miril rustled her wings, and her voice was stridently, piercingly beautiful. 'Then I will tell you that it is not so. The last step is to take responsibility, which is a very different thing from guilt. The world need not die. But you must let go of your guilt, and learn to place trust in those who know my true name, and let them guide you to the Quest's end.'

'You mean Estarinel and Medrian?'

'Yes. The Quest devolves equally upon all three of you.'

'I have not put trust in them, it's true,' he said quietly. 'I felt I dared not rely upon anyone but myself.'

'And for that you forsook every tender feeling that might have turned you aside from your doom?'

'Yes. How do you know these things?'

'Ah, Ashurek, I once told you, I know everyone, I can read your eyes and your heart,' Miril sang gently. 'Yet when you trusted Estarinel and Medrian so little that you would have killed them, you did not. Why did you stay your hand?'

'Because I am not yet wholly evil, I suppose,' he said mordantly. 'I don't know. I could not. It must have been some remnant of compassion.'

The sweet dark bird turned her head to one side and looked at him enquiringly. And at last he understood.

'Ah, you have found me, you have spoken my name, and I do not think I have ever been truly lost to you, after all. Can you yet believe that there may be a gentler way to complete the Quest?'

He nodded, his throat aching as if stuck through with knives.

'Then believe me when I say this: only compassion can truly win. Not guilt, not heartless, blind ruthlessness. Only compassion. And above all, Ashurek, before the end you must learn to spare some mercy for yourself.'

'I cannot – not as long as Silvren remains in the Dark Regions,' he grated. 'Miril, the Shana have almost destroyed her, made her think she is evil. I've lost faith in my ability to help her. Is there nothing you can do?'

'Alas, I cannot go to her. Only if she was to feel a little hope for herself, my spirit might enter even the Dark Regions.'

'No one could feel hope there!' he exclaimed bitterly.

'Still she must find hope in her own way, as must everyone,' Miril answered sorrowfully.

'She'd even lost faith that killing the Worm was the right thing to do. Miril—'

'Ah, no more questions now. It is enough,' she sang, 'enough that you have found me again. We must go back to your companions now, and then will I answer your doubt. Come, Ashurek, let me perch on your hand, and I will guide you.'

No. Not there – not to her. I hate her – loathe her – she is poison to me. I forbid it – I will not let you go there. The Serpent raged within Medrian, on and on, like a thrashing grey sea continuing to pitch the body of a drowning man long after he has ceased struggling. Its fear was her fear, vast and extreme, like the terror she had shared in its nightmares, but this was infinitely worse, something of which that remembered fear had only been a pale shadow.

The Serpent loathed and dreaded Miril.

M'gulfn had nearly taken Medrian over once, and since the time at the river, her control had been slipping, inexorably, day by day. There were blanks in her memory: she could not remember walking over the Tundra for two days. She could hardly recall being stung by the plant or crossing the sulphurous lake. Her only vague memory of that time was that she had somehow been someone else – still the Serpent's host – but someone who staggered on fractured limbs while the Serpent's mockery seared her flesh like a brand. Defeated and weeping with humiliation . . . but it had only been a glimpse of a previous host's life, brought on by fever . . . or by M'gulfn's will, as a warning. When she had awoken at Estarinel's side, she had known, instantly, that her precious wall of ice and steel was gone at last.

And yet . . . M'gulfn lay quiescent. It made no attempt to intrude upon her thoughts, though it could have ravaged her mind on a whim. It was laughing at her. *See, my Medrian, I have won. I do not even need to torment you. Your last defence against me is gone. And soon, very soon, you will be mine. There will be no warning . . . you must understand that every action you undertake of your own volition is by my grace only. When the time is ripe, I will enter your thoughts like a whisper. I will be you. It is almost over.* And with these words echoing venomously in her head, she had stood up like an automaton, and fought the flying things, and run to the Glass City, and listened to Hranna, all the time feeling her inward sickness and defeat permeating outwards through her body. It was as if something had laid an egg in her flesh at birth, and from it a worm had hatched and all this time it had been growing, feeding on her from within, so that now all that was left of her was a tenuous outermost skin, and in one mouthful the Worm would swallow that skin, and she would be gone, and there would be only a grotesque, bloated monster in her place.

And there was nothing, nothing she could do to fight the feeling. Tearing her apart was the most awful knowledge of all, that if she had not surrendered to her feelings for Estarinel in Forluin, she would never have become so weak. Their love for each other had betrayed them both, and the Serpent was laughing at her. *So, my Medrian, you are no more than human after all. Almost over . . .*

Ashurek was right. They should have left her behind. But that would not really have helped them; the Serpent could motivate her to do exactly as it wished. Once it decided to make its move they would be as defenceless against it as she was. Even if she could have warned them, it would have been futile.

Almost—

Then, suddenly, out of nowhere – the Serpent's awareness that Miril was on the Black Plane, and the Entrance Point hanging in the air before them. Its terror filled her like vertigo; she felt the emotion discolouring her face and crabbing her hands. Her whole body became nerveless and weak, and as violently as she desired to break away from Estarinel, she could not. Horror filled her like a torrent of viscous acid, bearing her mind away with it. It flooded her lungs and it overflowed and surrounded her. She was suffocating in a thick lake that stretched in every direction to the end of the universe. She had no self, but then, neither did M'gulfn. Together, they had become one amorphous mass of fear.

She saw nothing of the Black Plane. She did not hear a word that the nemen said. She knew nothing of the flight in the sphere. All she knew was a terrible, measured pounding – like the footsteps of a malevolent giant approaching, slowly but unstoppably, from a great distance. And each beat sent ripples through the lake of fear, grey shock-waves that filled Medrian-M'gulfn with an excruciating discomfort that was worse than physical.

Each beat was louder and more terrible than the last. Miril was drawing nearer and nearer. *I hate her, don't make me—*

And suddenly Miril was there, a silver-gold fire of unbearable sweetness. She instilled the Serpent with the same dread and disgust that it inspired in humans. Theirs was the repulsion of opposites, for she made the Serpent look where it could not bear to look.

Now Miril's breast was pressed to that of M'gulfn-Medrian, and at the touch the Serpent recoiled, screaming its cosmic abhorrence and misery. It contracted like an amoeba, and from being a mass of fear filling the universe, it continued to shrink inside Medrian, falling away into a void until it was but a speck, a mindless mote of terror. And Medrian fell with it, helpless, until at last she was in the centre of a gentle, quiet darkness. Here she found release from torment and, for once, dreamless sleep.

Estarinel felt horribly alone on the Black Plane, frantic with apprehension at Ashurek's disappearance. Somewhere behind him were the nemen; he could hear them talking, their melodious voices chillingly calm as they debated Miril's nature and other abstract topics. He did not trust them not to get tired of waiting and silently abandon them to the darkness.

After about an hour, although it seemed to Estarinel four times longer, he saw Ashurek approaching. His first reaction was overwhelming relief and not a little anger; his second

320

was amazement that he could see the Gorethrian. A faint silver radiance glowed round him, and it emitted from the small bird perched on his right hand.

'Miril,' Estarinel gasped, feeling a sudden urge to weep. Somehow, the idea of 'finding' her had been totally abstract to him; he had never expected it to be so literal, so heartrendingly real.

But she was black – not tawny-gold.

He stood holding Medrian's arm, watching as Ashurek and Miril came slowly towards them. And when they reached Estarinel at last, neither of them felt able to say a word. Even the nemen fell silent.

'Estarinel,' Miril chirped, flying to him. 'You know me, you know my name.'

'Yes,' he whispered. 'You've helped me so many times.'

'You understand that I was not destroyed, only lost. I am re-created in the hearts of men with each new sunrise, when they hear the piercing sweetness of the dawn chorus, and know that the previous night's darkness was not the whole truth of the world. And I give myself wholly again and again, for as long as life endures – but only where I am wanted.'

'Here you are wanted and desperately needed, Miril,' said Estarinel, tentatively stroking her silky head. 'Ashurek said your feathers were golden. Why are they so dark?'

'Sorrow had made me black, and only when this world reaches the sunrise beyond this night, will I find my true colour again,' she sang. 'Estarinel, you know love and compassion, but do you know that there is a difference between them?'

'What do you mean?' he asked.

She replied, 'Love may be selfish, but compassion is not. Remember this.'

She touched his hand with her beak and then flew to Medrian. She settled on her cloak and at once Medrian uttered a gasp and fell to the ground. For a long time Miril remained over her heart, uttering soft, sorrowful cheeps. Presently she said, 'Ah, alas, Medrian cannot hear me. But she will be well. When she awakes, tell her these words. She believes that her feelings are a despicable weakness, but it is not so: they will be her strength.'

Then she flew back to Ashurek's hand, and said, 'Ashurek, you spoke to me of Silvren's doubt that it was right to continue the Quest. Do you share this doubt?'

'Naturally,' he answered quietly. 'She was the only human who ever inspired me with faith, rather than cynicism. If she doubts, so do I.'

'The Hrunneshians also,' Estarinel added, 'have just told us that killing the Serpent would be wrong. That it is the same as destroying life itself. Hranna said much the same. Miril, are we doing the right thing, or are the Guardians just misleading us for their own ends?'

'They have their own ends, it is true,' Miril answered. 'But in the final evaluation, however it appears, they do not conflict with yours. You speak of "killing", but I know nothing of this. I only know that certain powers must be brought together: myself and the Egg-Stone, the Serpent and the Silver Staff. This is not destroying, it is creating. But it must be done with love and gentleness, as I told you, Ashurek.

'If you wondered why the Guardians could not essay this task themselves but had to send three humans, the reason must be clear to you now. They are not human. It is true that they could have destroyed the Serpent easily, and the Earth with it. But only through humanity can the Earth be redeemed. They sent you not because they are callous, but because they wished to give the world a chance.'

'If this is true, it changes everything,' said Estarinel.

'Ah, but there is still great risk, and your choices must be the right ones.'

'Miril, can you not come with us on the rest of the Quest?' Ashurek beseeched her.

'Oh, but I am coming with you,' she sang joyfully, to their relief. 'Don't you know that this is why you had to find me? Estarinel, take out the Silver Staff.'

Surprised, he obeyed. As he drew the Staff from its scabbard, he was at once overwhelmed by its joyous singing and a feeling of tranquil strength. It illuminated the blackness, splashing a silver light onto the wet stone. He wished he had thought to use it before.

Miril chirruped, and her notes were in exquisite harmony with the Staff's singing. 'You know that the power within this Silver Staff is that which is opposite to the Worm. Do you know also that I am a part of that power?'

'I had half-forgotten it, but yes, the Lady told us,' said Ashurek.

'In order to come with you, I must be absorbed into that power. This is why you need me. Without me, the Silver Staff is incomplete. Just as without the Egg-Stone, the Serpent is incomplete. Estarinel, hold the top of the Silver Staff against my breast.'

Ashurek began to protest, but Miril silenced him gently. Her voice was clear and lilting and gentle as she said, 'Do not fear: in this way will I escape the Black Plane, and show you an Exit Point to the Worm's domain, and fulfil my purpose. Although I will be with you, I will be invisible to you, and you must make your own choices. Yet you may call upon me in times of greatest need for my help. Now, Ashurek, hold me firm while Estarinel touches me with the Silver Staff.'

Then Estarinel raised the Staff and hesitantly pressed the blunt end to Miril's breast. She stretched out her wings and put her head back, beginning to glow from within so that her feathers were silhouetted like black lace against the light. Then they, too, absorbed the radiance until she shone as if afire. The Staff burned in Estarinel's hands with the same brilliance, while its carefree innocent energy reverberated through him like a paean. Miril cried out and leapt aloft, hovering on motionless wings, burning brighter and brighter until she blazed silver-white, and they could hardly bear to look at her.

She seemed to have lost her three-dimensional quality and transmuted into a heraldic symbol in front of them. When their eyes grew used to the brilliance, it seemed that they were looking at a bird-shaped hole in the fabric of the Black

Plane, through which they could see the sky of their own world. The corporeal Miril was no more.

'She said she would show us the Exit Point,' exclaimed Ashurek. 'Come on!'

Still in a daze of brilliance and warmth and immanent strength, Estarinel slid the Silver Staff back into its scabbard. Then he bent to pick up Medrian's unconscious, slender body. As he did so a voice near them said, 'Wait.'

It was Valcad, who seemed to be the only Hrunneshian still there.

'Must you go?' the neman said sadly. 'We had looked forward to many long and enriching talks with you.'

'Well, we must disappoint you,' said Ashurek. 'We have to return to Earth and complete our Quest. Where are your companions?'

'They went back to the other side,' Valcad said, 'because we could not understand the speech of Miril, and her presence was too disturbing to our basic philosophy. But I waited in case you needed further help.'

'Thank you, but we have found what we sought, and for your help in that we are profoundly grateful.'

'I must thank you, too,' Valcad replied, 'for we will be no longer troubled by Miril, and you have given us much food for thought. I ask only that in your "Quest" you bear in mind the philosophical paradoxes which we have brought to your attention.'

'Yes, we will,' said Ashurek with an ironic grin. 'There is some truth in them. Farewell.'

'What is truth?' they heard Valcad musing behind them as they turned and headed for the silver shape that was the Exit Point.

It was larger and further away from them than they had realised, and they walked for many minutes over the treacherous, dark rock before they reached it.

'If I'd had to spend any longer in the company of those philosophers, I would have gone mad,' said Estarinel as they walked. 'They could make nonsense sound as if it was profoundly true.'

'I don't agree,' said Ashurek. 'I think the Hrunneshians are quite right: there are no real answers to anything. And I think if they ever proved anything, they would all cease to exist.'

The surface beneath them began to slope upwards and they slithered and stumbled on the rock until they finally reached the bird-shaped window in the darkness. Ashurek looked through and Estarinel, behind him, called out, 'What can you see?'

'Nothing. It's too bright. It's all silver and white, and it's cold – freezing. Come on, let us go through.'

Side by side they stepped through the Exit Point, and the Black Plane vanished, and a cold, white brilliance embraced hem.

13

The Last Witness of the Serpent

As THEY stepped through the Exit Point it was several minutes before their eyes adjusted sufficiently for them to see where they were. Around them the air was cold and so still that it seemed they were not outside, but in an enclosed space. Then they saw that the brightness was not that of the sky at all: it was the whiteness of ice. They were in a cave, formed by a crevasse which had become sealed at the top. Walls of ice rose around them, shining like frozen glass, with hints of pale blue gleaming in their depths.

Estarinel saw a flat ridge on the far side of the cave and went over to lay Medrian down on it, skidding slightly on the ice floor as he went. He made her as comfortable as he could, reassured to find that her eyes were closed and her breathing steady. There was even some colour in her cheeks.

'Miril said she would recover,' Estarinel said pointedly, looking at Ashurek.

'I cannot withdraw what I said about her,' he replied softly. 'However, I'll admit I was wrong to want to abandon her. She is part of this Quest until the bitter end. The Serpent's victim, like the rest of us.' He walked slowly round the cave, searching for a way out. Presently he found a crack concealed by some tumbled blocks of ice.

'I think Miril has specifically placed us in here so that we'd be safe for a time,' Ashurek said. His voice echoed in the high-roofed cave. 'We'd better rest and eat before we think of going on. We'll stay here until Medrian has recovered.' Estarinel nodded, grateful for Ashurek's change of heart.

Having settled Medrian, he drew the Silver Staff from its red scabbard to check it. As soon as he touched it he knew that it had changed.

'Ashurek, look!' he exclaimed. On top of the argent rod, where previously there had been nothing, there was an oval orb the size of Estarinel's palm. It seemed to be made of the same metal as the Staff itself, but it had a translucent quality. At its heart, something stirred with tiny, soft, hardly discernible movements, like an unhatched chick.

'She said she would be with us,' Ashurek said. He touched the silver orb with a long, dark finger. 'I don't know exactly what this means. Except that she is somehow within the Staff, and may be called upon to our aid when we have great need of her.'

Estarinel replaced the Silver Staff carefully in its sheath. 'You don't still believe that there is no answer but the Earth's destruction, do you?'

'No,' Ashurek sighed. 'I was wrong about that as well. But it is still a danger, and it is up to us – all of us – to find the right way of finishing the Quest. I fear . . . well, I fear that I may have to face the Egg-Stone again. I don't know whether I will survive that.'

'But you said it was lost – with Meshurek—'

'Yes, it was. Ah, I don't know. Perhaps those philosophers have turned my brain. Now,' he said more briskly, 'it's very light in here – I think we are not far below the surface. The first thing I intend to do is to locate the way out of this cave, and see what is outside. I'll mark the way as I go if it proves tortuous. I'll be back soon.' He turned to go, but paused. 'There were many things I said on the Tundra which I now regret. Nothing has changed, about Silvren and the others, but Miril made me understand . . . well, that the path I had chosen was insane. As you so rightly pointed out. It was wrong of me to try to take the Quest upon myself. I now know that the three of us *are* the Quest.'

'It's all right,' Estarinel said, looking at him with a half-smile. He had not forgotten that when actually faced with the decision of slaying him and Medrian – by which means

327

the Serpent certainly would have triumphed – Ashurek had turned aside. 'It's over and done with.'

Ashurek nodded and gripped his shoulder briefly. Then he scrambled over the ice-blocks to the narrow opening in the cave wall, and his tall, lean figure vanished from sight.

Medrian found herself lying on a firm surface with something soft pillowing her head. She felt warm. She lay with her eyes closed for a long time, half-asleep, not wanting anything to disturb the peaceful, gentle darkness in which she drifted.

Where was M'gulfn? Ah, there it was, within her still, but very distant, like a child lost in the night. Let it stay lost. For the first time since the Blue Plane, she knew respite from torment.

She wondered where she was, but felt it did not really matter. She knew she was safe. There were a lot of strange memories within her, all confused and overlapping, though no longer disturbing. There was something about a Plane of black crystal on which tall, four-armed philosophers walked; a viscous grey sea of terror; and then a sweet silver-gold light, driving back the sea so that it shrank and shrank into nothingness.

Miril had restored Medrian to herself. She had complete mastery of the Serpent, such as she could never have achieved alone. There was no need for a great glacier to protect herself from it now. No need to encapsulate her thoughts in ice, or to force emotions to lie frozen in the pit of her heart. She could say and think and feel whatever she wished, and M'gulfn might writhe in her mind and groan and whimper all it wished, but it would never touch her. Never, never again.

She stretched and opened her eyes. The whiteness all around her made her blink, until she realised that it was ice. She propped herself up on her elbows, to find herself lying on a flat ridge, wrapped in her cloak and with her pack under her head.

Floating near her, about three feet above the ground, was

328

a soft sphere of starry blue and golden light. She looked at it in surprise, unable to think what it was, but noticing that it gave out a wonderfully cheering warmth. Estarinel was kneeling by it with a gold vessel in his hand, apparently heating some wine.

Medrian stared at him as if she had never seen him before, his long, dark hair, fair face and gentle brown eyes. She found herself so desperate to speak to him that it was like an ache of starvation within her. As she gazed at him he looked round and saw that she was awake.

'Drink this,' he said, handing the vessel to her. She swallowed the warm H'tebhmellian wine gratefully, feeling a pleasant heat and vitality spreading through her body. 'Now, how do you feel?'

'Better. Much better than I have for a long time,' she replied, and smiled at him. 'What's that?' She indicated the starry, floating lamp.

'Oh, a device the H'tebhmellians gave us. Look—' he reached into the sphere, which despite the heat it gave out was cool to the touch. At once the light vanished, and he showed her a small golden ball lying in his palm. 'To light it, you just press this indentation,' and at once the cloud of blue and golden stars appeared again. 'It floats in the air wherever you place it. It's to give us light and heat now that normal fires are impossible; it only works in Arctic conditions. So Filitha told me, anyway.'

'Where's Ashurek?' she asked, swinging her legs over the edge of the ridge and sitting up.

'He went to find a way out of this cave, only a few minutes ago. Medrian, do you remember anything about the Black Plane?'

'Hardly . . . There was something vague about nemen. But I remember Miril.'

'Do you? Did you hear what she said to you?'

'No. I couldn't see or hear anything. There was just a silver and gold light. Estarinel, will you come and sit by me?'

He seated himself next to her on the ridge and said, 'Miril told me to tell you that although you think your feelings are

329

a weakness, they will prove to be your strength.' She lowered her eyes and did not reply. Presently he noticed that her dark eyelashes, curved against her pale cheek, were glistening with tears.

'There's something I must tell you,' she whispered. She slipped her cold hands into his and looked up, her shadowy eyes as brilliant as rain. Estarinel could tell that something had changed within her, as it had when they had gone to H'tebhmella and Forluin, but in a subtly different way. She had always been intrinsically self-contained, but now there was also a tranquillity about her, as if she had come to terms with a lifelong fear. 'I always intended to wait until the very end of the Quest to say this . . . but things have changed. There's nothing to prevent me from speaking now.'

He remembered all the times he had tried to persuade her to talk to him, and the despair he had felt when she had doggedly kept her pain to herself. And now here she was, about to tell him everything, and he found himself dreading what she had to say, almost not wanting to know. He sat clasping her hands, waiting wordlessly for her to begin.

She hesitated. She was thinking of Forluin, which she had had to put from her mind of necessity, so that M'gulfn could not use it to torment her. But now she recalled with acute longing how it had felt to be free of the Serpent, the sad ache of finding love while all the time knowing she was going to lose it again. And here was Estarinel, regarding her with the love and concern which he had always shown her, steadfastly, no matter how strangely she had behaved or how hard she had tried to rebuff him.

Would he still love her after she had told him?

Perhaps he would pity her; but she did not see how he could fail to feel revulsion, or even bear to touch her. She hated herself for deceiving him, but she could not stop; she craved a few minutes more in which he did not know the truth, and still loved her.

'Medrian? What's wrong?' he asked gently.

'I've got to tell Ashurek as well. I can't say it twice.'

'That's all right; we'll wait for him. Don't worry.'

330

'You have been very patient,' she said faintly, and she leaned her head on his shoulder and put her arms round his waist. His astonishment only lasted a second, lost in the simple joy of holding her and kissing her. It was strange how effortlessly pain and loneliness could be eased, tragic that Medrian had for so long been trapped in bitter isolation.

He could not have guessed how confused her feelings were at that moment; in a way, she despised herself, but at the same time she was thinking, how good it felt to love and know she was loved, to feel his arms round her, his hands in her hair. And M'gulfn not touching her. Distantly she observed its jealousy, and she did not care. The detachment on which she had based her life was ashes.

But at the back of her mind, a small voice told her, In this way the Serpent will win.

Presently Ashurek returned, and Medrian drew away from Estarinel and sat stiffly upright, trying to regain her grim self-possession. But he kept hold of her left hand, and she made no attempt to release herself.

'I've found the way outside. It is long, but not difficult,' he said, stretching out his hands to the warmth of the H'tebhmellian fire. 'Is there any of that wine left?'

'We still have three flasks. We'd better make them last,' Estarinel said.

'I have something to say,' said Medrian, almost in a whisper.

Ashurek looked at her with some surprise. He seated himself on a block of ice and said, with unusual gentleness, 'Yes, go on.'

Her head bowed, her dark hair falling around her face, and her eyes fixed on her right hand which lay curved limply on her knee, she began, 'The Quest is almost over. I was always going to explain myself near the end . . . not this soon, but eventually. I could not – could not—' her voice was as fragile and cold as a crust of ice. She swallowed, and made herself continue, 'I could not tell you this at the beginning of the Quest, for two reasons. I was not allowed to speak of it anyway, but even if I had been, I still would

331

not have told you, because if I had . . . you would never have taken me with you.'

You are not permitted to speak of this. You will be silent, raged M'gulfn, but she ignored it.

As if her mouth was flooded with poison, she said, 'I am the Serpent's human host.'

She thought she could hear the sighing of the Arctic wind and the distant creaking of ice in the silence that followed. She felt Estarinel's grip on her hand lose its strength, as she had known it would, and she let her hand slide from his, and she felt metallic bitterness invade and petrify her soul.

'Ashurek, don't tell me you didn't know,' she whispered.

'I knew you were working for it,' he replied quietly. 'I should have guessed. Perhaps even I was unwilling to believe the very worst of you. And I suspected Arlenmia so strongly that it clouded my judgement. This explains everything, of course: how the Serpent always knew where we were, how it was able to thwart us so often . . .'

'Estarinel?' she said, her tone acidic and self-hating. 'Now do you understand why I warned you so often not to trust me or grow fond of me? The most selfish thing I ever did was to return your love in Forluin. Don't you agree?' But he did not speak, did not look at her.

'So everything we have said to you, or in your hearing,' said Ashurek, 'has been like speaking to the Serpent itself? And is so now?'

There was so much more she had to say to make them understand. She clenched herself against her bitterness and tried to ignore Estarinel's almost tangible abhorrence. 'No, no, you don't understand. I am not the Serpent. I hate the Serpent! It did not send me on the Quest to sabotage it: I came against M'gulfn's will, to kill it!'

'Yes, I can also believe that,' Ashurek said thoughtfully.

'I have so much to explain. I want to start from the beginning,' she said. And as she related her story she stared fixedly at her hands the whole time, and her voice was as low and chilling as a bitter wind sighing across a desolate plain of snow. 'The Serpent was within me from my birth. I never knew a moment without its presence. My earliest childhood memories in Alaak were of the rattle of looms in my family's cottage, my mother and father working – sometimes laughing, sometimes talking in low voices about Gorethria. And there was a pile of unspun fleece – I think that is the very first thing I remember, sitting on it, feeling how soft it was, picking out the burrs and bits of twig – but before that there was the Serpent. So that before ever I had a thought of my own, it seemed that I was a grey, ancient, mocking intelligence in the guise of a baby.

'As I grew, I realised that this mind was something apart from my own, and utterly alien. But I still had no idea that I was different from anyone else. I only wondered how it was that other children could laugh and play, how my parents could smile and hug me, how my brother could return their affection . . . I don't know how to describe to you the nature of M'gulfn. It is just – always there. And it is grey and reptilian and vast – as a nightmare seems tangible and frightening, although it is only something within your mind. And it is full of hatred – like a sickness – and because it has come to understand humans, through previous hosts, it knows the most subtle and insidious ways to torment them.

'It spared me no torment as a child. It could make me weep and scream with fear, it could make me attack other children, destroy things, whatever amused it. Even so there was nothing to make anyone suspect that I was the host. To all appearances I was just a fractious, ill-tempered child. My mother must have loved me, to tolerate it.' She fell silent for a few seconds, then continued, 'I don't know how I came to realise that not everyone had this nightmare presence within them. I think as I grew older I became aware that my real self was separate from M'gulfn and quite different from it. I realised that I was intensely disliked by the others in our village, even feared. And I think the Serpent itself had somehow explained to me that I was "special". "Chosen". I was an outsider, but my real self wanted to be loved, just as any human does.

'I believe that by this stage most of its previous hosts had gone insane. I don't know why I did not. Perhaps it is just the stubbornness of the Alaakian character, the same thing that made it impossible for us to accept Gorethria's rule. I remember being angry, and going off alone into the hills to fight it. I was about seven or eight, I think. And I found that the angrier I got, the more it tormented me, and the harder I fought, the more easily it controlled me, laughing and raging within me. But for that Alaakian obstinacy I would certainly have gone mad.

'But I didn't. I experimented. I found that the less I allowed myself to feel, the less M'gulfn could hurt me. First I suppressed anger, then slowly – oh, it took months, years – every other emotion, unhappiness, love. Fear was the hardest, but that went too, eventually. I became utterly cold. I think this must have puzzled and upset my parents more than my previous behaviour; soon there were no more smiles, no more hugs. I think my mother grew to hate me. Ye gods. Do you know I can't even remember what my parents looked like?' Medrian paused, expressionless, but knotting her hands together until the bones shone through the skin. 'But I was in control. The Serpent could not read a single thought of mine, unless I permitted it. Oh, but it made me suffer for it. It never stopped fighting me, whispering and straining against the icy barrier I had set against it. Sometimes I was certain it would burst through and swallow me, and sometimes it could still gain control of me, just for a little while. And all the time I was thinking: how am I going to end this?

'As soon as I was old enough – fourteen – I joined the army. Alaak was not supposed to have an army, as you know, Ashurek, but we trained in secret. Then came the uprising, and the massacre . . . and I survived, and I stood on the plain knowing that the Gorethrians had gone onwards to the village, and that I would never see my mother, father or brother again. I think that was when I realised that the Gorethrians were the Serpent's children as well, and that it was causing not only me to suffer, but the whole world. So I left Alaak, hardly knowing where to go or what to do, except that I must find a way to stop this damnable suffering.

'Don't think I hadn't thought of suicide: I attempted it, but the coal-black horse M'gulfn had sent to me died instead. Such horses have protected me from other death blows, as you know, and when one is dead, another always comes. I suspect that the one which came through the forest when I was with Calorn now lies dead from the sting of a venomous plant. M'gulfn does not want me to die. It has – a kind of possessive attachment to its hosts. If anyone should succeed in killing me, the killer would instantly become the host. But I think that to relinquish its hosts before extreme old age eventually claims them is agony to it. Nevertheless, it happily allows me to be wounded and tortured. The strange thing is that physical pain makes it shrink from me, so that I have greater freedom and control in those times. I came almost to revel in battle and danger because of that.' There was a note of disgust in her voice.

'I went into the Gorethrian Empire, and I was there for years, seeking an answer. I went to the palace library in Shalekahh, and found some books about the Serpent there. They weren't much use, except that they made me realise that I had access to the knowledge I needed within my own mind. M'gulfn's thoughts contained the memories of all its previous hosts. All I had to do was look there . . . and there were thousands, stretching back to the very beginning of man, one after another. All had suffered, most had gone insane, one had even tried to slay the Serpent and had been grossly tortured and humiliated for her efforts. And I learned that the Serpent is immortal and unassailable, filled with loathing of mankind, and that the only reason it had not destroyed us all long since was that the Guardians had taken one of its eyes, the Egg-Stone, so lessening its power.

'But the stealing of its eye also seemed to be what sparked off its hatred. It feared that they would come again and slay it. So it decided to take a human host, which would work in this way: if ever anyone succeeded in destroying its body, its spirit could flee and hide in the human body, until it regenerated itself. Only once has it had to do this. Hundreds of years ago a party went out from the North of Vardrav and injured it so seriously that they thought they had slain it. And M'gulfn itself was afraid, and hid within its host, but its wounds were healed by its gross energy, and it soon returned to life, and ravaged the North of Vardrav in return. All the others who have set out to kill it have died without touching it.

'And after I had learned this, there was the attack on Forluin.' Again she stopped, biting her lip. 'Sometimes I feel as if I am half in its body, and I can see through its eyes and . . .' She stretched her fingers out, rigid, and stared at them. 'I couldn't stop it, I tried, I offered it myself, anything . . . It paid no heed to me. And I knew – what I think I have always known – that it was no good seeking only an end to my own suffering. The Serpent must die. There must be no more hosts, no more witnesses to its depraved cruelty . . . I was going to be the last.

'I had no idea of how it might be done. All I knew was that the Serpent and the host, somehow, must die together. I was its ultimate protection, so any venture against it stood no chance at all without my presence. In the end I went to the House of Rede, wretched, with M'gulfn fighting me every inch of the way. I had no real hope. But when I met Eldor, he knew who I was, and he told me that others would soon arrive to form a Quest against the Serpent, and that we were to go to the Blue Plane. The Lady of H'tebhmella knew me as well. Yes, she knew, but she and Eldor agreed that no one should tell you this except myself. That was why she could not answer your question.

'You understand, Estarinel, that although I was in the deepest despair, I could find no comfort for it. If I had tried, M'gulfn would have swept away my defences and possessed me. Even to be offered help tormented me.

'Of course, M'gulfn was enraged by my setting out upon the Quest. It did everything it could to stop me. Sometimes my control would slip and it would force me into acting against you. I was always aware of this danger, and I did my best to warn you . . . But there was one occasion when I managed to bend its will to mine. When you summoned the demon Siregh-Ma, Ashurek, and it refused to obey you, I persuaded M'gulfn to send it back to the Dark Regions. But the demon recognised me as the host, and told Gastada, and Gastada purposed to seal my mouth so that I should never speak of who I was, and keep me imprisoned so that the Serpent would not be endangered.

'Ah, but I haven't told you about Arlenmia. Its "priestess".' There was bitter mockery in her voice. 'She also realised who I was. She wanted to be the Serpent's host herself – I'm sure she can't have understood what was actually involved, but she certainly possessed the power to transfer it from me to herself. Perhaps the power was no more than fanatical determination, but it was real. I feared her. It was so tempting . . . all my life I have craved nothing but to be free of it. Just to give in, and let the burden be taken away. But in the end I could not: I had already made my decision. I couldn't abandon the world's fate into Arlenmia's hands, just for my own sake. Of course, my refusal made her furious. She decided to murder me instead, thinking that she would become the host instantly. It was ironic that the horse protected me, because with Arlenmia as its host, the Serpent would have been invulnerable.

'On H'tebhmella, I had my wish; I was free of M'gulfn. It cannot touch the Blue Plane in any form, and the part of it that dwells within me was left in a kind of limbo when we passed through the Entrance Point. Oh, that sweetness was edged with pain. It was everything I had dreamed of, while all the time I knew it could not last, and I had got to go back into hell. It would have been better if I had never gone to the Blue Plane at all.

'And as for Forluin, the Lady assured me that I would also be free of it there. And I could not resist the temptation to walk on the Earth in freedom for a time.'

Ashurek said, 'No one can blame you for that.'

'I told myself I wanted to be sure that Estarinel didn't give up the Quest, and that I wanted to witness the evil of M'gulfn's work so that my own determination did not waver

337

. . . and these reasons were real, but the main one was my selfish desire for a taste of freedom, which became a weapon for the Worm to turn against me.

'Perhaps now you understand why I was so ill when we returned to Earth. At once the Serpent was within me again, and its anger almost destroyed me. Pain brought me back to myself, but my control was not what it had been before, because my experience of freedom had weakened me. And by the time we reached the river, Ashurek, M'gulfn was winning the fight, and by the time we reached the Glass City, it had won.

'But Miril saved me. The Worm is terrified of her. When she touched me, it shrank away in fear. And that gave me back my control, stronger than it has ever been before. This is why I am able to speak freely now. I am also able to think and act as I will without its intervention. You were right to be suspicious of me, but there is no longer a danger of the Serpent sabotaging the Quest through me. It is still within me, but I am free of it. Do I make sense?'

'Yes,' said Ashurek. 'Yes, you do.'

'I had to be careful about the Staff, of course. I have done my utmost to keep the knowledge from it. All it knows is that we have a weapon of some sort, and that troubles it. But it can no longer read any of my thoughts, or even see through my eyes. Miril has blinded it. I think she showed it a reflection of itself. And now my explanation is finished,' she concluded dully, still gazing downwards at nothing. Estarinel sat beside her as if frozen, expressionless and ashen-pale.

'I feel that I must apologise to you, Medrian,' Ashurek said. There was a quality of sorrow and understanding in his voice, even a touch of shame. 'I have misjudged you. And in a way that could have led the Quest to disaster. I am sorry.'

'There's no need,' she replied with the ghost of a smile. 'None of us can help being what we are.'

Estarinel was sitting absolutely numb, stunned by what she had said. He had known, of course, that she was somehow,

338

unwillingly, cleaved to the Serpent. Perhaps if he had cared to analyse everything she had done and said, he would have arrived at the appalling truth long ago. But he had had even more cause than Ashurek to shut his mind against the connections that might have led to this unthinkable conclusion: that Medrian, whom he loved, and the vile Worm, which was beneath loathing, were linked in such an intimate, obscene way as to be one being. His first reaction had been revulsion, and Medrian knew it, and he sensed how much this had hurt her. But his abhorrence was not really directed at her, and as her story unfolded – so much more terrible than he could have imagined – his disgust and outrage at M'gulfn for subjecting her to such anguish became over-whelming. Understanding her pain, and knowing that he had caused her further torment himself, he bled with inexpress-ible sorrow for her. And the admiration he felt for her strength, and tenuous, adamant determination, was poignant in its extremity.

Then he understood that he had known the truth all along. She was M'gulfn's victim, but more than that she was herself, and nothing she said could have made him love her less, only more.

Estarinel realised that she was no longer at his side. She had wandered out into the middle of the cave and was standing there with her back to him, dwarfed by the ice walls soaring around her. And on top of the dreadful burden of the Serpent, she believed that he had turned aside from her, and she hated herself, because she felt that she had betrayed him.

In a second he was at her side, pulling her into his arms and holding on to her, tight, until she eventually relaxed and returned his embrace.

'I'm sorry,' she whispered. 'I never meant to deceive you, but I couldn't stop myself. I despise myself for it.'

'Medrian, don't,' he said gently. 'Never, ever think such wrong of yourself. If you knew how much I love you – it's me who should say I'm sorry.'

'It must make a difference, now that you know,' she said tightly, looking up at him.

'Yes, it does – I never realised how much courage you had. I've always known that the Serpent was tormenting you in some way, but I never could have guessed it was this bad. What the Serpent has subjected you to is abominable beyond all reason. I never thought I could hate it more than I already did, but this—'

'No, don't say that,' she murmured. 'Anyone who has been tainted by the Serpent's hate as I have could never truly hate anything again.'

'Then say I am only more determined to stand by you.' He hugged her tighter. 'Never again doubt that you are loved.'

'No one could have had a more steadfast companion than you and have done less to deserve it,' she said, bowing her head against his arm.

'Why do you have so little regard for yourself, after all that you've achieved, and against such monstrous odds?'

'Because Miril was right, I see my feelings as a weakness, and I think I ought to be more than human.' Her smile was self-mocking. 'But I'm not.'

'You've been a steadfast companion to me as well, and helped me through so many dark moments.'

'There will be more darkness . . .' And darkness seemed to be distilled in her large, unnerving eyes as she gazed at him. 'I wish I could promise that you won't be hurt again, but I can't. I haven't changed so much: everything I do must be for the Quest still, and not for you. All I can say is I hope you'll forgive me – one day.'

'Whatever happens, there'll be nothing to forgive,' Estarinel answered softly. 'I wish I could help you find some hope that the future won't be as black as you expect. I won't allow it to be.'

Medrian felt herself weeping, inwardly and without tears, at this. She was so grateful for his love and his kind strength that she could not bring herself to warn him not to hold any hope for the future. It would be an untimely, unnecessary cruelty. She said, 'I dreaded the time when I would have to tell you the truth. But now I have, I feel relieved – almost

340

happy. Just to be able to talk freely, and know that you understand, and not to hurt you by my coldness.'

'The times I must have caused you torment, trying to make you talk to me . . .' he remembered with dismay. 'I'm so sorry. I just thought love was the answer to everything.'

'It is,' she answered. 'In the end, it is.'

Hand in hand they went back to sit on the ridge near the H'tebhmellian fire. Its blue and gold glow made firefly lights dance on the ice, and in the folds of their cloaks. Ashurek handed them some of the H'tebhmellian provisions – dark bread and a sweet, compressed cake that tasted of fruit – and they ate in a silence which was, none the less, companionable. There was no tension or sense of separateness between them now, nothing dividing them. Instead, there was renewed comradeship, much firmer than it had ever been, and although they were closer to the Serpent than ever, each of them felt calm in a way they never had before, far less apprehensive, even resignedly cheerful.

Presently Ashurek said, 'At least now we can discuss the Quest more freely. You're right in saying, Medrian, that had I known you were the host in the beginning – even if I had known the full story – I would not have risked going with you. Even on the Blue Plane I would have had serious doubts. But now I understand how essential your presence is, and I believe that you have M'gulfn sufficiently in check not to hinder us. I am wondering just how much further we have to go.'

'About a hundred miles,' said Medrian flatly. There was something unnerving in this unexpected preciseness; they looked at her in surprise. 'I don't know how many days that will take us: obviously our progress will be slow across the ice, and it depends on the weather as well. And on the Serpent, of course. It's all right, Ashurek – you could throw the compass away, and we would still find M'gulfn. I know exactly where it is. I usually know what it is doing. I will know if it moves, although it hates moving. Flights leave it torpid for months. That's how I knew it could not have attacked Forluin a second time, whatever Arlenmia said. That's why it attacks so rarely.'

'Your knowledge of it is going to prove extremely valuable. Do you have any idea of the actual mechanics of killing it?' Ashurek asked.

He saw her suppress a shudder. 'No, I'm afraid not. That is for us all to find out, as Miril said. There is still great danger. If it should attack us, above all we must not touch it with the Silver Staff, because that would cause a cataclysm such as you predicted. At least, it should be done only as a last resort.'

'Ah, I fail to understand how we are to use the Staff if we cannot attack M'gulfn with it directly,' Ashurek said, shaking his head thoughtfully.

'I don't know,' said Medrian. 'Somehow, we will find out. All I really know is that Serpent and host must die together.'

She said this so matter-of-factly that Estarinel had to restrain himself from crying out in protest. Out of nowhere he recalled the words she had spoken, what now seemed an age ago, when he had asked her (how cruelly!) if she did not have a home and family to return to when the Quest was over. 'Once . . . long ago . . . but there's nothing left,' she had said. 'Still, when choice is gone and the last journey is ahead, that has a kind of comfort of its own, doesn't it?' Now that the meaning of these words was acutely clear, they twisted in his chest like a barbed hook.

'Medrian, that can't be the only answer,' he said, clasping her hand. 'There must be a way—'

'Don't hope for too much,' she replied as gently as she could. 'I have always known how the Quest would end for me. It's all right: I want no more. I am prepared.'

'But after all you have been through, you deserve better than that – a chance of happiness at least,' he persisted. 'Listen, you were free of it on the Blue Plane – if there was some way for you to go back there, while Ashurek and I—'

'No, that would be impossible. When I was on H'tebhmella, the Serpent did not retreat wholly into its own body for that time, it waited for me. Besides, as soon as it thought itself in danger, it would find a new host anyway. It might even choose Arlenmia.'

'By the gods,' muttered Ashurek.

'Besides, without me to guide you and warn you of its movements, you'd stand no chance anyway,' she added. 'Don't raise your hopes over this, Estarinel, I beg you.'

Estarinel said no more, but he was still determined that she should be freed of M'gulfn without being harmed. The Serpent has taken enough from us, he thought. Medrian, I could not bear to lose you as well. I couldn't bear it.

'Do you really think we have any chance of killing the damned Worm?' Ashurek asked her morosely.

'Yes, we have a chance,' she replied. The dreadful sick, ashen look had left her face at last and although she was still pale, her visage was clear, almost radiant. 'I will tell you why I think so. The Serpent has nightmares. It is afraid of something. It was only because of these that I set out from Alaak, or thought we had a chance at all. Terrible, desolate nightmares.'

They slept for several hours in the ice cave, protected from the cold by their cloaks, and warmed by the H'tebhmellian fire. When they awoke they ate again, and then prepared to embark on the last stage of their journey.

The H'tebhmellians had given them extra clothing for the Arctic: leggings, belted jackets, gloves, and thick boots all made of the same supple, pearl-grey material that was so closely woven as to resemble kid. It was impervious to snow and wind and warmly lined with quilted layers of fleece. Over this they wore their stout, weatherproof cloaks, whose hoods could be fastened to protect their faces against blizzards, when necessary. Now all they had in their packs – apart from a rope, which Medrian was carrying – were the provisions they needed to sustain themselves for the next few weeks; as their journey had been shortened by their passage through the Black Plane, they had a plentiful supply. They also had vessels in which, using the H'tebhmellian fire, they could boil snow for drinking water.

They still carried a sword and a knife apiece. In addition,

Estarinel and Ashurek each had an axe, but Medrian had discarded her crossbow, having used all the arrows in the fight with the pterosaurs. And Estarinel carried the Silver Staff alongside his sword, its red sheath tied with thongs along the length of the scabbard so that neither inhibited free movement. The egg-shaped top of the Staff was protected by a piece of leather tied loosely over it.

Presently they were ready to leave the ice cave, which had been so welcome a refuge between Hrunnesh and what lay before them. Last of all, Estarinel extinguished the H'tebhmellian fire and slipped the weightless gold sphere into his pack, then swung his cloak over his shoulders.

'I'm almost too hot in this clothing,' he remarked.

'Aye, but we'll be more than grateful for it, out on the snowfields,' Ashurek grinned. He led them across the cave over the blocks of ice and through the aperture into a narrow passage, which tapered to a point above their heads. At once they discovered the value of the new, thick boots: they gave a sure grip on the frozen surface. This corridor was apparently no more than a flaw running through the ice, which might close when the massive sheets of Arctic ice next moved.

The flaw widened as they followed it but, disconcertingly, began to angle downwards, leading them deeper into the ice layer.

'There are a series of strange caves ahead,' Ashurek said. 'Nothing happened to me before: I think there is no danger.'

The passage led down into a smooth, milky-blue cave which they had to traverse bent almost double beneath the low roof. A thin, descending corridor led through three more similar caves, each smaller and dimmer than the last, like beads threaded on a strange necklace. Finally they entered a tunnel so low and narrow that only the slipperiness of its glassy walls allowed them to force their way through.

'Are you sure you came through here before?' gasped Estarinel, who had no love of confined spaces.

'Yes, it widens out ahead,' Ashurek replied, neglecting to mention that it first attenuated to a mere fistula through which they would have to crawl on their stomachs. However,

344

this proved to be more uncomfortable than difficult, and they soon gained the end of the constriction. Beyond, they found themselves in a wide, echoing cavern which resembled a subterranean grotto, all diamond-white columns of ice and blue shadows.

Something compelled them to cross it slowly and in absolute silence, looking about with wonder as they went. It seemed to be illuminated by more than refracted daylight, and the air reverberated with the distant cracking of ice. Estarinel became unpleasantly aware that there was no ground beneath the polar cap, only a slate-black, freezing ocean, and it seemed to him that there were tons of ice above them, and only a thin layer, like a pane of glass, below. He could almost see water swirling and bubbling angrily beneath the translucent floor, hear the ice groaning and giving under their weight . . . If this was an illusion, he did not know whether it had sprung from his own imagination or from an unseen sentience hovering in the frigid, motionless air.

But this sense of foreboding seemed to be unfounded. They gained the far side of the cavern without misadventure and entered a broad, glass-white passage, which began to slope upwards once more. As they drew nearer to the surface the light grew more and more brilliant, while the corridor widened into another ice cave. They could not judge its size, because they were everywhere surrounded by pure white, semidiaphanous curtains of frost, which chimed softly in an imperceptible draught. It seemed a weird, faërie realm in which humans were unwelcome intruders.

They trod silently through the cavern, feeling that every point of light sparkling on the frost sheets was a tiny eye, and the tinkling of ice flakes the rumour of eldritch voices, disturbed by their presence.

But there was no real sense of danger, only an unsettling otherworldiness. The cave narrowed and gradually gave into a rough fissure, at first enclosed by great slabs of ice leaning this way and that, and presently open to the sky. Then the fragile eeriness was crushed and blown away like dust by the imminent, stark reality of the Arctic. Estarinel quickly

345

convinced himself that the apparent sentience of the ice caves was merely a product of an over-sensitised imagination.

But even as he was telling himself this, Ashurek said, 'I have often thought that there must be forms of life which are so remote from us that we do not even recognise them as life. We are more akin by far even to the Grey Ones than such things are to us.'

'If it is so, they are still children of the Earth, and in as much danger as the rest of us from . . .' Medrian did not speak the Serpent's name. Perhaps she felt that to do so as they approached the Arctic proper would be too much like invoking it.

A jagged ribbon of pale blue ran above their heads, gradually widening as the walls of the fissure became lower. Presently the walls were below shoulder height, and soon after that they diminished into mere blocks of ice merging with the snow which had been blown into the end of the gully. They waded through the cold softness of the drift and came out, at last, onto a wide expanse of mirror-bright snow.

The fissure from which they had emerged ran back into a rugged mass of ice hills which stretched across the skyline from North to South. The polar cap had for countless years been cracked and forced up in gigantic, vertical slabs, then refrozen, the process repeated over and over again until there seemed to be massive, glacial teeth rooted in the landscape.

This range was to the East of them. To the North and West stretched a mantle of snow, shining like a harlequin coat of argent and silver-blue and white. Over it arched a clear sharp sky which was the delicate hue of a harebell. The air was as still as within the caverns, but it had a bitterly raw edge to it; the sun looked small and colourless, with no promise of heat in its dazzling rays.

It was now early autumn, but (Ashurek hoped) they still had the light on their side. If the sun set at all, it would only be for a few minutes each day. The weather was bound to be bitter, but by no means as intolerable as in the depths of winter. Things could have been worse.

'At least we don't have to cross those ice crags,' said Estarinel, as they surveyed the vista.

'I wouldn't be too sure of that,' Medrian replied. 'They may curve round and across our path eventually. M'gulfn has given me some vague concept of polar geography . . . but it is very hazy, and it is always changing anyway. I wish I could be more definite.'

'Any information is better than none,' said Ashurek. 'For the time being it will be useful to us to move parallel to those crags. They may afford us shelter if there is a storm.'

They began to tramp Northwards across the snow. Their cloaks, chameleon-like, had taken on a shadowy-white quality, so that any being watching from a distance would barely have seen them. The snow was firm, although a thin, fresh fall crunched under their boots and sprayed in a glittering foam around their ankles. As yet there was no real sense that this was the Serpent's domain; it seemed a neutral, untouched territory.

Encouraged by this, well-rested and heartened by the freshness of the sky, they made good progress on the first day. When the need for sleep overtook them, they camped in a niche within the ice crags, much cheered by the floating H'tebhmellian fire. Meanwhile the sun continued its slow circuit of the horizon, a floating fire of another sort. The moons appeared in the pale sky, like two flakes of worn ivory.

As he tried to sleep, Estarinel began to feel a disturbing awareness that the sun was in fact stationary, while the Earth was spinning vertiginously beneath them, and they were very near to the centre of that spinning. It was an awesome and dizzying sensation, like that which he had experienced in the Cavern of Communication, when he had glimpsed the true size and majesty of the universe, and had felt at once infinitesimal and infinite; less than nothing, yet part of everything. He fell asleep without realising it, and his thoughts became dreams.

It was odd that he had previously been haunted by phantasms of snow; now, here they were amid snow and he was dreaming of something different. A dim place; something greyish, bulky but half-hidden in shadow, uttering dull grunts. Another shape, dark with moisture, struggling within a glistening membrane. And there was his mother, kneeling in straw, her head bent, her fair hair tied off her face. Her bare arms were slimed with blood almost to the shoulder, and as she raised her face, it too was streaked with gore, and tears.

But as she looked at him he saw that she was laughing with joy.

'We are part of it, yet it reduces us to nothing,' she said. And then he realised that the grey shape was a brood mare, and the dark, wet form over which his mother was bending was a new-born foal.

He had helped his mother with such births so many times. How ordinary this scene was, yet how precious, how much more to be desired than even the transcendent, crystalline beauty of the Blue Plane. And yet utterly unobtainable. Gone. Destroyed by something that could not even comprehend what was being lost, could only envy and loathe it.

'Mother, the Worm is outside,' he said in the dream, as calmly as if he was mentioning a friend's arrival. At the same time he felt rooted to the spot by panic, knowing that his mother was in mortal danger. But she continued to smile calmly at him, with no trace of alarm.

'Already?' she said. Then, illogically, 'Tell it I am coming back.'

'Yes, I will. Everything I do is for this,' he replied.

He must have spoken aloud because he woke up then and found Medrian, already awake, staring at him.

'What did you say?' she exclaimed.

'I don't know. I was dreaming,' he replied, sitting up and trying to clear his mind of the dull pain which the images had induced.

'Do you often have such dreams?' Medrian asked. 'Prescient ones, I mean.'

'If that was prescient, I didn't understand it. It was only some muddled memories. I have had some presentiments of the future . . . not always when I've been asleep, either. How did you know?'

'I see it in your eyes, sometimes. There's no other look like it.'

'Isn't there?' he said, vaguely disturbed by this thought. 'But the things I think I see make no sense to me at all. It's only after the event that I come to understand what the vision implied.'

'But what you see turns out to have a meaning?'

'Yes, apparently. Do you know, Medrian, the night before the Serpent attacked, I dreamed of a woman with very white skin and black hair. I remember it vividly. It was you . . . although I did not realise until I had known you for some time.'

'Are you sure? The memory plays tricks . . .'

'No, I am sure, because that night I also dreamed about Arlenmia's horse.'

'Taery?' she exclaimed.

'Yes, a blue-green horse with a gold mane and tail. That was something I could not possibly have mis-remembered!'

'But nothing else to do with Arlenmia?'

'No, I only have the most random glimpses of things. There was always snow, but that's hardly surprising as I knew we had to come to the Arctic. I think I saw Silvren before I knew what she looked like . . . and Calorn before I even knew she existed. And the castle of the Guardians: red glass and grey figures. Yes, and the Silver Staff, before ever we reached H'tebhmella. And something to do with you and the Staff—'

'Oh, don't,' she said, gripping his arm with a gloved hand. 'Don't go on. Listen, you must not let this foreboding trouble you. I suffer it too, sometimes, and I promise you that it's for the best that it seems meaningless until you can see it in retrospect. Otherwise it would only cause you pain, and make you try to change what cannot be changed.'

'Yes, I'm sure you're right,' he said, and kissed her.

'We think we understand things,' she said, 'but that is to

save us from going mad. Everything is beyond our comprehension, really.'

They resumed their walk across the glittering snow plain. The air was as still and crisp as it had been before, the sky still a thin blue, bleached in the East by silvery sunlight. It was hard to believe that there was evil so close at hand.

'We'll be lucky indeed if this weather holds,' Ashurek said. 'Medrian, forgive me if this sounds like a fatuous question, but may we not have been misled in thinking that the Serpent inhabits the North Pole? I have no sense of it . . .'

'Be grateful for that,' she replied shortly. 'It cannot last.'

As if in answer, before they had walked on for another hour, a discolouration rose into the Northern sky, like venom blackening the skin around a snake bite. They stopped and stared at it. Estarinel felt such a sense of depression and dismay that he almost turned and ran; only with a great effort of will did he hold his ground, and restrain himself from crying out in fear.

It was like a ghastly parody of the aurora borealis, a curtain of semi-transparent darkness rippling across the skyline. There was light, of a sort, within it; a grimy ochre phosphorescence, which turned the sky behind it green. The sun seemed to flicker and quail before this violation of the atmosphere.

'No,' Estarinel protested faintly, closing his eyes and involuntarily gripping Medrian's shoulder. He felt he would sooner die than take another step towards the foulness undulating across the sky like brownish smoke. What a fool he had been, he thought, to imagine that he could even face M'gulfn, let alone attack it.

'Now I believe it,' said Ashurek. 'Is this a warning, or a welcome?'

Brown winds mourned across the Earth, heralding the Serpent's inevitable triumph. Everywhere people huddled shivering within their dwellings while grey creatures howled and moaned outside and unnatural birds flapped overhead, shrieking. Sickness and darkness were closing on the world like jaws. Some said, if only we had believed the Serpent existed, and fought it! And some said, if only we had worshipped it. Now it is too late. This is its revenge.

In Excarith, Setrel looked despairingly at a storm-tormented sky the colour of dried blood and murmured to himself, 'They have failed. Would that I had taken my family to the House of Rede with Benra.'

The House of Rede was the last bastion against M'gulfn on Earth, and refugees had flooded there from the Worm-racked continents. It had always been there, a house of sanity, kindness and wisdom. No one wanted to believe that its security had become a tragic deception. *The House of Rede will be the last to fall*, Silvren had said, but those words did not express what a very specific, gleeful act of vengeance its destruction would be, perpetrated by the Shana to celebrate the dawning of M'gulfn's age.

The demon Ahag-Ga made its way to the House of Rede, disguised as the neman, Benra. There Dritha was fooled by it for long enough to invite it over her threshold. But as soon as she recognised it for what it was, Ahag-Ga sloughed off the disguise and cheerfully eviscerated her.

Dritha was a Guardian, and could not be slain as such, but her soul was forced to flee her human body and take refuge in a distant domain. Then Ahag-Ga took on her corporeal form, and went smiling among the hundreds of refugees in and around Eldor's house, and began to torment and slay them. And they thought it was Dritha herself who had suddenly turned upon them, betraying them, and they knew then that the Serpent had triumphed. Those who escaped the demon fled and flung themselves into the chill ocean.

So fell the House of Rede.

14

The Arctic

THEY STOOD transfixed for perhaps half an hour before the bromine-dark curtain vanished. Its dissipation was sudden; it seemed to collapse onto the horizon like a piece of filthy gauze, and at once the sky regained its ice-blue purity, as if it had never been sullied by the Serpent's power. The sun gathered strength, and the snow once more shone like a sheet of white gold, over which handfuls of diamonds had been scattered.

But there followed a sense of absolute stillness, silence so overwhelming that it was beyond their power to disturb it by moving. They remained motionless, frozen with awe and apprehension. They felt as tiny as insects on an infinite, milk-white disc, set in a solid dome of pale blue glass, which was bound to shatter and tear the universe from end to end if they so much as breathed.

'Something's going to happen,' Medrian whispered. The sound of her voice seemed to break the spell. Shaking his head grimly, Ashurek began to stride forward again. Hesitantly, Estarinel followed, with Medrian at his side.

'Such as what?' Ashurek said. His voice sounded strange, as if despite the eerie, vast stillness of the Arctic around them, he had spoken loudly in a tiny room.

'I don't know,' she said.

'Do you know what the Serpent is planning? I thought it had been somehow weakened by Miril.'

'I can't read its thoughts when it is determined that I shan't,' Medrian replied. 'Its fear of Miril has not debilitated it. Miril has changed things in that the Serpent can no longer control me, but that doesn't mean that I can control the Serpent. Its fear has only served to make it furious, and while its fear fades, its anger grows. Don't imagine that it is less powerful than before because of Miril. Far from it.'

'That's encouraging,' said Ashurek drily. 'Was that foulness in the atmosphere a show of power, intended to dishearten us?'

'I think it just meant to say, "I am here",' Medrian replied chillingly.

'Well, it had the same effect,' Estarinel managed to say, his throat still spasmed with dread. 'It must wish to fill us with so much terror that we dare not approach close enough to attack it. It knows it can. What are we—'

'Don't think of it, Estarinel,' Medrian said. 'Let us only think of the journey, while it allows us to move.'

'Aye, we'll save worrying about M'gulfn until it next shows its power,' Ashurek agreed.

'Yes. I'm sorry. It's just that—' Estarinel shook his head and fell silent. He knew why he was feeling this fear more acutely than the other two; it was because he had actually seen the Serpent. It had stared at him with its tiny, malign eyes as it lay on the ruins of Falin's house and he had felt his soul branded by its pitiless grey evil. For a long time he had been able to forget about it . . . but now, every hint of the Serpent's presence brought back that horror tenfold.

In many terrible situations he had acted with what others saw as bravery. He did not think himself courageous; he had merely done whatever seemed necessary at the time, exigence overriding any qualms he might have felt. But this was different, it was more than fear; he was beginning to feel that he truly could not face M'gulfn a second time. It would be easier to take his own life. He could no more look upon the Worm again than he could coldbloodedly kill a friend.

But he did not want to believe he had come so far, only to turn aside and betray Forluin at the very end. He fell behind Ashurek and, fixing his eyes on the Gorethrian's resolute back, forced himself to follow, step for step, like a glassy-eyed automaton. Medrian saw that he was struggling, but she said nothing.

The silence around them grew no less weird as they trudged on. Contrary to Medrian's forecast, nothing happened, but the awful sensation that something was about to persisted. Strange colours began to gleam in the sky, not only in the North but in all its quarters. In the West was a pale green and lemon glow, shot through with points of rose light. A white-mauve radiance, imbued with a nauseating quality, insinuated itself across the Eastern skyline. Presently the whole sky was a-swirl with uncanny pastel hues such as were never seen in any natural sunset. The snow reflected them like a mirror.

Then sounds began to fill the silence as air fills a vacuum. A multi-voiced, disharmonious sighing rose above them, like the wailing of warped creatures bemoaning their lost humanity. The three trudged on, trying in vain not to let it disturb them.

Only when they saw white peaks lying along the Northern horizon, like glittering fangs tearing at the sky, did they realise that the moaning was caused by a distant wind in those crags. As Medrian had predicted, the jagged line of ice hills curved round in front of them. They walked on doggedly, and the discordant sighing grew more eerie.

Soon they walked into the wind. It lifted the surface of the snow into spirals of white frost and sent them streaming and whirling across their path. Even though they were not walking against it, it numbed their faces like a mass of frozen needles. Swiftly they fastened their hoods against it and walked with their heads down, grateful for the warmth of the H'tebhmellian clothing. Even their eyes were protected by a panel of some transparent stuff like pliable crystal. Totally enclosed by their cloaks and moving like pale shadows across the snow, they appeared no less spectral than the landscape which contained them.

'I suggest we gain those peaks and find shelter there,' Ashurek shouted above the wind, pointing ahead.

Suddenly all the strange tints fled the sky, leaving it colour-

354

less. Clouds began to stream overhead until solid white gloom enveloped them and thick snow filled the air. By the time they reached the beginning of the glacial slopes the wind had become a blizzard, sending whirlwinds of snow raging around them. Hints of aching cold penetrated even the stout H'tebhmellian clothing.

All the ways into the crags looked steep and forbidding. Ashurek chose a path that wound upwards between two spurs of ice and they began to climb in single file, bent against the storm. Soon they were surrounded by towering walls of ice, albumen-white and harder than glass. Here they had a certain amount of protection from the wind, although it still caught them in gusts as their path turned at different angles or crossed valleys. Streamers of snow were blowing out onto the wind from the peaks above them. But on lower ground the snow was drifting, and they were soon crunching through knee-deep mounds of it. The way steepened, presenting them with a treacherous series of steps and sharp ridges. Searching for foot- and handholds, they clambered slowly upwards until they gained a level stretch of ice.

At once the blizzard caught them full force, not allowing them a chance to catch their breath or rest their numb limbs. With the wind wailing savagely and hurling darts of steely snow at them they ploughed on in search of shelter. Presently they found a crevice in an ice wall, well-protected from the blizzard. They entered it gratefully, lit the H'tebhmellian fire, and sat watching the flakes drifting through the gloom beyond their refuge.

'Even this bitter weather is preferable to Serpent-sent apparitions,' said Ashurek, pulling his hood back from his face and brushing rime from the folds of his cloak.

'Isn't this storm M'gulfn's doing?' Estarinel said, feeling too tired to judge for himself.

'I think it is natural, but M'gulfn may choose to take control of it,' Medrian answered. 'If it does, it will swing round to the South.'

'Don't you mean the North?' Ashurek asked.

'No. If M'gulfn meant to stop us, it would use some more

drastic means than a storm. But if it meant to speed us towards itself, it would put the wind behind us.'

'Meaning that it is in as much of a hurry as we are to end the Quest, but rather more confident of the outcome?' Medrian did not reply to this.

They ate and rested in the crevice, hoping that the snowstorm would blow over within a few hours. It continued unrelentingly while they tried to sleep, huddled around the blue-gold sphere. After a few hours they were faced with deciding whether to brave the blizzard again, or to delay indefinitely in their shelter.

'This weather only makes our journey uncomfortable, not impossible,' Ashurek said. 'I would far rather be struggling through it than waiting days for it to subside.'

The others could not disagree with this. Fastening their hoods they emerged into a slippery valley, which they followed until it joined a path winding roughly Northwards between barricades of ice.

Medrian was right. The snowstorm had swung round to the South while they slept. They stepped out into its force and found themselves walking at considerable speed, the wind pushing at their backs like a giant, ghostly hand. Flurries of snow raced past them and diminished into the distance, giving a strange, hypnotic illusion of spiralling into a vortex. Apparently the Serpent was dragging its enemies avidly towards itself, eager to make an end of them. Estarinel did not even let himself think of reaching M'gulfn. He let the wind propel him and concentrated only on keeping his feet.

Soon the air was so thick with snow that they could barely see a couple of yards ahead. The wind was as bitter as a frozen knife; while their clothes protected them from the worst of it, their cloaks became stiff with ice. A polar wilderness of swirling, grey and white ice surrounded them, and within it they did not notice how dangerous their path had become until it was too late.

Ashurek, still in the lead, suddenly discerned that the walls on either side of them were no longer made of solid ice, but of an insubstantial, swirling mass of snowflakes. The way ahead lay along a blade-sharp ridge with a sheer drop on either side. Turning back was impossible, because it would have meant walking into the teeth of the gale. All they could do was to keep going, but they were being forced along at a pace that was too swift for safety. As soon as the ridge angled somewhat to the right, the wind drove into them like a ram, and the inevitable happened. All three simultaneously lost their footing and fell.

Their plunge off the ridge was sharp and breath-stopping. But it was over in an instant: snow saved them. Badly shaken, they dug themselves out of the deep, cold drift in which they had landed and stood shaking the snow and ice from their cloaks, trying to recover their breath.

The wind had dropped abruptly. Ashurek looked enquiringly at Medrian, but she only shook her head to say that she was no wiser than he. The snow, however, continued to fall thickly from the clotted, steel-grey sky. They resumed their walk, seeking a fresh Northerly route, with the white blanket deepening around them.

Their fall had left them in a crooked ravine, and it seemed they would face some sort of climb whichever route they chose out of it. They were already exhausted, so they decided to find shelter within the ravine and go on after they had slept.

When they emerged the next day – not that there had been any discernible night – gusts of wind were dancing along the ravine, raising a foam of ice crystals on the snow. The sun appeared briefly, transforming the grim, bitter landscape into a realm of exquisite beauty, all pearl-blue crystal and glittering whiteness.

Some hours later they had climbed out of the ravine, and reached a vast, smooth plateau. Pausing to get their breath and look back, they heard a soft rumbling noise, and watched as the entire face of snow which they had just negotiated collapsed in an avalanche.

They began to trudge across the plateau. Beyond it lay the pale, frozen fangs of the ice cap. They stretched in an unbroken line from East to West, but appeared to end some ten miles to the North. They hoped that another day's travelling would take them clear of the hostile crags, although they felt no optimism about what lay beyond. Meanwhile they tried to take advantage of the lull in the blizzard; only a few flakes of snow were drifting from the clouds, although a raw wind still prodded at their backs. Occasionally hints of Serpent-sent discoloration gnawed at the sky, deeply depressing.

Ashurek was somewhat ahead of Medrian and Estarinel, when he sensed the snow beneath his feet creaking and straining. Calling out a warning, he turned to retrace his steps. Even as he did so a chasm split open beneath him and he vanished in a flurry of white crystals.

Medrian and Estarinel hurried to the chasm and lay on their stomachs, peering anxiously over the edge. It was very deep, and its sides were sheer, diamond-hard ice. Ashurek was lying in the bottom, some thirty feet down, half-covered by the snow which had fallen with him.

'Take the rope out of my pack,' Medrian said to Estarinel, pushing back her cloak. 'Ashurek! We're going to throw you the rope!'

'It's no good,' was the faint response. 'My arms are pinioned. This crack extends below me. I can feel myself slipping further down.'

They cast the rope down to him, but it fell short by about four feet. Ashurek was unable to move to reach it. Even as they watched, helpless, they could see him sliding gradually deeper into the blueness of the crevasse.

'Pull the rope up,' said Estarinel. 'If we both tie our cloaks to it—' As he spoke the ice creaked again, and they watched, horrified, as Ashurek slid down another fifteen or so feet. Now they could barely see him.

'No, it's hopeless,' Medrian muttered.

The plateau began to creak and shudder beneath them and the crevasse narrowed, so that Ashurek was lost to sight, swallowed by the ice. They heard his voice, faint but very clear and calm, calling, 'Leave me. You must go on with the

Quest. Go quickly, before it breaks up any more and you join me. Go.'

'He's right,' said Medrian, her face adamant with resolution. She seized Estarinel's arm and pulled him bodily away from the chasm. 'Don't even think of arguing. Come on.' She was coiling up the rope with one hand and propelling Estarinel across the snow with the other even as she spoke.

They had walked perhaps fifty paces when the ground juddered so violently that they were both flung off their feet. Cautiously, they rose on their hands and knees, feeling an ominous certainty that another crevasse was about to open beneath them. A deep rumbling noise droned far beneath them, more sinister than the shifting of ice.

'Do you know what that sound is?' Estarinel gasped. Medrian shook her head. They both looked anxiously around them, gazing back at the place where Ashurek had fallen.

As they looked, they witnessed a remarkable sight. Ashurek's head – his hood thrown back – appeared over the edge of the crevasse. Slowly and smoothly his whole figure rose into view – just as if something was lifting him. Presently he was clear of the chasm and they saw that he was standing, feet apart for balance, on what looked like the back of a massive living creature. As his feet reached the level of the rim he leaped out onto the snow, rolling as he landed. Then he jumped to his feet and ran over to Estarinel and Medrian.

The rumbling grew louder. The crevasse groaned and widened and from it erupted a ghastly creature like a gigantic snake. Its head came first, a hideous visage that might have befitted a monster of the ocean, then a long, undulating body scaled with sickly purple and maroon. At the other end of it there was not a tail, but another head, with upward-staring eyes and a circular mouth stretched round too many hook-like teeth. It slid across the snow for perhaps fifty yards, then plunged its leading head into the surface and burrowed again. They watched it slide smoothly under the snow until it vanished; the plateau continued to crack and shudder beneath them as it continued on its underground route into the distance.

'Another sort of Amphisbaena,' Ashurek muttered.

'What?' Estarinel exclaimed. 'What was it?'

'A creature of M'gulfn's, without doubt. I had heard that such things wander about in the Arctic. Its passage must have caused the crevasse to open in the first place. Ironically, it also rescued me. I was trapped, unable to move, and I could feel the ice tearing open beneath me. But just as I was expecting to fall again, there was suddenly a firm, moving surface under me. I managed to bestride it and stand up. Perhaps it was irritated by my weight on its back and merely wanted to rid itself of me – whatever, I can but acclaim its decision to rise to the surface.'

Estarinel was laughing with relief. 'Oh, by the Lady, I'm glad you're safe! Are you all right?'

'Yes, I think so, just somewhat startled,' Ashurek replied. 'I never thought I'd have cause to be grateful to M'gulfn for anything.'

'You may not have now,' said Medrian. 'The Serpent probably did not want to be deprived of the pleasure of meeting you in person.' But despite her morose words, she looked as relieved as Estarinel at Ashurek's escape.

They crossed the plateau and were descending a slippery spur on its Northern edge when the blizzard began again. They found shelter in a sort of cavern formed by blocks of ice. Thawing and refreezing had caused massive icicles to form at the entrance. They ate and tried to sleep, but beyond their small circle of blue-gold light, lumps of snow were swirling past and the wind was howling off the plateau, and sometimes bromine-orange fires could be seen dancing amid the heavy clouds.

Estarinel became aware that some oblique perspective he had had on the Arctic was changing. At first it had seemed a raw, wild realm in which the Serpent had no place. But now, as he stared sleeplessly through the curtain of icicles, his viewpoint was transformed: the Arctic seemed wholly the Serpent's domain, while they were the unwanted intruders. It was as if the polar cap was a taut drumskin on which the Worm lay, feeling and understanding the tiniest vibration

360

therein. Nothing escaped its notice. This was its kingdom, where it was omnipresent.

Something Estarinel had not sensed when he had seen M'gulfn, was how deeply cleaved to the world it was, and how massive and all-pervading was its power. How could the slender needle of silver at his side possibly harm the Worm? Surely M'gulfn would feel it as no more than a flea-bite, if that; and how it would revel in mocking them, torturing them – he tried to suppress these thoughts, but they returned again and again. Somehow the deadly chill of the Arctic had seeped into his bones and he felt that despite the H'tebhmellian fire, the protective clothes – even Medrian, who was huddled against him, drowsing – he would never feel warm again. Even thoughts of his family did not make him feel resolute; it all seemed so pale, so far away. How clever the Serpent was to destroy people through their own despair, without ever touching them . . . he moved his hand to touch the Silver Staff, but its singing seemed to have grown shrill, nerve-jangling, and he snatched his fingers away. He felt exhausted, weak with fear, paralysed by the freezing cold . . . convinced that he could not go on.

They had now been in the Arctic for five days, and Medrian had estimated that they had covered about half the distance. How close that seemed – how final – Estarinel must have betrayed some reaction because Medrian had looked at him concernedly and said, 'Are you all right?'

'I'm terrified,' he admitted candidly. 'I don't know how much further I can go.'

'We're all afraid,' she said. But he already knew that, and she realised that it was not much help to him. 'The reality of it – being here – is worse than even I thought it would be. But there's nowhere for any of us to go except on to the end of the Quest. Nowhere. And I need you.'

'There's a certain satisfaction in doing what you know you must, however hard it is,' Ashurek added. And although these words had done nothing to reduce Estarinel's conviction that he could not go on, when the time actually came to resume their journey, he climbed stiffly to his feet and walked out into the blinding snow without conscious difficulty.

The sky was iron-grey, the air clotted with whirling flakes. The wind roared behind them, driving them onwards, crusting their cloaks with ice. All day they struggled through the glacial crags, as small and frail as moths blown across a hostile mountain range. The white blankets swathing the landscape looked deceptively soft and welcoming while concealing a heart as grim and bitter as frozen nails.

Wrapped in whiteness they came at last to the end of the ice crags, and took shelter beneath them to eat and sleep. When they awoke the snow was falling sparsely, so that they could see what lay ahead. It was not a heartening sight. Facing them was a vast, flat plain of snow unrelieved by any kind of landmark. The crags had seemed hostile, but at least they had offered refuge when it was needed. The frigid wind blew unremittingly across the snow, packing it like ice. Above it the sky was marble-white and sullen, but on the Northern horizon, malevolent olive and ochre lights danced like demons.

There was something moving on the snow, a bruise-coloured, many-legged thing that might have been coughed up from the Dark Regions. It did not attack them; it simply sat and watched them for several minutes, then dug itself into the snow and disappeared. But it was enough to instil them all with a sick disgust and wretchedness which made it even harder for them to set off across the plain.

Muddled with Medrian's own first experiences of the Arctic were M'gulfn's memories, so that each new place they came to, she felt she had seen before, from all different angles, in light and dark, fine weather and storm. And the sight of the white expanse, the Serpent-glow on the horizon, the silent, spidery watcher, filled her with unspeakable despair. What am I doing in this horrible place? she thought. The snow seemed to be reflecting a nauseating mauvish glare which mocked her dismay. She knew that there was nothing left between them and M'gulfn but this awful plain. Why did this have to be the last place I will ever see?

She turned to Estarinel and hid her face against his shoulder, and he held her, his eyes closed, trying to forget that the Arctic was there. But after a minute she straightened up and said, 'Now we must go on.'

Ashurek touched Estarinel's arm and pointed to the left. A few yards away, under an overhang of ice, stood another unpleasant creature. It was about four feet high, greenish-yellow in colour, with a huge head, dark, skin-covered swellings where its eyes should have been, and rudimentary arms. Obscenely, it resembled a foetus standing on spindly legs. As Ashurek made to draw his sword it opened its shapeless mouth and gave voice to a thin, piteous mewing filled with such uncomprehending hopelessness that it took away his resolve to kill it. It turned and burrowed mole-like into a snowdrift.

'Medrian, what are those things?' Ashurek asked.

'Just the Serpent's experiments in parodying life,' Medrian replied, her voice thick with revulsion. 'They will do us no harm. Not physically, anyway.'

Then they set out to walk across the snowfield. The gale pushed insistently at their backs, and the snow spiralled past them like splinters of ice. What beauty the Arctic possessed, however wild and raw, was utterly non-existent here. But the sense of malevolence and desolation which they felt here was not due to the physical aspect of the plain, but to the aura emanating from the Worm. It increased with every step they took.

In his imagination, Estarinel turned and ran any number of times; but in reality, with the wind at his back and Medrian's hand on his arm, he walked steadily on towards the Serpent, so afraid that he felt numb.

They saw more creatures emerging from the snow, staring at them, then disappearing. Perhaps some of them were not even real, but illusions sent by the Serpent to confound them; whichever, it did not really matter, because they served their purpose. The three tried to ignore them, but the phobic repulsion which they induced did nothing to improve their state of mind. Out on the plain they felt as exposed and vulnerable as if they were floating on a disintegrating raft in the middle of a freezing ocean . . .

'Does this snowfield extend all the way to M'gulfn?' Ashurek asked.

'Yes, I believe so,' Medrian said thinly. Ashurek was about to ask what the possibility was of the Serpent coming to meet them, but seeing Estarinel's expression, he thought better of it.

'How much further?' he enquired in a matter-of-fact tone.

Medrian did not have a chance to reply. There was a sudden creaking and groaning below them, followed by the deafening concussions of the ice cap fracturing. The surface heaved; they halted in consternation and hung on to each other, but a moment later they were pulled apart. The snowfield reared under them, tearing with a roaring noise like a great avalanche; then the whole Earth seemed to turn upside down and they were falling, falling, buried under tons of crumbling ice and snow.

Estarinel was floating. He had never dreamt it was possible to be so deeply, achingly cold. He could feel bands of iron gripping his chest and see red and black stars bursting across his eyelids, but at the same time he knew he was unconscious and close to death. Yet he did not mind. He felt quite calm . . .

Somewhere above him he thought he could hear a female voice which sounded vaguely familiar, saying, 'Ashurek, I need to know the words, can you remember?' Then it seemed that he was lying on a deadly hard surface, and it was cold, so cold; he opened his eyes and saw nothing but whiteness, as if he was trapped in a tiny room, like the hut in the domain of the Silver Staff – disorientated, he sat up violently, coughing water.

'Estarinel,' said a voice near him, not the disembodied voice he had heard while unconscious, but Medrian's. She was sitting at his side, and Ashurek was in front of him. 'It's all right, you're safe now. Comparatively, at least.'

'Oh, I'm frozen. I had this terrible feeling that I was drowning.'

'That's because you nearly did,' Medrian said.

He looked around and realised that they were sitting on a block of ice, roughly fifteen feet square, which was rocking gently beneath them. They were afloat on a slate-grey, apparently infinite ocean, with a great mass of ice packs jostling around them. It had almost stopped snowing and the sun shone pale and bright through the clouds.

'What happened?' Estarinel asked, shuddering with cold.

'The ice field broke up beneath us – whether due to a thaw, or something more sinister, I do not know,' said Ashurek. He lit the H'tebhmellian fire and made it float near Estarinel. 'Part of the plain must have been a mere crust, many feet above the ocean. It was only by luck that Medrian and I found ourselves on this ice floe. You went into the water, but we managed to haul you out. Your cloak trapped some air and kept you afloat.'

'It's fortunate that these clothes are waterproof,' Medrian added. 'Otherwise the cold would have killed you.'

'I can believe it. This journey would have been impossible without the H'tebhmellians' help,' Estarinel said, shivering and trying to warm himself by the starry fire. 'What are we going to do now?'

'The current is taking us North,' said Medrian, closing her eyes and trying to sense M'gulfn's thoughts. 'The Serpent has not been disturbed; less than two score miles from here the ice cap is undamaged. All we have to do is wait.'

The Serpent-fire on the skyline had turned to vivid green. It danced and spat, sending coruscating sheets of acidic light across the clouds. Flecks of discoloured snow fell hissing into the waves around them. Now that the initial relief of finding himself alive had subsided, Estarinel's spirits sank once more in the face of the Worm's grim power. Even retreat was impossible now; it was as if they were caught in a ritual dance of evil, drifting with a supernatural, leaden rhythm towards the heart of a nightmare. Again he felt that he could not go

365

through with confronting the Serpent. He found himself wishing that he had drowned after all; and although part of him knew that these thoughts were self-destructive, and that for Forluin's sake he should be facing the end with a bold and glad heart, yet it was completely beyond his power to feel anything but despair. Only the Worm's sickness was real; everything else was dreamlike, distant and ineffectual. For the time being he could function outwardly as if nothing was wrong, but he felt it was only a matter of time before this wretched sense of panic overcame him.

From the expressions on Medrian's and Ashurek's faces, they felt it too, although they were perhaps better able to cope with it. We were mad to think we could destroy it, Estarinel thought. The hypnotic rhythm of the ice raft as it carried them towards the Serpent seemed suggestive of something deeper, profoundly terrible but incomprehensible, like a half-remembered nightmare. And Estarinel felt that he was not afraid of dying – but of continuing to live in the Serpent's power.

Medrian slid her gloved hand into his and said, 'I know it's hard, but we must try not to look North. M'gulfn would dearly like to replace our determination with despair. We should talk of something else.'

'The Blue Plane, or Miril,' Estarinel suggested, although the words sounded hollow to him, as if such things had no more power here than frost against fire.

'There's something I would like to mention,' said Ashurek quietly. 'I thought I saw – well, just as we were hanging on to this piece of ice, and before we had rescued Estarinel, I thought I saw Silvren. Did you also see her, Medrian?'

'No, I'm afraid not.'

'Ah, it is as I thought: my imagination. She said she no longer had the power to project herself out of the Dark Regions. Strange, it was very real, and she seemed to be trying to say something.'

Estarinel was looking at Ashurek, startled by the memory that these words had awakened. 'I don't think it was your imagination,' he said.

'What do you mean?' The Gorethrian stared intently at him.

'Well, when I was more or less unconscious, I'm sure I heard a voice. I couldn't place it at the time, but now I realise it was Silvren's. She said, "Ashurek, I need to know the words, can you remember?" '

'You're certain of this? And she said nothing else?'

'That's all I heard. Do you know what it means?'

'No,' Ashurek sighed. 'Only that . . . if she somehow found the strength to contact me, it must mean that something has changed for her. What words? Oh, by the Worm . . .' He stared broodingly at the ice, one long-fingered hand tangled in his dark hair. Estarinel found it quite beyond his power to say anything remotely encouraging.

But as his gaze was drawn inevitably to the North again, Medrian exclaimed, 'Look, what's that?' and pointed across the sullen waves.

To their right, perhaps five miles distant across the jostling ice floes, floated a massive iceberg. It was not the only one they could see, but it was by far the largest. Most remarkably, it was sailing *across* the current towards them. It moved with the stately grace of a majestic ship, although in form it resembled a great castle of ice, rough-hewn yet beautiful, glowing beryl green, pale blue and amethyst where the light filtered through its translucent bulk. As it drew nearer, they could see the ice-floes spinning and tossing along its sides as it nosed them out of the way.

'We'd better be ready to jump to another floe if necessary,' Estarinel said, 'or we'll all end up in the water. I don't want to repeat the experience.'

The iceberg was travelling hardly faster than a man might walk, and it was over an hour before it drew close to them. Its size was awesome, and it seemed to give off a tangible aura of coldness. Its glass-white sides were ridged and faceted with uncanny symmetry. The three stood on their little ice raft, staring at it, trying to gauge just how much leeway it would give them as it passed.

But it did not pass by. As if someone had thrown down

an unseen anchor, it slowed down and came to rest a few hundred yards in front of them, rocking slightly with the swell of the waves. Their ice floe, meanwhile, continued its Northward drift, straight towards it.

'This looks deliberate,' Ashurek said, his hand on his sword hilt. Strangely, even the nearest of the other ice floes had floated too far away from them to be reached. They were stranded and could do nothing but wait, powerless, while they were carried towards the glacial castle.

Now they saw someone descending the side of the berg. The figure reached a ledge just above the level of the water and stood waiting for them, hands on hips.

Ashurek cursed, with great feeling, in Gorethrian. 'Oh, I should have guessed!' he exclaimed, and drew his sword. Medrian and Estarinel simply stared in shock and dismay at the figure.

It was Arlenmia.

Their floe crunched into the side of the iceberg and pitched wildly from the impact. They kept their feet, but the raft seemed in danger of breaking up beneath them.

'Here, I'll help you,' Arlenmia called, throwing them one end of a rope, which they all stared at as if it was a snake. 'Oh, come, take it! Ashurek, please put away your sword. I mean you no harm.'

'Ah, you've finally perfected the art of lying, have you?' the Gorethrian said acidly.

Arlenmia began to laugh. 'Look, you can stay on that piece of ice if you wish, but it would be easier for us all if you would step onto my iceberg now, rather than be fished out of the water in a few minutes' time. It's not much of a choice, I'm afraid, but it is the best I can offer.'

'She's right, damn her,' growled Ashurek, sheathing his sword and taking the end of the rope. He braced himself against it, pulling the floe tight in against the iceberg while Estarinel and Medrian – reluctantly – accepted Arlenmia's free hand to help them step onto the ridge. Then Ashurek followed. A few seconds after they quitted the ice raft, it split neatly into several pieces and bobbed away down the side of the great berg.

'What the hell are you doing here?' Ashurek demanded. Arlenmia smiled sweetly at him, and beckoned them to climb ahead of her up a series of steps cut into the ice. She was clad from head to foot in shimmering furs which were bizarrely striped with purple, black and green. Her fur-lined hood was pushed back and her hair spilled over it in a swathe of peacock-shaded silk.

'I would ask the same of you, except that I already know,' she said. 'All will be explained to you in time. Turn to your left, Estarinel – there is a tunnel there. I know you will not believe this but I am very, very pleased to see you.'

'You're right. I don't believe it,' said Ashurek. 'I dare say you were responsible for the break up of the ice?' Arlenmia smiled, but did not reply.

The tunnel led into a huge chamber within the iceberg, illuminated by a blue-green light which gave it an eerie, under-water quality. On one side a massive spiral staircase hewn out of ice evidently led to further chambers above and below. In the centre was an arrangement of ice blocks and ridges, covered with furs, which served as seats. Arlenmia motioned them to sit down.

'This is very impressive,' Ashurek said.

'Thank you. I had help, of course. One might as well travel in a reasonable degree of comfort. Now, can I offer you some refreshment?'

'We have our own provisions,' Medrian said flatly.

'Oh, I am not going to poison you!' Arlenmia exclaimed.

'Nor drug us?'

'No, I no longer have any need of drugs,' she said, an ominous note entering her voice. 'Listen, we are only going to be within this iceberg for a few hours longer. We will have to walk the last stretch. Do you understand me? So you had better eat and rest while you can.'

She was pacing slowly back and forth in front of them as she spoke. In the instant when Ashurek knew he was out of her line of sight, he glanced at Medrian and Estarinel and touched his sword hilt. Almost imperceptibly, they nodded. As Arlenmia turned they moved as one and surrounded her, Ashurek with the tip of his sword at her throat, the others on either side of her with their knives at the ready.

A look of annoyance crossed her beautiful, pale face but she stood quietly between them, not losing any of her statuesque poise.

'I know not what help you have on hand,' said Ashurek, 'but don't even think of calling for it, or you will never speak again.'

'This is very silly, and quite pointless,' Arlenmia replied calmly.

'Indeed? We have tasted your hospitality before. You have trapped us with admirable style, but we have no wish to be your prisoners a second time. You are going to be ours.'

'That will be nice,' she said, and a look of defeat came into her eyes, and Ashurek realised that she was feigning it, and began to feel horribly apprehensive. He pressed the sword against her throat, making a bluish mark in the silky skin.

'Now, tell us what you are doing here. Straightforwardly.'

'I was going to tell you anyway – there really is no need for this. I am here partly to prevent you from murdering the Serpent M'gulfn, of course. But I never intended to use force, or hurt any of you. You see, you stand no chance of success anyway, and I was hoping very much to make you share my point of view. You will be saved so much unnecessary danger and misery.'

'We have had this conversation before,' said Estarinel. 'It got us nowhere then, and it is not likely to now.'

Arlenmia looked sideways at him. 'I know, beloved, but I have not yet given up hope. However, I want to finish my explanation, and I am very uncomfortable with these blades pressing in on me, so as violence seems to be in order . . .'

There was a thud, felt rather than heard, like a silent splitting of the atmosphere, and for an instant the air was filled with a terrible dark light. When it faded, Arlenmia was still standing passively in the centre of the chamber, but

Medrian, Estarinel and Ashurek were lying, winded and half-stunned, in its furthest corners. The air seemed to be throbbing with a sickly, leaden power which was at once loathsome and seductively desirable.

Estarinel was the first to regain his feet. He staggered over to Medrian and helped her up, but Ashurek was still prostrate. As they went up to him he gasped, 'The Egg-Stone. She has the Egg-Stone.'

'Yes, that is correct, Ashurek,' Arlenmia said. 'I'm sorry I had to do that, but there was no other way to make you understand the futility of trying to capture me, threaten me, and so on. Please, come and sit down again. We'll have some wine. I hope you are not too badly hurt?'

The three staggered like dotards back to the centre and sat down, weak and dizzy from the Egg-Stone's power. Ashurek felt all his muscles clenched rigid against the molten fire running through his veins, the dreadful metallic voice whispering within his skull of the unspeakable torment he was going to suffer until he held the Egg-Stone in his hand once more, and did its will.

'But don't try to touch it,' said Arlenmia as if reading his thoughts. She bent over him and he could sense it, hanging around her neck in a little pouch as he had used to wear it himself. 'If you so much as think of taking it, I will blast you from the North Pole to the South Pole. Skord!'

'Ashurek? Are you all right?' Estarinel asked quietly.

'I will be. Damn her,' the Gorethrian gasped. 'With that thing in her possession, none of us can touch her. She's made herself invulnerable . . . and I cannot stop myself thinking about it. Its very presence weakens me.'

'What are we going to do?'

'There's nothing you can do,' Arlenmia answered, handing their weapons back to them. 'But perhaps now you will listen to me with a little more attention and respect for what I have to say. Ah, Skord. Will you bring us some wine, and some of those flat cakes, and the salted fish?'

They looked up in astonishment and saw, emerging from the stairwell, the youth Skord. He was dressed in similar furs

371

to Arlenmia. His brown hair was still neatly cropped, and his face looked even younger than before, despite its dull, strained expression. He gave the three an impassive glance; his once-bold, foxy eyes had a distant look. He knelt to Arlenmia and kissed her hand, then descended into the stairwell again.

'By the gods, Arlenmia, can't you leave anyone alone?' cried Estarinel, furious. They had rescued Skord from her and left him in the safe-keeping – so they had thought – of Setrel. 'What on Earth is he doing with you?'

'Oh, don't make a fuss,' she said, sitting down between him and Ashurek. 'He wanted to come with me. He realises how privileged he is to be with me on this most wondrous of journeys. In fact, I want you all to share that privilege: you see, I owe you so much. Everything you tried to do against me only aided me – this idea that you are working against the Serpent is but a delusion. We are comrades, all of us. We travel by different paths to the same goal.' Her blue-green eyes were shining as she spoke; again Estarinel felt her languid, enthralling quality beginning to ensnare him. He had forgotten that the magnetic aura of her personality was so powerful; with the Egg-Stone's force added to it she seemed omnipotent. Before, she had inadvertently broken the spell herself by making a careless remark about Forluin; but this time he knew that there could be no such simple release. A sudden pain in his hand startled him, and he found that Medrian was holding his fingers in a vicelike grip.

'You see,' Arlenmia said, 'if you three had not come to me, I might have stayed in the Glass City for ever, struggling through my mirrors to extend the tiny boundaries I had set for myself. I was furious with you all when you left, it's true. Your departure drained all my power out of the Glass City. Years of work, lost; I was faced with starting again from the beginning. Well might I have given up in despair. But I did not. I used that twilight time to think . . . to reflect, literally.' Her lips curved in a smile. 'Through all of you, though most of all through you, Ashurek, I saw that I had only been scratching at the surface of what I wanted, and that to achieve

372

it I must go straight to the heart. And I am grateful to you all for that. Suddenly I knew that I had been a fool, the answer had been before me all the time: I did not need the Glass City, messengers, and the rest, all I needed was the Egg-Stone.'

'How did you get it?' Ashurek asked hoarsely.

Arlenmia smiled and said, 'I had help. But once in possession of it . . . oh, what freedom! I had no more need of mircam or mirrors; all the power I had ever dreamt of was mine, flooding through me like a life-giving fire! But what should I do with it? Use it to conquer the Earth, as you did, Prince Ashurek?' Her tone was mocking. 'Ah, no. I spoke to the Serpent M'gulfn, and asked it what I should do.'

'You did what?' Medrian gasped, leaning forward to stare at her. 'That is impossible. It was a delusion – a hallucination.'

'You think so? You are wrong, Medrian. I spoke to M'gulfn. What it told me was so simple, something I should have known all along. The Egg-Stone is the Serpent's eye, and once the eye is returned, M'gulfn's power will be complete.'

Yes, so obvious, Ashurek thought, closing his eyes. Once the Serpent had possession of its missing eye, even the Silver Staff would not prevail against it. He could only wonder that the Shana, after sending him to fetch the Egg-Stone, had not taken it to the Serpent themselves.

'Have none of you anything to say?' said Arlenmia. 'Are you not going to inform me of how misguided, how evil I am? No persuasive speeches, no heartfelt pleas?'

Skord came up into the chamber and set a crystal table laden with food before them. Again he bowed to Arlenmia.

'Skord, please pour us some wine. And stay with us, have some yourself. Skord is sharing the honour of this journey, by the way, because it was he who first brought you three to me,' Arlenmia said. 'If you still have any thoughts of trying to stop me, I can only ask you not to waste your energy. I want you to understand that I could easily have killed you all by now. But why should I, when you are no danger to me?' She passed them goblets of wine. 'The reason I intercepted and rescued you was not so that I could harm you, but simply so that you could come to understand and share in the glory which awaits us. Won't you try these excellent cakes?'

Medrian forced herself to eat, knowing that they could not afford to be weakened any further by hunger. Ashurek and Estarinel followed suit.

'There's a lot I could say, Arlenmia,' Ashurek said. 'Unfortunately I doubt that I could persuade you to agree with any of it. It seems to me that you will find out how wrong you are only when it is too late.'

'But I am not wrong,' she said, somewhat venomously. 'I have work to do. I suggest that you take this opportunity to rest and consider whether you are so right after all.' She made her way to the spiral staircase of ice and ascended to the chamber above, leaving them alone with Skord.

Ashurek turned to him and asked, 'What are you doing with Arlenmia? Why didn't you go back to Setrel?'

Skord looked up at the Gorethrian, his eyes glittering with a mixture of emotions. They had seen him arrogant, murderous and half-crazed with the power Arlenmia had given him; later, when she had dismissed him from her service, they had seen him abject and mindless with fear. Now he seemed somewhere between those two extremes.

'I did,' Skord replied. He had hated them, especially Ashurek; yet they had saved him from Arlenmia, found him a new home. But perhaps, after all, he had not really wanted to be saved. He still loved Arlenmia, and they were her enemies, and yet . . . he also dreaded Arlenmia, and she spoke of the three now as if they were to be her allies.

'So what happened?' Estarinel asked. Skord feared Estarinel in a more personal, subtle way than he dreaded Ashurek, because the Forluinishman had possessed the power to bring back his memory of the terrible things which Arlenmia had made him forget . . . the Gorethrian atrocities in Drish.

'I don't have to tell you anything,' Skord said, his voice trembling under a thin veneer of arrogance.

'No, you don't, but we are concerned to find you here

when we thought you were safe with Setrel,' Estarinel said gently. 'What happened when you left the wood?'

Skord frowned, as if he had difficulty remembering. Ashurek strongly suspected that he had lost his reason – if he had ever managed to regain it. 'The wood . . . I rode a long way, I got lost. There were people shouting – nemale soldiers – and I was frightened. My horse bolted and carried me to Setrel's doorstep.'

'Yes – then what happened? Weren't you happy with Setrel?'

'I was . . .' he squeezed his eyes shut and shook his head as if with pain. 'Oh, damn you! You are the fools that my mistress said you were! You thought you were helping me?'

'We released you from the demon, Siregh-Ma, which was causing you so much torment. You said you hated Arlenmia,' said Ashurek. Skord stood up and tried to push past, but he grasped the boy's arm and held him.

'I wasn't myself,' Skord said through clenched teeth. 'I love her. I never wanted to leave her. Why did you make me? You dare to imagine that I ever needed your help? Putting me in a trance and making me remember those things I had forgotten – causing me to betray my mistress – abducting me – you think you were helping me? The happiest moment of my life was when Arlenmia came to fetch me, and knocked Setrel down so that I could go with her.'

'She did what?' Estarinel interrupted. 'Was he hurt?'

'How should I know? He tried to stop her coming in. It was his own fault.'

'And you just left him? After all his kindness to you?'

Skord's expression became one of confusion as he recalled how happy he had been with Setrel for that short time, how afraid he had been when Arlenmia came for him. But he suppressed that painful memory. 'My mistress is the only one who has ever been truly kind to me.'

'What happened when you went with her?' Ashurek asked, giving Estarinel a warning look; Skord would only make less sense if he was upset.

'I was proud to walk at her side. Proud! She had forgiven

375

me! Even after all I had done. She said that I was the best and most precious of her messengers. I went with her . . .'

'Where? Across the ocean?' Ashurek prompted.

'Yes. There was a ship . . .' Again the confusion flickered across his face. 'We went to a place called Terthria. It was dark and fiery and hot. There was a volcano.'

'What did Arlenmia do when she went inside the crater?'

'She – she made the demons go down into the lava for her.' Skord's voice fell to a hoarse whisper. 'And they came out, laughing, with the little blue Stone. I don't think they wanted to give it to her. But she always makes them obey her.'

'How many demons?'

'Three. One was Siregh-Ma.' Skord had gone ashen-faced even at mentioning the Shanin's name.

'So, you are happy with Arlenmia, are you?' Ashurek said sourly. 'She who is so kind to you, subjects you to the presence of a demon – the very demon I took such pains to release you from?'

Skord pressed a hand to his face as if he was trying to erase the terror in his expression. He was trembling. 'She does what she must. I serve her.'

'And then you came to the Arctic?' Estarinel said.

He nodded. 'I am loyal to her now. You can't make me betray her again!' he said defiantly.

'Ah, Skord, I do not blame you,' Ashurek sighed. 'You have had a miserable life. Even I find her will hard to resist. How then could you be expected not to succumb to her?'

'Don't patronise me!' Skord exclaimed, his eyes fever-bright. 'I choose to serve her. She says I am her comrade! We will defeat you. I don't want your pity! I warn you, I am your enemy!'

'If you are so dangerous, Skord,' Ashurek said softly, 'what are you so frightened of?'

'Nothing. I am not.'

'And you believe that Arlenmia's quest to make M'gulfn all-powerful is right, do you?'

'Of course. I know it. You three are just fools.'

376

'How would you feel,' said Ashurek, 'if I told you that the jewel of power she carries, the Egg-Stone, is the same stone which gave me the power to invade Drish?'

Skord's pale cheeks coloured with distress. 'I would say that you're lying,' he stammered. 'Leave me alone! Siregh-Ma never tormented me as you do! Just leave me alone!' He broke away from Ashurek and ran to the stairs, but there he hesitated, as if afraid to go up. Estarinel looked at Ashurek and shook his head despondently. Skord seemed intent upon clinging to his own weakness, and it was evidently more than they could do to save him from himself.

Arlenmia came half-way down the stairs and leaned round the spiral to look down at them. 'Why are you standing about there, Skord?' she asked impatiently, not waiting for an answer. 'Listen. I want all of you to come up here and join me. The view is quite breathtaking. I would not want you to miss it. Come.'

None of them particularly wanted to go with her, but it was then that they experienced a compulsion gentler, yet more horrible, than the violence of the Egg-Stone's power. They could not disobey her. Her will was tangible, like a heavy perfume. Oppressed by it, they stood up and walked, as if in a drugged trance, to the stairs, and followed Skord and Arlenmia up the icy treads to an observation chamber above. It was smaller than the one below, pyramid-shaped and much lighter, evidently hewn from the very top of the iceberg. On all four sides great holes had been cut out of the walls so that they could see for miles in every direction. But it was not the view that commanded their attention: the reason for Skord's fear had become evident.

In the chamber with Arlenmia were three demons: Meheg-Ba, Diheg-El and Siregh-Ma. Whimpering with terror, Skord backed into a corner and flattened himself against the ice as if hoping it would swallow him. Estarinel found himself edging away, clinging desperately to his sanity. Ashurek uttered a bitter curse and Medrian stared at them, blank-faced.

The demons hissed and giggled, their blood-red mouths

stretched in wide grins, lightning humming along their perfect humanoid forms.

'Now, you are not to possess them,' Arlenmia instructed the Shana, as if they were ravening dogs who obeyed only her. 'They are on our side now, or very soon will be.'

Searing argent light blazed around the chamber, merging sickeningly with the verdant fires in the Northern sky.

'On our side?' Meheg-Ba leered. 'Wonders will never cease, Prince Ashurek.'

'Be silent and do not touch them!' Arlenmia said commandingly. She turned her head so that her profile was outlined by the Serpent-fires, her hair backlit to a flaring green aureole. Three demons and four humans stood helplessly enthralled by her heavy, sweet, charismatic power, while she stood with her arms outstretched like an angel about to see the face of her personal god. 'There will be no more conflict now. We are all going to M'gulfn together.'

15

'They must open their eyes'

THE DEMONS crouched in a group, bouncing restively on their toes, muttering to each other. Their crackling silver forms were outlined by viridian fire. Skord still sobbed in a corner, his eyes riveted by paralysing fear to the Shana. Ashurek stood rigid, grim-faced, staring at the Northern skyline where a thin line of solid ice had become visible, reflecting the flickering Worm-lights. Estarinel and Medrian were clinging to each other like children, but Arlenmia stood oblivious to all of them, gazing ecstatically across the grey, white-flecked sea to her goal. One hand rested below her throat, where the Egg-Stone hung; her lips were parted and her eyes were huge and luminous, like sunlight shining through a blue-green ocean. The ghastly lights seemed to reflect the colours of her hair, as if she had conjured them herself, and the air was vibrating like glass. A dull, discordant humming had begun at the North pole, rich with power and evil.

'Thus will we all come to M'gulfn in glory,' Arlenmia murmured. 'Thus will we travel for ever more . . . the Serpent will be as a heart, from which energy will flow like liquid jewels. There will be no more human misery, no more death. I know not what form all our lives will take, but I know that we will live on, eternally, upon a level of being which we cannot contemplate, any more than an insect can imagine what it is to be human. Can you yet understand? Can you see that I am not doing this for my own gain, or because I am mad, or evil, but for the good of the world?' So sincere and earnest was her voice that they could almost believe that she was right, and that the Guardians and everyone else were wrong.

With difficulty, Medrian managed to speak. 'Arlenmia, I can see you believe this. But I don't know where you have got this vision from. If you understood the Serpent's nature, you would know that you are condemning the world to hell.'

'No!' Arlenmia exclaimed, reaching out to grip Medrian's shoulder. 'It is you who do not understand. It is so wrong to call M'gulfn a "Serpent". Corporeal forms are illusory. M'gulfn is energy. It knows nothing of your tiny standards of good and evil. You only think these things are "hell" and "evil" because of simple human fear. It is understandable. But if you would only show some trust in me, you would see the truth. My vision. My dream made real . . .'

'*Your* dream. No one else's,' Medrian said. 'And a dream is all it is. You think I have lived all these years alongside the Worm and not—' she trailed off, whether halted by Arlenmia's will, or some despair within herself, it was impossible to tell.

'My Lady Arlenmia, I warned you about her,' Siregh-Ma interjected, pointing at Medrian. 'She is dangerous. She is death. What are we going to do about her?'

'Siregh-Ma, you sound like a human fool. Be quiet and trust me,' she snapped, and the demon subsided, still glaring at the Alaakian woman.

'Fear, Medrian. Weakness,' Arlenmia continued. 'No wonder you have suffered, having tried to resist M'gulfn all this time. And Estarinel, what troubles you? You find now that you cannot face M'gulfn?' she smiled contemptuously at him. 'However can you presume to destroy the Serpent when you cannot even bear to approach it? Ah, but you will be forgiven. You will be the first to bend in awe when we reach it at last.'

'And Ashurek shall bend to me, shall he not?' said the demon, Meheg-Ba, stepping forward suddenly. 'He owes so much. More than he can afford. Is it not so, Prince Ashurek?'

'I have nothing to say to you, Meheg-Ba,' Ashurek said tightly, not looking at the Shanin.

'Oh, really? Nothing to say about the sorceress Silvren, who has undergone so much further unpleasantness since your ridiculous attempt to free her?'

'What?' Ashurek turned to stare into the demon's silver eyes.

'Oh, but it was not our fault!' Meheg-Ba cried, impersonating a flustered human. 'It was that idiot, Ahag-Ga – the one you so upset. We were away, and Ahag-Ga deemed she should be punished. But Diheg-El and I rescued her; she is safe now. She is working for us.' Ashurek looked away, knowing that he was risking possession by showing anger and curiosity. With an effort he suppressed his emotions; arguing with Meheg-Ba would achieve nothing. 'Do you not want to know what she is doing? We gave her Exhal's job.'

Then Ashurek did turn upon the demon, his control lost, but Arlenmia stepped between them and intervened. 'Meheg-Ba, be silent. I meant what I said. Forgo these petty ideas of revenge. Ashurek is not going to bow to you. We are all going to bow together to the Serpent.'

The Shanin fell back sulkily, and began to hiss and mutter to its two comrades. Skord tried to edge out of his corner, but Siregh-Ma sent out a lash of lightning that stopped him short. Estarinel, sickened, felt he could stay no longer in the demons' company, with the Worm's power permeating the atmosphere like a disease. He began to make for the stairwell, and Medrian and Ashurek followed him.

'Yes, you should go and rest,' Arlenmia said, an edge of mockery to her voice. 'I am staying here, but I will call you when we come into land.'

The three sat disconsolately on the fur-covered ridges in the chamber below. They felt defeated, but perhaps that feeling in itself had stirred some spark of defiance within them.

'I always felt we had not seen the last of her,' said Ashurek. 'And the damned Egg-Stone. Suddenly our battle is not just to kill M'gulfn, but to stop her reaching it first, and both tasks seem impossible.'

'Do you think she can hear us talking?' Estarinel asked.

'No doubt, if she wants to. But she is so sure of her power that she probably does not care what we say to each other anyway.'

'And do you think she knows . . .' he indicated the Silver Staff, which was concealed beneath his cloak.

'I don't know,' Ashurek sighed. 'But if she reaches the Serpent first and replaces its eye, nothing will prevail against it. Nothing. And with the power of the Egg-Stone and three demons, I can see no way to stop her.'

'What about Miril?' Estarinel said.

'I don't know . . . if we called her, the demons might just destroy her . . .' Ashurek began to dredge his memory for everything the Shana and Miril had ever said about each other.

'I can't believe that Arlenmia spoke to M'gulfn,' said Medrian. 'I am . . . I am the only one that can speak to it. But perhaps if she was determined enough, she might have communicated briefly with it; just long enough for it to tell her that it wanted its eye. But certainly she has never touched its thoughts, or she would have understood its true nature at once.'

'If we could make her understand—' Estarinel began.

'Even if she did,' Medrian said, 'still the Serpent's will would draw her on to return the Egg-Stone to it. But more likely, however much evidence she had, she would still twist it to fit her own vision. I think . . . well, I think she is insane in her way. Perhaps without this all-consuming obsession – religion – whatever it is, she would feel she was nothing. You see, she is just as much its victim as the rest of us.'

'My heart bleeds for her,' said Ashurek with bitter sarcasm. 'Nevertheless, she must be stopped. Miril must be reunited with the Egg-Stone. But I cannot touch the Stone myself; it would destroy me, put me in M'gulfn's power at once. In fact, it is not safe for any of us to touch it.'

'It all seems—' Estarinel began. 'Well, she is right about me: I feel I would rather die than go any closer to the Serpent. I don't want to let you down, but . . .'

'You won't. I know you won't,' Medrian said, putting her arms round him and holding him.

'Medrian, when we reach the ice cap again, just how far will we be from the Serpent?' Ashurek asked.

'About two days' walk,' she replied. 'Less, if the snow is flat and firm.'

'Two days! We have less than two days to stop her,' he groaned. 'Listen. The first thing we must do is separate her from the demons. That alone may give us a chance.'

'That's easier said than done,' said Medrian. 'Besides, she just uses them; she is no less powerful without them. Even if we could separate them, how would it help?'

'I don't know yet . . . it's just an instinct,' said Ashurek, standing up and walking slowly round the chamber. 'I must think.'

'And I must talk to M'gulfn,' said Medrian, so faintly that even Estarinel barely heard her. 'If I can only make it listen.'

As the iceberg continued its slow drift Northwards, Estarinel gradually realised what the rhythmic movement of their ice raft had symbolised: it was Arlenmia's terrible vision in which all life existed only to worship the Serpent, to pulse slowly towards it for eternity. He remembered the dreadful things she had tried to show him in her mirrors, Forluin a petrified landscape in which miserable figures made obeisance to M'gulfn, trapped as if within a jewel that was both beautiful and diabolical.

After about eight hours the iceberg grounded against a cliff of ice. The demons, under Arlenmia's instruction, held it steady while she directed Skord, Medrian, Ashurek and Estarinel to disembark. Again her will was irrefusable; they were fully aware that she was manipulating them, and yet they had no choice but to obey her like zombies. The cliff was fairly easy to climb and they soon gained the top. They found themselves on another perfect, flat field of snow, where the three demons were already waiting for them.

The sun was in the North, staring like a sick eye through the

383

poisonous green smoke there. The atmosphere reverberated with a dull, massive energy that was both nauseating and deeply depressing. Medrian felt M'gulfn stirring within her, gloating, whispering, *Medrian, come to me, come*. She thought she was going to fall and she hung onto Estarinel's arm, and it was only that which stopped him from turning back and plunging blindly into the freezing sea. Ashurek was filled with loathing and revulsion; yet the more he despised the Serpent, the more he felt akin to it, one of its own. Disgust overwhelmed him.

But Arlenmia looked quite ecstatic as she faced the North, her furs drawn up round her chin and her lips parted, her eyes sparkling with anticipation.

'We are nearly there,' she said. She turned and grasped Skord's shoulder; the wretched boy was glassy-eyed with dread. 'Do you feel M'gulfn's power, Skord? Do you see it? Soon we will belong to it . . . and it to us.'

'It will kill me,' Skord muttered wretchedly.

'Don't be foolish! Are you ready?' She turned to Ashurek and the others, laughing quietly to see the despair in their faces, to feel her power over them as if she literally held strings which moved their limbs.

She began to lead the way across the snow with Skord, Ashurek, Medrian and Estarinel following her helplessly. The demons trailed at the rear like dogs, gibbering to each other. Here, the Worm's control over the weather was total. Ghastly lights swathed the sky; the wind had dropped and there was thickness in the atmosphere, almost a stench, which filled them with despair and disgust. Instead of clouds, oily smoke rolled to and fro, spitting out a scanty fall of bitter-cold snow, the flakes of which fell like pebbles. The plain of snow seemed to stretch endlessly before them, grim and bleak and pitiless.

The walk swiftly became a nightmare. The snow seemed meat-coloured, raddled with maggot-holes, soft with decay. Behind them, demonic illumination flickered and hissed like acid, while before them a cold, cruel, impassive evil waited, grinning at their approach. From it radiated sickness, insanity, hate, bloodlust, like threadworms chewing through and through the Earth, causing it to suppurate and rot. Presently they were staggering rather than walking, drunk with horror and exhaustion, sobbing with despair as they went.

But Arlenmia strode on as if impervious to any sense of horror; and in contrast to the dreadful, carious surroundings, she seemed to glow with joy, like a bright emerald. She ignored the others as if they had ceased to hold any meaning or reality for her, and yet she drew them on in her wake, like an awesome and terrible beacon.

Delusions gripped all of them. Estarinel became convinced that he was in Forluin, and the Serpent's desecration was complete; all around him his loved ones were wandering about on an ash-grey plain, his mother and father, Lothwyn, Arlena, Falin and his family, Lilithea . . . all were crying out in misery and he knew that it was his fault. He had failed them. Again and again he saw Lilithea in front of him, tears running down her face, saying, 'There are some things I cannot heal, E'rinel.' And, worst of all, in the delusion he could not restrain himself from laughing at them, as if he had become as mad as a demon.

Ashurek felt that he was wandering on a black mountainside, and thousands of pairs of eyes were staring accusingly at him out of the darkness, Silvren and Orkesh and Meshurek among them. But all he felt was the desire to possess the terrible leaden power of the Egg-Stone, so that he might destroy all those sorrowful accusing eyes, punish them for laying bare his irremediable guilt.

And Medrian could no longer feel ground below her feet or see anything but a smooth grey void. She was drifting with M'gulfn and towards it at the same time. Its fear of Miril was forgotten and now it was speaking to her, gently and chidingly, *Come, my Medrian. No more will you shun me. Most precious of all my hosts . . . my last host . . . we will be together now, for ever* . . . and she felt that her sanity had been displaced at last, and the idea that she had ever existed independently of the Serpent seemed a bizarre and distant dream.

Skord, too, was locked within his own nightmare of memories: Gorethrians rising out of the sea like dark giants, cutting down his countrymen, conjuring a multitude of demons which surrounded him, their smooth bodies smeared with the blood of his sister and his mother . . . demons, always demons, laughing with malicious glee . . . and Arlenmia, whose image was like a splinter of diamond impaling his mind. For her he had cast a plague on two strangers who had claimed to be his parents . . . for her he had murdered a girl whom he had once thought he loved . . . for her he had forsaken the only peace he had ever known – with Setrel – and for her he now stumbled through a cacotopia towards an appalling doom.

Arlenmia halted and turned towards them. The sound of her voice brought them all back to themselves, only to find that reality was no better than the horrendous visions which had plagued them. The snow seemed like flyblown flesh and the sky resembled a black inferno.

'We are going to stop and rest now,' she said. Her face and eyes were radiant; the bright joy of such a beautiful woman at the Worm's loathsome evil struck a deep sickness to their souls. 'There is no need to look so afraid. M'gulfn will surely forgive you, if only you would admit defeat.'

'How far are we from it?' Ashurek forced himself to ask.

'Not far. It is just beyond the horizon. Can you not see?' She extended an arm towards the North, smiling. But what they could see was not, somehow, what they had expected. Like an incongruous mirage, they could discern glittering cliffs of ice, white and turquoise, half-veiled by great curtains of icy mist through which a topaz-yellow light glowed. Above, the green fires were beryl-pale, almost pure. The air throbbed with oppressive power.

'What is that?' Ashurek said, drawing his fingers across his forehead. Despite the cold, he was sweating; he felt unclean, contaminated by M'gulfn. 'Where is the Serpent?'

'It is as if we stand in a hellish pit, looking at heaven,' Arlenmia replied. 'And the pit through which we walk is but a test of our faith. Now will you believe that M'gulfn is not evil, but beautiful?'

'How have you—' Medrian began, but fell silent, shaking her head. She was wide-eyed and looked as confused, Estarinel thought, as he felt.

'Sit down, all of you,' Arlenmia went on. 'We must eat and rest before we come in sight of M'gulfn. And I have one last preparation to make. Then shall the Quest be completed!'

They did as she said – not that they had any choice – and seated themselves on the brown-grey snow. Grimy clouds roiled overhead, shot through with abscess-coloured lightning. Ashurek felt that the hint of weird, crystalline beauty at the North Pole, which was in such sinister contrast to their immediate surroundings, must hold some kind of warped revelation that would deal a death-blow to the last remnant of his spirit. He looked at Medrian and Estarinel, both of whom were as pale and wretched as Skord. They were all moving towards the Serpent animated only by Arlenmia's will; perhaps they would soon be wholly in her power, and even their thoughts would not be their own. But he knew no way to halt what was happening.

He made Medrian and Estarinel sit with their backs to the North, and lit the H'tebhmellian fire. For a few moments it gleamed like a mote of sanity in the Worm-defiled surroundings. But the Shana began to hiss with disgust, and at once Arlenmia exclaimed angrily, 'Put that out! It is an affront to the Serpent M'gulfn!' He had to obey. At least they were able to partake of the H'tebhmellian food and wine which, although they had little appetite, was immensely heartening. Arlenmia seemed to have relaxed her grip upon them somewhat.

'I saw such terrible things as we were walking,' Estarinel sighed. 'So real.'

'So did we all, I think,' said Ashurek. Silently he cursed the impossibility of speaking to each other without the demons and Arlenmia overhearing. Perhaps the best thing would be to initiate one swift battle now and get it over with; they stood no chance of victory, but it was certainly preferable to die than to live on under the Serpent's reign. He continued to think on this as they ate; it was doubtful that he could resist the weight of Arlenmia's will even long enough to start such a fight. And the chances were that even if they perished, the Shana would trap their souls in the Dark Regions. He felt he was going mad, blackness pressing on him from all sides. There was no escape, this insane nightmare was real.

'Medrian, I have something to discuss with you,' Arlenmia's voice intruded on his grim thoughts and he looked round to see her standing near the Alaakian woman, touching her shoulder.

Medrian stared at Arlenmia, white-faced. Estarinel put a protective arm around her and said, 'For pity's sake, leave her alone, Arlenmia. None of us have anything to say to you.'

'No,' Medrian silenced his protests with a meaningful look. 'It's all right, Estarinel. I will talk to her. But it must be alone, Arlenmia. Away from the others.' She stood up at Arlenmia's side with chilling calmness.

'Very well. I'm glad you realise how pointless it would be to argue. Besides, I only want to talk – there's nothing to fear.' Arlenmia slipped her arm through Medrian's, like a sister. 'We'll walk a little way over the snow. But in order that you shan't be lonely, Ashurek and Estarinel, I will of course leave the Shana to look after you.'

She and Medrian began to walk away Eastwards across the snowfield. They went for perhaps half a mile, but then they must have gone into a dip, because they were lost to sight.

'Arlenmia still wants to become the Serpent's host,' said Estarinel bitterly. Skord was sitting a few yards away, his head resting on his bent knees. The demons were stirring, surrounding the three humans.

'It will be the culmination of her dream,' said Ashurek.

'And we have to sit here, helpless, while she does some unspeakable harm to Medrian. Damn her!'

'But Medrian used the opportunity . . .' Ashurek glanced

at the Shana. 'I expect she will keep Arlenmia engaged and away from us for as long as she can.'

'Then how do we use this opportunity?' Estarinel whispered. Siregh-Ma was bending over Skord, poking at him with long argent fingers, muttering sibilantly. The boy was whimpering with terror and Estarinel felt sick to the core of his soul, knowing that they could do nothing to keep Siregh-Ma away from him, especially as Meheg-Ba and Diheg-El were now converging on him and Ashurek. Their eyes shone like white coins and they stank of metal and blood. Perhaps it would have been better if Medrian had not led Arlenmia away after all.

Ashurek jumped to his feet and said, 'Keep your distance, Meheg-Ba. Have you forgotten your mistress's orders?'

'Well, she is not here to give any orders at present, is she?' Meheg-Ba said gutturally. 'And she is not our mistress. We merely—'

'Use her,' finished Diheg-El. Estarinel now scrambled to his feet and went to Ashurek's side, fighting an uncontrollable revulsion that threatened to paralyse him.

'Indeed?' said Ashurek. 'Then I must congratulate you. Your impersonation of three abject curs was faultless.'

Meheg-Ba made a sibilant exclamation of annoyance. 'Don't make me angry, Prince Ashurek. She also makes the mistake of thinking we are stupid. However, I know more than she does. I also have something to discuss – with you and your Forluinish friend.'

'Don't look at them, Estarinel, however hard they try to make you,' Ashurek warned. 'Meheg-Ba, I don't know what you have in mind, but I will make no bargains with you. Not even – not even upon Silvren's life.'

'Bargains! What a fool you are!' exclaimed Diheg-El. 'What we require, we can simply take, so you are hardly in a position to bargain. We are only discussing it with you in order to taunt you.'

'That is in character, at least.'

'We are referring, of course, to the weapon which he is carrying.' Meheg-Ba pointed at Estarinel. Siregh-Ma had ceased his torment of Skord and was standing behind them, grinning.

'We both have swords,' said Ashurek evenly.

'Oh, do not pretend to be more stupid than you are. You think that such as we cannot sense a long, thin rod of silver which presents such danger to the Serpent? Not that you stand any chance of wielding it now, but that is not the point. It is still a nasty toy, and an insult to us.'

'Don't try to take it!' Estarinel exclaimed, horrified that he felt so helpless.

'Estarinel, don't speak to them,' Ashurek warned again.

'Take it?' said Diheg-El. 'You would be well advised just to give it to us, if you value your sanity. Which would you prefer: running about on the Earth doing our will, or languishing in the Dark Regions?'

'Alternatively, what an excellent joke it would be if he were to wield the Egg-Stone for us,' said Meheg-Ba. 'We would prefer it in hands we can control . . . I know that you would like the Egg-Stone back, Ashurek, but you cannot be trusted with it.' The Shanin leered and sent out a bolt of silver fire which crackled around Ashurek's shoulders until he groaned with pain. 'You would like it, wouldn't you? What a shame that you proved a greater fool than your brother. You are still going to work for us, though.'

'And so are you.' Diheg-El stretched out a hand and a searing energy surrounded Estarinel, filling his brain with malignant light. When it subsided he was trembling violently, gasping for breath. 'Now, are you going to give us the weapon?' Knowing he could not bear the Shanin to touch him like that again, he found himself reaching with shaking hands for the Silver Staff. He pulled the leather cover off the top, and drew it slowly from its red sheath. But as he grasped it, a different kind of silver fire filled him, something pure and calm. He held it by the shaft with the egg-shaped orb towards Diheg-El, offering it to the demon – yet at the same time determined not to let it go.

The demon, its blood-red mouth stretched in a grin,

390

reached out for it. In the same moment a word burst from Ashurek's mouth, a raw, despairing cry for help: 'Miril!'

And something happened. The tiny movements within the silvery orb became frantic. The translucent shell shattered. And a shining white shape fluttered out, straight into the arms of Diheg-El.

It was over in an instant. The demon's silver skin peeled back as if being consumed by an invisible fire; its flesh turned black, bubbling with blisters from which a yellowish fluid poured. It was screaming as it burned, a horrific, unearthly scream of terror and pain. Then, all at once, it was gone, crumbling away into a pile of black ashes, that swirled around on the snow at Meheg-Ba's feet.

Miril, shining like a star and singing loudly, alighted on Ashurek's hand. There were several moments of absolute stillness in which the two remaining demons stared at Estarinel and Ashurek, almost grey with rage and fear.

Meheg-Ba had had to send Ashurek to fetch the Egg-Stone, all those years ago, because the Shana could not fetch it themselves. 'The Stone is guarded by a creature,' Meheg-Ba had said, 'who could destroy a Shanin with the merest touch.'

Ashurek smiled malevolently. 'Well?' he said.

'Skord, help us!' Siregh-Ma exclaimed, but the boy only stood and stared, red-eyed.

'Don't be an idiot,' Meheg-Ba hissed at its comrade. 'Keep your head.' It raised its arms and began to mutter ugly words. Siregh-Ma followed suit and at once a dark knot appeared in the atmosphere to their right. Out of it stepped another demon.

Ashurek moved forward with his arms outstretched and touched Miril to the Shanin. It was destroyed at once. Meheg-Ba's and Siregh-Ma's voices rose. Another demon came through, and another, only to be consumed by Miril's fire as soon as they set foot on Earth. She could have flown free but she remained in Ashurek's hands so that no demon could touch him without touching her first.

The black entrance to the Dark Regions swelled. Demons

began to step through in twos, threes, fours, more than Ashurek could destroy at once. Meheg-Ba was shrieking now, issuing frantic instructions to its comrades in a sibilant tongue which was incomprehensible to humans. Siregh-Ma had laid hands on Skord, evidently hoping to make Ashurek desist by threatening the boy. Demon-created illusions began to dance around Ashurek and Estarinel; imps as red as fire skipped about their feet, while gouts of violet flame roared from the snow, forming the shapes of lions, humans, eagles, snakes, in confusing succession. Their perspective changed, so that they beheld impossible scenes: gullies in the snow became rivers that raged towards them, lumps of ice became mountains in whose valleys vast armies of bronze creatures marched upon them. A thousand copies of Miril thronged in the air; weapons flew at their heads – axes, morning stars, spiked chains; venomous crimson insects buzzed round them.

'These are only illusions!' Ashurek cried to Estarinel. 'Just stay behind me.' Estarinel had sheathed the Silver Staff, knowing that it was only to be used against the Serpent, and he had drawn his sword instead. But it was useless against the terrible demonic hallucinations thronging around them. Eventually he found his best defence was to close his eyes.

Demons thronged in a hellish horde from the Dark Regions, and the entrance grew wider and wider, a lightless pit gaping in the fabric of the atmosphere. But Ashurek strode surely among them, Miril blazing like a sun in his hands, destroying them one after another. Their hideous, inhuman shrieks filled the air as they were consumed by her fire, boiling and dehydrating and blackening to crisps.

Skord fled past Ashurek, shouting hoarsely for Arlenmia. Ashurek realised that Miril must have dispatched Siregh-Ma. But Estarinel caught him and the boy collapsed onto the snow, sobbing.

Abruptly, the hallucinations subsided. Ashurek swung in a circle but found that there were no longer any Shana round him. 'Miril, have we destroyed them all?' he gasped, disorientated.

'They have retreated, look,' she sang. He turned to see

392

the ragged hole still yawning down into the Dark Regions. And he was seeing it still with that distorted perspective, or with some kind of witch-sight. Meheg-Ba was standing just within it, its face ghastly with rage; behind were a whole multitude of demons, which he realised were all the Shana, summoned by Meheg-Ba to help against Miril. Now they stood glaring out at Ashurek like blood-famished wolves, knowing they would die if they dared to emerge. But overlaid on this scene Ashurek could see a second view, as clear and detailed and undeniably real as the Shana themselves.

He was looking down on the noisome swamp where he had once walked with Calorn. Milling about wretchedly in a herd of uncountable numbers were the pale forms of the human cattle. He could see them so clearly that he could even discern the individual lashes of their closed eyelids. In their midst stood Silvren. She looked pale and ill, her hair matted and her white robe ragged and begrimed, so desperately thin that she seemed no more than bone under the thin fabric. But still alive, and so close that he felt he could have reached out and touched her.

'Silvren!' he shouted. Miril added her voice to his.

And Silvren looked up, and saw him; and at once he knew what she had been trying to ask him when he had seen that brief vision of her, on the ice raft. *'Ashurek, I need to know the words, can you remember?'*

'Silvren!' he cried again. 'You must make them open their eyes . . .' He stopped, realising with horror that he no longer had the faintest recollection of how he had done so himself. 'Miril,' he said thickly, 'can't you help her?'

'Alas, I cannot go into the Dark Regions,' she chirped. 'But you are right. The human herd must open their eyes, but only Silvren can make them.'

'Prince Ashurek,' rasped Meheg-Ba, its eyes shining a ghastly pink as if through a film of blood. 'Don't do this. If the sorceress so much as opens her mouth, she will be killed at once. By Limir. You do remember Limir, don't you? Good. We have reached an impasse. You are very clever, but you will not prevail. I am going to close the entrance now. You damned fool! Don't you know that we were on the same side? I no more wish Arlenmia to achieve her goal than you do.'

'What do you mean?' asked Ashurek, certain that the Shanin had begun to bluff in order to win itself a fresh chance.

'Is it not obvious? If the Serpent gets its eye back, it will be all-powerful. It will have no need of helpers such as the Shana. It will destroy us. We don't want that! We want the world to continue as it was! And we only wanted the silver weapon in order to help us get the Egg-Stone back from that wretched woman. You will never do it alone, Prince Ashurek.'

'Don't listen,' said Estarinel over Ashurek's shoulder. 'It must be lying.'

'I strongly advise you not to take that risk!' Meheg-Ba screeched metallically.

'I believe you are telling the truth for once,' said Ashurek.

'Then allow me to come back onto Earth without destroying me!'

'Very well,' Ashurek said carefully. 'But on one condition. You must release Silvren. Let her come out before you.'

'Yes, yes, nothing could be easier. It was only Diheg-El who wanted her anyway!' Meheg-Ba said.

Estarinel looked questioningly at Ashurek, but he and Miril both remained intent on the entrance to the Dark Regions. He did not share Ashurek's witch-sight, and all he could see was Meheg-Ba, standing just inside a lightless abyss.

Meheg-Ba turned, apparently instructing one of the other demons to fetch Silvren. But in those few seconds, the frail, faint voice of Silvren reached Ashurek's ears. She was chanting. Her eyes were closed, her hands moving slowly as if she was stroking the heads of the herd without actually touching them.

Meheg-Ba gave a roar of rage. The other demons began to mutter with anxiety, their mingled glow becoming dim. In the overlaid vision, Ashurek clearly saw the eyes of three of the herd fly open, as blue as H'tebhmella. And he saw the hideous bird, Limir, appear as if from nowhere and flap purposefully towards Silvren.

'No!' Ashurek roared. Miril gave a piercing cry. But there was nothing they could do; Limir descended on Silvren like a sack of knives, and she fell, and was lost to view amid the human-cattle.

She had been silenced, and yet, somehow, the herd were continuing to open their eyes. The demons were wailing with consternation – Estarinel put his hands over his ears to block out that appalling cacophony – and they were becoming ash-grey, powerless. But the human-cattle had ceased their restless milling and were standing very still, all gazing upwards at Ashurek, their eyes clear and calm and intelligent, shedding sapphire light. And two of those pairs of eyes were those of Meshurek and Orkesh . . .

Hissing with dread, Meheg-Ba stumbled out of the gaping hole onto the snow. The rest of the demons began to follow, terrified of Miril, yet more terrified of what lay in their own Region. And as they came, one by one, Ashurek and Miril destroyed them.

Estarinel watched incredulously: Ashurek had become a larger-than-life, preternatural figure, cloaked in shadow, his dark face disturbingly calm while his green eyes burned with purpose. Miril sparkled on his hand like a fiery, avenging diamond. Unable to stop themselves, the Shana plunged out of the darkness, their skin as dull as mercury; and each met its painful end at Miril's touch, vaporising into wisps of ash.

It was over with unexpected, merciful swiftness. Within minutes the last but one of the demons had been reduced to cinders. Now only Meheg-Ba was still alive, its skin like rusted iron, its face almost human with dismay and trepidation. And close behind the demons, the herd of trapped souls began to wander out of the darkness.

Ashurek could not bear to look at them. He did not want to know which ones were his brother and sister, imprisoned in the Dark Regions in death because they had dealt with

395

demons in life. He shut his eyes. Miril flew free of his hand and proceeded to touch each of the wretched creatures in turn with her wings. As she did so, each one stood erect, losing its terrible deformity and taking a colourless human form; then dispersing to nothing on the air, silently.

'Ashurek,' said Estarinel, moving forward to shake his arm as he realised the Gorethrian was not watching. 'Look.'

Lying across the back of the last of the creatures was Silvren. Limir was still crouching on her shoulders, its shapeless grey body thrashing in frustrated anger. With a gasp, Ashurek sprang towards it, but Meheg-Ba got there first.

'You damnable – incompetent – negligent imbecile,' the Shanin hissed. It was addressing Limir not Silvren, and it stretched out a metallic hand and pulled the hellish creature off her. Limir did not even cry out as the demon broke its back and tore it apart, flinging the pieces back into the darkness like bits of rag.

At once Ashurek seized Silvren's body from the human-beast, and Miril touched it and freed its soul. And in the same moment, as if it had only been waiting to exact its revenge upon Limir, Meheg-Ba turned and deliberately stretched out a hand to touch Miril, and so perished.

Estarinel was standing with one arm round Skord, trying to soothe the boy's hysterical sobbing. Ashurek was holding Silvren's lifeless form in his arms, his head bent over her, his bitter tears falling onto her face. Miril circled over their heads, first brushing Skord with her wings, then Silvren, and finally alighting on Ashurek's shoulder. The great hole yawning into the Dark Regions remained, but all was dark and silent within it.

Silvren opened her eyes and said, 'I'm alive,' as if both surprised and pleased at this realisation.

'I think you know what I want to talk to you about,' said Arlenmia.

'Yes,' said Medrian without inflexion.

'Here is a hollow; is this far enough for you? Shall we sit

down?' Medrian did so, pulling her hood back from her pale and expressionless face. Arlenmia sat beside her, intently studying her sharp profile. 'I know that I tried to kill you once . . . It really was very foolish of me.'

'Don't apologise. I would have been happier if you had succeeded,' Medrian said acidly.

'Don't be bitter; I want to help you, truly. See, I am not wielding the power of the Egg-Stone over you. You could walk away now if you wished. But I think you half hope that I may help you after all.' Medrian smiled thinly at this. 'You would like to be free of the Serpent, wouldn't you?'

Medrian replied quietly, 'I have been free of it. I have known a few days of peace, and a few hours of happiness, which is more than many can say. I chose to take the burden up again, and carry it to the end. What you offer is empty, and false. I want nothing.'

Arlenmia slid her fingers into Medrian's hair and forcibly turned her head so that she could hold her gaze. Her blue-green eyes glinted with anger, but Medrian's were as shadowy and unreadable as her face. 'You mean it, don't you? You almost fell before, but not now. And I might as well save my breath.'

'Yes,' said Medrian.

'Well, I will waste no more time on gentle persuasion, then. I had not the strength to force you before, Medrian, but I have now. Besides, why would the Serpent wish to stay with one who wishes to destroy it, when it could come to me?'

'If it wanted you, Arlenmia, it would have gone to you years ago,' Medrian said with a touch of malice. The fingers tightened in her hair, and she felt a languorous, hypnotic force flowing from Arlenmia's eyes to her own. She could not resist it. She was being drawn from the physical world to a mental battleground, an indigo void where Arlenmia's strange thoughts and visions became real.

'Look at my dream,' said Arlenmia's voice in her head. And Medrian saw a sphere like a perfect glittering topaz with a pulsing sapphire heart. It was enmeshed by a net of shining capillaries in which corpuscles like jewels pulsed towards the heart, singing their worship of M'gulfn, which no longer resembled a Serpent . . . And each of the corpuscular jewels had once been a human, but was now elevated to a higher level of being in which there was nothing but joy . . .

Medrian stared at the vision for hours, years. It was beautiful. It was freedom from the pain of life and the oblivion of death. It was the fulfilment of ecstasy beyond the dreams of mortals . . . she was weeping, falling towards it with outstretched arms. So this was what Arlenmia intended! If only she had known—

Medrian, said a voice somewhere in the darkness. *Ah, my Medrian. Must I tell you of the unspeakable pain and loneliness you have caused me? None of my former hosts did to me what you have done. Yet none of them really mattered to me either . . . not in the way that you have been precious to me.* Medrian turned round and round in the void, and she could feel the Serpent's presence all about her. And she realised that it could not see Arlenmia's vision; it could only see her, its host. *Ah, you mean much to me, my Medrian. What have I done to deserve your hate? Why, when I cherished you from birth, did you turn away from me? Why return my care with despite? Such pain I have suffered, because I would not forsake you. But I cannot allow you to slay me. They shall not slay me. Even now I do not want to leave you . . . it will cause me excruciating pain . . . but I must go instead to someone who does love and worship me.*

Then Medrian felt a terrible pulling and tearing sensation in her limbs and stomach and eyes, but worst of all, in her mind. And although she could see nothing, she was aware of Arlenmia's face very close to hers.

'M'gulfn, no, don't leave me,' she cried out in her thoughts. The pulling lessened.

Why not? said the Serpent. *Now you plead with me? Now, when it is too late?*

'Please. It is not too late. You don't want Arlenmia, you know you don't. It's true I wanted to be free of you before, but that's changed now. I want – I want you to stay with me to the end.'

The tearing began again. She realised that it was the Serpent's own pain that she was feeling. *No, Medrian, it is too late! You should have surrendered to me years ago. This is your fault. You have betrayed me over and over again. No more. I am going to her . . .*

'No. You won't like her, she won't like you. And you can't bear this pain. Stay with me.'

She worships me. She will never betray me . . .

'Oh, but she will. I promise you, she will betray you. You are not going to leave me, are you?' The Serpent screamed and groaned in its confusion.

Somewhere at once very distant and very close, Arlenmia was calling, 'Leave her, M'gulfn. Come to me!' And Medrian felt that she and the Serpent were falling together, tumbling over and over as they hurtled towards the crystalline sphere of Arlenmia's vision. But the sphere was dull and cold.

Promise you will betray me no more. Promise you will not spurn me nor share yourself with other humans. Promise—

'Hush, now,' said Medrian. 'You are not going to leave me. I won't let you. We will be together until the bitter end.'

The pulling stopped.

Arlenmia found her own powerful vision wrenched from her, and replaced by another. The Earth was grey . . . Of all colours, she hated grey. And it was not round and crystalline, but shapeless and bloated, filled with glutinous matter that could never be expelled – dead and worm-ridden and decaying. And across its desolate landscapes bent figures wandered, knee-deep in ash, weeping, endlessly seeking a way to end their misery . . . but they could not comfort each other, because all they felt for each other was hatred. And the heart of this hell, the perpetrator, itself lay atop the husk in a despairing torpor, alone and wretched and devoid of intelligent thought. And enclosing the Earth was a leaden membrane through which nothing could pass, so that the outside forces, which might otherwise have helped, did not even know that it existed.

With a mixture of relief and anger she suddenly realised that this nightmare vision was only one conjured by Medrian to trick her. She gathered the power of the Egg-Stone and flung it at the vision, destroying it with a thud of energy.

All at once, she and Medrian were in the physical world again, sitting on a snowy slope in a grim landscape, looking at each other. With an exasperated curse, Arlenmia released Medrian's hair. 'Damn you,' she said.

'You see, it is futile,' Medrian said. 'M'gulfn cannot leave me even if it wants to. You will never be its host.'

'You prevented M'gulfn from coming to me!'

'How do you know? Did M'gulfn actually speak to you?'

'No . . . but it wanted to!'

'Then how can you be so sure that you understand its nature, when you have never touched it? Did you not see the true vision of how the Earth will be if the Serpent gets the Egg-Stone back?'

'True? If you cannot believe my vision, how then can you expect me to believe yours?' Arlenmia retorted icily. 'More likely it is the world's doom if fools like you persist in fighting the Serpent.'

'Arlenmia, please listen to me. Hate is all that motivates the Serpent. It doesn't care about you. It is using you to get its eye back, that's all. You are no more to it than – than anyone. It knows nothing of your vision! All it knows is hate, sterile and destructive, and all it cares about is taking revenge on the life which it thinks has usurped its supremacy on Earth. Why would I want to lie to you about this?'

'I really do not know, Medrian.'

'You still cannot believe that you are wrong. I know of no way to convince you.'

'I should kill you!' Arlenmia exclaimed, her face bright with anger. 'I would, if I knew how! I have shown you the future – and still you deny it! Still you cling to this nonsense of hate and decay. You are all the same. The human race does not deserve what I am trying to do for it.'

'That's true,' Medrian murmured, and Arlenmia made as if to strike her. But in that moment she became aware of a strange cacophony issuing from the direction of Ashurek and the others. It had been going on for some time, but so intent had she been on Medrian in their shared trance that she had been unaware of it. Now she leaped to her feet with a cry of rage.

'What on Earth are they doing?' she demanded.

'It looks as if the Shana are disobeying you,' Medrian said as she stood up.

'So this is why you wanted me away from the others!' Then Arlenmia did strike her, with such force that Medrian sprawled several feet away on the snow. She was stunned for a moment, but she quickly dragged herself upright and followed the figure of Arlenmia, striding furiously across the snow.

Ashurek and Estarinel both took off their cloaks and wrapped them around Silvren's frail form. Having moved several hundred yards from the grim entrance to the Dark Regions, they floated the H'tebhmellian fire near her and made her sip the reviving wine. She was very weak, but the warmth of the blue-gold sphere seemed to ease the pain of the wounds Limir had caused, while the wine visibly restored her. 'Now I must return to the Silver Staff,' Miril had said when the purging of the Dark Regions was over. 'But understand, all of you, that I can be called to your aid only once more before you reach the Worm. You must choose that time well. Fear not,' she added, 'you have chosen well so far.' Then she alighted on top of the Staff and, while retaining the form of a bird, became as inanimate as a carved figure.

There was much that Ashurek had wanted to ask her, but it seemed that she was unwilling or unable to spend time talking to them. As for Estarinel, Miril's appearance, her transformation from living creature to statuette and all that had gone between were so miraculous that he was left speechless. Even in this terrible polar waste, so close to the Serpent, she had given them a short respite from dread.

'Ashurek, why does this place feel as terrible as the Dark Regions?' Silvren asked. She seemed disoriented and half in a dream, which was not surprising after what she had undergone. 'And so cold. It is Earth, isn't it?'

'Yes, but we are very close to the Serpent,' he said gently.

'Oh – oh, the Quest,' she said. 'I am sorry – I've forgotten so much, and I am not myself yet. I thought perhaps it was all over – but no, I'm glad that I will be there at the end of it, after all.'

'Don't try to talk, beloved,' Ashurek said. He was holding her in his arms, unspeakably relieved that she was alive, but aware that she was very frail, while the worst danger of all still lay ahead of them.

'No, I want to talk: I am all right, truly. Is this Estarinel?' she said, looking sideways. Warmth was returning to her previously dull eyes. 'Ah yes, I remember you. The Glass City. And who is the other young man?'

'His name is Skord,' said Estarinel. The youth was sitting cross-legged on the snow with his head bowed, silent but seeming calm and composed since Miril had touched him. But Estarinel hesitated to explain who he was, having a strange intuition that Silvren would be somehow disturbed by the knowledge that Arlenmia was with them.

'The demons are all dead, aren't they?' Skord said suddenly, looking up at Silvren.

'Yes, all destroyed,' she replied kindly, as if she understood his fear; and in that moment Ashurek could have wept for joy to realise that the Shana had failed to change her after all. She seemed to know what he was thinking, and went on, 'Now that the Shana are gone, I can look back clearly upon how they deceived me, as if it had happened to someone else. I know that I am not evil. Only human. And I am so, so sorry for the pain I caused you by making you leave me behind that time.'

'Silvren, I am only glad that you were able to see the Shana's lie for what it was. I knew that Miril would help you.'

'Oh, but it was not just Miril; it was those poor trapped souls,' she said. 'They did not think I was evil, and they needed me; and I felt their judgement was surer than my own. And it was.'

'And now they are free.'

'Yes. The words to open their eyes were within me. You see, all that had been negative within their souls had been absorbed by the Shana to feed their power. So all that was left within them was the positive, which was the very antithesis of the Shana's evil. When they opened their eyes it was as if Miril's eyes shone upon the Dark Regions, rendering the Shana powerless, and making them see the horror and futility of their own existence. That was what they feared. That alone made them walk out to Miril and destroy themselves in their despair.'

'When that white bird touched me,' said Skord, seeming somewhat dazed, 'everything that was confusing me began to make sense. As if I am not two or three different people after all, but just myself. None of it hurts so much now. I think – I think I should help you.' He glanced hesitantly at Estarinel. 'And when we go home, I will go back to Setrel. I think he cared about me.'

'Yes, he did,' said Estarinel.

'Damn it, she is on her way back,' Ashurek muttered, looking across the snowfield. 'I'd almost forgotten about her.'

'Who?' asked Silvren.

Arlenmia, closely followed by Medrian, descended on them like a viridian tongue of fire, blazing with rage. She seized Skord by the shoulder and jerked him to his feet, shaking him violently. 'Why didn't you call me? Where are my demons?' She did not seem to have noticed that the cloaked figure in Ashurek's arms was Silvren. She closed her eyes briefly and rested one hand on her chest, apparently using the Egg-Stone to glean the knowledge of what had transpired. Then her eyes flew open and the malevolent energy of the Egg-Stone seemed to be concentrated within them.

Skord was cringing at her feet like a dog, instantly plunged back into the nightmare from which Miril had woken him. Estarinel had gone straight to Medrian and was hugging her, relieved to find that Arlenmia had not harmed her. Ashurek remained seated, looking levelly at her. She approached him, knocking the H'tebhmellian fire out of the way as she came, and pulled back the hood of the figure in his arms.

'Silvren,' she said. All the anger seemed to leave her face as she gazed at the woman who had once been her dearest – her only – friend. Silvren reached out of the cloak and seized her hand before she could move back.

'I can see the Egg-Stone round your neck. How did you get it? Oh, Arlenmia, if you will listen to no one else, please listen to me—'

'No,' said Arlenmia, jerking her hand from Silvren's grasp. 'I have suffered enough of this pernicious nonsense. Least of all will I suffer it from you. Now hear me, all of you.' Her compulsive will, joined to the Egg-Stone's energy, began to reassert itself over them. 'I suppose you think that this escapade was very clever. I suppose you are now full of hope that I may be stopped after all. Well, you are wrong. The Shana, although they served me, were conspiring against me. You think I didn't know?' She laughed mockingly. 'They also thought they were clever, but to me they were transparent: they did not want M'gulfn's power to be whole, because then it would have had no need of them. They saw that they had no place in the future; their motive was utterly selfish. I knew that before the end they would have risen up and tried to thwart me. Who knows, Ashurek, they might have succeeded, if not for you.' Her tone was acerbic. 'So all you have achieved is the destruction of my enemies. I give you my heartfelt thanks for saving me the trouble. If you doubt what I am saying, ask yourselves why M'gulfn did not come to the Shana's defence. It was because it wanted them destroyed.'

Her power engulfed them, as sweet and languorous as sleep, yet as suffocating and inescapable as a heavy green sea. And while their thoughts remained their own, it was beyond their ability to disobey her. 'I don't need to deprive you of that silver needle, nor destroy the bird who is a mere ghost of the human fear of change. I don't even need to become the host. It is all irrelevant. Nothing stands in my way now. And you still imagine that you do not work for the Serpent? Come, get up. We are going to M'gulfn now, and we shall not rest again until we can repose within its glorious shadow.'

16

Night Falls

So IT was that their final journey to the Serpent was like nothing they had ever envisaged. Arlenmia led the way, and the others stumbled after her, cold and helpless with exhaustion, lost in grey despair. Skord staggered along just behind her, and then came Ashurek carrying Silvren's weightless frame. Medrian and Estarinel helped each other along as best they could. What was real and what was illusory became inseparable; they seemed to be floundering thigh-deep through treacherous, rotten snow, while Arlenmia walked lightly on the surface, a froth of ice crystals glittering round her feet. The sun glared at them like a colourless eyeball from which no light came. They were drowning in a grim, greenish twilight, but Arlenmia sparkled like a rare aquamarine, drawing light from the curtain of cold Serpent-fire which hung before them. They could not see M'gulfn, but they knew it awaited them within that rippling veil.

It seemed a bizarre chase in which Arlenmia was rushing to deify the Serpent while the others struggled along behind her to prevent it; and yet she was drawing them along behind her, almost dawdling so that they could keep up.

Now they were crossing mounds of snow like heaps of pewter-dark ash in the gloom. Horrible creatures kept pace with them. There were white bears with bright blue eyes; amorphous, tentacled reptiles; bald grey things with fanged jaws; primeval birds whose faces were as harsh as iron. These creatures hovered always in the periphery of their vision, but disappeared when looked at directly. And they all felt a continual sense of panic that made them long to turn and retrace their steps, crying out in madness and horror. But Arlenmia drew them on like a star. Everything seemed to be converging towards a central point; all life was gathering and rushing towards the Serpent. Sickly yellow lights glowed behind dark, indefinable masses, guiding them on their way.

It seemed they walked for hours, days, for ever, with each step becoming more aware of their smallness and helplessness, the futility of their existence compared to M'gulfn's. Once or twice Ashurek thought he had called out to Arlenmia, begging her to stop, but if he had she ignored him, drifting onwards like gossamer on a purposeful breeze. They were her abject prisoners, but they found no relief in giving up the struggle against her, only deeper anguish and misery.

The snow-blanketed ground rose and the Serpent-fires grew paler and brighter, shining through Arlenmia so that she was like a diamond, filled with flashes of green fire. She led her captives up a slope which ended in an ice ridge, and there she held out her arms and stopped them. The Worm-fires flared.

'Behold,' she said.

The journey had seemed endless and terrible, but how much worse it was to arrive. And it seemed sudden, as if they had drifted into sleep unawares, only to wake violently and find that it was later than they had thought.

The fires turned to white; white lights burning on snow. All hints of discoloration and disease were miraculously bleached away. Before them stretched a valley of pure, smooth, untouched silver perfection, so vast that it took the breath away.

Arlenmia turned to them, power streaming from her like wings of sapphire light. 'We only have this dip to cross now,' she said. 'And thus we shall come in glory to M'gulfn!'

The lights on the snow were dazzling, and on the far side of the valley they soared into the heavens through layer upon layer of ice crystals. The Serpent lay somewhere within that effulgence, veiled in magnesium-bright fire.

Silvren was weeping, her head hidden against Ashurek's

shoulder. Medrian and Estarinel clung to each other, their black hopelessness compounded by overwhelming awe. And Ashurek was thinking, how Meheg-Ba must have been laughing at me, all along, to know I imagined such a power as this could ever be vanquished.

'Medrian,' he whispered, his throat spasmed. 'Did you know that it would be like this?'

'No,' she choked. 'I had no idea. Never a hint . . .'

Arlenmia turned towards them, smiling triumphantly, exhilarated with power. 'Come, let us not delay,' she said.

They began the descent. The valley seemed infinite, and the further they went, the more the lactescent fires towered over them and the more helpless they felt. They stumbled along with heads bowed, blinded and confused, but Arlenmia walked with her arms outstretched towards the aching light.

And as they drew nearer, the white blaze paled and transformed so that touches of blue and green could be seen through it. As soon as they were able to look at it, they could not look away.

Then, as if a veil had been torn aside, the Serpent itself was before them.

It had the appearance of a statue many thousands of feet high, a vast and terrible dragon formed of blue-green ice, towering into the sky. It was glassy, translucent. An ultramarine core glowed through the shining ice layers of its body, and its surface was scaled and sparkling as if sprinkled with millions of stars. Chasms of sapphire and amethyst ice lay all around it.

Terrible and splendid it was, its mighty head dripping white fire. It was poised motionless, yet it seemed to be gazing impassively down at them, and its eyes were like indigo moons, omniscient and soulless. All life seemed to be centred around it, going to and fro like blood in the veins and arteries of an all-powerful heart. They were servants and messengers going about its work, and its work covered the entire world, and every living thing thereon was its slave. And it seemed that the world was there before them, dwarfed beneath the vast Serpent-deity, a god formed of azure and emerald, flooded with diamond light.

And although they were still half a mile away from it, its vast glory overshadowed them.

'Who can see it and not worship?' cried Arlenmia, falling to her knees. She was weeping with joy.

Beside her, Skord prostrated his body full length on the snow. Unable to help himself, Ashurek dropped to his knees. He did not know how it had happened, but Silvren was no longer in his arms; she was kneeling at Arlenmia's left side, and Estarinel was on the right. Arlenmia had her arms round them both, inducing them to join her in adoration of M'gulfn.

Medrian was curled up on the snow near Ashurek, turning her head from side to side like a blinded animal. 'We will never destroy it now,' she was groaning repeatedly. 'Never.'

The Serpent's splendour beat down on them with cruel fierceness, and the intensity of its might vibrated outwards into space like the singing of an infinite choir. It was a song without words, yet it spoke of the Serpent's eternal glory.

And now Medrian was murmuring in a voice that was not her own, 'Come to me. It is over.'

Estarinel felt he had knelt a lifetime under the Serpent's shadow, its radiance burning down on his head. He was poised at the peak of some excruciating pain, intolerable but not to be escaped by losing consciousness. And he felt that he was doomed to be here for ever; and the despair and rebellion inspired by that knowledge only increased his anguish. Every pain he had ever suffered came crowding back into his memory; again and again he saw the attack on Forluin and the deaths of his family, so that the Serpent seemed to be mocking him, whispering, *See how they needed you and see how you have failed them* . . .

'Arlenmia,' he managed to say.

'Yes, beloved, what is it?' she asked, her voice melodious and gentle.

'That is not the Serpent,' he gasped. She betrayed no

reaction, nor did her adoring gaze waver from M'gulfn. 'The Serpent is low and foul – a vile colour – with a hideous head.' She did not answer him, and somehow he must have pulled himself out of her grasp, because he suddenly found himself on his feet, wandering to and fro on the snow like a madman.

'This is not the Serpent!' he cried. None of the others seemed able to hear him. 'I have seen it. Alone of all of you, I have seen it. This is an illusion!' He stared with dismay at the wide eyes and blank faces of his companions. 'What is the matter with you? It's only a Worm!'

But they were all ensorcelled, and he fell to the snow again, weighed down by M'gulfn's will and his own despair. And they stayed there for what must have been hours, although time was distorted beyond meaning within the Serpent's awesome domain.

'Estarinel, the Serpent you saw was false. This is its true form,' came Arlenmia's voice out of the burning-cold nightmare. She was standing before them and looking down at them, seeming more than human, robed in a dire light. 'All of you, attend to me. You have permission to look away from M'gulfn now. I don't want you to stay in this trance of worship, because I wish you to be in full possession of your senses in order to witness the final act.' Her voice brought them back to themselves. Silvren stood up unsteadily and helped Skord to his feet. She led the youth over to the others and seated herself at Ashurek's side. Medrian straightened up, pushing her black hair away from her ashen face. Estarinel put his arm round her, but it seemed an empty gesture; they could not comfort each other, and there was nothing to be said.

'I am going to M'gulfn now,' Arlenmia said. She loosened the neck of her fur garment and drew out the chain on which the Egg-Stone hung in a pouch. Ashurek gasped, the Serpent momentarily forgotten; and yet, it was all part of the same power. The dark part of him had triumphed; it seemed that all he had ever wanted, and striven for, was to become the Serpent's emissary. He felt like laughing, striding to Arlenmia's side to share her victory – or take it from her.

410

Only Silvren's hand on his arm – of which he was not even conscious – stayed him. 'Know that you are privileged to witness the most glorious event – the only true event – in the history of this Earth, or any other. Watch carefully, and understand, and be joyous.' She stepped forward, and bent down to kiss Silvren. 'I am sorry for the pain I have caused you, but I forgive your misguidedness. I am glad you are with me to see this after all.'

Silvren wanted to beg her not to go, but her mouth was too dry; she could only shake her head like a frightened child.

'What makes you so sure you will be able to relinquish the Egg-Stone?' said Ashurek, his bitter feelings surfacing. 'You will be unable to give it up, and as soon as the Serpent realises it will kill you.'

'No, you are wrong there, Ashurek,' Arlenmia replied. 'I am no slave to the Stone such as you were. And M'gulfn is not going to harm any of us: we have all served it in our way. I know not if we will meet again – in our present forms, at least. When M'gulfn's power becomes whole, we may all be transformed beyond recognition. So I bid you farewell. Have no fear: M'gulfn will forgive your doubts, even you, Medrian. Soon we will all share the glorious rewards of worshipping the Serpent.' She turned away and began to walk across the blazing valley.

All they could do was stare at her, helpless. Into the silence Skord said brokenly, 'I want to go back to Setrel. I will go back, won't I?' He was pulling at the edge of Silvren's cloak, as if she was the only one whom he trusted and did not fear.

'Of course you will, Skord,' she said as calmly as she could, wiping the tears out of her eyes. But Arlenmia must have heard him, because she turned round and glared at him.

'Skord,' she called. 'I think you should come with me, dear.'

'No!' he cried, his face blank with terror. Simultaneously Silvren exclaimed, 'Oh, no, Arlenmia, let him stay here. As if he isn't frightened enough—'

411

'Skord, come to me,' she repeated sternly. And the youth, unable to disobey, stumbled towards her, convulsed with dread. 'You should share this glory. Truly, I do not know what is the matter with you – don't you realise how honoured you are?' And she gripped his shoulder and began to march him towards the Serpent.

As if in a dream the others watched them dwindling, like two flies crawling infinitely slowly up a vast white wall.

'Medrian, is that its true form?' Estarinel asked. So intent was Arlenmia upon the Serpent that her will no longer weighed them down, but their awe of M'gulfn was as paralysing in a different way.

'I – I don't know,' she said. 'I can't read its thoughts, it's closed to me. All I can see is that awful light, and – and confusion. Terrible confusion.'

'We must stop her,' he groaned, as if articulating the need could make it less impossible. As he spoke, Ashurek stood up, his expression sinister and distant.

'Ashurek, what are you doing?' Silvren asked, alarmed.

'I must have the Egg-Stone,' he stated. And with a movement at once so unexpected and so deft that Estarinel had no chance of protecting himself, Ashurek seized the Silver Staff.

'Meheg-Ba implied that the Staff might be used to get the Egg-Stone from her,' he said, a pale, terrifying light in his green eyes.

'Don't – she'll kill you!' Silvren cried, but he disregarded her and began to stride mechanically after Arlenmia. Estarinel jumped to his feet, his fear of the Serpent suddenly swamped by his distress at the Silver Staff being taken from him. He remembered the Lady of H'tebhmella's warning that the Staff might become like another Egg-Stone in Ashurek's hands, and he began to run after Ashurek, shouting, 'Miril! Miril, aid us!'

Silvren stood up, but almost passed out. Medrian caught her, and said faintly, 'There's nothing you can do. Please stay with me. When M'gulfn sees the Silver Staff—' she

412

trailed off, her face chalk-pale. With no choice but to wait, she and Silvren sat huddled together, supporting each other as best they could.

Ashurek caught up with Arlenmia and she swung round to face him, contemptuously angry. She prepared to use the power of the Egg-Stone against him, but the sight of the Silver Staff in his hands made her hesitate.

'What on Earth do you imagine you are doing?' she asked coldly. She gave Skord a push and said, 'Go on. I will catch you up,' and the wretched youth had no choice but to stagger on towards the Serpent alone.

'Give me the Egg-Stone,' Ashurek said. 'This weapon is more powerful than it.'

'You've gone mad!' Arlenmia exclaimed. 'And I strongly advise you not to touch me with that silver instrument – the consequences could be disastrous.'

'Miril!' Estarinel cried again as he ran towards them. 'Ashurek, give me back the Staff – you'll kill us all, it is not to be used like this.' But Ashurek ignored him. On top of the Staff the silver figure of Miril began to move stiffly, like an exquisitely crafted mechanical toy. She turned her head from side to side, her wings creaking as she stretched them out. Gradually her carved feathers became soft and silken, but at the same time they began to darken. Presently she was not silver-white but soot-black. She sprang from the Staff and hovered in the air between Ashurek and Arlenmia, who backed away looking mildly surprised, but more irritated than afraid.

At the sight of Miril, the deadly light faded from Ashurek's eyes and he handed the Staff back to Estarinel without a word. The Forluinishman sheathed it with relief. But the Serpent had seen it, and the air began to throb with its anxiety.

Medrian uttered a terrible, deep cry, an echo of M'gulfn's terror as it understood what the Staff was, and saw Miril before it. She writhed in Silvren's arms, fighting M'gulfn's dread and rage, trying desperately to speak to it and soothe it. But she could not make it listen; she could only hang on to it grimly, just as Silvren was hanging on to her in an attempt to quiet her.

'What is this – this sparrow supposed to be?' Árlenmia exclaimed scornfully. 'Should I be afraid of it?'

'I am Miril,' the bird sang. 'And you do not know me, Arlenmia, but the Worm knows me. You must give the Egg-Stone to me, not to the Worm.'

'Whoever taught it to talk was wasting their time,' Arlenmia remarked, and turned away to resume her pilgrimage. Miril flitted after her and landed in her hair, causing Arlenmia to swat her away with a cry of rage.

'I must be reunited with the Egg-Stone,' Miril chirped again. Arlenmia turned to glare at Ashurek and Estarinel, one hand gripping the pouch which contained the Stone.

'Will you call off this ridiculous bird!' she exclaimed. She called the Egg-Stone's power to drive Miril away, but, of course, it had no effect against Miril, who had been its guardian. She went pale with shock and frustration, and in that moment while her attention was on the bird, her control over Estarinel and Ashurek was lost. They felt the release and began to converge on her. She turned to confront them, preparing to flick them away with a lash of the Stone's energy. But the leaden power was melting and sliding through her hands like ice . . . and nothing happened.

Ashurek saw the expression of alarm on her face and realised what this meant: Miril's presence had somehow neutralised the Egg-Stone. At once he and Estarinel seized Arlenmia and pinioned her arms, and so stunned was she by her loss of power that she made no attempt to resist. As she stood stiffly in their grasp, Miril swooped and danced infuriatingly around her head. At this her face became livid, and she found her voice.

'M'gulfn, aid your servant!' she shrieked. But the Serpent, towering above them in its swathes of white and sapphire and emerald light, showed no sign of having heard her. Then she began to struggle in earnest, and they discovered with dismay that her physical strength had not deserted her. With a lightning movement she evaded their grasp, and in the split

414

second before they could lay hold of her again, she had slipped the Egg-Stone from its pouch and flung it in a wide arc at Skord.

'Skord!' she yelled. 'Take it and run! Quickly now, straight to M'gulfn!'

Skord would not have dreamt of disobeying her. He bent to retrieve the Stone from the snow and began to hurry towards the Serpent. Immediately Ashurek was after him. Estarinel managed to hold Arlenmia back for a couple of seconds before she broke free and dashed in pursuit, but Ashurek had already reached Skord. He grabbed the boy's arm, seized the Egg-Stone from his hand without difficulty, and Skord collapsed into the snow, moaning.

The Egg-Stone lay in Ashurek's palm, just as it had when he had first stolen it from Miril, a small thing like a sparrow's egg, pale blue with silver flecks. It was lead-heavy and gelatinous to the touch. It called to him, filling him with a terrible dark light which drove back the pain he had suffered since losing it, assuaged all his guilt and anguish, soothed him with the sweet promise of power . . . Power to avenge Meshurek, to fulfil their father's hopes . . . And yet, it was only a fleck of the far greater power that towered above him, just as a tiny stream leading to an ocean of pale fire.

He turned and began to walk towards the Serpent. Somewhere behind him, he heard Arlenmia laugh.

Then a streak of black crossed his vision and Miril was on the snow in front of him. Faint silver and gold lights shimmered on her darkened feathers and she gazed at him, just as she had when he had first taken the Egg-Stone from her and seen his guilt in her eyes. Those shining black orbs transfixed him now, dazzling in their simplicity and honesty, speaking the forgiveness he did not deserve.

Memories impaled him like arrows. *You have found me – but have you found me?* He did not want to hear her say those words again.

But Miril said only, 'I will not prevent you. It is your choice.'

By the gods, no! he screamed inwardly. The Egg-Stone,

the Serpent, allowed only one decision. Their imperative will was drawing his muscles as taut as wire, compelling him to fulfil their irrefusable need to be reunited. And Miril offered him *choice*? She should have seized the Stone from him, relieved him of that responsibility—

You must let go of your guilt. The last step is to take responsibility.

Ashurek took two more compulsive steps towards M'gulfn, willing the Stone's fell energy to obliterate Miril from his mind. But she was still in front of him, he could not escape her eyes. And he thought, she looks on me with pity. M'gulfn's wretched puppet. Yet it should be me who has pity on her.

I have waited for you, Ashurek, waited to be reunited with the Egg-Stone so that my pain may end.

'For your sake, Miril,' he whispered hoarsely, 'this is my choice.' He stretched out his hand and the Egg-Stone slid through his limp fingers and thudded into the snow at Miril's feet.

At once she seized it and was on the wing, flying away from him with the eye in her beak. And, as he had known it would, a familiar agony flooded him. He could not bear to part with it a second time – drowning in fiery pain, he stumbled after her. Arlenmia and Estarinel were pursuing her as well, but she easily outflew all of them and landed in the snow near Silvren and Medrian. As the others reached her, she put back her head and swallowed the Egg-Stone.

Arlenmia cried out. Ashurek would have done, but he mastered himself, determinedly driving back the pain of loss. He had been its slave for long enough. Miril leaped into the air, chirping stridently as if in anguish. For seconds she fluttered there; then she looked round at all of them with her sad, black eyes. 'My child is back with me,' she sang. 'I have fulfilled my task as world-protector. Only remember me, and you need have no fear.'

Then she folded her wings and dropped like a stone into the snow.

Ashurek knelt down and scooped her up in his hands; but her body was limp and tattered and lifeless. Miril was unquestionably dead. She and the Egg-Stone had destroyed each other. Weeping, Ashurek laid her down in the snow where she had fallen.

At Miril's death, Medrian felt the Serpent's fear subside abruptly. Gasping with relief, she drew herself upright, pushing her hair from her face and trying to orientate herself. She found herself facing the huge statue-like figure of the Serpent, but now that M'gulfn's thoughts were less muddled, she suddenly discerned the truth about it. And as she realised, she saw that it was changing. 'Look,' she gasped, and the others also stared at it in astonishment, except for Arlenmia, who witnessed the transformation with tears streaming down her cheeks.

As they watched, the brilliant fires burning around it flickered and faded. Dull mustard-coloured flames sprang up in the ice chasms and a deep rumbling filled the air as they began to tremble and cave in. The towering form of the Serpent was swaying as shimmering rivulets of molten sapphire began to pour down its scaled, shining sides. Cracks were branching through its ultramarine depths. Soon, it began to disintegrate, its glassy surface sloughing away first in fragments, then in great chunks, until it became a mass of crumbling ice layers, molten glass and foam. Slowly, with the roaring of an earthquake, it collapsed into itself, and the collapsing seemed to take a century.

The wide valley with its flaring lights, vast chasms, and the awesome shining effigy of M'gulfn, was gone. It was as if night had fallen; all daylight had been obliterated by dense, tarry clouds. They found themselves facing a flat, rough snowscape under a pitch-dark sky.

And before them was the Serpent in its true form.

It was not thousands of feet high, it was more like fifty feet long. It was a thick, tapering tube of foul-coloured flesh wrapped in a loose, greyish membrane. Rudimentary claws and small, leathery wings protruded from its sides. Its head was huge and misshapen, with two tiny, pale blue eyes and grinning jaws. It lay on its belly in the snow, staring at them. Its stench was overwhelming; grey-green fires spat around it, and from it there emanated a sense-numbing aura of evil.

And Skord was a bare few yards from its head. None of them had given him a thought; only now did they realise that he had not followed them when they had chased after Miril. Fear had overcome him, and he now lay huddled on the snow, a tiny abject figure beyond their help.

It was Arlenmia who started out towards him, shouting, 'Skord! Come here!' They saw him lever himself up on his hands, instinctively trying to obey her call. But it was too late. In the same instant, the Serpent launched itself into the air.

Panic gripped them, so that none of them were able to move or make a sound. It was just as Estarinel remembered from the attack on Forluin, its swift, impossible movements, its loathsome shape, its aura of diabolic malevolence. They could hear Skord's terrified sobbing as the Serpent lurched into the air and swooped towards him. Paralysed with horror, they saw it swing its head and seize the boy in its maw like a rag doll. The jaws moved and a froth of blood and foam ran from the Worm's lips and Skord was gone.

'No,' Arlenmia breathed. She turned to the others, and they saw that her expression was one of horror and disbelief. 'It has slain my messenger. This cannot be . . .' And she cried out and sank to her knees in the snow and tangled her hands in her hair, mourning her shattered dream with infinite bitterness.

Later, they came to understand the meaning of what had happened more clearly. So total had been Arlenmia's devotion to M'gulfn, so compelling her belief that it was a kind of god, that the very strength of her conviction, linked to the Egg-Stone's power, had created the illusion that it was vast, magnificent and beautiful. It was like the illusion she had created around the Glass City, but on a far greater scale. The Serpent itself knew almost nothing about it, except that something strange and confusing was happening; the vision had been solely the product of Arlenmia's ambitious imagination.

She knew that the Serpent had attacked Forluin; she knew what it really looked like. But these had been abstract ideas, glimpses in mirrors which, because they did not accord with her vision, she could not accept as reality. To her, what she believed was real, and if it was not to start with, she could make it so.

But deprived of the Egg-Stone, her manufactured reality had collapsed, and she was faced at last with the truth of the Serpent's ghastly appearance and evil nature. She had not been lying when she had claimed to abhor violence, but she had always found ways to disregard it, or excuse her own use of it, by convincing herself that as a means to an end it was not as terrible as it seemed. But confronted with the murder of Skord, she could not turn away, could not deny the horror or excuse the evil of it. Disgust shook her to the core, and her dream was demolished.

Perhaps it was true that only the Serpent itself could ever have convinced her that her vision was wrong. Here before her was incontrovertible proof of M'gulfn's infernal nature. It did not care about those who served it; it had eaten her messenger. It was not beautiful; it was loathsome and mean-spirited and vile. As Arlenmia was finally forced to accept this as the truth, the enormity of its deeds and of her own came crowding upon her. Crushed by their weight she fell into the snow, powerless and grief-stricken.

And as complete as her devotion had been, so absolute was her disillusionment.

The others realised that she had given in and presented no more danger, but they could spare her no attention. The Worm was watching them, its head swaying from side to side, blood hissing into the snow from its cruel jaws. Ashurek had gone so far beyond his initial terror that he now felt icily calm. Silvren was trembling, but fiercely keeping herself under control. Estarinel, however, was less fortunate, and the panic which had been gnawing at him ever since they had first glimpsed the Worm's aura swamped him at last. He did not know where he was. He almost thought himself back in Forluin, running and running through a grey fog to find M'gulfn in front of him, grinning like a ghoul as it lay on Falin's ruined house . . . And now here it was again, and he knew only that he must get away from it at all costs. He turned and fled blindly across the snow, unaware of everything except his need to escape.

Medrian was after him at once. She seized his arm – as she had once before, in a valley in Forluin – and dragged him to a halt.

'Stop – Estarinel, it's all right, don't be afraid,' she heard herself saying, ridiculously. 'The Egg-Stone is destroyed. M'gulfn won't attack us, because it knows we have the Silver Staff. It is afraid of us, too. And you were right: its appearance before was an illusion, just Arlenmia's distorted vision. Estarinel?'

As she spoke to him, his breathing slowed and she saw the panic fade from his eyes – only to be replaced by despair. He stared at her for a few moments and then half turned away, although he did not make to run off again. He stood still with his back to the Serpent, seeming somehow remote from her.

'Come back with me,' she said.

'I can't,' he said stiffly. 'Medrian, I'm sorry, I can't. I can't face it.'

'You must,' she whispered. But he only shook his head, and then she felt a kind of panic herself, a cold viscid realisation that it was beyond her power to restore his resolve. She reached out to touch his arm, yet he seemed to be slipping away from her.

'Estarinel, there's something I haven't told you—' her words were urgent, yet lost as soon as they were spoken, like a whisper swept away on a blizzard. 'Something you should know.' But it seemed to her that her hand was an elusive thing sculpted out of ice, melting and sliding from his arm so that she could not keep hold of him; and that she was herself only a small figure made of frost, insubstantial and transient. This is just a moment of my life, she thought – then I will be gone. I must make him understand before it's too late . . . But he was staring straight through her as if she had no more substance than ice vapour.

'It's no good,' he said.

'In Forluin,' she persisted desperately, 'you remember when we went into the wheelwright's barn, where they had laid your family?' Oh, this is hard, she thought. 'I had resolved not to tell you this, because it would only have caused you pain. But now I know no other way to make you see the Quest through.'

'Medrian, what are you saying?' He gripped her shoulders and a wild look came into his eyes. At least he was listening to her.

'Their bodies were perfect. There was a reason for that. You see, even without the Egg-Stone, the world will still fall into M'gulfn's power. Not at once, but within half a year, if you recall Setrel's prediction, and then its venom will reduce the rest of Forluin to ash. And it will reanimate those that it killed in order to torment and enslave them. Do you understand me? Your family are not truly dead. M'gulfn holds them in suspension until its power is total. You remember what you said Silvren told you, about the world becoming a poisoned sac – you know that its rule would be hell on Earth. Without the Egg-Stone the Serpent is vulnerable, we have a chance to kill it. But if we don't – if you turn aside – you are condemning your family and the whole of Forluin to something infinitely worse than death.'

'You knew this, and you didn't tell me?' he exclaimed.

'It would only have hurt you.'

'Or you kept it back so that you might use it if I lose my nerve?'

The accusation shocked her; mainly because it was, she realised, half-true. 'Yes, in a way. Not deliberately,' she whispered. And he continued to stare at her so that she felt more than ever that she had become a ghost.

Then the moment was over. He was embracing her, and

she was real again, living flesh and blood. 'Oh, Medrian, what am I saying to you?' he cried. 'Forgive me. You should not have to persuade me to go on; I feel ashamed. I gave you my word that I would not let you down, and I will not. I'm all right now.'

'Are you sure?'

'Yes,' he said, taking her hand and walking determinedly back to Ashurek and Silvren. 'I am ready. Let us finish it.'

'I love you,' she said faintly.

They stood together on the snow, a group of five figures: one apart, bowed down by her private wretchedness, the other four close together, gazing grim-faced upon the evil creature which they must somehow destroy.

'I am glad that I am able to be with you at the end after all,' Silvren murmured to Ashurek. 'I wish only that I could summon my power to your aid.'

The Serpent was edging slowly towards them, smearing the snow with blood and grey venom as it came. Its insatiable malevolence thrummed in the air, making it almost intolerable for them to stand their ground against it, let alone launch an attack on it. Silvren would not say it, but Ashurek knew she felt, as he did, that the Worm had proved to be indomitable after all. It was laughing at them, gloating.

'Why does it not attack us?' Ashurek asked. He had one hand in a reassuring clasp on Estarinel's shoulder; far from despising the Forluinishman's near-surrender to fear, he could only admire him for overcoming it. 'Is it because of the Silver Staff?'

'Yes,' Medrian replied. 'It knows what it is now, and it is not so stupid that it does not fear it.' Estarinel had held the end of the Silver Staff to Miril's breast as he had on Hrunnesh, but nothing had happened, the bird had remained lifeless.

'We seem to be in a sort of stalemate,' Ashurek said. 'Always I had faith that once we had come this far, how to end it would have become obvious. It it has not. We must have gone wrong somewhere, or Miril would not be dead.'

'I've thought and thought,' Medrian said, 'but still I arrive always at the same answer. I don't know whether it is right, but it is all I can think of.'

'Well, what is it?' Ashurek asked. 'We must do something. I would rather take a chance than stand here discussing it for ever more.'

'I think I know what should be done,' Medrian said, 'but I am not confident of how to achieve it. Its body must be destroyed with ordinary weapons. It is not invulnerable to them.'

Ashurek looked at her with surprise. 'Maybe not. But all the same, how do we get close enough even to touch it? It will snap us up as it did poor Skord. What about the Silver Staff?'

'You know that we cannot use the Staff to slay its body without causing a cataclysm. It must – it must not be used until afterwards. Besides, if we approach the Serpent with the Staff, it will flee.'

'So either we spend eternity chasing it about, or else we advance on it with earthly weapons only to be killed at once?' Ashurek exclaimed. 'Medrian, you are making less sense, not more.'

'No, hear me out,' she said. 'I can see only one way for us to succeed. This will be the way of it: I will go first to the Serpent and speak to it. It's all right, Estarinel – it cannot touch me, any more than I can physically harm it. I will induce it not to defend itself. Then you two must advance with axes and slay it.'

'Induce it?' Ashurek sounded incredulous. 'To have gained independence of its will is one thing, but to convince it to lie quietly while we murder it is—'

'But it is our only hope!' Medrian replied flatly. 'Can any of you think of a better way? Estarinel, take off the Silver Staff and leave it here.' He unbuckled the red scabbard and Silvren took it from him. 'Now, I will go to it. Stay twenty or so yards behind me, and only advance when I signal to you. The H'tebhmellian clothes will protect you from its venom. Are you ready?'

'Yes,' both replied, taking their axes from their belts.

'Remember what Miril said. It must be done with gentleness. Try to kill it swiftly, as if—' She swallowed, 'as if you were putting an animal out of its misery.' She seemed icily calm and resolute, and in fact she was not feeling any fear in that moment. To her the physical presence of M'gulfn was no worse than the mental presence she had endured all her life. Ashurek felt something like battle-fever gripping him, which drove out even the strongest doubt and terror. And Estarinel felt so sick and weak with dread that he was sure some outside force must be propelling him towards M'gulfn; or perhaps it was simply that no fate could be worse than betraying Medrian's and Forluin's faith in him.

'How should we best attack it?' Ashurek asked.

'Behead it,' Medrian answered matter-of-factly, 'then dismember the head.'

And the three who had set forth from the House of Rede now walked together towards the end of their Quest, in darkness.

The air swirled thickly about them as they went, like a sea of bromine gas. They moved through it in agonising slow motion, choking on the Worm's stench, the snow sucking at their feet like viscid flesh. Before them the Serpent M'gulfn lay waiting, grinning like an impassive cockatrice.

Presently Medrian signalled the other two to stop while she went on ahead. Estarinel found it terrible to watch her advancing towards that vile creature alone, a small, brave figure outlined by green-brown phosphorescence. The Worm was bigger than he had realised; she looked tiny by its head. How shameful his own fears seemed in the face of her courage. He held his breath, thinking, surely she is not going any closer—

All the time Medrian was talking to M'gulfn, trying to draw it from the depths of her mind where it was sulking and make it listen to her. For a time there was no response. Only

424

when she drew so near to it that she could have reached out and touched its great, wrinkled head, did it speak: *Ah, my Medrian. You have come to me at last.*

'Yes,' she replied.

The loss of my eye was painful to me, but at least the hated bird was destroyed thereby. I devoured her. I have nothing to fear now. They dare not bring the silver weapon near me. I am safe, and you will stay with me for ever.

'Yes, I will stay with you, M'gulfn,' she answered quietly. It seemed quiescent, not fully aware of what was happening. Arlenmia's tricks had left it shaken and confused. Perhaps this was not going to be so hard after all.

You are not lying to me, are you, my Medrian?

'No, I am with you now. Hush, be still,' she whispered. She could feel its mind sliding away within her own, as if in torpor or sleep. She probed at it cautiously, but it seemed utterly tranquil. Slowly, never looking away from its tiny blue eyes, she raised a hand. Behind her she heard the crunch of Estarinel's and Ashurek's boots as they began to advance. Those few instants seemed to drag on interminably, as if a fleeting nightmare had been crystallised in time—

Suddenly she was on her back in the snow, while overhead the Serpent hurtled into the air, the whirring of its wings deafening. A scream died in her throat. *Traitor! You think I did not know what you intended?* Its thoughts raked into her brain like poisoned barbs. *How dare you do this? I warned you I would make you sorry. You are going to suffer, suffer until you grovel for pity.*

'No!' she cried, trying desperately to control and quiet it. But as the Serpent had lost its power over her, so had she lost what little power she had had over it. It circled in the air, strings of blood and acid falling from its mouth. She struggled to her feet – skidding in the befouled snow – and saw Estarinel and Ashurek staring up at it, blank-faced and frozen, like figures of stone.

It dived over their heads, turning round and round in the air with hideous grace, like an eel chasing its tail in a murky sea. And Medrian knew that it was not going to kill them

425

quickly, but very slowly and systematically, if at all. It wanted more than anything to humiliate them.

'Stop,' she gasped. 'I won't let this happen. M'gulfn, stop!'

They shall not slay me, not me! it kept crying, and its emotions seared her lungs like an acrid gas. *I will give them confusion and pain and death, just as I promised when they took my eye!*

Estarinel stood gripping the shaft of his axe, so numb and faint with terror that the Serpent itself seemed tiny, miles away from him in a grey-brown fog. He could do nothing to defend himself, it would spew its poison onto him as it had onto Forluin. He was trapped in a leaden nightmare from which there was no escape. And Ashurek stood determined to deal it at least one blow before it felled him, thinking all the time of Silvren.

The Serpent swooped. But it did not touch any of them; it plummeted heavily onto the snow, sending up great pinkish-grey gouts of the stuff. It writhed there and they waited, petrified, for it to rise again.

Yet it did not. Medrian was standing rigidly upright in front of it, her arms by her sides and her head back, and she was singing. Her voice was low and the words of the song were strange, if they were words at all; but they seemed to have paralysed the Serpent. It lay thrashing on the snow, but it could not rise.

Medrian had remembered the Guardian's song. It was a deep, weird chant with which they had pinioned it all those millions of years ago in order to steal its eye. Perhaps they had forgotten the song, or perhaps they had not thought to suggest its use; but the Serpent had not forgotten it. It still had nightmares about it. And now the song came directly from M'gulfn's memory into Medrian's mind, and she sang the slow, strange melody back to it so that it sank helpless onto the ground, fear running like paralysis along all its muscles.

And there she held it, the song looping between their minds, until it became a cacophony of terror within M'gulfn's skull; but she remained detached, not allowing herself to be drawn into the vortex of its fear. And as she continued to sing strongly, she raised both hands and beckoned Estarinel and Ashurek to come forward again.

They saw that she had the Worm in check and once more they went cautiously forward. But as they approached it, it opened its mouth and gave voice, not to a roar, but to a terrible groan. And the groan went on and on; and the utter desolation of it filled their heads, so that they cried out in horror and staggered as if buffeted by a gale. The Serpent was pinioned, but it was still swollen with fell power.

Its head was flat out on the snow, and its pale eyes – siblings of the Egg-Stone – glinted at them, filled with implacable malice. And it seemed to be looking down at them, as if it was towering above them, ballooned to many times its actual size, like a grotesque parody of Arlenmia's vision, while they were trapped by their own arrogance in the bottom of a slimy, grey pit, helpless and humiliated.

Fires spat around the Worm, brown and ochre and olive-green; and in their glow basked obscene creatures; discoloured, malformed creations of the Serpent. Some were laughing and some were weeping and some were expressionless, but all were so pitiable and so repulsive that just to look upon them induced madness. Estarinel and Ashurek both cried out in horror, and awful thoughts began to crawl about in their minds. In danger of forgetting who or where they were, they wandered about before the Serpent as if blind.

Medrian knew they were struggling, but she could do nothing to help except to sing on above the Serpent's groan, praying that they would not lose their sense of purpose altogether.

Silvren was pacing up and down on the snow, clasping the cloak round herself with one hand, gripping the Silver Staff in the other. She was shivering involuntarily, unaware of how cold she really was. She watched as the three approached the Serpent, saw it take off and held her breath for ten heartbeats before it dropped to the snow again. Now they were trying to approach it, their figures rimmed by its baleful, sick aura. Silvren felt as distressed by her helplessness as by her anxiety.

Unable to bear watching alone, she went to sit by Arlenmia, who was kneeling in the snow with her back to M'gulfn.

'Arlenmia,' Silvren said. 'I know how you feel.' Arlenmia looked up at her, her face as white as alabaster. 'Do you?' she said expressionlessly.

'Well, I suppose I do not. What can I say?'

'I don't know why you want to say anything. It is no thanks to me that you are still alive, is it? You warned me, and I would not listen, and now you are proved right.'

Silvren took her hand, and held onto it when she tried to pull away. 'It was a dream, Arlenmia. Only a dream. This is real.' She held up Arlenmia's hand in her own. 'You and I, talking to each other. There is nothing else; but this is everything. This is what we are fighting to save.'

'Must you be so forgiving?' Arlenmia exclaimed. 'You make things very difficult.'

'Good,' Silvren replied. 'Listen, my power is all but gone. But they need help, I must do something.'

'Such as what?'

'Their weapons. If I could only imbue their axes with some degree of sorcerous energy, it would give them a greater chance of killing the Serpent. I can't do it alone, but if you would only link hands and help me—'

She expected a flat refusal, but to her surprise Arlenmia turned to her and said, 'Yes.' Colour had come back to her face and her eyes were burning. 'M'gulfn has betrayed me. Yes, I would like to help them kill it.'

Medrian's throat was raw, scoured by the Serpent's acrid stench. Its groans were echoing in her ears and head, but still she continued the chant. She saw Estarinel and Ashurek stumble past her, going to the left and right of M'gulfn's head. Its tiny eyes swivelled to follow them and it writhed frantically against Medrian's restraint.

Ashurek's axe was trailing in his hands like a dead weight. With an effort he lifted it, balancing it ready for battle. He was trying grimly to shut his mind against the Serpent's confounding aura and remember his purpose. Its head and neck loomed before him, thickly roped with muscle under the flaky membrane. Close to, it seemed huge, and he could not see Estarinel on the other side of it.

He swung the axe in an arc and it bit into M'gulfn's neck, sending a shuddering, painful shock through his arms and shoulders.

The membrane parted like paper and the edge sank into its flesh as if through a putrescent gel, only to be stopped by an iron-hard sinew. Ashurek pulled the weapon clear and staggered back, gasping. The Serpent flung its head into the air and howled with rage. Its body contracted into an S-shape, and despite the restraining song, it tried to attack.

Its hideous mouth was gaping before him and Ashurek saw between its jaws a glistening scarlet cavern, with fangs like stalactites of ivory, glutinous with bloody slaver; and its hot-cold, foul breath caught him full in the face.

By reflex he hefted the axe and struck again. This time the edge cut into its lips and gums, and a virulent crimson liquid oozed from its mouth. The shock of the blow sent Ashurek reeling away onto the filthy snow, while the Worm half-rolled away in irritation.

On the other side, Estarinel was caught off-guard. He had aimed one blow at it, but it had barely nicked the membrane. The Worm's creatures were sighing around him, worsening his disorientation. He felt that he was sinking slowly through a brown ocean, and that the corpses of those tragic monstrosities were drifting down with him . . . Even as he was struggling to shake off the illusion, the Worm's thick body lurched into him and he fell with his legs trapped beneath it. The shock brought him back to himself, and he cried out in terror. The Serpent righted itself, releasing him, but before he could regain his feet, its head snapped round and he found himself caught in its lips.

Thick, heavy folds of soft flesh enveloped him and its

stench was overwhelming. He could see every detail of its skin: the ridges and furrows crusted with dried venom, the pores like pits clotted with dark blood. Somehow he held onto his axe; in fact it was dragging painfully on his free arm, but he could not let it go, his fingers were spasmed. He waited for the Worm's jaws to crush him.

Instead, the Serpent spoke to him. Each word seemed as tangible as a monolith of fossilized bone, and each letter of each word was in itself a terrible image. Forluin, Medrian, Skord – all real yet distorted and imbued with a nightmarish, profound meaning, as if he was seeing them with subconscious, greater-than-human perception. He saw the Earth itself groaning in immedicable despair as it drifted through eternity under the Worm's rule, and Miril, lying dead in the snow . . . On and on the Serpent spoke. The images were like weights, crushing him with insufferable pressure. And at the same time, he felt that he was himself the words that M'gulfn spoke.

Medrian saw Estarinel caught in the Serpent's maw, Ashurek prostrate on the snow, and it seemed to her in that moment that she had misjudged everything. There was no easy way to slay M'gulfn. Her only hope now was to retreat towards Silvren and take the Silver Staff from her, chanting all the while so that M'gulfn remained pinned to the snow. Then she must approach M'gulfn with the Staff and pierce its throat. Their lives would be lost and the Earth torn apart, but at least it would all be ended . . .

No. Even that last, drastic solution was beyond her power. She was exhausted, her grip on M'gulfn was slipping. She knew that she could not slay it herself; and at that moment she could not even believe that the Silver Staff possessed the necessary power. She felt that they were all victims of some ghastly joke played on them by the Grey Ones, who were now smiling down at them, their impassive callous amusement worse even than the Serpent's mockery.

Ashurek regained his feet. He could not see Estarinel, but he knew something had happened to him. Perhaps M'gulfn had killed him. Fury possessed him and he determined to do it some dire harm before it destroyed them all. He struck at its neck, once and twice, his blows stopped short by its wire-hard muscles. He was gasping for breath, choking on the thick atmosphere. To bring the axe down a third time seemed a monumental, impossible task. It was dragging at his arms like an anchor, while his whole body felt nerveless, as if some paralysing fever had drained all his strength from him. He managed to half-lift the weapon, only to stagger and almost fall, put off his stroke by astonishment.

There were golden fires running up and down the length of the axe, stars scintillating on its sharp edge. He recognised Silvren's sorcery, and it was for her sake that he made a renewed effort. Bracing his feet apart, he hauled the axe into the air and brought it down onto the Serpent's neck with the full weight of his body behind it.

This time the sinews split like fruit, and Medrian and the Serpent screamed in unison.

Estarinel was still glued to the Serpent's lip, helpless, but as it shrieked with pain he became vividly aware of his situation and desperate to escape it. Almost involuntarily he swung up his free hand, which held the axe. Showering silver-gold sparks, the edge caught M'gulfn across the eye. It flung up its head in agony, hurling Estarinel into the snow.

He rolled clear and leaped to his feet, experiencing a wonderful exhilaration; he was no longer in the slightest degree afraid. He bore down on it, the axe held two-handed above his head, scattering sorcerous light. He was thinking, what gave this loathsome Worm the right to destroy a people whose gentle lives were beyond its understanding; the right to cling like a diseased tick to a world whose beauty was outside the compass of its mean soul? It had gone far enough.

In unison he and Ashurek hacked at its neck, and at each blow they felt the snapping of blood vessels and tendons. Medrian had collapsed barely two feet from its cavernous mouth, and she was no longer singing, but crying out with shared pain. It was just as well that Ashurek and Estarinel were too intent on their work to see her, and that the

431

Serpent's terrible moaning drowned her cries. The ghastly creatures which thronged around it were dying, collapsing shapeless onto the snow, and the virulent Worm-fires were burning as pale as dead skin. The sky throbbed like a bruise.

Now a hideous greenish-white light began to stream from M'gulfn's body. Its wrinkled membrane glistened with moisture, as if it had broken out in a dark sweat of fear. Viscid blood was pouring from its wounds, steaming like acid as it fell to the snow. Ashurek and Estarinel struck again and again, their axes blazing like suns as Silvren poured sorcery into them.

Those weapons bit into M'gulfn's soul like bitter-cold iron, because they were a taste of a power which should not exist, which could only exist if it died. It lost the strength even to scream. Still it clung to its Wormish body, but its grip was becoming feeble, and it was whimpering inwardly, begging Medrian to help it.

'Leave your body. Come to me,' she said to it. 'Quickly, so that this terrible pain will cease. Please, M'gulfn . . .'

There was a massive split in its neck now, and its head was half off. Chunks of flesh flew into the air with every blow, spattering the snow and their clothes. The sickly glow exuding from its sides had faded and they knew that it was dying. By the time their axes met its spine, it had ceased struggling altogether. There was a cracking and splintering of unnatural bone, then the remaining flesh of the neck parted like butter; a moment later the head lay severed. Then Ashurek and Estarinel proceeded to split the eyes and cleave the skull, striking manically as if they could not believe it was truly dead.

Indeed, M'gulfn clung desperately to its body for as long as it could bear to. But at the cold touch of that baneful sorcery within its skull, it could tolerate no more: it forsook hope of regenerating its physical form and, gathering up the cognizant atoms of its being, it fled wailing into Medrian.

As Estarinel's and Ashurek's axes cut through the brain,

a leaden burst of dark power throbbed into the air, flinging them backwards. They lay winded on the snow, braced for a further shock. But it seemed that nothing was going to happen. The sudden, absolute silence was eerie. They dragged themselves to their feet and looked with objective disgust at their surroundings: the flat, defiled snowscape under an oppressive sky; the brown-tainted atmosphere; the ghastly body of the Serpent lying in the snow, its head severed and horribly crushed, its blood and glutinous venom smearing the snow for yards all around it.

And Medrian, lying unconscious in the snow just in front of the head.

Estarinel rushed over to her and lifted her gently off the ground. 'She's still alive. I don't think she's hurt,' he said. Ashurek, trying to wipe the gore from his hands, looked at him holding Medrian in his arms; and he suddenly understood about the Silver Staff. Feeling that he was going to weep, he turned away, only to find the ghastly remains of the Worm before him.

'Ashurek, come on, let's go back to Silvren,' Estarinel said. 'It's dead. How can you bear to stay near it?'

'Have you still got the H'tebhmellian fire?' Ashurek asked as they walked back across the snow, begrimed and too exhausted to feel anything about the Serpent's death – not elation, not even relief, nothing.

'Yes, I retrieved it after Arlenmia knocked it into the snow. Why?'

'Because I think the Worm's body should be burned, and the H'tebhmellian fire is the only means we have to set it alight,' Ashurek replied.

Silvren and Arlenmia both looked equally numb; it was partly the aftermath of their horror of M'gulfn, and partly the feeling that the horror was not yet quite over. There was no sense of release, the world still seemed to be sinking into a swamp of brown and grey filth.

But Silvren came forward to meet them, embracing Ashurek with no regard for the blood on his clothing. 'Oh, thank the Lady!' she cried. 'I was sure you would be killed.'

'Only because of you were we able to destroy its body,' he whispered into her hair. 'But it is not yet over.'

Medrian! the Serpent groaned. *How could you permit this? You have betrayed me, you should have let me go to another host. This pain is intolerable. I will make you sorry yet.* It raged on and on within her, swamping her as it had done when they had left the Blue Plane. Medrian knew that its body was dead and that its psyche was now wholly within her; the shock of its transference had caused her to faint, but she now listened to its ravings in the smooth grey void of unconsciousness. Its anguish and indignation were boundless. *How dared you sing that song of death? I could despise you as I have always despised the others. How shall I avenge—*

'But I saved your life,' Medrian interrupted. It paused in its flow of outraged thought.

Yes, yes, you have. How foolish you were to think that you could slay me, when all the time you were my protection. You were bound to fail. And now you lie humiliated before me, as I promised.

'Did you really want me to fail?' Medrian asked, but it did not seem to understand her question.

What a fool you are. I will rest within you awhile, for as long as it takes me to regenerate my body, and then I shall punish those others.

'No, you don't want to regenerate your body,' she said softly.

What? What are you saying, my Medrian? She could feel its mind writhing like a scaly, grey snake within her skull.

'Think of it. How hard it can be to move, how tired and heavy it makes you feel. The snow grating against your skin. Your vulnerability.'

The Serpent began to moan to itself. *No. No. I must—*

'No. You haven't the energy. Rest, stay with me.'

Ah, but you are right. Most precious of all my hosts . . . I said you would be my last host. What need have I of a Wormish body? From now on we will be as one. My Medrian, you will share immortality and power with me. It is fitting that I should now take a human form. I have no more need of helpers or servants now. Just you. For ever.

'Not for ever,' she said, her thoughts now soothing and persuasive and as strong as M'gulfn's. 'I said we would be together until the end, but the end will be very soon. We will die together.'

No! How can you say this? It became frantic again, crying out with angry denial. *Still you betray me . . . Ah, the silver weapon. I should have known! But you would not dare. You do not dare to destroy me. I was meant to endure for ever . . .*

'You don't want that,' Medrian replied calmly. 'You are so old . . . and tired, so tired. You do not even have the energy for anger and hatred. You want to rest. To die.'

No. You shall not slay me. It struggled against her, but its efforts were half-hearted, fading into confusion.

'Not slay, it will be gentle, a falling into sleep. No more nightmares. No more pain. Peace. You desire peace, don't you?'

Yes. No. I cannot die . . . But it did not resist as Medrian showed it the vision she had shown to Arlenmia: the Earth, drifting through an eternity of utter desolation, and itself lying alone and wretched on the dead husk for ever. For the first time, she made it look at that cold grey vista, and like a great rock being crowbarred away to reveal the creatures teeming and scurrying in the dark hollow beneath, so the Serpent's doubt was laid bare. It was forced to accept the truth, and the truth was unbearable; the grief and despair it had sought to bring to humans, it had only brought to itself. *No*, it wailed tormentedly within her. *No . . .*

'This is how your eternal life would be,' she said. 'You don't want this, do you? You don't want the torpor and desolation and loneliness that would be your future. You want release from them. Rest from your pain. Not to lie on the ice listening to the cold winds for ever . . .'

Help me, it cried. *Please help me . . .*

'Yes, I will help you. Only stay quietly within me, and it will soon be over.'

No more nightmares. Peace . . .

435

'Be still. We will find peace together,' she murmured. And the Serpent ceased crying and struggling against her, and it curled up and became utterly quiescent.

Medrian opened her eyes. Estarinel was bending concernedly over her. He helped her to sit up and she looked around and saw Ashurek sitting on the snow with Silvren in his arms. She was still holding the red sheath containing the Silver Staff. Arlenmia was a little apart from them, staring fixedly at the grisly remains of the Serpent. A cleansing fire of blue and gold was dancing along the length of the body, the only clear light in the murky surroundings.

'Why is it burning?' Medrian asked.

'We set fire to it with the H'tebhmellian lamp,' Ashurek replied. 'And we put the body of poor Miril there, so it is also a pyre for her – and Skord.'

Medrian nodded. 'Yes, it's for the best,' she said resignedly. She sensed that the others were waiting for her to tell them what should be done next; perhaps they knew, but it had to be her who said it. Estarinel was pale and grim-faced, and she could hardly bear to look at him. She took a deep breath and tried hard to stop herself from shaking.

'You destroyed M'gulfn's body swiftly and bravely. It was my fault that it nearly – but anyway, it did not.' She shook her head and went on, 'I'm so relieved that none of you were hurt. Except for Skord, of course. It was a nightmare, but it is nearly over.'

'How did you manage to subdue it, after all?' Ashurek asked.

'A song, which the Guardians sang to it when they took its eye. I think it was to do with Miril. M'gulfn was literally paralysed by fear. And its fear was of what Miril forced it to look at, which was a reflection of itself.'

'We could not have slain it without the help of Silvren's sorcery, either,' Estarinel said.

'I know,' Medrian said, managing to smile at the pale sorceress.

436

'It was Arlenmia, too,' Silvren said. 'Together, we just had enough strength.'

Medrian looked at Arlenmia and said, 'The reason you failed was that the Serpent did not want to be invulnerable. It was confused. On the surface, all it desired was eternal life and power over Earth, but underneath there was always doubt gnawing at it, no matter how hard it tried to deny it. Miril tried to show it that the desire was false and the doubt was real, but the truth terrified it. So it hated her and fled from her, refusing to look. But I made it look. I made it understand the wretchedness of its existence, and that if it won, its desolation and misery would only grow worse, not better. Being forced to accept the truth has destroyed it. Now all it desires is death and peace. Perhaps even such a creature as M'gulfn cannot bear immortality. I discovered something as well: all the torment I have suffered through being its host, was its own. I was feeling its pain.'

'Medrian, is it dead or not?' Estarinel whispered.

'Not yet. It is within me.' She held his arm in a futile attempt to reassure him. She tried to go on but faltered, thinking, how terrible it is to know that when the others go home I will not be with them; that everything I say and do in this awful place will be for the last time. I can't do it, she thought, closing her eyes. But I must.

'I think you all understand the use of the Silver Staff by now,' she said. She tried to keep her voice steady but it sounded hoarse and faint to her own ears.

Ashurek said, 'Yes.' His face was grim with sorrow and she could not look at him, could not look at any of them. She made herself stand up before her resolve wavered.

'Estarinel,' she said. 'This must be the way of it. Take the Silver Staff from Silvren and – and come with me. I want to talk to you alone.' Numbly, he did as she said. They put their arms round each other and began to walk away from the others, close together but not speaking. She led him to a hollow some distance away, where they would be out of sight and hearing of the others.

They sat down in the snow. Neither was wearing a cloak now, but they were oblivious to the cold. Medrian pulled off her gloves and twined her fingers with his, and although he could feel her hands trembling, her face was diamond-clear and calm.

'Do you remember, in Forluin,' she began, 'I said that I would one day have to ask you to do something terrible? That time is now here.'

'Yes,' he replied faintly. 'And I gave you my word that I would do whatever you asked without protesting.'

She nodded, gripping his hands, hoping desperately that she was not going to give in to the knot of tears in her throat. 'You understand, don't you? This is the only way. The Serpent is wholly within me now. It must be absorbed into the Silver Staff. I can't do it myself . . . and you are the wielder of the Staff. There is no danger of the Serpent passing into you. It will go into the Staff, and there meet its opposite power, and so be annihilated.'

Inside, he was crying out in bitter denial; surely, surely there must be another answer. He had sworn to himself that he would save Medrian from this fate, and he could not accept that it was going to be impossible after all. But knowing that his protests would only torment her, he swallowed them, forcing them to remain unspoken, like iron barbs in his throat. He was shamed by the knowledge that he had almost let her down more than once; he could not break his word and fail her again. He longed to hug her, fiercely denying her doom, as if that could magically change things; but he constrained himself. Now, above all, she needed him to be strong.

'When I am gone, light will return to the Earth,' she said. 'Forluin will be saved. Those whom the Serpent did not truly kill may even be restored to life. Your family, Estarinel.'

But that was so far away. Here and now he was with Medrian, and it seemed to him that the Serpent had won after all. It was having the worst revenge against them that it could have devised. Now he understood: it was this that he had foreseen and dreaded from the beginning, this, that he had felt unable to face. Even this that made the Serpent impossible to slay, after all . . . All the grisly horror of the Worm paled in comparison to the simple, quiet despair of this moment.

'You have known that this was inevitable from the beginning, haven't you?' he said, as gently as he could. 'And Eldor and the Guardians knew, and the H'tebhmellians.'

'Yes,' she said. 'But how could anyone have told you? You would never have accepted it. I always knew I would have to wait until the very end. Estarinel, I know how very hard this is for you. I can't bear to cause you this pain. But please believe that it is inevitable.'

With an effort, he said, 'Yes. I believe it.'

'Then would you prefer not to do this yourself?' she asked him softly.

He shook his head. He was unable to keep the grief out of his voice as he answered. 'No, if it has to happen I would far rather it was by my own hand. I said I would not fail you, Medrian, and I will not.'

'Oh, bless your steadfastness,' she said. As if she could not stop herself, her arms slid round him to embrace him and he held her, thinking, this is unbearable, I would rather take my own life. 'You understand now why I tried to be remote from you. It wasn't only the Serpent's presence. I thought that if you cared too much about me, it would make this impossible. I tried so hard to stay detached, hoping that you might even begin to hate me. What a fool I was to think that! In Forluin, when I could no longer pretend that I didn't love you, I was sure I had doomed the Quest to failure by my weakness. I had accepted that I must die, and I wanted nothing else. But because of you I found out that life could be good, and that made it so much harder to see the Quest through.'

'Medrian, I'm so sorry, I never—'

'Hush, let me finish. Oh, I am making this terrible for you, and I swore I wouldn't. I was going to say that in the end, your love has made me stronger, not weaker. The Serpent can only be defeated, this final act carried out, with love.

Not hate, not indifference. Only love.' She kissed him and went on, 'Even though I must die with it, it has not defeated me. I used to hate myself, which was what M'gulfn wanted, I suppose. I hardly knew I was alive. If it had gone on, the Serpent's coldness would have consumed me in the end. But you seemed to see through me to my real self, which I did not even know existed. Because of you I can say that my life wasn't wholly wretched, that I knew what it was to be alive, and happy, and loved. Against that, even M'gulfn's hate could never truly win.'

He held her tighter, unable to speak. He was still struggling against his inward denial: how could this happen to her, after what she had already endured? He wanted her to go back to Forluin with him; she could not die here, where it was so desolate, so cold.

'Now,' she said, drawing away from him a little. 'It must be done quickly, while the Serpent is still quiescent; it won't wait for ever. Take out the Silver Staff.' He hesitated and she said, her voice shaking, 'Please, Estarinel. I cannot live on with it inside me. We must find peace together. Peace is as sweet as happiness.'

Fighting down his distress, he drew the long, slim Staff from its red sheath and held it across his palms. He tried to ask her what to do, but he was unable to find his voice. It glinted like dull steel and there was no song within it to ease his anguish.

'Put – put the sharp end to my throat,' Medrian said, 'and support me with your other arm at my back. As swiftly as you can—' There was something raw and obdurate in the stabbing gesture she made, and he saw how her hand was trembling.

He began to do as she asked, but slowly, almost faint with the feeling that there must, must, *must* be some way to avoid this, something he had failed to do or say, a miracle that would reprieve her if only they waited a few moments longer. He gripped the Silver Staff with the needle-thin end poised in the hollow of her throat, knowing that he was about to break his heartfelt promise not to fail her.

Medrian looked steadily at him, her face white with both fear and diamond-hard resolve. How could he hope to equal her strength? Faintly – the words turning in his heart like a cry for pity – she said, 'I'm ready, Estarinel. Let it be over soon. Please let it be over.'

It was then that he understood what Miril had meant when she said that love was selfish, compassion selfless. In his love for Medrian he was hopelessly seeking ways to redeem her, but every moment he delayed could serve no purpose except to increase her misery. What she needed from him was compassion, the understanding that there was no choice and that to end her life swiftly would be the truest, kindest proof of love. He did not know where he found the strength to act, except that compassion won.

She closed her eyes as she finished speaking, and he seized the instant as if his will had been suspended. The point of the Silver Staff slid deep into her throat. Her body spasmed, but there was no blood, and she did not make a sound.

The Silver Staff began to glow.

Silvren, Ashurek and Arlenmia were staring towards the hollow in anxious silence, though they could not actually see Medrian and Estarinel. It was many minutes before anything happened, but just as Ashurek became sure that the Quest had failed, a whisper of light began to glow there. Swiftly it grew brighter until they were privileged to witness an extraordinary, breathtaking sight. From the hollow, a pillar of silver fire sprang up to stand silently between the snow and the sky.

Energy was pouring upwards in a silver-white blaze. The negative force that formed the Serpent's spirit joined to the positive force within the Silver Staff, creating a fresh power, which was neutral, yet vigorous and cleansing. The very fabric of the Silver Staff was fraying away to form that column of joyous light. Where it touched the sky, it spread out like a fountain, and the layer of oily cloud began to dissipate, incinerated by diamond-bright purity. Then from the base of

441

the column, argent flames came pouring over the snow like a swift, foaming tide.

Before Ashurek even thought that they might be in danger, the white fire was lapping all around them. But it was heatless, as sweet and soothing as fresh air. And as it reached the Serpent's remains, the flames licking half-heartedly along them leaped into a gold and sapphire blaze. Paler and paler the H'tebhmellian fire burned until it became one with the greater incandescence of the Silver Staff. The Serpent's hideous body caught like tinder and within minutes it had flashed into vapour. And all the blood and filth that lay around it was also burned away, leaving the snow blessedly clean.

But then a cataclysmic noise began, a deep, tearing roar that vibrated painfully through their skulls. They flung themselves flat on the snow, wondering if the world was to be annihilated after all. Over their heads hurtled a vile flood of darkness, a viscid river swirling with grit and clots of filth. But the silver fire had spread to fill the whole sky, and as the dark flood touched it, it too was consumed. Then Ashurek realised that the fabric of the Dark Regions was being disgorged through the gateway that Meheg-Ba had opened. The Silver Staff's power was drawing out and cleansing all the Serpent's effluent.

At last the putrescent flood ended. The world was still intact, the air as pure as birdsong. Silvren, Arlenmia and Ashurek sat up slowly, dizzy with relief to realise that it was finally over. Then they looked around in amazement.

All traces of M'gulfn's defilement had been eradicated, and the snow was a blanket of pure white, illuminated by a light that was brilliant, yet soothing. The whole sky had become a vast ocean of pale silver fire. Within it the sun floated like an apricot-gold orb, the twin moons like iridescent opals. All around them stars were scattered, winking like diamonds from white to red to blue; and around each one circled planets which, with the exquisite illogic of a dream, could be seen in perfect detail. Each was different: a soft purple-blue sphere, an ellipse striated with ruby and amber, a jade globe encircled by flat, shimmering rings . . . their number was infinite.

And now the column of argent itself seemed to be singing, voicing the innocent cosmic joy that Estarinel had experienced in the domain of the Silver Staff. It was as if each of the billion drops of white fire was a wordless voice, swelling into a paean as wild and forlorn as infinity, as vast and vital as the birth of stars; powerful, ungentle, yet without guile. Even the Guardians did not understand what the Silver Staff was, for it was greater than them, but the song seemed to say, *We are a vessel; as the land holds the sea, and the body contains the mind, so are we a vessel for this pure and perfect energy* . . . and as they watched, the pillar appeared to take on a sentient form. It could have been Miril, a winged child, a hippogriff . . . all or none of those. It was a mythic being formed of countless glittering, oscillating motes of light. In that form it began to ascend towards the sky – its task upon Earth complete – there to continue its enigmatic dance amid the stars.

Being within the column of fire, Estarinel could hardly see it and was mainly aware of it as a cool upsurge of energy from the Silver Staff. The substance of the Staff itself was dissipating within his hands, channelling awesome energies from Earth to sky; presently the slender metal rod vanished altogether. There was nothing in his hands, nothing piercing Medrian's throat.

She opened her eyes and murmured, 'Do you see the sky?'

'Yes,' he replied, cradling her in his arms. But all he really saw was the blood which sprang from the wound as soon as the Staff was no longer there. He tried to stem it, but she whispered, 'Let it flow. There's nothing you can do.'

He saw that she was right. More than a mortal wound was draining the life from her. All he could do was to hold her, kissing her hair, while her blood poured over his hands and she slipped towards oblivion.

'I'm cold,' she said presently, like a child. 'I'm frightened.'

Bitter misery was tearing his heart out, but he could not let himself weep, not while she needed his comfort. 'Don't be afraid. I'm with you, beloved,' he said gently, saying anything, anything to make her feel less alone. 'Look at the sun, the stars; are they not beautiful? We won, Medrian. Everything is all right. You will always be loved . . .' he carried on even when he was sure she could no longer hear him. Only when her eyes were closed and her heart stilled did he begin to sob, his tears falling onto her dark hair and ice-pale face.

Some stubborn part of him still could not accept that she was dead. Why could not those heartless forces leave her alive? he cried inwardly. Surely she must live – half-mad with grief he chafed her cold hands, rocked her despairingly in his arms. But all the while he knew that his efforts were futile; and black sorrow claimed him, and he gave up.

A distant concussion shook the Earth, a shock-wave from far off forces. The silver sentience had vanished into the heavens, and the fantastical vision of moons, stars and planets was lost. The scene returned to one of earthly normality; but the delicate blue of the sky and the purity of the sun were refreshing in their simplicity. All trace of the Worm was gone, and the Earth had survived to witness a new and sweet dawn.

But Estarinel was not looking at the sky, and did not even notice. There was a wheel of ice turning in his heart, darkness pressing on his eyes. Medrian was gone, no comfort could reach her; but still he remained there, hugging her to him, weeping silently. So he was still when Ashurek found him.

17

The Far Side of the Blue Plane

'ESTARINEL,' ASHUREK said. 'Come on. You can't stay here.'

Estarinel insisted on carrying Medrian's body, but Ashurek had to support him as they walked back to Silvren and Arlenmia. 'The sooner we leave this place the better,' the Gorethrian said. 'I know it is hard, but we have to think of the return journey. There's a possibility that it may not be as arduous as I'd feared.' Estarinel said nothing. Ashurek went on, 'There was something more fortuitous than we dreamed of in the purging of the Dark Regions. You know they were on the far side of H'tebhmella; if only that Entrance is still there, we may be able to go directly to the Blue Plane.'

'Are you all right?' Silvren cried as Estarinel reached her; and when she saw Medrian, she also wept. Ashurek held her; only Arlenmia showed no emotion, and he felt unreasonably angered by her.

'Come,' he said. 'Let us go and see if the Entrance is still there. If not, we will have to think of something else.'

'Well, I am going back to my iceberg,' Arlenmia said. Ashurek turned on her.

'You are what?'

'You do not expect me to come to H'tebhmella with you, surely?'

'On the contrary,' he said quietly, his eyes burning, 'you must come with us. The Lady of H'tebhmella should decide what to do with you, what form your punishment should take.'

'Punishment?' Arlenmia echoed, an uncharacteristic look of fear crossing her face.

'You assumed that your deeds would go unremarked? I believe that this is not the only world to which you have brought near-disaster; however, you will answer to this one first. Arlenmia, you show no remorse; a ghost of attrition at best. You should have died! You and I – not Skord, not poor Miril. And not Medrian!'

'Ashurek, don't,' Silvren said. 'She feels sorrow, but she is too proud to show it. She helped against M'gulfn. The truth about it almost destroyed her. Show her some compassion.'

He sighed, turning away from Arlenmia. 'Ah, Silvren, you think too well of people for your own good. If she feels true remorse, let her prove it by coming with us.'

The Entrance was still there, now radiating light instead of yawning into darkness. To their astonishment, where once had stood a vile multitude of demons, there was now a throng of H'tebhmellian women. The Lady of H'tebhmella herself stepped forward to greet them, her beautiful face bright with relief and joy. The dark-haired Filitha and fair Neyrwin were at her side.

'Oh, we are well met!' she said. 'No words can encompass the joy and sorrow of this moment. Only come through to us and receive the healing of H'tebhmella.'

'We are grateful, my Lady,' said Ashurek, and he took off his sword and threw it away onto the snow. He helped Silvren through the Entrance, and propelled the reluctant Arlenmia after her. Estarinel went through last with Medrian.

Then they found that the H'tebhmellians were not standing on ground, but in a number of crystal boats that were bobbing gently in thin air. Each was shaped like a coracle and exquisitely figured with a pearly substance that shimmered all shades of blue and copper as the light changed. The Lady directed Arlenmia to step into another sky-coracle in the custody of Filitha and Neyrwin; then she bade the others to take seats in her own vehicle.

'Alas, Estarinel,' she said very softly to him, 'although the Blue Plane can heal the living, it possesses no power to

446

restore the dead. I know that you loved Medrian, but this was the only possible end. Be consoled by the knowledge that you acted rightly, and that Forluin has been redeemed thereby.'

Estarinel only shook his head, too lost in grief to answer her.

The sky-coracles began to drift through an infinite heaven which was of a rich, clear blue never dreamed of on Earth. Above and below and on every side were cloud banks of breathtaking strangeness and beauty – if clouds they were. They seemed to hint at other, exquisite worlds, as if they contained the essence of those strange planets seen in the vision after the Serpent died, no less distant and yet heart-rendingly real. The feeling they induced was like that of emerging from a windowless cell into a dew-clear spring morning caught in a net of light, and the contrast filled them with poignant and mixed emotions. For Estarinel, it made his loss unbearable.

Around the vehicle they shared with the Lady floated several others, crewed by H'tebhmellians. Presently, however, Silvren noticed that one, some way below them, contained a number of bewildered-looking humans, as thin and pale as herself.

'They were the prisoners held in the Dark Regions,' the Lady explained. 'The Serpent's death brought much good; that vile clot of darkness was torn away, and this, the far side of H'tebhmella, has been restored to its untainted glory.'

These revelations brought questions thronging into Silvren's throat, but in the end, all she could manage was, 'Are we staying on this side?'

'No, we are returning to the other one,' the Lady replied, smiling slightly at her evident relief. 'The tranquil side.'

'Forgive me, it's not that this place is not beautiful – but I think my heart will stop if I am here much longer. It is overwhelming.'

'It was never meant that humans should come to this side,' said the Lady, adding enigmatically, 'at least, not until they are ready to stay here. I know not how to explain it – except

447

to say that it touches the subconscious mind, which is far simpler and far wiser than the conscious mind.'

After several hours they saw land below them. It was unlike the H'tebhmella they knew; rather, it contained everything that was most familiar, sweet and beautiful about the Earth. There were violet-blue mountains, wild hills, towering fjords plunging into shimmering seas, sunlit forests, orchards and flower-filled meadows. But each of them saw something different in the landscape, so that Ashurek thought he was looking at the mountains of Gorethria, Silvren at Athrainy's hills, Estarinel at some part of Forluin he had never seen before.

The other sky-coracles flew on, but the Lady caused her vehicle to land in a green-velvet glade shaded by graceful chestnuts.

'E'rinel, there could be no lovelier place for Medrian to rest than here,' she said. 'Lay her down in the centre of the glade.' Estarinel did as she asked, covering Medrian's slight form with her travel-worn H'tebhmellian cloak; there was something pitiful, tragic in its tattered edges and snow-stains. He knelt on the grass at her side, his head bowed. Then the Lady cast a sphere of white and sapphire light – similar to the one that had sustained them in the Arctic – onto her. Soft flames sprang up along her body, like the ghosts of snowdrops and harebells. Gently and gradually she was consumed, like frost dissolved by a breath. Soon there was nothing left to mark that she had ever existed, save for a slight flattening of the velvet grass.

The Lady, Ashurek and Silvren withdrew to the edge of the glade, but Estarinel remained kneeling on the grass long after it was over, weeping in forlorn, unreachable despair. Eventually they left him by himself.

He felt more alone than he had ever believed possible, here in this place, which was soft and beautiful yet more remote and comfortless than the Arctic. He stared at the empty place where she had been, the meaning of the prescient visions he had had of her turning like a cold blade in his heart. Images came crowding back to him, heartbreakingly real and yet distant, gone for ever. Medrian, sitting white-faced and grimly quiet at a table in the House of Rede; walking with him through the white tunnels of Hrannekh Ol, trying to ease his doubts; a shadowy figure in a dusty hayloft in Belhadra, or in a circle of firelight in Excarith, her eyes always terrifying, yet so compelling . . . and again and again, Medrian in Forluin. Lying with her arms around him, whispering, 'I wish I could stay here for ever.' The hem of her blue H'tebhmellian robe brushing the ground as she turned to embrace him, saying, 'I was alive here.'

After an hour or so the Lady returned alone. When she took his arm and led him towards her sky-coracle he went without protest, dimly realising the futility of staying in the glade. Medrian was not there. He sat without speaking as the little craft skimmed above the strange landscape, presently entering a crystal tunnel which led through to the other side of the Blue Plane. It was not the tunnel through which Calorn and Ashurek had forced a way, but a wide one that had been unblocked when the Dark Regions had ceased to exist.

On the other side – the Plane of tranquil blue lakes and exquisite rock formations, which he knew – the Lady caused the sky-coracle to land on a secluded shore. She led him to a stream running between banks of moss, shaded by willows with leaves like jewels. There was no sign of the others.

'They are resting, and you must do the same,' the Lady said gently. 'Here fresh clothes have been left for you, and food and drink. Here you may sleep for as long as you wish. I know it is hard for you to believe that this sadness will ever leave you, but let H'tebhmella comfort you, at least.' She kissed him on the forehead and walked away through the trees.

He was exhausted, and it was good to strip off the travel-worn Arctic clothing and bathe in the clear, reviving stream. He felt too tired to eat, but he drank the honeyed wine that they had left for him. Then he lay down on the soft moss and, with the calming power of the Blue Plane pervading his mind and body, he fell at once into a dreamless, healing sleep.

'Skord seemed beyond help, but I don't believe he was,' said Ashurek. 'At Miril's touch he seemed to regain reason and self-awareness. But Arlenmia's hold on him was too strong. No sooner had he found hope – for the first time in his life – than he fell prey to the Serpent.'

'Ah, the poor child,' said the Lady sadly. 'Would that he could have been saved from that fate.' It was a day later, and Ashurek and Silvren were sitting on a sapphire shore in the company of the Lady, and several other H'tebhmellians.

'His death was as much our fault as Arlenmia's,' said Ashurek with harsh self-condemnation. 'She used him, but we used him also. From the very moment we met him.'

'He was M'gulfn's victim—' Silvren began.

'We cannot escape blame so easily. The fact is, he was the wretched and innocent victim of all of us – not just of the Serpent.'

'Perhaps it is so,' the Lady said, 'but, Ashurek, I believe that you are putting all your own sense of guilt onto this one boy. His end was tragic, but remorse cannot bring him back.'

'You are right,' Ashurek replied, looking levelly into her clear grey eyes. 'Yet I speak not of guilt, but of responsibility. It has been easy to blame all evil upon the Serpent. Now that it is no longer there to blame, how much better shall we fare? M'gulfn is dead, but so is Miril. How long will it take us to learn that good and evil are inside ourselves, not outside?'

A new voice said, 'This is a wise question, but the answer is beyond me.' They looked up and saw Eldor standing at the edge of the group. With him were Neyrwin and Calorn.

The tall chestnut-haired woman rushed forward, smiling, to embrace Ashurek and Silvren. 'We knew that you were back safely,' she said, 'but the Lady would not let us see you until you had rested. Oh, Silvren – both of you – I'm so glad. Neyrwin has been telling me something of what happened. Where is Estarinel?'

'Here he is,' said the Lady. Approaching from another direction were Estarinel and Filitha, who had gone to fetch him. As he reached the group he stopped in surprise to see Calorn and Eldor there.

They greeted him with unbounded relief and joy, and while on one level he returned their warmth and could have wept with happiness to see them, on a deeper level he felt detached from everything, as if the core of his soul had turned to ice. Calorn embraced him and then stood back, her hands on his shoulders, looking at him. Yes, she was thinking, he has been destroyed, just as she had feared he would be.

'I'm glad you're safe,' she said. 'I'm so sorry about Medrian.'

He nodded, not looking her in the eye. 'It's good to see you,' he said quietly.

Now he was wearing a loose white shirt and blue breeches, and went barefoot. Ashurek had on a simple, long robe of ultramarine hue, Silvren a silver-blue one tied by a cord at the waist. Already H'tebhmella had worked its healing power upon her. She had been weak and ill from her ordeal in the Dark Regions, and Ashurek had always feared that she might die in the harsh cold of the Arctic. He was sure that only her will had kept her alive. But now she looked healthy again; her ashen skin had resumed its golden hue, and her hair was glossy. It was hard for all of them not to think of how clear-eyed and tranquil Medrian and Skord would also have looked if circumstances had been less unjust.

While Estarinel was greeting the others, Neyrwin came to speak to Ashurek. 'It is simply a matter of your horses,' she said. 'Filitha is going to take Shaell back to Forluin today. What do you wish us to do with your Vixata?'

'She is the last thing I have of Gorethria,' Ashurek said thoughtfully. 'She is no longer young; I would ask no more of her. Let her be taken to Forluin with Shaell. She deserves peace for the rest of her days, and I know they will care for her there. What about Taery Jasmena?'

'The blue horse? I was told that he belonged to Arlenmia.'

Ashurek laughed. 'Aye, indeed, that is so. Let her have him back! Then she cannot accuse us of worse than "borrowing" him.'

Neyrwin added softly, 'Say nothing of Filitha's visit to Forluin to Estarinel. The Lady thinks it best that he be told nothing – until he is ready to ask.' Gravely, Ashurek agreed, and went to rejoin Silvren.

She had not seen Eldor for years, and was joyously hugging the sage. Ashurek, remembering all that had transpired between the Guardians, the H'tebhmellians, and themselves, was looking for signs of unease between the Lady and Eldor, but he sensed only a certain coolness, rather than actual hostility.

'Master Eldor and I have talked for many hours,' the Lady said, realising what he was thinking. 'He and I are not in disagreement about the rights and wrongs of the Guardians' deeds. However, I know that he is not in total accord with the other Grey Ones; there is much that must be resolved. But for now, it is enough to know that our joint efforts have resulted in the destruction of the Serpent and the preservation of the Earth and Planes.'

Ashurek said, 'Miril told us that the Guardians sent humans upon this Quest so that the Earth would be saved. If they had cared nothing for the world, they could have slain the Serpent themselves – and Earth with it.'

'It is so,' Eldor said. 'I feel that no apology can atone for what you have undergone; their manipulation of you was to induce you to make the right decisions. Ah, but the Grey Ones are proved shallow and short-sighted in their inhumanity.' He shook his grey-white head. 'The wisest choices were your own.'

'Perhaps the Guardians should all be forced to live on Earth for a while, as you have, Master Eldor,' said Silvren, but the sage did not smile at this. Instead, he looked grave and thoughtful.

After a minute he said, 'Alas, I have some sad news to impart. The House of Rede is no more. A demon went there and slew Dritha and most of our poor guest-refugees. The

452

rest fled and perished in the sea.' Exclamations of dismay greeted this news; Eldor raised a quieting hand and went on, 'Only Dritha's earthly body was slain; she has returned to the Guardians' domain. And the demon itself died the instant the Serpent was destroyed. But Dritha and I have decided that we will not return to Earth. The House of Rede's time was over with M'gulfn's. I only regret that it had to end in such violence and bitter sorrow.'

Ashurek, Silvren and Estarinel remained on the Blue Plane for many days, resting in its healing tranquillity. They spent much time talking to Eldor, Calorn and the H'tebhmellians about the Quest, the Earth's future, and many other things, except for Estarinel, who became more and more withdrawn. He often wandered off to be alone with his thoughts. It was not that he liked solitude: it was simply that whenever he was in company, he found himself looking around for Medrian, and the shock of sorrow when he recalled why she was not there seemed to grow more intense each time. 'I finally understood what the Guardians wanted of me when they insisted that I prove "clear of purpose",' he said to Eldor one day, when the sage had come looking for him. They stood together on the flat top of a great, mushroom-shaped stalk of rock. All around them delicate gazelles grazed on flower-spangled moss; beyond lay the lovely azure lakes and rocks of H'tebhmella. 'It simply meant, was I so determined to slay the Serpent that I would even kill someone I loved to achieve that end?'

'Don't torment yourself, Estarinel,' Eldor said, placing a hand on his shoulder.

'Don't—?' the Forluinishman said bitterly. 'How can I avoid it? Why should I not be tormented?'

'Because – because it was inevitable from the beginning,' the sage said inadequately. 'You acted rightly.'

'That makes it worse,' he replied flatly. 'It was just one of the many things you wouldn't tell us. Inevitable! If it had been a mistake – an accident – I could have borne it better; I could simply have made an end of myself without a qualm.

But to think that it was *right* for her to die—' he broke off, shaking his head.

'I know nothing I can say to lessen your pain, except that you should look to the future, think of Forluin—'

'It was so unjust – that after all her misery, her courage, she had nothing better to look forward to than death! Right?' He turned away, pulling his fingers through his long, black hair. 'Eldor, forgive me, I know you're trying to help. But you're right, there's nothing you can say. I know it wasn't the Guardians' fault. It was the Serpent's fault, and the Serpent is dead. But I don't want revenge; I just wish Medrian was alive. I wanted her to come back to Forluin with me. To be happy. I miss her.'

Arlenmia was being held prisoner in a small crystal cavern, guarded by H'tebhmellians. However, she was suffering no hardship, beyond the anguish of her disillusionment. She had expressed no remorse, the Lady said, but neither had she shown any inclination to escape captivity. Neither Ashurek nor Estarinel wanted her to be drastically punished for her misdeeds; in fact, they did not want to think about her at all, and were happy to leave her fate in the fair and merciful hands of the H'tebhmellians.

Only Silvren went to see her.

'What do you want of me?' Arlenmia greeted her. She was looking across the Blue Plane through a natural embrasure in the cavern wall.

'To talk to you,' Silvren replied.

'Why? I don't know what we have to say to each other. After all that I have done; after causing you to be imprisoned in that terrible place. I have not the effrontery to ask for forgiveness! But perhaps you are not intent on forgiving me. Perhaps you merely wish to point out that you "told me so".'

'Oh, don't,' Silvren exclaimed. 'It's only that for some reason I can't forget that we were friends for ten years. I wish I could. I still feel that I know you, although that is obviously an illusion. If you hated me – if you had wanted

454

to destroy this world – I could understand you better. But you believed you were doing right! And I don't think you hate me – obviously, I never knew you at all.'

'No, Silvren, I don't hate you,' Arlenmia said quietly. 'And yes, I believed I was right. But now I know I was wrong. And I am sorry that I caused you suffering. What more can I say?'

'I am concerned about you! I want to know – well, what are you going to do?'

'That rather depends upon the Lady of H'tebhmella,' Arlenmia replied icily.

Silvren went to her side and slipped her hands through Arlenmia's arm. 'I mean, what would you like to do?'

She turned to look at Silvren, her blue-green eyes startled. 'How can I answer that? What I dreamed of proved hollow . . . Never can I settle for lesser dreams, transient mortal ambitions, but I have lost faith in my own judgement. Yes, I have lost faith, and I am nothing without it. What is there left for me?' She stared out of the embrasure and said softly, 'They say it is impossible to kill yourself on H'tebhmella. The wound heals before a drop of blood escapes. Ashurek was right, dear heart: I should have died with M'gulfn.'

'Don't – don't talk like this. Could you not go home – wherever that is? There must be people there who love you – miss you . . .'

Arlenmia was silent. After a few moments she said, 'Where will you go? You and Ashurek . . .'

'I don't know. I hadn't thought about it.'

'Well, don't tell me. And I beg of you, don't come to say goodbye. I could not bear it.' Unexpectedly she turned and kissed her on the cheek, and Silvren felt a tear fall from Arlenmia's face on to her own. 'Whatever you think of me, I wish you well. Now go.'

'No, I have no wish ever to return to Gorethria,' Ashurek said. He and Silvren were sitting alone by a jewel-like waterfall, their arms around each other.

'Are you sure? You feel like that now . . . but you may come to think that you should have gone back, or—'

'No, my love, I will not,' he replied. 'What I miss about Gorethria is my own distant past, which cannot be recreated. And I would not wish it to be. As for feeling responsible for Gorethria's future . . . well, I do; but whatever wrongs I perpetrated there, I am not so arrogant as to suppose I can also put right. Her fate must repose in other hands.' After a pause he said, 'You would like to return to Athrainy, would you not?'

Silvren shook her head quickly. 'All I want to do – if my sorcery is yet strong enough – is to make sure that my mother is all right. Setrel too, if you wish it.'

'Yes, it would set my mind at rest, and Estarinel's. He was a good man. Well, there is nowhere in Tearn that I could live at ease; nowhere that I could expect to suffer my presence. I am outcast from the Earth, in essence.'

'But you have freed the world from the Serpent!' Silvren exclaimed.

'Aye, but I will not be remembered for that. I will only be remembered as the fell Gorethrian wolf, the bringer of bloodshed throughout Vardrav and Eastern Tearn. No, perhaps I have not even the right to set foot upon Earth again. But where I go means nothing to me, as long as I am not separated from you again.'

She kissed him in heartfelt agreement. 'Then I have a suggestion,' she said. 'The world where I learned to use my sorcery. Ikonus, some of us used to call it. I would like to go there . . . they wanted me to go back – the people at the School of Sorcery, I mean. I think there is much work to be done there, and I would like to help. And it is more home to me than this world has ever been.'

'Then that is what we shall do,' said Ashurek, 'if Calorn or the Lady of H'tebhmella will aid us in finding a way there. Yes, a new beginning in a new world . . . that would be the best of all.'

There came a time when all those who had participated in the Quest of the Serpent parted at last. Eldor had already returned to join the other Grey Ones in their domain. Calorn was to take Silvren and Ashurek to Ikonus; it was her own home world and as yet she had mixed feelings about whether she wanted to stay there or not. Arlenmia was to remain in the custody of the Lady of H'tebhmella until she was deemed harmless, although Ashurek had reservations about how that could be judged.

'Aren't you going back to Forluin?' Calorn asked Estarinel as they walked along the mossy shore of a shining aquamarine lake. 'I thought you would have gone back almost as soon as you set foot on the Blue Plane.'

'I suppose I will go back,' he said.

'You sound as if you don't want to,' she exclaimed, astounded.

'I'm not sure that I do. So much has happened. I am not the same, and Forluin is not the same . . .'

'But it's your home, which you fought so hard to save—'

'For others, perhaps not for myself. I'm not sure I could bear to go back to somewhere I was once happy, and be happy no longer. I don't know how to explain it.'

'I think I understand,' Calorn said.

'When Miril died . . . it was as if she died for me personally, as if to say, there is no hope for you in Forluin. No hope for you without Medrian.'

'You need time to grieve, you won't feel like this for ever,' she said gently.

'It doesn't matter,' he said, half-smiling. 'I think the worst thing of all is the feeling that nothing matters. Medrian tried to warn me not to care too much. This is the result: you end up not caring about anything.'

'I don't believe you mean that.'

'No, perhaps you're right. It's strange. When the Quest began, it was terrible to me to be away from Forluin and my friends, and in the company of these two frightening strangers, Medrian and Ashurek. But I grew to love them, you, too, and Silvren. Now you and they seem real, and

Forluin seems distant, like a dream. Maybe your heart belongs with whatever you have grown used to.'

'Then come with us to my Earth!' Calorn exclaimed. 'That may be the answer—'

'No – that is Silvren and Ashurek's future. Not mine,' Estarinel replied. He smiled to show that he was grateful for her concern, but as he walked away from her, she felt saddened by the feeling that she could not help him. He seemed closed away, beyond even the reach of H'tebhmella's healing beauty.

Estarinel did go back to Forluin, but not until after Silvren and Ashurek had gone to Ikonus. Under Calorn's direction, several of the H'tebhmellian women created a special Exit Point which would take them to that other world. It was not a soft blue cloud like an Exit Point to Earth, but a sphere of crackling green and silver light.

The Lady of H'tebhmella kissed Ashurek and Silvren on the forehead. Tears shone in her lovely, agate-grey eyes. 'I hope that you will find happiness,' she told them. 'And, Calorn, whether you return to my service or remain on your world, I wish you joy also. Fare you well.'

Ashurek said, 'I know that I can never atone for the evil I have brought to the Earth. Not even the Serpent's death – nor my own – can eradicate the past. However, I will do what little I can to show that I remember what Miril taught me. From now on I will wear only the robes of a scholar instead of a soldier's garb, and never again will I take up a weapon.'

Then he and Silvren both embraced Estarinel, all three of them weeping. This parting proved harder than they had imagined it would. Then Ashurek, Silvren and Calorn turned away and vanished into the silver-green light.

The Lady touched Estarinel's arm with her white hand and said, 'Estarinel? You are still sad. I fear that even H'tebhmella has no power to touch your pain. You are welcome here, but I think that only human warmth can heal you. They must miss you very much in Forluin. Do you not want to return there?'

She was telling him, however gently, that it was time to leave. And why not? Perhaps he would feel even more rootless in Forluin than he felt here, but it did not matter, because he really felt nothing at all beyond a persistent cold sadness. Resignedly he replied, 'Yes, my Lady. I will go back now.'

He stepped out of the Exit Point in almost exactly the same place into which he and Medrian had emerged before: Trevilith Wood, about five miles from his home. A feeling of numb shock gripped him as he looked around. This wood had been undamaged a few months before; now the trees were leafless and scorched, every blade of grass and twig in the undergrowth coated with a grey substance.

So the Serpent's venom, which had flooded his family's farm long after its initial attack, had spread further. He would have cried out, if he had had any capacity for feeling left; as it was, he just stared at the greyness with blank despair. It was twilight; there was no colour anywhere. This meant that the village had been destroyed also, he thought. He wondered if Falin and the others had escaped. Perhaps, after all, the Serpent's poison had covered all of Forluin and killed everyone, perhaps they had slain M'gulfn too late. A number of confusing thoughts passed through his mind, but he did not dwell on them. He began to walk woodenly towards the village to see if there was anything left.

Presently he realised that while the substance which destroyed his home had been glutinous and deadly, the stuff flattening the grass was as dry as dust, and it cracked and crumbled away beneath his sandalled feet. The terrible Serpent-stench was no longer in the air. Sometimes he had found it hard to believe that they would ever be free of its curse, but now he knew that its power to destroy had truly gone at last. Even if it was too late.

The gloom deepened. It was cloudy and cold. Autumn, of

course, he thought. He decided to walk past the Bowl Valley where his home had been, because the sight of it could not possibly cause him further pain. As he approached, the sky began to clear and the last of the sunlight spread an even, topaz-yellow glow across the sky. He came to the edge of the valley and stood still, convinced that he had somewhere walked out of consciousness and into a nightmare.

Below him were figures standing in a grey landscape, frozen under a dome of topaz glass . . . the hellish vision which had haunted him ever since he had seen it in Arlenmia's mirrors. Uncomprehending, he stood swaying on the lip of the valley, staring down at this impossible scene, which was the culmination of his worst fears.

I must be dreaming, he thought vaguely. The figures seemed to be moving very slowly towards him in a ragged line. Some appeared to be scattering a substance – dust, or water? – onto the ground, while others moved behind, bent in a gesture of sweeping the ground with brooms. Dreaming . . .

One of the figures looked up and stopped. Faint but clear he heard a voice say, 'Who's that?'

'I don't know,' another replied. 'Run up and see, will you, dear.'

He was walking down into the valley now, seeing the figure rushing towards him but not really registering that the person was real until she collided with him. There were arms round his neck, a voice crying with breathless disbelief, 'It's E'rinel! Mother, it's E'rinel!'

It was his younger sister, Lothwyn.

Then there were faces all round him, hands touching him, people laughing and smiling and hugging him . . . his mother, his sister Arlena, Falin, Lilithea, and others, Falin's aunt Thalien, his mother's and father's parents, Taer'nel, other men and women from the village and nearby farms . . . voices asking questions which he could not understand, something about how long had he been back, where he had come from, how was he . . .

'I think he's ill,' someone said.

'Oh – come – we'll take him to the village. Falin, help him. Hurry!'

Slowly he came back to himself. He found himself wrapped in a patchwork blanket, propped up by pillows on a bed in a room he vaguely recognised. There were uneven, creamy walls, woven rugs on the floor, a window framed in dark wood . . . Falin was sitting beside him, holding a cup of some hot, reviving drink to his lips.

He took the cup in his own hands and Falin grinned at him and said, 'Are you back with us yet?'

'I – I think so. It was just . . . I was so shocked, seeing my mother and sisters.' He sat up, looking at Falin anxiously. 'Or did I dream it?'

'No, you didn't. It must have been a terrible shock.'

'Where are they?'

'Lie back, everything's all right. You would only let me stay in the room with you. You insisted that the others were – ghosts, or something.'

'Did I? Oh, by the gods,' Estarinel exclaimed in dismay. 'When I came over the edge of the valley and saw you all, it was like – like an awful—'

'Will you be quiet? Finish the drink – Lili put something in it. There's plenty of time to explain tomorrow.'

'Tomorrow? It will take me a month. Falin, I can't tell you how glad I am to see you.'

'And we thought we'd never see you again,' his friend said warmly. 'Can I send in your mother yet? She is wearing holes in Thalien's rugs.'

'Not yet – you must tell me what's happened here since I left. I don't understand. What were you doing in the Bowl Valley?'

'Clearing the poison away,' Falin replied. Seeing that Estarinel would be unable to rest until he was told everything, he continued, 'Well, after you left, we went on fighting the Serpent's venom as best we could. There was little we could do. Neither fire nor water would destroy it, no barriers would halt its progress. All we could really do was flee. We left the village for several weeks. Some people became trapped

461

within pockets of it. But the rest of us were driven slowly towards the South. There's not much to tell of that time, really. You can imagine how terrible it was. Almost the whole population of Forluin – the survivors, I mean – were crowded upon the Southern coast, and some in Maerna and Ohn. We had to eat fish, there was nothing else. I hope I never see a fish again.' Falin pulled a face. 'Nearly all the farmlands were destroyed. The venom was only a score of miles behind us. And in that time, the sun never showed itself; there was just a perpetual greenish-grey haze in the sky and this appalling reek, like metal, and things decaying—'

'Yes, I know,' Estarinel said.

'And it hardly rained. I don't think any words can ever make it sound as horrible as it actually was.' He shuddered involuntarily and went on, 'Anyway, we had some ships ready to sail if it became essential; but there was only room for a few hundred of us, and how could we decide who was to be saved? So none of us went. And one morning when we were sure there were only a few days left, someone walked back to see how far the venom had come, and he found it dry.

'As that day went on, a clean wind sprang up and blew the haze away. The sun shone. We could walk over the dried venom without harm. Then we knew that the Serpent was dead, and we wept for joy. So, with what animals were left alive, we came North again. We found that the village was undamaged, although there was venom all around it, but now it was all dry, harmless.

'It was then that the most remarkable thing of all happened. Some of those whom we thought were dead, were not.' Tears came into Falin's eyes and he swallowed. 'We had laid them on pallets in the wheelwright's barn – oh, you remember, you saw them, of course. But some of them rose up and came out of the barn wrapped in the pale green gowns and still wreathed with yellow flowers, blinking in the sunlight like children who had just awoken from sleep. Or like creatures newborn. They seemed to have no memory of what had happened to them – not at first, anyway. When it had

462

been explained, they remembered. We couldn't believe it at first, but they were alive and undoubtedly well.'

'You said "some",' Estarinel said anxiously.

'There seemed no logic to who recovered and who did not. But when we thought about it, we realised that those who died in the Serpent's attack, or not long after, had remained truly dead, but those who "died" more recently were brought back to life. E'rinel, your father did not return. Neither did my parents nor my sister, Sinmiel.'

'Falin, I'm sorry.'

'We should be glad for those who were restored to us. Your mother and sisters. But I can't explain how or why this miracle can have happened.'

'I think I can. Oh, it is too complicated to explain now, but I will tell you one day. Who else?'

Falin recounted as many people as he could remember who had been restored to life. 'And Edrien and Luatha are still well. They stayed in the South. But Thalien and Lilithea came back here with me. Oh, we rejoiced when we knew that the Serpent was dead, and how much more so when Filmorwen, Lothwyn and Arlena were restored to us, but we were also . . . dazed, I suppose. There was so much damage to be repaired, and we hardly knew where to start. Then a message came from the Elders at the Vale of Motha. They said a H'tebhmellian – Filitha, I think – had come to see them, bringing with her two horses. One was your Shaell and the other a Gorethrian horse. She said that you were safe on the Blue Plane, and that the Serpent was dead. But the message wasn't very clear, and we thought it must be wrong, because the days went by and you hadn't returned. We really thought you were not coming back, E'rinel.

'But the other purpose of Filitha's visit was to tell us that the H'tebhmellians would help us in the healing of Forluin. Somehow they caused water from H'tebhmella to fill a lake and river near Motha. Wherever we sprinkled this water, she said, it would speed the healing of Forluin.'

'I wasn't told any of this,' Estarinel exclaimed. But then, he had not even asked for news of his country. He would have returned sooner if he had known these things, and perhaps the Lady had wanted him to go back to Forluin in his own time. 'And will it work?'

'When you came upon us in the Bowl Valley, we were cleansing it. We throw water onto the venom, then brush the grass, and it vanishes into the ground. We have to use the H'tebhmellian water very sparingly, so we are only clearing selected areas to begin with. Eventually rain and wind should do the job for us, but Filitha said that the areas we cleared with H'tebhmellian water would be producing grass and crops by next spring. Meanwhile we have to live on salted fish, I'm afraid.'

'There's a great deal of work to do, then.'

'Yes,' Falin said, putting out a hand to restrain him, 'but, please, have a night's rest before you begin.'

'You've got very thin, Falin,' said Estarinel, looking down at his arm.

'So have you. Now can Filmorwen come in to see you?'

'I'll come out, I feel better now.' Estarinel made to get up, but even as Falin opened the door, his sisters burst into the room and both hugged him at once. He put his arms around them, dark Lothwyn and silver-fair Arlena, and over their shoulders he saw his mother in the doorway, smiling at him, her golden hair escaping the ribbon she had tied it back with. How could he have ever considered not coming back?

'Don't suffocate him,' she said to her daughters. Arlena turned and hugged Falin instead, and Lothwyn still hung onto his arm as his mother came forward to embrace and kiss him.

'I dreamed about you, Mother,' he said, when he had recovered his breath. 'You were in one of the stalls, helping a mare to foal. I told you that the Serpent was outside, and you just smiled at me and said, "Tell it I am coming back".'

'And here I am,' Filmorwen said, laughing. 'And I have dreamt of this moment a thousand times. Are you sure you are all right?'

'Yes. It's all over now. The nightmare is over.' He saw Lilithea standing almost shyly in the doorway, and he remem-

bered that he had not seen her at all for a year. She hesitated
and then ran to embrace him. She was painfully thin, as they
all were, but there was still a wiry strength in her arms as
she hugged him for longer than even his mother had.

'We knew it was dead,' said Lothwyn with awe in her
voice, 'but did you actually . . .?'

'Yes, but not just me,' he said. 'None of us could have
achieved anything without the others.'

That winter was grim and hard, but the Forluinish faced it
with joy. Now that M'gulfn was dead and its evil removed,
nothing could daunt them. Snow and rain and wind were a
blessing, sweeping the last traces of virulence from the land.
Long before spring came, grass was growing vigorously again,
the trees were heavy with buds, and the places where
H'tebhmellian water had been strewn promised to be more
fruitful and beautiful than ever before. Long years of work
still faced them before life returned fully to normal. There
were forests to be replanted, farmhouses and villages to be
rebuilt, and animals – both domestic and wild – to be nurtured
until their numbers were replenished. Food was short and
their tasks never-ending, but they worked eagerly and with
good cheer, because everything they did was for Forluin and
for each other.

Only Estarinel, his family and friends noticed with distress,
seemed melancholy. He was Forluin's hero, but he determinedly refused to be singled out for special attention. He
worked unstintingly with the others, and was outwardly as
friendly and affectionate as ever he had been. But he hardly
mentioned the Quest and he often seemed withdrawn, as if
concealing a bitter sadness. He told Falin some of what had
happened, but it was only to Lilithea that he told everything,
and even then, the story only emerged bit by bit over a
period of months. But because he spoke to her the most, she
discovered that he was more deeply depressed than anyone
realised. She would never forget how pale, how emotionless
he had been when he told her about Medrian; he did not

weep but, oh, she thought afterwards, how much more hope she would have had for him if he could have done.

'I am so worried about him,' she said to Falin one day. 'You have noticed how distant he seems.'

'Yes, but he talks to you, doesn't he?' Falin asked.

'Oh yes, he talks to me,' Lilithea replied, an almost bitter note in her voice. 'I think I know almost everything that happened. He had a terrible time.'

'He feels that his experiences have set him apart from us.'

'Yes. But is he going to feel apart from us for ever? If so, he'll never be happy.'

'And neither will you,' Falin said gently, taking her hand.

She was silent for a moment. Then she said, 'I know about Medrian. It's all right, I understand why you didn't tell me that he came back that time. I told E'rinel – and I meant it – that I would have loved her if I had known her. And if she had come back with him, and he had been happy, then I would have accepted it and been happy too. But she's dead. Is he going to mourn her for ever?' She paused, biting her lip. 'I shouldn't have said that. But do you know how wretched it is to love someone who looks on you as – as a sister?'

Falin shook his head, trying not to smile. 'Why don't you tell him?'

'I could not. I should not have to.'

'That's not necessarily true . . . He gave me the same advice himself once, about Arlena. "Don't tell me, tell her." '

'But you were just being circumspect. This is different. Oh, I could not tell him. It would make things worse. He would be forced to say that he does not love me, and then I would be less than a sister to him. I would have to go away.' She looked up at Falin, her large eyes at once dark and bright. 'Perhaps that would be for the best. To carry on like this is unbearable.'

Spring came, and the grass grew lush and the trees heavy with blossom. Their branches became full of nests and chirping fledgelings apparently overnight. No foals were born that year, but there were many more lambs and smaller animals than they could have hoped for. But to Estarinel, the life and beauty all around him made it more intolerable than ever that Medrian had had to die in that lonely, frozen wasteland. He looked on the happiness of others and felt objectively glad for them; he would not have wished things otherwise. But inside he felt cold and dark, as if nothing of Forluin could ever touch him or warm him again.

That spring, Falin and Arlena were married at last, the simple Forluinish Ceremony of Flowers, followed by a day of riotous celebration. Amid the rejoicing, Estarinel thought, I would have undergone the Quest a hundred times over for this. This makes everything worthwhile, this is what it was all for. But at every joyous sight – Falin and Arlena dancing past him, dressed in green, white and gold, his mother and Lothwyn laughing as they deluged the couple with blossom – he could not stop himself from wishing that Medrian had been there to share it. Every moment of sweetness brought him a cold stab of pain.

When the wedding was over he felt that he must be on his own for a time, before the contrast between his family's joy and his own inner coldness drove him mad. He decided to walk to the Vale of Motha, a journey of several days, to fetch Shaell and Vixata.

To his surprise, Lilithea asked if she could go with him.

'I was going to go on my own, but . . .' he paused, reconsidering. Perhaps it was not good to be alone, and of all people, he found Lilithea's quiet company the most soothing. 'Yes, I would prefer it if you came as well,' he said.

They wore the usual garb of Forluinish farmers, brown breeches and soft boots, a sleeveless jerkin belted over a wide-sleeved white shirt. They took nothing with them, because every traveller in Forluin received hospitality wherever they went, and at this time of year it was no hardship to sleep in the open.

Lilithea had lost the strained, ill look that she had had when he had first returned from H'tebhmella. Her pretty,

467

delicate-featured face had regained its healthy colour, and she was once more slender rather than thin. The spring sunshine gave a golden lustre to her rich, bronze-brown hair.

Their walk took them through glorious woods and soft valleys. The last time they had passed this way together it had been just after the Serpent's attack, when a grey haze had hung in the air like death. Now, all was green-gold and fresh, as Forluin should be. At first Estarinel thought Lilithea was so quiet because she was awed by this joyous contrast, but presently he realised that she was not so much silent as uncharacteristically morose. He asked her if anything was wrong.

'I am worried about you. You are not happy,' she replied.

'What makes you say that?' he asked. 'Forluin will soon be whole again. How could I not be happy?'

'The way you ask me that betrays you!' Lilithea exclaimed. 'Where are you, E'rinel? You are not with us. You are with strangers in distant landscapes. Somewhere I can't reach.'

Her words startled him, and he was quiet for a moment. He answered in a low voice, 'I can't help it, Lili. I'm not the same person I was. Part of me died with Medrian.'

'But you are still alive. Are you going to stay in the cold for ever, only half-living? How can that help Medrian?'

'It's not that simple. Yes, I feel apart. I no longer feel truly Forluinish. They want to call me a "hero" but that is false. They don't know of the times I almost ran away, the blood on my hands—'

'And they call me a healer,' she said harshly, 'but that is false too. There are some things I cannot heal, E'rinel.' She strode ahead of him so he could not see her tears, but he caught her up.

'Lili, don't worry about me,' he said, cursing himself for having upset her. 'I am all right, really. It's enough for me to see others happy.'

'Do I look happy?' she burst out. He stopped and stared at her. In the silence some young thrushes began to sing in the trees around them.

'Lili, what is wrong?' he asked concernedly.

'You're breaking my heart!' she cried. She had been so determined to stay calm, but she had failed. 'You say you're not the same person. Well, none of us are. You are far away in some bleak and miserable place and you don't want to come back because you think only Medrian and Ashurek could understand you, and they are gone. But you are not unique! The Serpent happened to all of us! I was with you, don't you remember? When it came, and we ran across the valley and saw it lying on Falin's house. It was me with you!'

'Yes – yes I know—' Estarinel floundered.

'And while you were away, I have been here trying to cure people of the Worm-sent illnesses, and failing, and watching them die. How do I know if I tried hard enough? I may have more blood on my hands than you. You are not the only one who has suffered. We have to go on living! It's a sin not to! E'rinel, you're giving up, you're frightened to care about anything. Would Medrian have wanted you to give up? Did she die so that you could stop caring? Oh,' she turned away from him, 'I'm sorry. I should not – please forget I said these things.'

'Lili, I have never, ever known you to get upset like this before,' he said, shaken. 'Now I am as worried about you as you are about me. I've missed something, or I'm being very stupid . . . What is it, really?'

'Isn't it obvious? How long have you known me?'

'Since we were six or seven . . .'

'And why do you think I stayed in the cottage when my family moved away, instead of going with them? It wasn't that I thought myself indispensable to the village—'

'But you are,' he put in quietly. She hardly heard him.

'– I stayed, because I loved you. The brother I did not have . . . but I'm not a child any more. I still love you. The reason I have not married was not for want of opportunity. I hoped – if you knew how much I have missed you, feared for you – E'rinel, I can't bear being no more than a sister to you. Perhaps I'm wrong to want more. Oh, I swore I would never tell you this.' With an effort she composed herself and said calmly, 'It's because I love you and you don't love me that I can't stay with you. Let the village find another healer. I can't even heal myself.'

She turned away and began to walk slowly back the way they had come. Estarinel knew that she was leaving him, but for a few moments he could not move. What she had said was true. *The Serpent happened to all of us* . . . And he had taken her for granted, because she had always been there, like Arlena and Lothwyn, but that did not mean he did not care about her, or that he wanted her to go. The Serpent should have taught him never to take anything or anyone for granted again. What a fool he had been, not to realise—

She was almost out of sight, her slender figure and waist-length bronze hair vanishing among the trees, when he began to run after her. He reached her, caught her arm so that she had to face him. 'Lili, I do love you. Why do you think you're the only one I've told everything to? Why do I seek your company when I don't want to be with anyone else?'

'I really don't know!' she replied acerbically. 'Because I am a good listener? There can't be any other reason.'

'Then listen to me now. We've always been friends and I've always loved you. But I didn't know that you felt like this. It's not that I don't – oh, never mind.' He stopped trying to explain and kissed her in an unbrotherly way instead.

'I shouldn't have said those awful things,' she whispered eventually.

'But they were true. I have been selfish and blind. Everyone's been too kind to me. I needed you to shout at me, to bring me back to my senses.' He smiled at her, and she realised that she had not seen him smile – as if he meant it – since the day of the Worm's attack, more than eighteen months before. 'But I am not the only one guilty of isolating myself, Lili. Do you know that as long as I've known you, this is the first time you've told me what you really feel?'

'Yes, I know. We are both to blame in our way.' She looked warmly at him; he wondered how he could ever have missed the love in her eyes.

'If you still mean to leave me, I deserve it,' he said.

470

'But please stay with me, Lili. If – well, I have nightmares sometimes. If you can bear that, please stay.'

'I can bear it,' she answered, and kissed him again.

They had fetched Shaell and Vixata and were on their way home again, several days later, when they saw her. They had spent the night in a wood, resting in the friendly shelter of the trees; Estarinel and Lilithea were lying in each other's arms on a bank of soft grass, while the horses grazed nearby. It was just dawn; soft light was filtering through the mass of young leaves, but the undergrowth was still deep in shadow. Lilithea was asleep, but Estarinel was in that pleasant state of being half-awake, when all thoughts seemed limpid and painless.

Because of Lilithea, he had begun to feel that he belonged in Forluin again. She had brought him back to reality, shown him that the future was not to be feared. Forluin had been changed for ever by the Serpent; nothing could be the same again . . . but it could be better. He had wept in Lilithea's arms that first night, as he had not wept since Medrian died. And he knew that he would perhaps never cease to dream of Medrian, and wake up crying out, with the memory clutching his heart like an ice-cold hand, but at least there would be Lili to bring him back to the present, make him forget. It was not that he loved Medrian less; rather, he loved Lilithea as much. There was nothing strange in this: no Forluinishman or woman believed that one love excluded all others.

It was as he lay there, gazing sleepily through the misty wood, that he saw the figure. The tree trunks were a myriad shades of grey in the half-light. But clearly, as if she shone with a light of her own, he saw a woman walking between the trees. She was small and slim with long, black hair and she was clad in a white robe. Over it she wore a shimmering cloak of pale gold, and there were blue flowers glowing in her hair, their petals like glass. A corona of misty light enveloped her, and Estarinel knew that she was only a phantasm, but all the same she seemed vividly real.

She walked slowly through the trees until she drew level with him, and then she turned to face him, her face radiant. He was afraid he would wake up if he tried to move, so he lay utterly still, gazing at her without even trying to speak. It was the strangest dream about Medrian he had ever had, the first one that had not been acutely painful.

'I had a nightmare,' Medrian said. 'A terrible, impossible nightmare that an ancient being lay coiled about the Earth and coiled within me at the same time. And everything the being touched turned cold and grey until the whole world became desolate. And I lay stained with blood and tears, alone in my pain, because I *was* that being and although my existence was unbearable it was also eternal. And in this nightmare I witnessed horrors too great for any human to bear . . .

'But it was only a dream. Someone who loved me more than I could have guessed woke me gently, and I saw that it had only been a nightmare after all, something that could never have happened, something that was over and forgotten. Then I smiled at my fretful dreams, and I rose and walked out into the light.'

For the space of three heartbeats she looked straight at him, her eyes no longer full of shadow but clear as starlight. Then she turned and went on her way through the trees. Estarinel wanted to call out to her, but the words would not leave his throat. Trails of light lingered in the trees after she had passed out of sight . . . He realised that they were just wisps of mist, catching the first faint sunlight. Somewhere a bird began to sing, the first bird of dawn, an exquisite, liquid melody that seemed to lift all the sadness from him.

He sat up and looked round to see that Lilithea was awake, her dark eyes very wide. 'I've just had such a realistic dream,' he said, smiling at her.

'E'rinel,' Lilithea said, her voice somewhere between a gasp and a whisper, 'E'rinel, I saw her too.'

The horses were standing with their heads up and ears pricked, startled by the bird. As the chirping grew more strident they saw the large female blackbird singing in the branches of a tree a few yards from them. Her beak was like burnished bronze and her feathers had the sheen of rich, tawny-gold silk. And as she sang, she gazed at them with a dark, liquid eye in which leaves and trees and woodland animals were reflected. The look seemed to say, 'What made you think such as I could perish? Am I not reborn with every sunrise?'

Tears were running down Lilithea's face, because she had never seen any creature more beautiful than that simple blackbird, who was the embodiment of love and hope. 'Her name is Miril,' Estarinel whispered, and Lilithea replied softly, 'Yes . . . I know.'

They watched her without moving, hoping that she would come to them, or at least stay singing in the tree. But Miril was swift to follow the direction that Medrian had taken. With a last, sweet note she stretched out her sunlit wings and soared out onto the misty, woodland air. Then she, too, was gone.

interzone

SCIENCE FICTION AND FANTASY

Quarterly   £1.95

● *Interzone* is the only British magazine specializing in SF and new fantastic writing. We have published:

BRIAN ALDISS	GARRY KILWORTH
J.G. BALLARD	DAVID LANGFORD
BARRINGTON BAYLEY	MICHAEL MOORCOCK
GREGORY BENFORD	RACHEL POLLACK
MICHAEL BISHOP	KEITH ROBERTS
RAMSEY CAMPBELL	GEOFF RYMAN
ANGELA CARTER	JOSEPHINE SAXTON
RICHARD COWPER	JOHN SHIRLEY
JOHN CROWLEY	JOHN SLADEK
PHILIP K. DICK	BRIAN STABLEFORD
THOMAS M. DISCH	BRUCE STERLING
MARY GENTLE	IAN WATSON
WILLIAM GIBSON	CHERRY WILDER
M. JOHN HARRISON	GENE WOLFE

● *Interzone* has also published many excellent new writers; graphics by JIM BURNS, ROGER DEAN, IAN MILLER and others; book reviews, news, etc.

● *Interzone* is available from specialist SF shops, or by subscription. For four issues, send £7.50 (outside UK, £8.50) to : **124 Osborne Road, Brighton BN1 6LU, UK.** Single copies: £1.95 inc p&p.

● American subscribers may send $13 ($16 if you want delivery by air mail) to our British address, above. All cheques should be made payable to *Interzone*.

● "No other magazine in Britain is publishing science fiction at all, let alone fiction of this quality." *Times Literary Supplement*

- -

To: **interzone** 124 Osborne Road, Brighton, BN1 6LU, UK.

Please send me four issues of *Interzone,* beginning with the current issue. I enclose a cheque/p.o. for £7.50 (outside UK, £8.50; US subscribers, $13 or $16 air), made payable to *Interzone.*

Name _____

Address _____

_____

FREDA WARRINGTON

A BLACKBIRD IN AMBER

The great serpent M'gulfn was dead, its power dispersed and all save one of its demon-servants destroyed.

Now was the time when the power of sorcery might be harnessed for good or for evil.

Journeying disguised to Gorethria came Mellorn, daughter of Silvren and Ashurek, by training and by will eager to use that latent power for good.

But to Gorethria, summoned by the usurper Duke Xaedrek, there came also the demon Ahag-Ga in the guise of an old woman. Together they plan to use the power: he to rebuild the terrible authority of the old empire: she, silently vengeful, determined to unleash the dark forces of Chaos on a world that, saved, is yet in peril.

A BLACKBIRD IN AMBER, sequel to A BLACKBIRD IN DARKNESS is the third in the series begun with A BLACKBIRD IN SILVER.

HODDER AND STOUGHTON PAPERBACKS

GEORGE ALEC EFFINGER

THE NICK OF TIME

At noon on February 17th, 1996, Frank Mihalik becomes the world's first time traveller. His odyssey is to be a simple one: a quick day trip to the past and back again. Unfortunately, the time-travel process still has a few kinks in the system. He finds himself stuck at the 1939 New York World's Fair, reliving the same day over and over again. Just as he is about to lose hope his girlfriend Cheryl arrives to lend support. With a little boost from the past, the pair are soon on their way again, hurtling through time at a breathless pace, down an endless path filled with lively, intriguing – and often dangerous encounters: riding with the Three Musketeers, serving in a war between the Queen of the Past and the King of the Future, even visiting the futuristic Land of Oz ('If we come to a yellow brick road . . . I'm going to give up').

HODDER AND STOUGHTON PAPERBACKS

ROBERT E. VARDEMAN

THE JADE DEMONS QUARTET

Kesira, beautiful, last survivor of the sacred Order of Gelya, looked about her. Demon-destroyed, all her past, all learning and companionship lay blasted into nothingness by the liquid jade fire that had lanced down from the apocalyptic skies.

A terrible understanding grew and flared in her mind. She knew now that the time for her Quest had come. Accompanied only by the magical, future-seeing bird Zolkan and Molimo the changeling man-wolf, she must challenge the Jade Demons.

Gigantic, fearful creatures, they loomed and battled in the skies, destroying the land and the people, as they fought for final supremacy.

Kesira, votive maiden turned she-warrior, set forth on her fate-ordained path ...

Never before published in the UK, THE JADE DEMONS QUARTET comprises THE QUAKING LANDS, THE FROZEN WAVES, THE CRYSTAL CLOUDS and THE WHITE FIRE in one volume.

HODDER AND STOUGHTON PAPERBACKS

MORE SCIENCE FICTION AND FANTASY FROM HODDER AND STOUGHTON PAPERBACKS

FREDA WARRINGTON

☐	05849 2	A Blackbird in Silver	£3.50
☐	41903 7	A Blackbird in Amber	£3.95

GEORGE ALEC EFFINGER

☐	41736 0	The Nick of Time	£2.50

ROBERT E. VARDEMAN

☐	41351 9	The Jade Demons Quartet	£4.95
☐	39001 2	The Keys to Paradise	£3.95

ROBERT L. FORWARD

☐	05197 8	Dragon's Egg	£2.50
☐	05823 9	Flight of the Dragonfly	£2.95
☐	41908 8	Starquake	£2.95

All these books are available at your local bookshop or newsagent, or can be ordered direct from the publisher. Just tick the titles you want and fill in the form below.

Prices and availability subject to change without notice.

Hodder & Stoughton Paperbacks, P.O. Box 11, Falmouth, Cornwall.

Please send cheque or postal order, and allow the following for postage and packing:

U.K. – 55p for one book, plus 22p for the second book, and 14p for each additional book ordered up to a £1.75 maximum.

B.F.P.O. and EIRE – 55p for the first book, plus 22p for the second book, and 14p per copy for the next 7 books, 8p per book thereafter.

OTHER OVERSEAS CUSTOMERS – £1.00 for the first book, plus 25p per copy for each additional book.

NAME..

ADDRESS ....

....